S W A N

S O N G

A NOVEL

ELIZABETH

B. SPLAINE

Woodhall Press
Norwalk, CT

woodhall press

Woodhall Press, 81 Old Saugatuck Road, Norwalk, CT 06855
WoodhallPress.com

Cover design: Asha Hossain
Layout artist: LJ Mucci

Library of Congress Cataloging-in-Publication Data available

ISBN 978-1-949116-83-0 (paper: alk paper)
ISBN 978-1-949116-84-7 (electronic)

First Edition

Distributed by Independent Publishers Group
(800) 888-4741

Printed in the United States of America

This is a work of fiction. Names, characters, business, events and incidents are
the products of the author's imagination. Any resemblance to actual persons,
living or dead, or actual events is purely coincidental.

This book is dedicated to a special lady—
Mischling, Friend, and Seamstress Extraordinaire

It is also dedicated to all persecuted people who suffered through the madness.
I am humbled by your strength and perseverance.

May we apply what we have learned in an effort to promote peace and awareness.

But never, *ever* forget.

The silver Swan, who, living, had no Note,
when Death approached, unlocked her silent throat.
Leaning her breast against the reedy shore,
thus sang her first and last, and sang no more:
"Farewell, all joys! O Death, come close mine eyes!
More Geese than Swans now live, more Fools than Wise."
—Orlando Gibbons, 1612

PROLOGUE

Hitler was a monster.

Except he wasn't.

He was a narcissistic sociopath who convinced millions of people to join his cult.

In his early years, observers might have called him a simple man. Or a man who lived simply in a tiny apartment with as close to a friend as Adolf Hitler would ever have. Hitler met August Kubizek at the Linz opera after Hitler's family moved to Linz following the death of his father. Like all of Hitler's relationships, the friendship was largely one-sided. As Hitler vacillated between silence and raving diatribes about perceived wrongs, his roommate was doomed to listen and nod appropriately until Hitler finally exhausted himself. His friendship with Kubizek ended abruptly when the young man returned from the holidays to find that Hitler had moved out, leaving no trace. For reasons known only to Hitler's troubled mind, he had decided to end the relationship as suddenly as it had begun.

Hitler's relationships with women were no less muddled and one-sided. While living with Kubizek, he fell in love with a young woman whom he spotted on the street. Over a period of months, he loved Stefanie from afar and never approached her. Instead, he fantasized about their life together and imagined he communicated with her through telepathy. According to Kubizek, Hitler truly believed Stefanie understood his thoughts and shared his unspoken passion. He even discussed the idea of kidnapping her, until Kubizek astutely pointed out that he had no money to support her. The fact that kidnapping is legally and morally wrong never came into consideration.

Hitler's "love" was all-consuming, volatile, twisted. To him, loving someone meant possessing her, smothering the person's spirit and will until she became a part of him. If, for some reason, the supply of love was severed, the victim suffered greatly, having poured herself—heart, mind, and soul—into Hitler. Subjugation was an unspoken requirement when becoming involved with Hitler. In the process, the person lost her own identity, her sense of self. And when that has happened, what remains? A husk, a shell, with roiling emotions and a desperate sense of loss. Stefanie escaped by never actually engaging with the megalomaniac. Other women were not so fortunate. At least seven women committed suicide after being involved with Adolf Hitler.

But of the seven, only one adversely affected Hitler.

Hitler was forty years old when he became the legal guardian of his half sister's daughter, Angela "Geli" Raubal, who was twenty-three. They lived together in a well-appointed apartment in Munich, her bedroom located right next to his. According to all accounts, Hitler adored Geli, and she enjoyed being the object of his attention. He showered her with gifts and paid for voice lessons when she showed some interest in the craft. He preened with her on his arm and thundered when she showed interest in spending time with other men.

The relationship had limits, however, as Geli had no desire to marry him, and he was unable (or unwilling) to force his will on her. Still, he yearned to possess her, to control her every move. Seeing himself as a talented artist, he painted lewd pictures of her in the nude, which were stolen in an effort to blackmail him (and reacquired through purchase from the blackmailer). There are stories that he slashed her with a bull-hide whip he often carried. But she remained by his side, like so many abused partners. She stayed until she could stand it no more. On the night of September 18, 1931, following yet another screaming match, Geli shot herself in the heart with one of Hitler's Walther revolvers. Hitler was out of town. Geli's body was discovered the following morning by the housekeeper, Annie Winter.

Next to the passing of his mother, whose picture he carried with him until his death, the suicide of Geli had the most dramatic effect on Hitler's psyche. He ordered the suicide covered up, and, for the next two weeks he barely ate and rarely slept. According to confidants, he had to be physically restrained from committing suicide. In Hitler's twisted mind, the death of Geli elevated her to a saint. Her bedroom became a shrine in which fresh flowers were placed each day to honor her memory. A full-length painting of Geli hung in Hitler's alpine home near Berchtesgaden, commonly known as the Berghof. Underneath the painting always sat another bowl of fresh flowers. Hitler carried Geli's picture next to his mother's until his own death (by the same pistol Geli had used) in 1945. As his memory reinvented the young woman, her suicide became regal, an honorable, heroic choice to which he would refer again and again over the ensuing years.

There were several events in Hitler's life that drove him closer and closer to the insane, autocratic tyrant he eventually became. But the guilt he felt at Geli's suicide was the trigger that fully unleashed his complete lack of morality and conscience. As Robert Payne so aptly describes Hitler's mental deterioration in *The Life and Death of Adolf Hitler*, "She was of his blood and flesh, almost a daughter and almost a wife, closer to him than anyone else in the world. To have caused her death was to have committed the ultimate crime; the guilt would remain, never to be washed away. Henceforth, he was free from all of the conventional ties of morality . . . He had gone beyond good and evil, and entered a strange landscape where . . . all the ordinary human values were reversed. Like Dostoyevsky's Grand Inquisitor, he succumbed to 'the dread spirit of death and destruction.'"

It is important that you, dear reader, understand Hitler's state of mind as he makes the acquaintance of a beautiful young opera singer named Ursula Becker. In this story, he has been following her career from afar, much as he followed (and courted) Stefanie only in his mind. It has been several years since the death of his beloved niece when he finally meets Ursula Becker, who so closely resembles Geli that Hitler cannot help but be drawn to her. He yearns to possess Ursula, to consume her. But her will is strong and her personality rebellious. As she continues to defy him, his broken mind conflates the two women and, over time, the truculent Ursula *becomes* Geli. Hitler is left with two choices: once again cause the death of someone he cherishes or allow her to live and openly defy him. The personal decisions he makes, as seen through Ursula's eyes, reflect the turmoil he continues to create throughout the world.

This is not a novel about Adolf Hitler, who died like a coward in an underground bunker instead of facing the atrocities for which he would have been held accountable. This is a story that represents the victims, a tale of one woman's struggle to survive against overwhelming odds as the object of a crazy person's possessive passion. This is a love story that spans continents and time, war and cruelty. This is a story of the worst and the best that human nature has to offer, a tale of the resilience of the human spirit, of the Light against interminable darkness. And we all know that, in the end, despite the unthinkable atrocities that were waged on the innocent, the Light overcame the darkness.

Respectfully Yours,
Elizabeth B. Splaine
October 2021

I

1933

1

The tall, raven-haired beauty stood motionless in the cavernous space and appraised the sea of red velvet seats. Placing her hands on her slim waist, she adjusted the belt of her knee-length, lightweight wool dress and kicked off her brown leather pumps. Shapely calves sheathed in seamed stockings offered the casual observer a tantalizing glimpse of her delicate bone structure.

Sudden, bright light stabbed her large brown eyes, and she threw up her hand to shield them. Straight ahead, the lighting director waved as he tested various colors. She smiled as the spectrum splashed blue and purple across the perky cherubs who never tired of supporting the balconies.

Ursula closed her eyes and inhaled deeply, allowing her lungs to expand until her midsection bulged. The musty, woody scent that wafted up from the worn, pine floorboards snaked its way into the olfactory portion of her brain, reminding her that she stood in her most favorite place in the world. She blew out the air she'd been holding, then stretched her lips to relax the tension that had settled there. She opened her eyes and scanned the auditorium where, in just a few short hours, the most wealthy and influential Berliners would be seated, the men chattering in hushed tones about the blossoming economy while their wives furtively evaluated the competition outfitted in the latest haute couture.

Following the Wall Street crash four years prior, many countries were in financial ruin. Germany had not been immune to the economic downturn, so Ursula was grateful that people still regularly attended the opera. Her father believed that an operatic performance allowed a brief respite from the drudgery of daily life, if only for a few hours. A chance to soar with the eagles on some of the most majestic music ever composed. He liked to say that Ursula's work was critical to Germany, her small part in maintaining and growing the cultural icon that Berlin had become.

Ursula reached her arms toward the auditorium's domed ceiling where angels danced among the clouds, and then quickly bent forward, dropping her hands to the floor. She allowed herself a moment of silence and stillness as she simply hung there, the tiny muscles in her arms, shoulders, and neck slowly achieving full release with her repeated, low breaths. She inhaled deeply once more, enjoying the expansion in her lower back. Someone cleared his throat.

"Excuse me, Fräulein, but you cannot be in here. We have a show in two hours, and we must prepare."

Ursula slowly raised her torso and grinned, her even, white teeth completing the image of elegance and refinement. "Do you not recognize me out of costume, Fritz?"

The diminutive, white-haired man blushed, and he removed his wool cap. His rheumy blue eyes found the floor as the cap writhed in his large, veined hands. Shifting his weight from one foot to the other, he mumbled, "Oh, please excuse me, Fräulein Becker. I did not know it was you. Take as much time as you need."

Ursula approached the theatre's property custodian and placed her hand on his crepe-paper, mottled arm. "I have asked you many times to please call me Ursula, Fritz. After all, I refer to you always as Fritz. In fact, I just now realize that I do not know your surname." He gazed at her with unsettling sincerity.

"Rosen. Rosen is my surname."

"Fritz Rosen." Ursula rolled the name around her tongue. "It flows nicely, does it not?"

"Ja, Fräulein."

"Ursula."

Fritz's entire countenance lit up as he smiled, revealing two missing teeth. "Ja, Fräulein Ursula."

Ursula shook her head and laughed. "I suppose that Fräulein Ursula will have to do for now."

As Fritz retreated, Ursula stepped forward until she was aligned with the proscenium arch, the most advantageous acoustical point on the stage. She dropped her head and closed her eyes, allowing her imagination to morph her into Adele, her character in the upcoming opera. After a few moments, she lifted her head, smiled brightly, and launched into vocal exercises that slowly and deliberately climbed the pentatonic scale until she'd reached her goal, a quiet but solid high E flat. Satisfied, she waved to Fritz, who had seated himself in the balcony to listen to her abbreviated

2

concert, and hurried to her dressing room, where her hair and makeup stylist awaited her.

"Ursula, where have you been? You're late! You are not the only person for whom I work, you know."

Ursula rolled her eyes. Hilde Mayer had been employed by the opera house since the age of sixteen when she'd been apprenticed by her father. She had started as a costume seamstress until she discovered a passion for makeup artistry, which she deftly parlayed into a new career by marrying the former opera house manager. Her husband had since passed, leaving Hilde the unofficial mistress of the opera house and the uncontested lead makeup artist. Hilde was now in her mid-thirties and had seen divas come and go. Her righteous indignation was matched only by her expansive bustline, which heaved as if she'd run a fair distance prior to Ursula's arrival. Her thin, platinum-blond hair was plaited down her back, and her eye makeup was as elaborate as the outfit she'd cobbled together from various costume scraps.

"Hilde, we have this same conversation over and over. You don't need to do my hair and makeup first. Why don't you start with Frau Baumann and then come to me?"

"Because she's a contentious snot. She's been singing for far too long and believes that her vocal prowess is unrivaled."

Ursula sat and acquiesced to the horsehair brush being dragged through her long hair. She grimaced as Hilde's strokes matched the vigor with which she continued to denigrate the aging opera star.

"Helga Baumann used to be like you, Ursula. Kind and humble, bordering on insecure."

"I am not insecure," Ursula balked.

Hilde stopped brushing and stared at Ursula in the mirror. "Not about your singing. But you are insecure about men."

Ursula crinkled her nose and Hilde recommenced brushing. "But her years in the spotlight have altered her demeanor. She's haughty and believes that each man she encounters desires her. I've seen it happen over and over again. Young ingenues enter the door of this glorious Statische Opera house and conceited, overbearing women emerge. Don't let the same fate befall you, my dear."

"I'll do my best, Hilde."

Hilde stopped brushing and jutted out a hip. "You're unique, Ursula. Your voice is beautiful, but great voices are common. No, there is something else about you." She shook the hairbrush as she considered her words. "I have the belief that you were meant to do something special."

"I am doing something special, Hilde. I have the unparalleled opportunity to sing in this glorious theatre and get paid good money to do it! There is nothing more important than that."

A knowing smile grew as Hilde resumed her task. "You're wrong, Ursula. There are many more important things in this awful world. I pray that as long as you live, the most challenging task you encounter is how to embrace a difficult new role."

"Hilde, as usual you're being dramatic. I assume you're referring to current politics? You do like to prattle on and on about that."

Hilde halted, mid–brush stroke. "Yes. I do. Because the situation is frightening, Ursula. You need to pay attention."

Ursula sighed heavily. "I'm sorry that you lost your husband in the Great War. You know that my father fought as well and continues to suffer because of it. But Papa says that the world has experienced enough bloodshed for a lifetime, and that Germany is repaying its debt through the Treaty of Versailles."

Hilde shook her head as she gathered sections of Ursula's silky hair and twisted them into unfathomable knots, cementing them in place by driving metal hairpins into Ursula's scalp.

"Your father is wrong. I would have agreed with him before two years ago, but now von Hindenburg is ailing and may not run for re-election. There's no one suitable to replace him. People are tired, Ursula. Although our economy is on the rise, their memories of war and post-war reparations are strong. They'll turn to anyone who offers them security. I don't trust the new chancellor. His thugs held a book burning, for goodness' sake! Trust me, unless something changes, Germany will suffer, maybe even worse than it did after the Great War."

A perfunctory knock was followed by the fastidious opera house director sweeping into the small room. "There's my beautiful princess!" Carl Ebert was dressed in a fitted, pin-striped gray suit that matched the color of his closely cropped, salt-and-pepper hair, and he clutched a black walking stick that sported a silver handle in the shape of a ram. As far as Ursula could figure, the cane was not a physical requirement. Rather, Herr Ebert liked to use it as a prop as he spoke, gesticulating madly in the air to hammer home a point. He held his stick aloft, his arms wide.

"Herr Ebert, what a pleasant surprise," Ursula said. "Please forgive me if I don't rise to meet you, but I believe that Hilde's hairpins might skewer me clean through if I make the attempt."

Carl waved his cane. "No need, my love. I just came to wish you the best on your opening night. I'm so proud that you're my Adele in this production

4

of *Die Fledermaus*. I could not be happier and cannot imagine anyone more fitting or talented to assume the role."

"You are too kind, Herr Ebert. I hope that my interpretation of Adele will make Johann Strauss proud."

"Of that I have no doubt!" Carl approached Ursula and whispered conspiratorially. "You should know, my dear, that there will be some important people in the audience this evening."

Ursula smiled. "I'll do my best."

Carl withdrew and flared his eyes as he regarded Ursula in the mirror. "I mean, *really* important people."

Ursula cocked her head, causing a hairpin to miss its mark. "Ouch!"

"Don't move, Ursula!" Hilde ordered as she wound another section of hair.

"What really important people?" Ursula asked.

"President von Hindenburg."

Ursula's eyes widened. "I was under the impression that he doesn't care for opera."

"That's true. But rumor has it that his guest is an opera connoisseur, and that his favorite opera is—"

"*Die Fledermaus*," Ursula finished.

"Exactly!" Herr Ebert waggled his eyebrows. "Apparently this gentleman knows many wealthy people who funded his campaign for the National Socialist German Workers Party. Perhaps if he enjoys your performance this evening, you might meet him afterward and then, who knows? He might want to make a contribution to our humble opera house." Herr Ebert threw his arms wide, the silver ram barely missing Hilde's head. Hilde sniffed loudly.

"Frau Mayer, do you have something that you'd like to add?"

"We have all seen this 'gentleman' to whom you are referring, and he is a boob. A loud, barking boob."

Carl leaned close to Hilde and spoke quietly. "You're speaking ill of a powerful man who is considering running for president, Frau Mayer. Be careful. You never know who is listening."

Ursula turned in her chair. "Of whom do you speak? You can't be referring to Herr Hitler, as he was just recently appointed chancellor. My father says that he's an unproven politician. He wouldn't be so brash as to consider running for president so soon."

Hilde grunted. "He's more than brash, Ursula. He's dangerous. Mark my words. There's something about him. Although he's small in stature, he carries himself with an air of authority and assuredness. I'm sad to say that he can be quite riveting and convincing. People are listening."

Carl's cane crashed against the floor, causing Ursula to jump in the chair. "Enough, Hilde! Silence!"

Ursula watched in the mirror as the two overbearing personalities faced off. She wondered who would blink first. "I will do my best, Herr Ebert. You have my word."

The statement broke the stalemate and Carl smiled broadly. "Of course you will, my love. And you will meet him afterwards. He has followed your career closely, from your early days when you were studying with the incomparable Lilli Lehmann in Salzburg. You know Herr Hitler is Austrian by birth."

"I didn't know that."

"Yes, and he saw you sing 'Song of the Moon' when you performed in *Rusalka*."

Ursula's mind floated away to the small apartment she had shared with her parents in Prague. Her mother, a talented singer herself, had studied music under the great Czech composer Antonin Dvorak, and she had sung "Song of the Moon" to Ursula as a lullaby. Ursula had memorized the aria before she learned how to read music. After her mother died, she and her father had moved to Berlin, where her father had met and married a talented violinist and had another daughter named Anna. Unfortunately, her stepmother had passed away two years ago, leaving her father twice a widower with two daughters to support.

"My mother taught me that song," Ursula mumbled in Czech.

"I beg your pardon?" Herr Ebert asked.

Ursula shook her head, returning to German. "Forgive me. All I have left of my mother is songs she taught me and fluency in Czech. I haven't been able to use either recently."

Herr Ebert smiled tightly. "Yes, well, tonight is all in German, my dear. As I was saying, Herr Hitler has followed you since you sang in small opera houses in Austria and Germany, but tonight you make your debut as the lead on the Berlin operatic stage. It shall be glorious!" His cane swung wildly, and both women ducked to avoid being struck.

Herr Ebert stilled his cane and set his gaze on Ursula. "I know you will make us all proud. You belong to Germany now and will be considered one of its treasures once Herr Hitler deems it so." He clapped his cane against his open palm. "I must go and attend to our guests." He exited with a flourish, the door slamming behind him.

Ursula met Hilde's hard stare in the mirror. "Be careful, Ursula."

Ursula rolled her eyes.

Hilde shook her head slowly. "Do not dismiss my words, Ursula. There are rumors that Hitler has his eye on ruling not just Germany but surrounding nations as well. He believes that Germany requires room to spread out. 'Living room,' he calls it. He's looking to undo the Treaty of Versailles. He's treacherous."

"Hilde, my job is to sing well and that's what I shall do. When I meet Herr Hitler afterwards, I will be polite. Then our relationship will be over."

Hilde shook her head. "I hope so, Ursula. I really hope so."

2

The applause rumbled like thunder across the cavernous auditorium. The crowd leapt to its feet as Ursula crossed to center stage for her curtain call. Hans Schmidt, who had played the role of Eisenstein, received rousing accolades, as did Marie Geistinger, who had played Rosalinde. But it was Ursula's interpretation of Adele that had the audience on its feet yelling "Brava!" and tossing flowers. At only twenty-six years old, she was the youngest singer to successfully present the aria "Mein Herr Marquis," or the "laughing song" as it was colloquially known, in such a grand theatre. Ursula's expression of genuine, grateful surprise crowned her the immediate audience favorite, and the ovations continued for several more minutes before Carl Ebert joined the cast on stage.

"Damen und Herren, please sit down." Carl motioned with his cane for the audience members to retake their seats. "We are so pleased that you have enjoyed tonight's performance." The crowd rose once again as a new round of applause burst forth. Ursula laughed out loud, amazed at the enthusiasm. Berliners were known to be staunch supporters of opera, especially German and Austrian works, but the current response was overwhelming. Ebert's cane took on a life of its own as it bobbed up and down, motioning for the group to be seated.

"As I said, we are extremely pleased that you have enjoyed this evening's performance of *Die Fledermaus*. We are fortunate to be privy to established talent such as Frau Geistinger." The audience stood once more as shouts of "Brava!" resounded against the gold-leafed dome. Ursula smiled broadly as Frau Geistinger stepped forward and raised her hands outwards toward her swooning fans. She waved and then brought her fingers to her lips, kissed them, and threw them to the raucous crowd before collapsing into an elaborate bow/curtsy combination known simply as "the Geistinger." *How wonderful it would be to be adored like that,* Ursula mused as her eyes swept across the ebullient crowd.

"And, of course I would be mightily remiss if were not to mention the, how shall I say, up-and-coming talent of Fräulein Ursula Becker." Ursula was shocked that she had been singled out of the large cast and stood frozen in place as the applause rose to a deafening roar. She glanced at Herr Ebert, who motioned with his head that she should acknowledge the adulation. Hesitant, she stepped forward and curtsied deeply as she bowed her head to the roaring crowd. Flowers landed at her feet and she picked them up, one by one, until she had formed a ragtag bouquet, which she cradled in her right arm like a baby. She glanced at Frau Geistinger for guidance and found a tight smile and hard eyes. As Ursula scanned the thousands of well-wishers, she realized with astonishment that she was being anointed the new grand diva of opera. And Frau Geistinger knew it. Ursula raised her head and waved to the adoring crowd before blowing a kiss and walking briskly off stage, where she dropped to her knees and started sobbing.

"Fräulein, are you hurt?" Suddenly Fritz was at her side, a concerned furrow firmly planted in his generous brow.

"I am . . . I am . . . overwhelmed," she stuttered. Carl Ebert rushed to the wings and searched Fritz's face for assurance that Ursula was alright. Fritz nodded, and Ebert visibly relaxed and returned to speak to the audience. Ursula caught her breath and wiped her eyes. Fritz offered her a handkerchief, which she accepted with a sigh.

"You are very kind, Fritz. A true gentleman. I don't believe there are many of you left in this world." Fritz blushed. On stage Ebert was informing the audience about a reception in the lobby, an opportunity to meet the cast. Ursula dabbed at her eyes, certain that her heavy makeup had melded with her tears to form a colorful, grotesque mosaic.

"I must look a fright, eh, Fritz?" She laughed as she considered her pitiful bouquet of wilting flowers—fresh roses that had sat on the warm laps of patrons for several hours before being hoisted through the air to land with a thump on the hard, wooden stage floor.

"You look beautiful, Fräulein. Always."

Ursula smiled at Fritz, who immediately averted his eyes. "You are too kind, Herr Rosen."

"Let me help you to your feet, Fräulein. Your public awaits you at the reception."

Fritz extended his arthritic, calloused hand to help Ursula stand. At her full height she towered over him as she straightened her wig and smoothed her dress.

"I'm going to hug you now, Fritz, whether you like it or not."

Before he could protest, she wrapped her arms around him and squeezed tightly. "Thank you for being my friend."

Fritz grunted and cleared his throat as Carl Ebert appeared. "Ursula, what on earth are you doing? Come. We must go to the lobby. There are literally hundreds of people waiting to meet you."

Ursula allowed herself to be led away and placed atop the grand staircase that greeted operagoers as they entered the remarkable building. A line snaked its way down the Italian marble stairs and out of her sight as she shook hands and accepted accolades, repeating "thank you" and "you're so very kind" over and over again. After what seemed like an eternity, Ebert appeared at her side and ushered her away, leaving many attendees frustrated that they didn't have the opportunity to chat with her.

As they passed Frau Geistinger, Ursula smiled and received a frosty glare in return. Ursula noted that the line of people waiting to meet the aging diva was only one third of the length of her line. She felt a rush of sadness for the singer, appreciating the swiftness with which tastes can change. Now it was Ursula's turn to shine. But before too long she realized, even in this most precious of moments, that her starlight would wane, and she would be regarding her own replacement with a quizzical tilt of her head, much like Frau Geistinger was doing now. Ursula decided that she must cherish the fleeting moments. She understood that everything can change in an instant.

Ebert guided her to a large, ornate door. Although Ursula had never entered the room, she was aware that receptions for dignitaries were often held there. Ebert knocked twice. She noted that he was sweating as he smoothed his suitcoat and hair. His posture was stiff, and his grip on her elbow had tightened.

"You seem tense, Herr Ebert." He threw her a stern look as a voice ordered, "Enter!" Standing a full inch taller than usual, Ebert switched his cane to his left hand and offered his right arm to Ursula.

"Don't be flippant, my dear. Just be your mesmerizing self."

She looked at him. "I don't know what that means, Herr Ebert."

The door opened slowly to reveal a group of about twenty people, the men in crisp Party uniforms and the women wearing gowns and silk gloves. Upon the newcomers' entrance, all heads swiveled appreciatively toward Ursula. The group broke into polite applause, stifled by the fact that each person held a champagne flute. A man emerged from the group and fixed his gaze on hers. He approached and raised Ursula's right hand to his lips. He kissed her hand, then openly evaluated her round face. His deep blue eyes settled on her warm brown ones.

"Fräulein Becker. Your performance this evening was simply astonishing. Your interpretation of Herr Strauss's glorious Adele left me speechless." He leaned forward and stage-whispered, "And that is saying something, my dear." Polite chuckles rippled through the onlookers.

"Thank you, Herr Hitler." Hitler's probing eyes examined Ursula's face, as if he were trying to memorize the details. His eyebrows came together, and,

1 1

to her surprise, his eyes became dewy. The moment stretched for so long that she glanced to Ebert for guidance. Hitler broke the silence. "Your hairpiece must be itchy and warm." Ursula paused. His reaction to meeting her was confusing and bizarre. His stare was disconcerting, heavy with familiarity, yet they had never met. She didn't know how to respond, so she offered a half smile, revealing a dimple on the right side of her mouth. Hitler's eyes jumped to it.

"Yes. The wig is warm."

Without removing his eyes from the indentation, he said, "I have seen your real hair in a production in Vienna. It is a glorious brown that draws attention to your eyes." His unsettling gaze moved to her eyes once more, and she found herself mesmerized by his intense stare. Hilde's words came back to her. *He can be quite convincing. People are listening.* Hilde was correct. He commanded attention and respect without demanding it. His expression was austere, and his small moustache twitched. His pupils flared and then became pinpoints as he awaited her response.

Ursula held his steady gaze and smiled demurely. "My father refers to my eyes and my hair as mud brown."

For several moments time slowed. The stillness and silence in the large room closed around her, and she felt her pulse quicken. She glanced at Herr Ebert and then at the man who stood unmoving before her. Eventually, a small smile played on Hitler's lips, and he dipped his head forward to adorn her hand once more with a kiss. "On the contrary, Fräulein. Your bright eyes are riveting." He turned so the crowd could hear him. "And how refreshing it is to meet someone who speaks her mind so plainly and without remorse. Much like myself," he added as he winked at Ursula. "Will you dine with me this evening, my dear?"

"Thank you, Herr Hitler, but I cannot. I must return home to attend to my father. He's ill."

"Oh, my dear. I am so sorry to hear that. I shall send my personal physician to see him tomorrow."

Ebert cleared his throat. "I'm certain, Fräulein Becker, that you can spare an evening with Herr Hitler if he's willing to send his personal physician to see your father tomorrow, can you not?"

Ursula turned to face the director. "Unfortunately, Herr Ebert, I would be remiss if I didn't return home immediately, per my father's instructions."

She turned back to Hitler and offered her most winning smile. "I'm sure an important man like yourself will understand that I cannot disobey my father."

Hitler's eyes burned brightly as he patted her hand. "Oh, my dear. Germany should have more women like you. Intelligent, talented, and simply breathtaking. Of course, you shall return home per your father's directive. Expect Dr. Brandt in the morning."

"You're too kind, Herr Hitler. Thank you for your generosity."

He inclined his head. "I wonder, though, if I might have the pleasure of your company on another occasion? Perhaps a small dinner when I am hosting some close friends?" His intimate gaze lingered on her lips.

Ursula paused as Hilde's concerns ran through her mind. Although his overtness disconcerted her, he had been nothing but kind. "I thank you for your gracious invitation."

"Perfect." His piercing stare went through her, as if he were gazing into the past. "I shall have my personal secretary be in touch, my dear. Until then."

He kissed her hand once more, released her, and the room came back to life. She realized that no one had moved during her interchange with Hitler, as if the crowd were hanging on his every word. Indeed, when he had spoken to her, everything else had seemed to fall away, as if she were the most important person in his world. Ursula understood why Herr Ebert was so impressed with Adolf Hitler. He had a charisma about him that drew people in. She couldn't wait to tell her father about the kind man who was sending his personal physician to her home tomorrow.

3

"Absolutely not!" Otto Becker thundered. "Under no circumstances is anyone affiliated with that crazy man allowed in my house!"

"Papa, how can you say that? You bleed when you cough. You're unable to take care of Anna and me. We need help, and Herr Hitler has offered it. How can we possibly turn his physician away?"

Otto stood with the aid of thirteen-year-old Anna. Leaning on her thin arm, he rose to his full height. His clear blue eyes were wide as he shook his crooked finger and spoke with great clarity of tone. "Ursula, I have known men like Hitler before. Nothing good will come from associating with him."

Her father turned toward the small kitchen in their two-bedroom flat. Using the sparse furniture as touchstones, he slowly made his way to the kitchen table and sat down heavily in a wooden chair that groaned under his weight. Ursula watched him wince as pain shot up his back and settled into his neck, which sat at an awkward angle against his left shoulder. A bullet from the Great War had lodged against his spine and was slowly putting pressure on the surrounding nerves. That, combined with a phlegmy cough that had recently turned bloody, left him unable to work consistently. Ursula looked on mutely, afraid to intervene lest he lash out in frustration. Her heart sank as she watched Otto remove a small flask from the windowsill and toss back its contents. He held the flask aloft and shook it to ensure the last drops fell into his mouth, then turned suddenly to Anna and ordered her to get him some more.

"Papa, you've had enough," Ursula said. "It's only ten o'clock in the morning."

Otto turned quickly and sucked in breath as new spasms of pain shook him. "I will determine when I have had enough." He breathed heavily and stared at her, daring her to challenge his authority.

Ursula glanced at Anna, who had sunk to the floor and pulled her knees against her chest in an effort to appear smaller and less conspicuous. She knew that Anna detested when they had disagreements, which were certainly more frequent since he'd been working less and drinking more. Ever since her stepmother had died from breast cancer two years prior, Ursula had assumed the home responsibilities. She'd watched her father sink into a depression that had started with understandable sadness but had slowly morphed into a barely controlled fury fueled by constant pain and his inability to provide for his family. As their circumstances had gone from bad to worse, pain in his chest had appeared, quickly followed by coughing fits that culminated in spitting up blood. Ursula knew that he needed the help of a well-trained physician. If he could get better, she reasoned, then the burden of supporting the family would once again fall on his shoulders. He would feel strong once more, and she could focus on singing. That was the plan in her imagination, but the conversation wasn't playing out as she had hoped.

She knelt by Otto so he could look at her without straining his neck. His tired eyes met hers and she saw tears gathering. "Papa, I love you. I want you to get better. For me, for Anna, and, most of all, for yourself. You are the strongest man I know. Please, see this physician."

Otto placed his large, calloused hand on Ursula's cheek and offered her an uneven, tobacco-stained grin. "I love you too, Ursula, and that's why I want you to stay away from Herr Hitler. Come, sit." He patted the chair next to him. "Anna, you come too. I want you both to hear this story. It might save your lives."

Anna rushed over, clearly relieved that the tension had eased. Ursula knew that her sister loved Otto's stories, the more dramatic the better, as she dreamed of one day being a movie star like Greta Garbo. Papa had a different plan for Anna, however, as she had exhibited an almost prodigious talent for the violin at a very early age. Initially Ursula's stepmother had taught Anna, helping her place the tiny fingers of her left hand on the neck of the violin while her right hand would slowly draw the horsehair bow across the strings. But when Anna had outgrown her mother's tutelage at the age of eight, Otto had ensured that, no matter how financially burdened the family became, Anna received top-notch training from a professor at the Berlin Conservatory. Similarly, Otto ensured that Ursula continued studying voice as well, urging her to apply for a one-year scholarship to study at the renowned Mozarteum in Salzburg, Austria. It was there that she'd worked with Lilli Lehmann prior to her death in 1929. It was there where she'd debuted on the professional operatic stage, and where Herr Hitler had first set eyes upon her.

Given Ursula's recent vocal achievements from last evening, it would seem that their parents' hard work was paying off for Ursula. But being only thirteen years old, Anna still had a long way to go before she could potentially make a living wage as a violinist. Ironically, it was now Ursula, not Otto, who insisted that Anna continue her music. In fact, Ursula had taken on extra washing and sewing to pay for Anna's most recent lessons. Anna revered her older sister and took the opportunity to curl up in her lap to listen to Otto's story. Ursula wrapped her arms around Anna and rocked her as she planted a kiss on the girl's soft blond curls. Otto cleared his throat.

"There was a man named Klaus who owned a cobbler shop. He was known throughout Berlin as being a most talented cobbler, honest and fair-priced. He prospered in his business as his reputation grew by word of mouth. Klaus had a friend named Peter who also owned a cobbler shop in Berlin, albeit smaller and not as well-known as Klaus's. Klaus was living comfortably and had no need to expand, but he was greedy. He visited Peter and suggested that he purchase Peter's smaller business. Peter politely declined, angering Klaus. Klaus returned to his own shop determined to put Peter out of business. Using most of his money, Klaus purchased all available supplies—leather uppers and soles, laces, additional machinery to enhance production—leaving nothing for Peter to purchase. As there was no room in his shop, Klaus stored the new supplies in his home, thereby angering his wife, especially when she learned why he had hoarded the supplies. Peter, unable to buy necessary supplies to create new shoes, sent out word to his neighbors, who brought him their older shoes to be mended. He started mending other items as well, such as belts and buttons, thereby expanding his business. Once word spread about what Klaus had done, people stopped going to his shop, preferring to give their business to the frugal Peter, who had altered his methods in order to survive and even prosper. Klaus realized his error and sold some of his horde of supplies to Peter, but it was too late. As Peter's business grew, Klaus had to close his shop. Klaus's wife, embarrassed to be married to a greedy louse, left him. Last I heard, Klaus was working for Peter. Many thought that Peter should turn Klaus away when he came looking for a job, but Peter took pity on the weak man and took him in."

Her father finished, leaned back in his chair, and crossed his arms. Anna smiled up at him. "Do you know this Klaus man, Papa?"

"I do," he said.

"And Peter?"

"Him too, yes."

Ursula smiled at how easily Anna could be entertained. In the midst of their chaotic lives, sometimes she forgot how young Anna was. "Papa, forgive me, but I don't understand what your story has to do with whether or not you will see this physician today."

Her father sighed heavily. "Ursula, Adolf Hitler is trying to be a Klaus. Kaiser Wilhelm made the exact same mistake, and it led to the Great War. Wilhelm wanted Germany to expand its navy to match Britain's. He succeeded, but the result made Britain wary of Germany. Wilhelm allowed his generals to commence the war, even though he knew it would be a mistake. But once it started, the conflict took on a life of its own and two million Germans died. The kind man, as you describe Herr Hitler, who is sending his private doctor to see me, is trying to do the same thing. He's trying to be a Klaus. Instead of being happy with what Germany is, he has designs to make it into a dominant European power. I love my country, and I don't want to see it ruined by a fanatic who uses his love of Germany as an excuse for another war, or worse."

"What could be worse than war?" Ursula asked.

Her father's eyes softened and took on a worried squint. "Annihilation."

Ursula burst out laughing. "Papa, you always tell me that I should save my drama for the stage. Now look who's being dramatic."

Before she could react, her father grabbed her hand and squeezed it hard. "Listen, you foolish girl!" he hissed. Shocked, she tried to pull away, but his grip remained.

"This Adolf Hitler is far worse than the general public knows. His Nazi thugs are terrorizing the city, and rumor is that he plans on creating an Aryan paradise where many people will not be welcome."

"What is . . . an Aryan paradise?" Anna asked.

Ursula ignored her. "How do you know this?"

Her father released her hand and looked away, embarrassed. "Because when I couldn't find construction work, I attended one of his rallies. I went searching for a purpose and returned terrified of what anger and power can do to a man."

"Papa, you're scaring me," Ursula said.

"You *should* be scared. That's my point."

Anna scuttled from Ursula's lap and dashed to a corner of the room, where she sank into her protective position, arms grasping her knees close to her chest. Ursula glanced at her and offered a tight smile. "Papa, you're scaring Anna."

Her father's eyes found Anna and calmed. He took Ursula's hand and rubbed it gently with his thumb.

"It's just that I don't want you involved with anyone like that, especially that man."

"I'm not involved with him, Papa. He simply offered his physician's services."

Before she'd finished her sentence, he was shaking his head. "A man like that always expects something in return for a favor."

Ursula blushed and averted her eyes. "Papa, I would never do such a thing."

"No, not *that*, Ursula. He can get that anywhere. He will want loyalty. And loyalty can be deadly."

"Papa, please—"

"Do you know that Germany is split right now between the communists and the worker's party? The political situation is becoming dire. People are looking to Hitler to fix the nation, but it's a serious mistake. Are you aware that he wants to rid Germany of all Jews?"

"What does that have to do with us?"

Two loud raps on the door made Ursula jump. Her father's glare morphed into a pleading stare as he looked from the door to his elder daughter. "Ursula, for the love of all that is good, do not let that man into our home."

Ursula, torn between wanting to help him but not wanting to disrespect her father, made a decision. She opened the door to the flat, where a dark-haired man with a high forehead stood holding a brown leather bag. He clicked his heels together. "Fräulein Becker, it is my pleasure to make your acquaintance. I am Doctor Karl Brandt, at your service."

His face was angular, and he sported a jaunty, full moustache that lifted as he offered a warm smile. Ursula found it challenging to hold his brown-eyed gaze and decided to look at his bag as she spoke. "Doctor Brandt, how extremely kind of you to make a house call. Unfortunately, I believe there's been a mistake. My father, who was quite ill yesterday, has rounded the corner today into full health and will, therefore, not require your services. I do thank you for your kindness and wish you a good day." Ursula started to close the door, which stopped abruptly as it bumped against Dr. Brandt's shoe wedged against the jamb.

"Fräulein, you must excuse me, but I cannot return to Herr Hitler without issuing him a full report on your father's health. He told me that the matter is of utmost importance to him."

Ursula lifted her eyes and matched his smile with her own. "Of course. Please tell Herr Hitler that Herr Becker is well and no longer in need of your services."

They stared at each other until Doctor Brandt finally nodded. "Will you not even invite me in for some tea perhaps?"

Ursula raised her chin. "Unfortunately, we are out of tea at the moment."

Dr. Brandt's smile faltered, then he backed away from the door and nodded efficiently. "I understand. Good day then."

"Good day to you, sir." Ursula closed the door and breathed a sigh of relief. She was shocked to find that her knees were trembling. Otto emerged from the bedroom where he'd hidden with Anna. "Well done, Ursula. Well done."

Ursula crossed to her father, who gathered both of his daughters in his arms. "As long as I have my two beautiful girls, I am whole."

1938

4

"My dear, you must embrace the character. Let her inside of your body. Or, better yet, inhabit the character and then let her emerge from you as a gift to your adoring audience."

"Of course, Maestro."

"Now, sing the aria once more and let me hear your new interpretation based on my suggestions."

The tall, wiry maestro tapped his baton twice on the music stand that held the massive opera score, drawing the attention of the fifty musicians who awaited his direction. He raised the baton, inhaled deeply, and commenced sweeping arm gyrations that guided the various instruments to play as one. Ursula crossed to her mark and drew a full breath, then opened "Du bist der Lenz" from *Die Walküre* with a warm timbre that drew a smile from the elderly conductor. As she worked her way through the aria, she moved with the music, winding her way across the expansive stage until she was embracing the actor playing Siegmund. Her voice crescendoed on the surging waves of music, the tension building as the musicians' fingers flew up and down the scales. She lifted her head as she held the final note, her declarative tone soaring up to the silent, marble cherubs. As the orchestra closed the aria, Ursula slowly collapsed in Siegmund's arms. The echoes of Wagner's masterpiece reverberated, creating the magical, heavenly effect of being transported through time and space while remaining completely still.

Ursula glanced at the conductor, whose hands were frozen in midair. He exhaled, washed ashore from the exhilarating musical tide. "Congratulations, my dear. You have just bested yourself."

"Thank you, Herr Maestro."

"It has been five years since your debut on my stage, and during that time I have observed you fully emerge from your cocoon. It has been my pleasure to see you successfully metamorphose into an exquisite butterfly. Alas, I would love to see your interpretation of the role of Madama Butterfly, but we both know that is not possible."

Ursula walked to the edge of the stage and lowered her voice so that only he could hear her. "I don't understand why we must perform only German opera when the Italians and the French have written such beautiful music as well."

"Sshhh!" commanded the maestro. He turned to the orchestra. "Get some fresh air, everyone, and return in ten minutes." The musicians exited the auditorium, and the maestro shook his head. "Ursula, you must mind your tongue. If word were to travel to the Führer that you've spoken ill of German opera ..."

His words hung in the air. Ursula recalled the previous day when she had watched in horror as a man had been dragged out of a bank and beaten. The sound of a heavy leather boot finding its mark in the man's ribs made her wince, and, if she closed her eyes, she could vividly recall the stench of vomit as his stomach emptied its contents on the SS officer's boot. That unfortunate action had enraged the soldier, and he'd erupted in a renewed torrent of kicks and verbal abuse that ended with the poor man's head being staved in. Ursula had willed herself to look away but found that her eyes would not oblige. Instead, she had stuffed her hand in her mouth to keep from screaming and swallowed the bile that rose to her mouth. As sickening as the scene was, no one had dared to intervene, lest they become the next victim.

When she was certain that the man's suffering had ended, Ursula had run home and sobbed in Otto's arms.

"You shouldn't watch such things, Ursula."

"But how can I not, Papa? If I don't witness it, then I can pretend the mayhem isn't happening. I believe that's what the Nazis want. They want us to become accustomed to the hate, violence, and fear. If we do, then perhaps it will be easier to control us."

Her father had held her at a distance and smiled. "You're a smart girl, Ursula, and I agree with you. But—" He had tapped her nose with his forefinger. "Keep your opinions to yourself. You do not know who is a Nazi spy."

That conversation had been less than fifteen hours ago, and Ursula was once again speaking too plainly with the maestro.

"I'm not speaking ill of German opera. I'm simply stating the obvious. German opera is wonderful, but there are—"

The maestro held up his hand to silence her as a tall, athletic man dressed in a navy blue, double-breasted suit sauntered down the middle aisle of the theatre. His suit jacket nipped in at the waist and flared at the bottom, enhancing his broad shoulders. His trousers were creased perfectly, and his brown leather wing tips shone.

"Excuse me for interrupting, Herr Maestro, but I noticed that the instrumentalists were on break, and I wondered if I might take the opportunity to say how much I enjoyed the performance of *Die Zaubergeige* last Saturday evening."

The conductor cleared his throat. "Why, thank you, Herr—"

"Hitler. The name is Hitler. Tell me please, who is this exquisite young lady I see before me?"

The man turned and fixed his dark blue eyes on Ursula. His chestnut brown hair was combed straight back and held in place with a generous amount of pomade. He angled his head and offered her an enigmatic smile.

She had the feeling they'd met before. "What did you say your name was?"

The man approached her and gently took her hand. After kissing it and commenting on her alabaster skin, he met her gaze. "I'm William Patrick Hitler, but my friends call me Willy."

Ursula pursed her lips. "Any relation to—"

"The Führer? Yes, but please don't hold it against me."

Ursula's discerning eyes narrowed like a cat. "You are not from Germany."

"I am not. I was raised in England."

Ursula nodded. That explained his peculiar accent. "And you are here because . . .?"

The maestro cleared his throat. "Ursula, I am certain Herr Hitler doesn't need to tell us why he came to Germany or to our humble opera house."

Still openly staring at Ursula, Willy waved his hand in the maestro's direction. "It's fine, my good man. I don't mind a woman who speaks so directly. In point of fact, I rather enjoy it. I am in Germany because my father, the Führer's half brother, lives here and I don't have the opportunity to see him very much. Additionally, I'm now employed by the Reichskreditbank and have taken up residence in this beautiful city. As for why I'm in this astounding opera house—" He swept his arms wide and looked around the cavernous space trimmed in gold relief. "I came to show my appreciation for the maestro's talent and attention to detail."

The maestro stood taller and bowed his head in thanks before glancing at Ursula. "You are aware, Herr Hitler, that Fräulein Becker sang the role of Gretl in the production that you attended."

He nodded curtly. "I am aware, yes."

"I am sure that you would agree that she did an outstanding job in the role."

"She was enjoyable, to be sure."

It wasn't his words. It was the manner in which he'd stated them that made Ursula's blood rise. She had received nothing but positive reviews regarding her performance, both in person and in print. To be receiving a mediocre report from an egotistical Anglophile was an affront.

"Well, Herr Hitler, I am so sorry to hear that you had to *suffer* through my performance."

Willy turned to her with a playful glint in his eyes. "Are you aware that your eyes take on a deeper hue of brown when you're angry, Fräulein? They are quite off-putting, if I may say so. I certainly did not mean to offend. You should understand, I detest the opera. I attend only because my uncle insists that I gain more culture in my life. You were exquisite, but you see, your grandeur was lost on this ignorant troglodyte."

Ursula tried not to smile but lost the battle. She burst out laughing.

"My God, but you're beautiful," Willy said.

She brought her hand to her mouth and blushed. "And you are quite forward, Herr Hitler. I'm sure that my father would not approve."

The maestro, fearing that his presence had been forgotten, shifted on his feet and cleared his throat. Willy tore his gaze from Ursula. "Forgive me, Maestro, but I must take my leave. Again, it was a pleasure to meet you. Both of you." Willy turned to Ursula and took her hand. "If I promise to behave, may I present myself to your father so that you and I might dine together this evening?"

Ursula knew that she should say no. Warning bells rang in her head about this suave man who had inadvertently insulted not only her singing, but her chosen profession as well. As a performer, Ursula possessed a vivid imagination, and there was no way the situation ended well in any version of events. But before her brain could fully process a response, her mouth spoke.

"Yes. That would be lovely."

"Splendid. I shall pick you up at, say, six? That will give me enough time."

"Enough time for what?"

Willy smiled and Ursula felt her pulse quicken. "To persuade your father that I'm not the cad you will make me out to be upon your arrival home."

Ursula had never met anyone so brash in his speech. No German man would utter such nonsense and expect the date to occur. And yet, somehow, the confidence fit him, this nephew of the one and only Führer.

5

"A date, Ursula? You have finally secured a date?" Otto shook his head, then looked up and raised his hands in a supplicating gesture. "Mein Gott, you are truly up there. My daughter has a real date."

"Papa, please." Ursula rolled her eyes. She wrapped her arms around Otto's waist and lay her head against his barrel chest. He responded by kissing the top of her head and enclosing her in one of his bear hugs. She smiled as she took in his scent, then sighed in contentment. Not one moment was taken for granted since Otto had come so close to death several years ago. When Ursula had turned Doctor Brandt away at the door, Otto's health had steadily declined until she had insisted that he see someone. Although many of the best physicians had left Berlin in search of a stable political climate, Ursula had managed a barter agreement. In exchange for doing his family's washing for one month, Dr. Gottlieb had agreed to see Otto. He could do nothing about the bullet lodged against his spine but had diagnosed Otto with high blood pressure and a severe lung infection.

In confidence, Dr. Gottlieb had told Ursula that the illness was well-advanced and would most likely worsen. In Otto's presence, however, the doctor was more positive. He had instructed Otto to lower his stress level and had prescribed strong herbal tea to aid healing. Over the next six months, Otto had meticulously followed the doctor's orders and his health had slowly improved. He now coughed only intermittently and had been able to do sporadic jobs that boosted his pride and contributed to the family budget. He had lost most of his hair during his recovery, however, and blamed it on the tea. But he was grateful to be alive, and his only wish, which he voiced every chance he could, was to see his two girls grown and happily married.

"Yes, I have a date. But I've told you many times, Papa. I do not need another man in my life. You are most important, and I don't see that changing anytime soon. Besides, we're more financially sound now. I don't want you to worry about me."

Otto glanced at Anna and sighed. "And what of your sister if something happens to me, Ursula? She's only eighteen years old. How would you manage then? You wouldn't have a life of your own."

Ursula reached up and took Otto's face in her delicate hands. "Papa, Dr. Gottlieb told you not to worry. I'm also telling you not to worry. Nothing will happen to you. And if it did, I'm very capable of taking care of Anna. My goodness, she is almost grown. Before you know it, she'll be playing in the orchestra. Another well-paid musician in your house." Ursula smiled proudly.

"Things can change quickly, Ursula. Look at what's been happening to the Jews in the city. Herr Kravitz's shop windows were broken. He was dragged into the street and beaten in front of his own family. Trust me when I say that things will get worse before they get better."

"Papa, I'm sorry for the Kravitz family, but the fact is that we need to care for our own family. Right now, we're doing well. Please, just be happy with that. You speak often of the plight of the Jews. Again, I ask you, what concern is that of ours?"

"It matters because they're human beings and aren't being treated as such. It matters because, well . . ." Otto paused and examined his hands. "I just want to ensure your safety and security, whatever it takes." A soft knock sounded.

Ursula grinned and jumped up. "Your speech will have to wait, Papa. How do I look?" She touched her hair and smoothed the skirt of her flower-print dress.

Otto raised an eyebrow. "Why do you care how you look for your date if I'm the most important man in your life, dear daughter?"

Ursula narrowed her eyes and twisted her mouth into a grin as Anna crossed to the door. When she opened it, Willy touched the brim of his hat and beamed at Ursula. He removed his fedora, then inclined his head politely toward Otto. "Herr Becker, it's my honor to make your acquaintance." Turning toward Anna, he said, "I assume this beauty standing before me is your sister?" Anna giggled and ran into the bedroom, closing the door quickly behind her.

Otto stood at his full six-foot-two frame and nodded once. Walking quickly forward, he gripped Willy's hand. "So, you are the young gentleman who has my Ursula tying herself in knots."

"Papa!" Ursula bit her lip and stood next to Otto.

"In all of her excitement, she has told me little about you. I know you only as Willy, the man she met at rehearsal. Come, sit, and tell me about yourself."

Ursula drew a quick breath. "Papa, we have a reservation . . ."

Otto glared at her. "The young man can take a moment to tell me what he does for a living and what his future plans are."

Ursula offered Willy a tight smile and pulled out a chair at the kitchen table. Willy sat and cleared his throat, turning his fedora round and round in his hands. Otto sat heavily in the chair opposite him.

"Well, sir, I grew up in England. I'm currently employed at the Reichskreditbank."

"In what position?"

"Assistant manager."

"I see. A fine position. Do you anticipate advancement at the bank?"

Willy smiled. "I do, as the current manager will be... retiring soon."

Otto paused and leaned back. "I know Herr Bronstein. He is in his forties, yet he is retiring?"

Willy glanced nervously at Ursula before responding. "That's my understanding, Herr Becker. He is a . . . he is . . ."

Otto nodded and slowly leaned forward in his chair, carefully placing his large palms on the table. "Son, you're clearly taken with my Ursula. But, more importantly to me, she is taken with you. So, I could sit with you all evening and converse, but I really need to know only one thing."

Willy's gaze intensified to match Otto's. "Yes?"

Ursula knew that her father would choose his next words carefully. Having already lived through one war, he understood that he must be perceived as loyal to the current president, or risk losing everything.

"I, of course, support our Führer's decisions. Do you support his regime as well?"

By using the word "regime," Otto was implying a dictatorship without stating it outright. Willy immediately recognized the verbiage that Otto had employed and responded in kind.

"I, too, support the Führer's ... reign and wish him only the best. I recognize that my advancement at the bank will be due to another's loss, and I feel genuine sadness at that. However, I'm also a practical person and understand that if I intend to support a wife and family, I must use the advantages that are presented to me."

He held Otto's gaze as he spoke. Ursula understood that Willy would be leaving soon, either with her on his arm or alone.

She glanced nervously from one man to the other and watched Otto consider Willy's words. After an interminable length of time, she pursed her lips and cleared her throat.

"Papa, may we leave now?"

Otto squinted at Willy for another moment before responding, "Yes. You may." Relief melted the tension in her shoulders. "I believe you've found a fine young man here, my dear."

Ursula glanced at Willy and then at the ground, knowing what was still to come. *But maybe, just maybe, we can exit the apartment before Papa remembers to ask Willy about—*

"I haven't asked you your full name, young man. I know you only as Willy."

Otto stood and shook Willy's hand as they crossed to the door. Willy nodded once and met Otto's eyes.

"It's Hitler, Herr Becker. My full name is William Patrick Hitler."

Otto paused and glanced at Ursula, whose heart hammered in her chest. Otto's eyebrows drew together, and he inhaled deeply. Ursula steeled herself for the angry bellow she was certain would emerge. To her complete astonishment, Otto guffawed and slapped Willy on the back. "I see that you have found a man with a good sense of humor! Yes, you are Willy Hitler, and I am Franz von Papen!" Otto roared with laughter as he ushered the young couple out of the apartment and closed the door.

Stunned, Willy and Ursula stood outside the apartment door listening to Otto's laughter fade. Ursula's wide eyes searched Willy's face, for what she didn't know.

"Should we go back inside and tell him?" Willy asked.

Ursula shook her head. "You did tell him."

"Yes, but he thinks I'm joking."

Ursula thought a moment, torn between loyalty to her father and her desire to spend time with Willy. The last words Otto had spoken prior to Willy's arrival rushed back to her. "I just want to ensure your safety and security, whatever it takes." She genuinely hoped that he meant it.

"I think we should have an enjoyable evening and deal with Papa afterwards. Or, better yet, another day."

Willy raised his eyebrows and smiled. "I was really hoping you'd say that."

6

Willy and Ursula walked along Wilmersdorfer Strasse until they came upon the Kurpfalz-Weinstuben, a restaurant that had recently debuted to stupendous reviews from the Berlin elite. One needed to have either a lot of money or a lot of clout to secure a table, so Ursula was surprised when Willy stopped in front of the entrance.

"I thought only high-ranking officers and the inner circle to the Führer dined here."

"It's true," Willy agreed.

"In which of those two categories do you fall, Herr Hitler?"

He shook his head. "Neither."

"So how is it that you obtained a reservation?"

Willy smiled. "You'll see. After you, please."

Ursula entered the courtyard and was quickly approached by a fawning maitre'd. "Fräulein Becker, when your companion called to say that you would like to dine here this evening, I was simply overcome. Overcome, I tell you!"

Ursula offered him a tentative smile. "Why were you overcome?"

The maitre'd drew his left hand to his chest. "Darling, your Elsa was impeccable! Exhausting and exhilarating at the same time. How anyone cannot love Wagner's *Lohengrin* is simply beyond me, but you, my dear, you brought Elsa to life as never before! Where are my manners? Please sit. I offer you our best table, outside under the linden tree." He pulled out her chair. "I've prepared our best meal for your arrival, the chef's Pfalz Platt, a trio of spicy stuffed pig's stomach, liver dumplings, and bratwurst served with roasted potatoes and red cabbage. In addition, our sommelier has paired your meal with a succulent Alsatian pinot noir. Light and fruity. I do hope that it will be to your liking!"

With a rousing hand flourish, he was gone. Confused, Ursula faced Willy, who gazed at her evenly. She looked away and then back again. "You secured a reservation here by using *my* name?"

Willy smiled. "I don't think you understand the depth of feeling you produce in your audience when you sing. You have many, many fans."

She tilted her head. "Yet, you are not among them."

Willy reached across the table and took her slender fingers in his. "Perhaps I have not been clear, Fräulein Becker. I'm a great fan of *you*, just not of your singing."

Ursula withdrew her hand. "You are quite a talker, Herr Hitler, but you need to understand that when you are an artist, it is not what you do, but rather who you are. My art comes from the inside, like a painter or a poet. Therefore, when you disparage my art, you are, by default, disparaging me and who I am." They locked eyes over the gauntlet that Ursula had thrown.

Willy inhaled deeply. "Then I suppose I love the opera."

Ursula smirked, wary of his newfound enthusiasm. "We shall see, Herr Hitler. Perhaps you might attend the opening of *Die Walküre* this Friday evening?"

"Nothing would give me greater joy."

Ursula laughed. "In addition to being quite dashing, you are an able liar. I'll need to remember that. But I do appreciate that you're making an effort."

The sommelier approached and poured each of them a generous portion of wine. Ursula looked at Willy, who wore a sly grin. "Why are you smiling?"

"Because you think I'm dashing."

Ursula sat back in her chair and shook her head. "You are incorrigible."

"I am not. I am very corrigible, actually."

Their meals arrived and, true to the maitre'd's word, they were impeccably plated and incredibly flavorful. At home, she and Anna prepared simple meals, not only because of their budget, but because neither enjoyed cooking. Ursula finished her entire platter of food and then commented on the variety of flavors.

Willy smiled. "Do you not prepare meals such as this at home?"

She thought he was joking and then realized he wasn't. "Do *you* eat like this at your home?"

Willy paused.

"Of course. You are lodged with your uncle, who eats only the finest foods prepared by skilled hands, I'm sure."

Willy touched his napkin to his mouth. "My uncle eats vegetables, Ursula. No meats. He does like spicy foods, although they do not agree with his . . . delicate intestinal nature."

"That's unfortunate for him."

"For all of us." He looked at her and raised his eyebrows, silently asking if she understood his implication.

Fork still in hand, Ursula covered her mouth and laughed loudly. She leaned forward and whispered, "That is something I believe most Germans don't know about their president," before breaking into giggles once more.

They ordered dessert, and Willy said, "I do need to ask you about my uncle, Ursula."

"What of him?"

"He didn't seem pleased that you and I were dining together this evening. I think he would have preferred it were him sitting here instead of me."

Ursula stared at Willy. After refusing Dr. Brandt's medical visit several years ago, the Führer had extended at least four dinner invitations that she had declined. Her reasons were always valid—an upcoming performance, an illness, a prior engagement—and she'd hoped that the Führer would forget about her. She thought her plan was succeeding. But several months ago, she'd been asked to attend an event for generous opera donors. When she'd entered the reception hall there was a table set for two, and Adolf Hitler stood to greet her. Seeing no reasonable way out of the awkward situation, she had dined with him. He was attentive and polite, if not a little too intimate with his gestures and speech. After an hour, she thanked him and excused herself. She hadn't told her father of the encounter and silently vowed she would avoid future interactions. Since the dinner, she'd heard nothing from him. She hoped that he had moved on from his obvious infatuation. And perhaps he might have, if Willy hadn't entered her life.

"Ursula?" She met his eyes and he smiled. "The Führer thinks very highly of you."

Ursula dropped her gaze to the pavement and examined an ant making its way across the cobblestones with a large crumb in its pincers. Her hands wrung the cloth napkin that lay across her lap. "That is kind."

"It might be a good idea for your career if you were to spend some time with him."

She continued to scrutinize the ant. "Is that why you asked me to dine with you, Willy? To recruit me for your uncle?" She lifted her eyes and searched Willy's face. She saw no deception or guise.

"No, Ursula. It is just that Uncle Alf—"

"Uncle *Alf?*"

Willy nodded. "That's what I call him. Anyway, he likes to surround himself with pretty things—artwork, music, and, yes, women. Not because he wants to bed them, but because they are unique, like him. Like you." He took her hand and enclosed it in both of his. She wanted to resist but found that her hand would not disengage from his tender grasp. "You *are* unique, you know."

She stared at his perfectly buffed nails.

"Uncle Alf isn't interested in you romantically. He just wants to get to know you. You fascinate him."

Ursula shook her head. "Why is he so interested in me?"

Willy smiled. "Well, he adores the opera, and you embody the art. Secondly, you remind him of someone he loved."

"Who?"

Willy leaned back in his chair. A cloud crossed his features. "His niece, Geli."

"I see. We're the same age, Geli and me?"

"Yes. Well, you would have been, if she were still alive."

Ursula was quiet as she examined his face. His eyebrows were knitted, and his gaze had fallen to the tabletop.

"Did you know her?"

Willy shook his head. "No, I arrived in Germany years after she died."

"Was she ill?"

"Physically? No. She shot herself with uncle's pistol."

Ursula drew back. "What? Was it an accident?"

Willy shrugged. "It's difficult to know. No one talks about it. It's an unspoken rule that no one is to speak of it in Uncle Alf's presence. Her bedroom is a shrine in the Munich apartment he shared with her."

Ursula raised her eyebrows. "They must have been very close."

Willy fixed her with a stare. "*Extremely* close."

Ursula looked at her hands, embarrassed at the implication. She couldn't imagine that the most powerful man in Germany, a man who could have almost any woman he wanted, would choose to consort with his own flesh and blood. His niece, no less. She shuddered.

"You could be her twin, you know."

Ursula's head shot up.

"It's true. Your hair and eyes. The way you carry yourself. Your dimples." Willy smiled, then looked away. "Everyone says that there was something about her, a star quality. Apparently, she was captivating. From her photographs she was beautiful, full of life." He returned his soft eyes to meet hers. "Like you."

Ursula blushed and averted her gaze. "I believe that you're being a brash Englishman, Herr Hitler. I'm sure that I might resemble this unfortunate young woman, but to be her twin?" Ursula shook her head. "It's difficult to believe."

But doubts niggled at the back of her mind. If what Willy said were true, it would explain the lingering looks the Führer had thrown her way, the manner in which he repeatedly touched her hand as they dined. As she had risen to leave, his hand had found her lower back, an intimate gesture that bespoke care and concern . . . and ownership.

Ursula shook her head to clear the ugly memories. "What do you think happened to Geli?"

Willy smiled sadly. "Ursula, I don't want to speculate. Besides, we've spoken enough of my uncle. You and I are together on this beautiful evening eating wonderful food. Let us speak of happier topics."

Ursula found herself trembling as she imagined how unhappy someone would have to be to take her own life. "Willy, you raised the issue of your uncle. Not me."

Willy took her hand again. His touch felt comfortable, as if she'd known him a long time. "You're right. I did, so let me finish the thought. Please, just dine with him one time. I will be in attendance as well, and I assure you that if he were to try anything untoward, I would be there in an instant to defend your honor."

Ursula noted how small her hand appeared encased in his. His fingers gently caressed her palm, and she felt herself softening. She looked at his eyes, so clear and blue. So warm and honest.

"I suppose if you're attending the opera this Friday, then I can attend a dinner with Uncle Alf."

Watching his face light up made her happy she had agreed. "But—" She raised a finger toward him. "You do realize that I must lie to my father, which makes me feel ill."

"Why must you lie to your father?"

Ursula sighed heavily, then took a large sip of wine. "Papa doesn't believe that your uncle is good for Germany."

Willy glanced around nervously. "Ursula, mind your tongue."

Ursula blinked, astonished that Willy would speak to her like that. "Excuse me? Did you just tell me to *mind my tongue?*"

He held up his palms. "I'm sorry, but you must be careful how you speak about my uncle."

Ursula's blazing eyes narrowed. She crossed her arms over her chest.

Willy leaned forward and held out his hand, which she regarded with a haughty stare. His shoulders slumped as he withdrew his hand and whispered, "You need to understand, Ursula. The Gestapo is everywhere."

Ursula looked at the unoccupied tables and onto the near-empty street. His stern reprimand annoyed her, and the wine loosened her tongue. "I don't see any Gestapo, Willy."

Willy closed his eyes in a silent appeal for patience.

"Am I not able to speak freely anymore, even with the Führer's nephew?"

Willy leaned forward again, a pleading edge in his tone. "You need to be careful, Ursula. Being well-known can protect you and harm you at the same time. Just like knowing me can protect you and harm you at the same time."

"You're speaking enigmatically, Willy. All I'm saying—"

Willy placed his index finger on his lips in an effort to quiet her. She rolled her eyes and leaned across the table to whisper, "All I'm saying is that Papa disagrees with your uncle's political philosophies, and I'll need to lie to him in order to dine with the Führer."

"Fine. Lie to you father. Just, please, keep your opinions to yourself or share them only with me. *Quietly.*"

Ursula leaned back in her chair and studied him, a sly smile forming on her full lips. "I thought I *was* sharing them only with you. Tell me, do you agree with your uncle's decision to rid Germany of the vermin he calls the Jews?"

Willy gazed into her eyes. She didn't want him to see how much his opinion mattered to her. He smiled and she had to remind herself to be strong, not to concede her point. She noticed that he focused on her dimple as he spoke. "I wholeheartedly disagree with him!"

Her fears appeased, she nodded her approval and offered Willy a double-dimple grin. "I knew there was a reason I liked you."

7

When Otto realized that Willy's surname was truly Hitler, he had forbidden Ursula to see him again. It had taken much convincing to assuage Otto's fears that Willy was sympathetic to his uncle's tenets. Truly, it was the passion and vehemence with which Ursula spoke of Willy's impeccable character that finally convinced Otto. Willy and Ursula became almost inseparable over the ensuing months, and Otto had continued to quietly voice his displeasure about their relationship.

"There are things in this world out of Willy's control, Ursula."

"Papa, Willy loves me."

"I know that. But what about his uncle?"

"What of him?"

At this point Otto would usually turn away and shake his head, as if speaking of Adolf Hitler would summon bad luck.

Although he admitted he liked Willy personally, Otto was concerned for Ursula's safety due to her being involved with a Hitler. He told her, in no uncertain terms, that he hoped that she and Willy would have a falling out so she could find someone else. She had responded that Willy loved her and would keep her safe no matter what.

When Ursula and Willy were alone together, however, outside influences were mostly forgotten and the rest of the world fell away. Often Willy would go the opera house and sit quietly while Ursula rehearsed. Afterward, they would stroll along the river or lounge under a tree, discussing music or art, until one of them complained of bitter hunger. At that point they would either find somewhere to dine or Willy would walk Ursula home. They would linger outside the apartment door until Otto opened it and cleared his throat, at which point Willy would tip his hat and bid Ursula good-bye until the following day, when they would do it all over again.

In the last several weeks, Willy had repeatedly raised the issue of dining with his uncle. In deference to her father's concerns, Ursula would either change the subject or simply not respond when Willy pressed her on setting a date. Finally, out of frustration, Willy decided to arrange the dinner himself. The previous night he had informed her that they would be dining with his uncle immediately following the final performance of her current show. She had started to object but was silenced when Willy had thrown her a pleading look. Although she didn't want to disappoint Otto, she realized that she was falling in love with Willy and didn't want to risk losing him.

For the first time in her life, Ursula planned not only to deceive her father, but to openly defy his wishes. If only she could keep her father's concerns at bay long enough, Otto would see what a wonderful man Willy was and how much he cared for her.

She primped in the mirror while evaluating her father's mood. He had just finished a meal of bratwurst with onions, courtesy of Willy's generosity, and sat smiling and rubbing his belly in contentment. *It's now or never.* She tried to appear casual as her stomach churned. "Papa, I shall be attending a party immediately following our final production and will not return home until the wee hours."

Otto smiled. "Then I shall meet you at the close of the festivities to ensure your safe return."

Ursula's heart skipped a beat. She turned slowly to face him, her most winsome smile affixed to her lovely face. "Papa, I'm grateful for your kind offer, but I'm old enough to attend to my own security."

"Don't be foolish, Ursula. It's not a bother." He stared hard at her. "Unless Willy will be attending as well?"

Ursula resumed her self-evaluation in the mirror and steeled herself for another outright lie. "No. But I have many admirers who would be more than willing to see me safely home."

"That is precisely what I'm worried about," Otto responded. "Who will be attending this party?"

Ursula paused, warming to her own deceit. She pictured the last post-performance party she had attended. "Oh, just the usual, Papa. The rich, the powerful, the hangers-on."

"You have hangers-on?" He laughed. "My, my, daughter, you must be more popular than I realized."

She kissed his cheek and hugged him. "You know what I mean, Papa. The people who like to be seen."

"Again, those are exactly the people whom I do not want escorting you home."

She knelt and grasped his large hand. "Have I not made meticulous choices in friends over the years?"

Otto crossed his arms. "Until recently I would have answered yes to your question, but your choice of late saddens me, as you are well aware."

"And yet you currently enjoy a full stomach because of Willy's generosity." The comment had escaped her lips before she'd considered its implications. Although her words rang true, she immediately regretted her rash statement. How could she blame her father, who had lost so much weight due to stress and illness, for taking advantage of an opportunity to dine on such delicious food? Otto's face registered surprise, then hurt and guilt as he considered her words. He hung his head.

Ursula placed her hands on his crossed arms. "Papa, please look at me."

Otto's mouth twisted and his eyes remained focused on his knees.

"I really enjoy spending time with Willy. As I've said, he strongly disagrees with his uncle's principles and actions."

"Yet he works at the Reichskreditbank and benefits from the misfortune of a displaced Jew." Otto shook his head.

"Papa, we've discussed this. You want me to find a gentleman who cares for me and is able to provide. I want to find a gentleman for whom I care. Willy meets our criteria."

"But his uncle . . . mark my words, Ursula, Adolf Hitler will lead this country to ruin."

Ursula knitted her brow. "Papa, this country was already in ruins. Although I don't particularly care for some of the Führer's methods, the fact is that most people are working again and can afford to put food on the table."

"But at what cost?"

"Papa, sometimes I believe you're too smart for your own good. Try not to think so much. Just enjoy the bounty that comes our way. Willy is kind to me, and to you and to Anna. Did you see the new violin he gave Anna? She cried when she opened the package, Papa. She was so grateful. Willy has all but promised that Anna will soon be playing in the orchestra."

"Soon is an elusive word, Ursula. Soon can feel like an eternity."

Ursula's shoulders fell as she realized the depth of her father's concern. She wished she could relieve him of the mental burden, but she didn't know how. She sighed and wrapped her arms around him. "Papa, we have our health, each other, and good food on the table. We cannot look a gift horse in the mouth. We must acknowledge and show gratitude for what we've been given. From God and from those made in his form."

Otto sat still for a moment and then returned Ursula's embrace. She felt the tension melt away as she held him, much as he had done when she was a child. "Of course, you are correct, my smart daughter. I just worry. That's all." He withdrew from her and took her face in his hands. "Now go. Have a wonderful performance and enjoy the party afterwards. You've earned it."

* * *

Ursula took a fourth curtain call before flitting back to her dressing room, flying high on adrenaline and sweet accolades. She pulled off her false eyelashes and removed her wig, then slipped out of her floor-length gown and threw it on the chaise for the dressing assistant to collect. She plucked out the sixty-four hairpins that Hilde had used to segment her mane into small rings, then shook her head, allowing ringlets to cascade down her back and shoulders. She glanced in the mirror and was pleased with her reflection. She slipped into a simple lavender frock that fit snugly against her small waist and flared towards the hem. She twirled several times and giggled as the skirt lifted, and she stopped abruptly when the door to her dressing room opened.

"Forgive me, Ursula, but I knocked twice. Did you not hear me?"

Ursula rushed over to Willy. "I'm sorry. I was being a silly girl, twirling and admiring my reflection."

"Admiring you is my job. Please don't put me out of a job," Willy joked.

"Never." Ursula stood on tiptoe and kissed him, catching him off guard.

When they parted, he said, "That's also my job, Ursula. Initiating kisses."

Ursula put her hands on her hips. "Who says it's only your job? Are you complaining because I kissed you?"

He stepped forward and placed his hands around her waist. "I would never in a million years complain about that."

He smiled and kissed her deeply, leaving her breathless. "I was wrong, and you were right. You should be in charge of that."

Willy laughed. "We should leave now. Uncle admires promptness."

* * *

Ursula squeezed Willy's hand as they approached the Old Chancellery. He turned to her. "There's no need to be nervous, Ursula. Uncle Alf is one of your biggest fans, truly."

"I have not seen him in some time."

"Well, you should know that he absolutely adores you."

Ursula fidgeted. She didn't care to be adored by Adolf Hitler any more than she already had been.

Willy stopped to face her, then took her hands. "Ursula, please, don't worry. Just have fun."

She didn't want to disappoint Willy, so she allowed his warm gaze to calm her nerves. She realized that in addition to her own feelings toward Hitler, she had taken on her father's concerns as well. She admonished herself for being so foolish and decided to enjoy the evening. It was a simple gathering in which she would say polite things and laugh at mediocre jokes. She squeezed Willy's hand and smiled. "Alright. Let's go."

They entered the Chancellery and were shown to the reception hall, where Ursula immediately recognized the Reich Minister of Public Enlightenment and Propaganda, Joseph Goebbels. When Willy excused himself to get some champagne, Goebbels sauntered over. Although his shoulders sloped down, his posture was ramrod straight and his brown hair was slicked straight back, accentuating his beaklike nose and deep-set brown eyes. She was shocked to find that he was several inches shorter than she, yet he somehow managed to give the impression of looking down at her.

"Fräulein Becker, what a lovely surprise to see you."

"Herr Goebbels, the pleasure is mine."

"I must tell you that you took my breath away with your performance this evening."

"I was not aware that you were in attendance."

"I was, and you were simply magnificent. Tell me, what do you think of the changes made to the performance venue?"

"I love singing in our opera house. The air is less dry, and my voice favors the acoustical advantages. I must say though, Minister, that I don't understand why the seating was altered. The house sits two hundred people less than it used to."

"My dear, the changes were made to accommodate our Führer's vision of what an opera house should be. The Führer's special seating boxes were incorporated so that he might maximize his viewing and listening pleasure."

"I see." Ursula nodded as she considered the fact that two hundred less people could now attend a performance simply because one man wanted a better view.

The minister's eyes wandered around the reception hall. She was reminded of a hawk scouring a field for a mouse. "The Führer redecorated this space."

Ursula followed his gaze around the large room highlighted with embroidered tapestries, crystal candelabras, and a stunning Steinway piano. "It is lovely. He has a good eye."

"He's an artist to be sure. Take the rug on which you stand, for example. It was designed for the League of Nations—"

"The same League of Nations from which Herr Hitler resigned Germany some years ago?" Ursula asked. She caught her breath, immediately regretting her impulsive outburst. She was glad that Willy was out of earshot. He would not have been pleased at her inauspicious comment.

The minister paused. "Yes. There is only one League of Nations. Now, as I was saying, this rug was designed for the League, but when the final payment became due, the League could no longer afford such opulence. Luckily, our Führer intervened and purchased the rug at his own expense, thereby saving the League great embarrassment."

Before Ursula could respond, Goebbels slapped his heels together. His entire body quivered like a hunting dog on point. She turned to find the Führer approaching, a half smile fixed on his waxen face. His eyes caressed her as he waved his hand at Goebbels, silently telling him to stand down. Hitler's movements were graceful, almost effeminate, as he swept his bangs away from his eyes. He took her hand and brought it to his lips, brushing it ever so gently against his tiny moustache. His lewd scrutiny, coupled with that tiny gesture, made her want to flee to the restroom and wash herself.

"Fräulein Becker, it is my honor to see you again. It has been several months, I believe, since I last gazed upon your lovely countenance. Tell me, how is your father's health?"

As he spoke, he raised his gaze to meet Ursula's. In an instant, she knew that Willy's rosy assessment of his uncle had been incorrect. Ursula may resemble the niece he loved, and he may be taken with her singing, but by raising the issue of Otto's health, Hitler was referencing the fact that she had rebuffed his kindness five years ago. *Five years ago!* She had hoped they were past the slight, but clearly not. Hitler's eyes narrowed slightly, and Ursula instinctively removed her hand from his grasp.

"He's very well, thank you."

"I trust that the new opera director is treating you well?"

Ursula paused, sensing a trap. Carl Ebert had left Germany several years ago in response to growing Nazi extremism. Since then, a flurry of artistic and administrative directors had taken the role, vying for Hitler's favor. Knowing that she should answer one way but wanting to respond differently, Ursula managed to find a middle ground. "Each director with whom I've had the pleasure of working has been more than accommodating. I miss Herr Ebert, but I understand that he has found a new opera home in England."

A small smile played upon Hitler's lips. "Carl Ebert did not appreciate the perfect nature of German opera, my dear. He is better suited to a capitalist society in which he can impart his non-Aryan talent on less artistically proficient minds."

Goebbels snickered as Willy and another man walked toward them. Willy smiled encouragingly at Ursula, and she was reminded how much he wanted her to like his uncle. She swallowed, then smiled shyly. "You would know best, Herr President."

"What are we discussing?" Willy asked as he handed Ursula a glass of champagne. She took a sip and met the piercing gaze of the man with Willy.

She recognized him as Heinrich Himmler, Hitler's leader of the SS. His brown hair was tidy, and over his thin lips sat a caterpillar moustache. His weak chin and droopy cheeks gave him the unmistakable resemblance to a hound dog. His beady eyes ran the length of her form, then summarily dismissed her by turning his full attention to the Führer.

"We were discussing the superiority of Aryan musicians," Hitler responded. He winked at Ursula. "Despite one notable exception, it is a fact that Jewish opera singers are not as talented as Aryan singers. The Jewish musculature is different. It does not allow for the depth and breadth of tone that Aryan forms do."

Ursula stifled an urge to laugh out loud at such a ridiculous comment. Instead, she glanced at each member of the small group, waiting for someone to disagree with the Führer. No one did. In fact, most were nodding in agreement. Willy stared at his champagne.

"I sang with Ali Kurtz, and I found her timbre and tone to be exquisite, exceptional even. I haven't seen her in some time, however."

Hitler's steady gaze never wavered from Ursula's face. Goebbels said, "Yes. It is unfortunate that Fräulein Kurtz is no longer able to sing."

Ursula turned to him. "What do you mean?"

Goebbels looked sad. "Well, I have heard that she fell ill. The Jews are not hearty. It is not in their natures to accommodate changes in the climate."

Ursula clenched her teeth. She wanted to reprimand these dolts on their bigoted views but knew it would end badly. She glanced at Willy, whose eyes held an unspoken plea. She tried to end the subject by saying, "I suppose I should pay a visit to Fräulein Kurtz, if for no other reason than to wish her well."

Hitler placed his hand on her arm. She glanced at it and noted that his fingernails were chewed to the quick.

"I would not do that, my dear."

Adrenaline flooded her.

Hitler's mouth formed a moue, and his pupils flared. "It is not a good idea for someone of your exceptional talents to be associating with such swine. One might believe that you lower yourself to their mediocrity, or worse, that you sympathize with them." He patted her arm. "We wouldn't want people thinking that, would we?" Hitler met each person's eyes before rounding back to Ursula. "Just think what it might do to your blossoming career and how your family might suffer because of it." Hitler smiled condescendingly. "No. We cannot have that. Not when your star is still on the rise."

For the first time in her life, Ursula was speechless. She wanted to scream at him, to run from the room, to release the torrent of anger that threatened to overwhelm her. She looked to Willy. His eyes registered embarrassment and sadness as they begged for her compliance. She returned her gaze to Hitler, who observed her carefully. His veiled threat was real, she had no doubt, and she finally understood what her father had been trying to relay to her for the last five years. Adolf Hitler would stop at nothing in his quest for dominance.

8

Ursula rose early the following day and dressed quickly, hoping to avoid questions from her father regarding the previous evening. To her dismay, she exited her bedroom to find Otto sitting at the kitchen table, a steaming mug in his hand. The aroma filled the small apartment, and Ursula's mouth began to water.

"Papa, is that coffee? Where did you get it? Did you steal it?" she joked.

Her father offered her the mug.

"Willy dropped off some grounds this morning."

She inhaled the richness before taking a large gulp that burned her tongue. "Willy was here?"

"Only for a moment. He said that you left the party quickly last night and that he was worried about you."

Ursula froze, knowing what was coming.

"You told me Willy wasn't attending the party."

Caught in the lie, Ursula had a choice to make—tell her father the truth or continue the deceit. Her stomach heaved at both choices, but she decided quickly. She handed the mug back to Otto and turned toward the window. "He wasn't planning to attend but changed his mind and showed up at the last minute." She turned around and smiled.

The lie seemed to appease Otto's concerns, as he settled back in his chair and wrapped his hands around the warm mug. "I see. Did you quarrel with him?"

She turned away quickly so he couldn't see her face. "No. Why do you ask?"

"Because he left so quickly this morning. I invited him inside, but he declined. He said he didn't want to bother me. He seemed different somehow. What are you not telling me, Ursula?"

She tried to hold his earnest gaze but failed. Her eyes traced a crooked gouge in the wood floorboard, created by an errant pull of a kitchen chair. "I spoke to Hitler, Papa."

Otto drew a quick breath and dropped his head. "I knew it."

Ursula sat across from him. "You're correct. He's not well in the head. The way he discusses the Jews . . . it's scary. He wants to rid Berlin of all Jews."

Her father laughed mirthlessly. "If only it were just Berlin, my love. No, it's all of Germany."

"You cannot be serious." Ursula blanched. "What will he do with all of them?"

"He wants them to move east, out of Germany. He's making their lives more difficult in the hope that they will just go away. I've seen signs on shops owned by Jews that say 'Defend yourself against Jewish atrocity propaganda. Buy only at German shops.'"

"I've seen those signs as well."

"He's rebuilding the army, and now that he's invaded Rhineland, the Jews are no longer welcome there either."

They sat quietly for a moment, taking turns sipping from the coffee mug. "So, if you and Willy didn't quarrel, why did you leave the party so quickly?"

Ursula looked at her hands, which picked at a small tear in her light blue dress. "You won't like the answer, Papa, but you'll be proud of me."

She stole a glance at Otto and saw kindness and concern. She took a deep breath. "I stood up for a Jewish singer who is no longer performing due to illness. You know her. Ali Kurtz."

Otto narrowed his eyes. He stretched his fingers and then folded them into fists that he rested carefully on the tabletop. They reminded her of a coiled snake whose latent power was deadly when unleashed. "Go on."

Ursula swallowed, then described the evening, starting with her initial lie and finishing with the quiet walk home. Following her discussion with the Führer, Ursula had quickly excused herself and Willy had followed, trying to engage her in conversation, but she had remained mute. There had been nothing to say. Well, that wasn't quite true. There was a lot to say, but she didn't want to quarrel with Willy, so she had remained silent.

After hearing the entire story, Otto leaned back in his chair and sighed. "Ursula, you lied to me. I understand that you were trying to spare my feelings, but please don't do that again. It's imperative that we remain honest with each other. You and your sister are all I have. I cannot lose you." His voice caught.

She reached across the table and grabbed his hand. "Please forgive me, Papa. I won't lie to you again. It was wrong of me. Immature. I should have trusted that you have my best interests in your heart."

He gazed at her with such unconditional love that she thought her heart would break.

"Always," he whispered. "I *always* have your best interests in my heart. Your colleague, Ali Kurtz. I'm sure that she's not ill. She's most likely not allowed to perform anymore because she's Jewish. I'm proud of you for standing up for her, but you must be more careful. The Führer might tolerate your insolence if he believes that your voice is a benefit to Germany. But do not be fooled. The second you become a liability you will be expendable. Do you understand?"

Ursula nodded and wiped away tears.

"This is a dangerous time to be alive, and you're walking a tightrope. It's not just you on that rope, Ursula. It's Anna and me as well. Please don't forget that."

Hitler's words ran through her mind. *How your family might suffer.* An involuntary shudder shook her. "I'll remember, Papa."

The sound of breaking glass drew them to the window where they watched in horror as an elderly man was dragged into the street. Two SS officers screamed questions at him, and each time he tried to answer, they kicked him. Ursula turned away and returned to the table, where she lay her forehead on her arms. "We should help him," she whispered.

"We cannot. If we do, we will be laying in the street as well."

"What's happening, Papa? The world has turned on its head."

Anna emerged from the bedroom, escaped strands of plaited blond hair standing on end. She yawned and rubbed her eyes. "Who is screaming?"

"It's of no concern to you, my dear. Go back to sleep," Otto said.

Ignoring her father, Anna crossed to the window and observed the wretched scene unfolding outside. Ursula noted that Anna didn't flinch or turn away. It saddened her to realize that her younger sister had seen so much violence that the spectacle of a man being beaten meant little. "That's Herr Liebovitz," Anna noted dully. "Oh. Someone is coming to help him. A woman."

Ursula stood and placed her arm around Anna's shoulders, pulling her close. Together they watched the woman approach the SS officers. One of them rounded on her and slapped her hard enough to send her reeling backwards, where she landed hard on the cobblestones.

"Oh, my God," Anna whispered.

Otto ordered, "Anna, step away from the window!"

"That's Frau Bergmann!"

Ursula squinted to better see the woman's face. "Your violin teacher?"

"Yes. I must help her!"

Before they could stop her, Anna bolted out of the apartment and down the stairs. They watched from above as she rushed to Frau Bergmann and knelt beside her, gathering the small woman in her arms. Anna touched her left hand to the back of Frau Bergmann's head, then looked at it. She turned to Ursula and Otto framed in the upstairs window and held up her hand toward them. It was covered in blood.

Ursula's hand flew to her mouth. Until this moment the Nazi movement had been an abstract thing, an ugly monster that had affected others. A plague that had mercifully avoided her family. An inconvenience in terms of roadblocks and curfews. But Ursula knew this woman who now lay unmoving on the street for attempting to aid a man who was treated unfairly. Frau Bergmann was a pillar in the community. She had four children of her own and a husband who was bedridden due to a muscular disease. She worked tirelessly, for her family and for her community. Ursula ran toward the door.

"Do not leave this apartment!" Otto's voice thundered through the small space. Ursula froze in mid-stride. She turned to argue but stopped short when she saw her father's face. His eyes were wild, and tears flowed freely down his cheeks. She had never seen her father cry, not even when her mother and stepmother had died.

"Papa, I must help Anna and Frau—"

"I cannot lose you too! I could not bear it, Ursula. I cannot lose my two girls. If you go out there—" Sobs burst from his mouth, uncontrollable ejections of sound and spittle. Otto collapsed into a chair as Ursula looked on helplessly, torn between her father and her sister. After a moment of impossible, frozen indecision, she whispered, "I'm sorry, Papa, but I must help Anna."

She took the stairs three at a time and exited the building to find Herr Liebovitz cowering against a fallen bicycle. He was desperately trying to make himself less of a target for the black leather boots that continued to find their mark. Ursula winced as another blow landed, but she hurried over to where Anna knelt.

"How is she?"

"Still breathing. Can we carry her to our apartment?"

"Yes. You take her arms and I'll take her legs. Come on."

It took them three tries before they maneuvered the unconscious woman into a position that allowed them to securely transport her. As they passed the two Nazi soldiers, the smaller one sneered and narrowed his eyes.

"Halt!" he ordered in a clipped tone. Ursula and Anna stopped and cast their eyes downward. Frau Bergmann's body suddenly seemed very heavy and hung low between them.

"Schau mich an, junge Frau," he ordered. Ursula obliged and raised her blazing eyes to meet his. He evaluated her for a long time before breaking into a smile.

"Ich kenne Sie."

"You know me?" Ursula asked. "I don't believe that we've had the pleasure of meeting, mein gutter Herr." She offered a winning smile, acutely aware of how bizarre it was for the two of them to be conversing over an unconscious body.

"You are the opera singer, Ursula Becker!"

"You are correct. And you are?"

The soldier lowered his rifle and placed his right hand on his chest, bowing formally. "Heinz Braun. I enjoy your singing immensely. Might you sing for us, Fräulein?"

"Right now?" Ursula asked as she looked at Frau Bergmann and then back at the soldier.

"Of course, you cannot. You are busy. Perhaps another time then?"

"I would love to sing for you, Herr Braun." She smiled. Ursula's eyes flitted to the beaten older man. "Might you do me the favor of allowing Herr Liebovitz to return to his family?" Ursula's arms burned from the strain of holding Frau Bergmann. Anna remained silent, but her arms shook from the strain.

The soldier glanced at the broken man curled in a protective ball and spat on the pavement. "Gehen! Judisches Schwein! Get out of here!"

The older man threw Ursula a grateful look and then stood slowly and limped away, cradling a dislocated arm. The second soldier joined Ursula and Braun. He leered at Anna in her nightgown. "Is this your sister? She is very pretty."

Ursula raged inside but smiled serenely. "She is my sister. Only eighteen years old, sir."

He leered at Anna while sucking on rotting teeth. "You should be careful, Heinz."

"Why?"

"Do not become enamored with the elder Fräulein Becker. There is a rumor that she is on the mischling list. We must leave. Come."

The younger soldier's eyebrows came together, and he examined Ursula with renewed interest. "That would be a shame," he mumbled as he sauntered away.

"Ursula, I cannot hold Frau Bergmann much longer," Anna whispered breathlessly.

"I agree. Let's go." They struggled up the stairs and were breathing hard when they lay her on the tattered couch.

"Get some water and a clean cloth, Anna. Papa, come look at Frau Bergmann. You have more experience than we do." Otto sat unmoving at the kitchen table, his eyes locked on a scratch Anna had made in the wood when she was four years old.

"Papa, we need your help. *Papa!*"

Ursula's directive tone roused Otto. Anna walked by him with a bowl of water and a piece of white cloth she had torn from a dress that no longer fit. He watched in fascination as his daughters attended to the wounded woman.

"I had no idea you knew how to care for someone who has been hurt," he mumbled.

"I don't know what I'm doing, Papa, which is why I could use your help," Ursula said as she wiped blood from the back of Frau Bergmann's head. "Oh . . . my."

Anna gasped as Ursula picked pieces of bone from the cloth. Ursula looked desperately at her father.

"Her skull has been fractured," Otto said dully.

"What does that mean?" Anna asked.

"It means that she will most likely die."

"Papa, what is a mischling list?" Ursula asked.

Otto's head shot up. "Why do you ask me that?"

"Because one of the soldiers said that he heard a rumor I'm on the mischling list. What does that mean?"

Her father's shoulders slumped, and his eyes became vacant.

"Papa? You're scaring me. What is it?"

He slowly raised his gaze to meet hers. "Mischling means mixling."

Ursula shook her head, impatience needling her. "What does *that* mean?"

"It means that you are one-quarter Jewish, so—"

The air felt suddenly cold and Ursula found that she couldn't inhale. Otto gazed into the distance and finished his sentence. "—according to the Nazis, you should not exist."

9

Ursula stared open-mouthed at Otto as a thousand spiders crawled up her back. She had heard his words, but her brain wouldn't process their meaning. It was unthinkable. "I don't understand."

"Your grandmother was Jewish," Otto said quietly as he shrugged his shoulders. Ursula was incredulous. His stabbing words didn't jibe with the nonchalance with which he'd spoken them.

Anna's eyes darted between Ursula and Otto. "What does this mean for us?"

Ursula glanced at Anna but didn't acknowledge her question. "Which grandmother?"

"Your maternal grandmother, but your mother didn't practice the Jewish faith growing up, and we decided that we weren't going to practice any specific religion either."

Ursula shook her head, refusing to believe. "You must be mistaken."

Otto raised his eyebrows and blew out a mouthful of air. "I wish I were. I was hoping I wouldn't have to tell you. That we could get through this awful time without your knowing."

Ursula stared past him as she considered the fact that he'd just passed her death sentence. Her brain felt fuzzy, and she shook her head to clear it. "But I'm only one-quarter Jewish, which means that I'm three-quarters Christian. Surely the weighted percentage should win out."

The look in Otto's eyes shattered her hope.

"Why have you not told me this before now?"

"Because it never came up in our everyday lives. None of our friends knew that your mother was Jewish and, as I said, we decided not to practice the Jewish faith. It was better that you didn't know, because then you were not carrying a burdensome secret. Knowing makes you vulnerable. Before now, you carried yourself with the haughty indifference that a gentile can enjoy in this wretched period of history. And now . . ." His threw up his hands, then rubbed his face. "Well, now you know."

Ursula glanced at the window. "And *they* know," Ursula whispered, the horrible truth washing over her. *My life, as I know it, has ended.*

Anna paled, and her eyes frantically searched Otto's face. "Is Ursula going to die?" Then she stood quickly and drew a sharp breath. "Am I Jewish too, Papa?"

Otto sighed heavily. "No, Anna. Your mother was Catholic, although we didn't practice that faith either."

"So, I am safe?" she asked.

Otto cringed. "Yes. You're safe. Relatively."

"But Ursula is not because she's a Jew."

Anna's blunt words sliced into Ursula. She turned to face her sister and saw a mixture of disgust and relief on her face. Ursula had grown up in a tolerant Germany, whereas Anna's opinions had been formed during the last few years when Nazi propaganda of division and hatred spewed from the mouths of the brainwashed. As Ursula stared, she felt a chasm open between Anna and her. Papa had taught them that all lives have value. But when everyone else in your life tells you otherwise, when your friends and teachers constantly remind you that "the Jew" should not exist, over time, perhaps a young mind begins to believe. No just go along but actually believe.

She wanted to scream at Anna, but she knew it would do more harm than good. Instead, she focused on Frau Bergmann.

"Is your beloved violin teacher not Jewish, Anna?"

Anna's eyes darted to the injured woman, who lay prone on the couch, a puddle of blood growing larger beneath her head. "That's different, Ursula."

"Is it?" Ursula shot back. "I'm your sister, for God's sake!"

"Half sister," Anna corrected her.

Ursula closed her eyes and breathed deeply. "Papa is correct. Our family is vulnerable because of me." She turned to face Otto, who had tears in his eyes. "Papa, what is it?"

"It's starting," he said. "This is what happens. Friends turn on friends. Family betrays family." He shook his head. "I cannot bear it."

Ursula turned to Anna and shot her a furious look before crossing to Otto. "Help me understand, Papa. Why am I considered a Jew if our grandmother was Jewish? What does that have to do with me?"

Otto shrugged again. "According to Nazi law, if someone's grandparent was a Jew, then you carry one-quarter Jewish blood in your veins, making you a mischling. But the good news is that you are a mischling of the second degree."

"Papa, what are you talking about?"

"If you had two Jewish grandparents, then you would be considered a mischling of the first degree, a more ominous classification to be sure."

Ursula blinked quickly while shaking her head. "This is pure insanity. Are you having me on, Papa? Some strange joke that I don't understand? Are you trying to scare me so I won't take risks?"

Otto's eyebrows came together as he sucked in a breath. "I wish I were, but, no, Ursula. I am telling you the absolute truth."

Suddenly Frau Bergmann's back arched and her eyes rolled back. Every limb became rigid and blood spurted from her mouth as she bit through her tongue. "Papa! What should we do?" Ursula asked frantically. Frau Bergmann's left arm shot out and caught Anna in the eye, knocking her from the couch to the floor. "*Papa!*" Ursula screamed.

Otto rose and closed the distance from the table to the couch in two large strides. He placed his knee across Frau Bergmann's legs and held her arms with his hands to cease her flailing. "Ursula, take your sister and go into the bedroom."

Terrified, Ursula grabbed Anna's nightgown and dragged her into their room. She closed the door and evaluated Anna's wounded eye, already starting to swell and bruise. "Can you see?"

Anna nodded through her tears. "It hurts a lot, though."

"I'm sure it does." Ursula gathered Anna in her arms and stroked her golden hair. *How can a ridiculous classification cause such a rift with a country, within my family?* Jew. It meant nothing to her. She held no grudge toward them, but she knew little of the Jewish faith. How could *she* be a Jew? Ursula pictured her mother, a raven-haired, green-eyed beauty whose smile filled the room. She had never once mentioned her Jewish faith to Ursula. Indeed, her family had celebrated Christmas. *Did my mother look Jewish?* Ursula wondered. Then she realized that she was applying Nazi doctrine. *What does looking Jewish even mean?* She knew how the Nazis would answer, and she chastised herself for even entertaining the question.

As if reading Ursula's mind, Anna sniffled and whispered, "I'm sorry I called you a Jew, Ursula. I know that you're not really one."

Ursula stopped stroking her hair. "What do you mean?"

"Well, you're beautiful and talented. You're not the least bit selfish or greedy. Your nose isn't big."

Ursula felt her limbs stiffen. They had never discussed their personal opinions because they hadn't needed to. Ursula had naïvely believed that their little nuclear family shared the same morals. But clearly, she was wrong. Anna was giving voice to feelings Ursula didn't know she harbored. She shook her head to clear it. It had been five years since Adolf Hitler had come to power and used his thugs to spew vile rhetoric throughout the country. Five years was a long time for a young, developing mind to be told the same thing over and over without finally truly hearing it. Anna had been brainwashed, and Ursula had missed the warning signs. *Or did I simply ignore them because it was easier?* she wondered.

"Anna, you know what the Nazis say isn't actually true, right?" Anna's large blue eyes searched Ursula's, trying to understand why her sister was so upset. "It's all lies, Anna. You must know that."

Anna looked away. Her lack of response spoke for her. Ursula's heart sank as she stared at her sister, and she realized with sudden horror that Anna was the spitting image of an Aryan— blond curls, blue eyes, a hearty bosom, and child-bearing hips.

"How did the soldiers know that you're a mischling, Ursula?"

"They must have family records." Then a thought struck. *If the soldiers know I'm a mischling, then Willy must know as well . . . which means that the Führer knows too.* She thought back to a casual comment Hitler had made the previous evening. "Despite one notable exception, it is a fact that Jewish opera singers are not as talented as Aryan singers." *Am I the notable exception?* The soldiers had said that her voice was protecting her. *Maybe they're right. But . . . how long will that protection last?* she wondered. An involuntary shiver rattled her.

"Are we going to be alright, Ursula?"

Ursula regarded her younger sister, whose petite frame made her seem younger than her eighteen tears. Her large eyes searched Ursula's, willing her to quell her fear. But Ursula didn't know what the future held for either of them and she wouldn't lie to her. Instead, she sat in front of Anna and took her sister's alabaster hands in her own. "You are vulnerable because you're related to me, but your hands are your assurance of safety, Anna. I'll speak to Willy about getting you into the Berlin orchestra this coming season. If my voice is what's keeping this family safe, then perhaps we double our value to the Reich by making your exceptional violin skills evident to the Führer."

Anna's eyes bulged. "The Führer?" she asked in astonishment.

Ursula didn't want to heighten Anna's unease, so she grinned. "Let me tell you about our fearless leader. He is a small-statured man with a little moustache whose breath smells of sulfur, and he always has dandruff on his shoulders. Yes, he is powerful, but he's also ridiculous."

Anna slitted her eyes. "Really?"

"Really. And—" Ursula looked about as if they were not alone. "—he suffers from severe flatulence."

"What is flatulence?"

Ursula leaned in. "The Führer farts a lot." Anna drew her lips in and then burst into giggles. Ursula followed suit and before they knew it, Otto was standing over them wearing a confused expression. When they looked at him, they burst into laughter once again.

"What are you laughing about?"

Ursula covered her mouth in embarrassment. "Nothing, Papa. How is Frau Bergmann?"

Otto glanced behind him into the living room. "She's dead."

Anna stood quickly. "What did you say, Papa? She's what?" Anna rushed from the room. Ursula and Otto watched as Anna sank to her knees next to the slack form draped on the couch.

Otto spoke quietly but firmly. "She is dead, Anna. We need to contact her family and let them know. They will want to make arrangements for her burial."

Ursula observed her sister process what Otto had said, marveling at how Anna's childhood had all but vanished in a few short minutes. A myriad of emotions crossed her countenance before she spoke. "Her husband is bedridden, and her children are small, Papa. We must make the arrangements. What of the man who killed her?"

Otto said, "What do you mean?"

Anna continued to kneel by her former violin teacher, stroking her long fingers. "What will happen to the soldier who caused her death?"

Otto placed his hand on Anna's shoulder. "Nothing."

Anna looked at Ursula, desperation in her wide eyes as she sought a second opinion. "That cannot be correct. Surely the soldier will be punished."

Ursula paused, but she decided Anna needed to hear the truth. The entire truth. "Anna, you need to understand that the justice system no longer works as it used to. Now that we know of my heritage, we need to be careful. I would love to see the soldiers receive a just punishment, but Papa is correct. Right now we are protected, but if that changes, who knows what might happen? We can't take the risk of exposing ourselves. As much as it pains me, we must not make a fuss."

Anna turned back to Frau Bergmann, whose tongue lolled out of the left side of her mouth. Thick blood continued to drip onto the threadbare carpet. "But she's dead, Ursula! Surely we must do something!"

The accusatory expression on Anna's face made Ursula marvel at how quickly her own morality had been replaced by practicality. Survival was paramount. But what good was surviving if one lived in an amoral state? She looked to her father for guidance and, finding none, made a decision that she hoped bridged the gap. "We will do something. We will commemorate Frau Bergmann by performing a concert in her honor."

Anna stared at her, considering the idea. After a moment, she smiled. "Ursula, what a splendid idea! I'll perform pieces that Frau Bergmann taught me, and you'll sing in order to draw a crowd. We will educate the large audience as to Frau Bergmann's kindness and talent, as a teacher and as a violinist." Anna retrieved her violin case from atop the bookshelf and removed the instrument, a strained smile firmly fixed on her face.

Ursula had spoken from her heart when she'd suggested a concert. But given her newly discovered mischling status, she quickly realized that drawing attention might not be a good idea. As she opened her mouth to speak, Anna started playing Bach's Sonata No. 1 in G minor. Ursula held her tongue and listened to Anna pay homage to her deceased teacher. Time stood still as Anna coaxed a story from the instrument's strings. Ursula was moved to tears by the beauty of the music and Anna's mastery of her instrument. When she had completed the Adagio section of the piece, Anna lifted her bow and whispered with her eyes closed, "That was for you, Frau Bergmann. Rest in peace." She opened her eyes and regarded Ursula with a solemn expression that carried the weight of her grief. Ursula knew she couldn't deny Anna this last chance to say good-bye to her beloved mentor. She forced a smile and spoke with more confidence than she felt. "A concert it shall be then."

* * *

Frau Bergmann's memorial service was to be held at Olympiapark's Waldbühne amphitheater the following Sunday. With Willy's help, Ursula and Anna printed and pasted posters around the city inviting people to the service, which was to be followed by a concert featuring diva Ursula Becker and her prodigious violinist sister, Anna Becker.

As the preparations progressed, the tribute to Frau Bergmann began to take on a larger purpose in Ursula's mind. The incident that had led to her death forced Ursula to face an ugly truth—she felt slightly ashamed of her heritage. She held no grudge against the Jewish people and certainly didn't want them harmed. But she didn't want to be considered one either. What bothered her most is that she wasn't sure *why* she felt this way. In conversations with herself at night, she silently acknowledged that Hitler's vicious propaganda had seeped into her consciousness and poisoned her psyche. Embarrassed, she decided that although she may not embrace her lineage, she could work harder to counter the daily atrocities that were becoming more frequent. To that end, she endeavored to use the concert to make a statement: The Nazis who killed Frau Bergmann might go unpunished, but the sacrificed life would not go uncelebrated. In a daring move, Ursula had asked Willy to advertise the free concert in the Nazi newspapers *Völkischer Beobachter* and *Der Stürmer*.

Immediately following the well-attended memorial service, several hundred people arrived for the concert, making the final headcount close to one thousand. Willy hugged Ursula and Anna. "I'm proud of you girls," he said. "You're doing a really wonderful thing here today." Ursula smiled warmly at him as Anna simply nodded. She seemed overwhelmed at the number of people. "Ready?" he asked. Without waiting for an answer, he stood, crossed to the microphone, and held up his hands to quiet the crowd.

"Ladies and gentlemen, we are gathered here today to remember the life of a remarkable woman who contributed greatly to the artistic community. Not only did she play in the Berlin symphony for many, many years, but she trained some of the world's finest violinists, all of whom reside in our beautiful fatherland. I am proud to present to you today two sisters, one of whom you already know—" The crowd whooped and hollered, and Willy glanced at Ursula. "Yes, I am referring, of course, to Fräulein Ursula Becker."

The audience leapt to its feet. At Willy's urging, Ursula stepped forward and waved, eliciting a new round of cheering. Once the crowd had quieted, Willy continued. "As talented as Fräulein Ursula is, wait until you meet her younger sister. Anna, please come forward."

Anna turned to Ursula for support. Ursula nodded. "Go ahead. Just like we practiced." Ursula wasn't sure if Anna was excited or terrified as she tentatively stepped forward, her violin and bow clutched to her chest while her large blue eyes drank in the horde of people. As the cheering increased, she raised her bow to the crowd. The audience roared in response, and Anna beamed as she glanced at her smiling sister. In Ursula's experience people either came alive on stage or shut down. There was no maybe. No in-between. Anna relished the attention; she was a performer. That much was clear.

Willy held up his hands for silence.

"But let me be clear, we're here to honor Frau Ilse Bergmann, a mother, a wife, a talented violinist who did so much to honor her colleagues, her city, and her country. Frau Bergmann died in a tragic and needless accident while trying to aid a fellow human being. Each piece you will hear today was taught to Anna by Frau Bergmann, and Anna dedicates her performance today to her beloved teacher." Ursula commended Willy on his choice of words. Anyone else might have been arrested for such audacious words in support of a Jew.

Anna opened the concert with the "Melodie" from Gluck's *Orfeo ed Euridice*, followed by Ursula singing "Che faro senza Euridice" from the same opera. They had chosen pieces meant to evoke strong emotions, so by the time the duo had finished their forty-five-minute presentation, the audience was exhausted. Most people were silent as the final musical note floated across the broad, open space. Anna lifted the bow and opened her eyes. She took a moment to return from her emotional, musical journey, then bowed deeply to the stunned crowd, who had never before heard someone so young master such challenging pieces.

Taking advantage of their silence, Willy thanked everyone for coming and wished them good health in the coming days. As people filed out of the amphitheater, many well-wishers stopped to chat with Ursula and Anna, thanking them for the gift of music. Ursula watched Anna handle the accolades with aplomb, as if she'd been performing publicly for years. When the space was empty, Ursula turned to her sister and asked how she felt.

"I feel like Frau Bergmann is smiling down from heaven."

Ursula nodded. "I couldn't agree more, Anna. And through this concert you've been introduced to the public—"

"—who clearly love you," Willy finished.

"Yes, they do," a voice said from nearby. Anna, Ursula, and Willy turned in unison. Adolf Hitler stood staring intently at them, his blue eyes focused on Anna, who blanched as he approached.

"Herr, Herr, mein . . ." Anna stuttered.

The Führer chuckled and placed his hands on Anna's shoulders. "No need, my dear. I came to hear you play, and, by God, you are magnificent! What musical gifts you Becker girls possess. I should like to thank your father for sharing you with us. Is he present?"

Ursula interceded. "He has already left."

Still smiling at Anna, Hitler asked, "I trust his health is well?"

Ursula felt the silent jab at their shared past. "He is fine, Herr Führer. He simply wanted to return home."

Hitler turned to Ursula now, his face an inscrutable mask. He stared at her, then smiled and waved his hand. "No matter, my dear. Anna shall play in the Berlin symphony orchestra. She is more than capable, do you not agree, Willy?"

"Yes, Uncle."

"See to it that she meets the maestro and finds suitable placement."

"Certainly."

Hitler's eyes remained locked on Ursula's. "I must take my leave, but it has been a pleasure to hear your exquisite voice again, Fräulein. I find there are some talented Jews that are worth keeping in Germany. Would you not agree, Willy?"

Willy recognized the impossible nature of the question and paused before answering. "Yes, Uncle."

Hitler broke eye contact with Ursula and turned to face Anna. He gingerly took her hand, still clutching the bow, and lifted it to his lips. He kissed it as he held her gaze. "You are exceptional, my dear."

Without acknowledging Ursula, he turned and walked away, followed closely by his toadies. Watching him, Ursula's earlier excitement evaporated. "At least Anna is valuable to him now." She turned to Anna and whispered, "See? Didn't I tell you that he is a buffoon?"

Her sister was silent. Her unblinking eyes were focused on the spot where Hitler had been standing.

"Anna, are you alright?" Ursula asked.

Anna turned slowly and looked through Ursula. "He was amazing," she breathed.

"Who? Hitler?" Ursula asked, astonished.

"Yes. He has the bluest eyes I have ever seen."

1939

10

Over the next months, financial conditions improved in the Becker household. Not only did Ursula continue to sing, but Otto's physical condition strengthened to the point that he could work. Because of his health history, Otto was unable to seek employment through the National Labor Service. But Willy had intervened and found him jobs that ensured a reasonable wage that kept food on the table and pride in his soul. In addition, Ursula had noted that whatever they couldn't afford would simply appear in a basket on their doorstep, courtesy of Willy.

Other people padded their own pantries by trading information to the Nazis in return for food. The previous week two families from their apartment building had been seized in the middle of the night. Ursula had covered her head with her pillow in an effort to muffle the terrified screams from Frau Heileman and her five-year-old daughter as they were hauled away. Based on the bulging waistline of an elderly man named Hans Stille who lived on the third floor, Ursula assumed he had informed on the Jewish family. By the way he sneered at her when they passed on the stairs, she also believed he knew her secret. She was meticulous in her greeting each time they met, ignoring his leers as she lowered her gaze and used the most formal tone in her speech.

Anna knew little of this, as she had been spending increasing amounts of time away from the apartment. True to his word, Hitler had found her placement in the Berlin orchestra, and she had quickly risen to second chair violin. Their infatuation with each other had grown such that they spent most leisure time together. When she wasn't rehearsing, Anna was whisked away in swastika-ornamented cars that delivered her to wherever Hitler was at the moment.

Although Ursula and Willy had done a yeoman's job of trying to keep the relationship from Otto, he discovered the affair.

"Anna, you will no longer see this man. Ever!" Otto's hands shook as he spoke.

Anna glowered. "You can no longer tell me what to do, Papa. I'm a grown woman—"

"You are nineteen years of age!" Otto bellowed.

Anna continued as if he'd not spoken. "—and I can do what I want, with whom I want, and where I want."

"Do you hear yourself, Anna? You speak like a child throwing a tantrum!"

"Adolf says that I'm capable of making decisions. And I choose to carry on my relationship!" They squared off, and Ursula knew that Otto's cause, albeit just, was lost.

Anna raised her chin in defiance, then exited the apartment, saying that she'd return later that evening, or perhaps the following day. Ursula and Willy exchanged worried looks and sat next to Otto, who collapsed on the couch with his face in his hands.

"Papa?"

Otto shook his head. "I've already lost her, Ursula. I lost you, and now I have lost Anna."

Ursula bit her lip. "You haven't lost me, Papa. You have gained Willy."

Otto smiled weakly. "Forgive me, Willy. You're a good man. It's just—"

Willy lifted his hand. "No need, Herr Becker. I understand what you're saying. Or *not* saying."

Otto's gaze turned far away, and he remained silent and still.

"Papa, what are you thinking?"

Otto remained mute.

Ursula glanced nervously at Willy. His face expressed the concern Ursula was feeling.

"Papa?"

The corners of Otto's mouth turned up, and Ursula thought he was going to cry. Instead, he started laughing. It was quiet at first, but then blossomed into large, loud guffaws that filled the small apartment. Never having seen her father so out of control, Ursula sat back and watched, unsure. When he calmed, he whispered so quietly that Ursula leaned forward.

"I didn't hear you, Papa. What did you say?"

He looked directly into her eyes. "Belly of the beast. That's what I said. We are in the belly of the beast now."

"I don't understand."

"Neither do I. I don't understand why or how this has happened, but desperate times call for desperate measures. How better to control a man than through his heart, eh?"

Otto abruptly stood and rubbed his hands together. "Yes, we shall remain close to Herr Hitler and thereby gain some control over our situation. Perhaps that was Anna's plan all along. Come, let us dine on the delicacies Willy has brought. You told me once, Ursula, that we should focus on what we have instead of what we don't have. Having lost two beautiful wives, I cannot bear another loss. I will do what it takes to keep my family together. For the sake of our survival, let's enjoy the here and now."

Ursula, Willy, and Otto sat at the small kitchen table. Willy had brought ham, flour, sugar, and salt in such quantities that Ursula was able to create Eisbein with sauerkraut and Pfannkuchen for dessert. When the aroma of freshly baking pastry escaped the apartment, neighbors came calling and were rewarded with a small packet and a promise from Ursula to share if more food windfalls came the Beckers' way. Otto closed the door on the last neighbor and said, "We won't be sharing any more, Ursula."

"But Papa, Willy brought enough for—"

Otto raised his hand. "We don't know what the future holds. From now on we'll keep our food to ourselves."

Ursula accepted the not-so-subtle reprimand and sat quietly as Willy apprised Otto of Hitler's strategic plans. "He has signed a pact with Stalin."

Otto placed his fork carefully on his plate. "For what purpose?"

"A non-aggression agreement if war should break out in Europe."

"But that would put a target on Germany's back. If Germany is making agreements with other countries, the rest of Europe will think we want war."

Willy nodded. "He does want war, Herr Becker. He intends to take Poland with the Soviets' help. Germany and the Soviet Union will divide the spoils."

Otto blanched. "When?"

"The pact was signed two days ago. I know about it only because I over-heard von Ribbentrop and my uncle discussing it over lunch. He plans to invade on September first."

Otto leaned back in his chair and ran his hands over his haggard face. "My God. And then?"

Willy shrugged. "That's all I know, but we need only look to the past in order to determine the future. Consider my uncle's vision of Europe as a chess board. He manipulated Mussolini by meeting with him in 1934 and creating a gentlemen's agreement to stay out of Austria. And then, weeks later, Austria's chancellor was assassinated. Coincidence? I think not. Mussolini was furious, as you can imagine, and distanced himself from my uncle. And then, miraculously, when Italy invaded Ethiopia, they were friends again when Germany supported the barbarian attack."

Ursula leaned in, horrified at how easily lives were used as currency in the egotistical warmongering between two sociopaths.

Otto shook his head. "I don't understand, Willy."

Willy leaned forward. "When my uncle sent 22,000 troops into Rhineland, he armed it to the teeth. All of Europe's collective attention, including Mussolini's, was on the western side of Germany, on Rhineland."

Otto drew a quick breath and sat back. Ursula looked from him to Willy, who crossed his arms and smiled as Otto's quick mind put the pieces together. "And that's when he invaded Austria," Otto breathed.

"Exactly. Now he plans on invading Poland. Why would he do that?"

"To distract so that he can invade elsewhere?"

"Yes. Belgium and the Netherlands is my guess."

"To what end?"

Willy took a deep breath. "Again, this is just a guess, but I think his ultimate goal is Britain. He often talks of their dominance during the Great War. He is afraid of the Brits, and I think controlling them would be his goal."

Ursula's mind reeled. "But certainly someone will stop him!"

The two men turned to her but didn't speak.

"What if he's successful in attacking Belgium and the Netherlands? What would that mean?"

Otto groaned. "It would mean another war, Ursula. One in which Germany would be fighting all of Europe and, perhaps, even Britain. I can't survive another war."

Ursula violently shook her head and stood, knocking her chair over. Willy reached out a hand to calm her, but she pulled away. "No, Willy. Someone has to do something! People are literally being dragged through the streets. Good men and women who have worked their whole lives to build foundations for their families are being sent away to God knows where, leaving their children to wander the streets in search of food or be taken in. Neighbors turn on neighbors in an effort to please their captors. They receive rewards to turn in solid citizens who have committed no crime. It's insanity. Pure insanity!" She picked up her chair and sat heavily. "Someone has to do something. I have to do something." Ursula felt suddenly nauseated by the tasty, expansive meal she had prepared. She stood again, her chair scraping the floor.

"I don't care what you say, Papa. I'm offering our leftover food to our neighbors. I can't stop Hitler from driving Germany to war, but I can take care of my community to the best of my ability. It starts with one person, one gesture, and this is mine." As Otto looked on mutely, Ursula crossed to the door and opened it wide, then yelled into the corridor. "There's food here for anyone who is hungry!" Within seconds four people appeared at the door, the smallest of them only three years old. Hanna Weinman gazed up at Ursula with an earnestness that cut straight to her heart. "Danke," she whispered as she hugged Ursula's legs. "Thank you, beautiful lady."

1940

1 1

Each of Willy's predictions came to fruition. Two days after Hitler invaded Poland, the rest of Europe declared war on Germany. Hitler stormed the Low Countries and, just recently, had successfully invaded France. The world had split into warring factions, and the German economy was now almost entirely focused on supporting the war effort. It was true that unemployment had fallen dramatically, but the reality was that most jobs were focused on constructing Hitler's war machine. Men who had been milliners, butchers, and bakers were now employed by the Reich, riveting and assembling in armament factories. The result was that the average German was starting to feel the pinch as the supplies of flour, sugar, and coffee dwindled. Ursula had noticed that fewer and fewer people attended the opera, and she wondered how much longer it would remain viable ... and how much longer she would remain relevant.

She turned to the dressing room mirror and evaluated her reflection, seeking any remnant of the ingenue who had graced the stage only seven years prior. The opera house had seen more changes, as the most recent director was discovered to be a mischling of the first degree. Ursula hadn't learned this information firsthand, but rather through opera house gossip, as no one spoke openly any longer for fear of being reported.

She and Willy had dined with Hitler and Anna on several occasions over the last year, and Ursula had gone out of her way to ensure that she was respectful and kind. In response, Hitler had treated her with deference, often commenting on how maturity had enhanced her beauty, much like someone he'd loved very much. Ursula knew he was referring to Geli but never responded to his comments. She didn't want to encourage his obvious infatuation, so she averted her gaze or changed the subject. She would catch Hitler watching her, staring at her mouth when she spoke, brazenly holding her gaze when she met his eyes. She had recently commented to Willy that his attention made her uncomfortable, but Willy had reminded her how fortunate she was to be valuable to the Führer, so she had remained silent.

Hitler and Anna now spent nearly every free moment together. Anna had noticed Hitler's fascination with Ursula and had ordered her to stop flirting with him. Ursula had protested at first, explaining that the obsession was completely one-sided. But eventually she'd given up trying to reason with her sister. Anna was so taken with Hitler that she considered every other woman a threat. Like all bewitched partners, the flirtation—as Anna saw it—was never Hitler's fault. It was much safer for Anna to blame Ursula than to confront Hitler and risk losing the man she adored.

Ursula sighed and turned her attention to the letter that sat on her makeup table. It was penned by Carl Ebert, the opera house director under whom she'd premiered. Herr Ebert was writing to request that she emigrate to England to join him at Glyndebourne, the opera house he'd been managing for the last few years. Apparently, Herr Ebert had teamed with renowned conductor Fritz Busch, another anti-Nazi émigré, and together they were finding great success and growth in the fledgling company. "The only puzzle piece that is missing, dear Ursula, is you," the letter stated. Ursula leaned forward and spoke aloud to herself as she applied eyeliner.

"Ursula, what should you do? Go to England or remain in Germany? Well, Ursula, you do not speak the English language," she answered herself. "And your entire life is in Germany. Everything you love is here, including Willy." She paused as a thought struck. "Would England even accept you, you silly girl? Willy says that people in England do not like Germany's behavior. I can't say that I blame them. Would I be welcomed there?" Ursula drew back quickly, poking herself in the eye. "Ouch! But it's a good question. Would I be welcomed there?"

A knock sounded and the door opened. Anna appeared, her eyes scanning the dressing room. "Ursula, are you losing your mind? To whom were you speaking?"

Ursula smiled. "I was speaking to myself, dear sister. Sometimes I'm my own best company."

Anna crossed to Ursula and kissed both cheeks. "I came to wish you well this evening. Yet another premiere for my esteemed older sister."

"Emphasis on 'older,'" Ursula commented as she examined her visage for premature, unseemly lines.

"Oh, Ursula, don't be ridiculous. You're at the height of your beauty. All of Berlin speaks of the diva who brings men to their knees. I have heard you described as a siren by none other than the Führer."

Ursula rolled her eyes. "A siren? I think not."

"What is this?" Anna asked as she picked up the letter. "Herr Ebert wants you to go to England?"

"Yes."

"Will you?"

"I don't know. That's what I was discussing with myself when you entered."

"Do you want to go?"

Ursula thought a moment. "No. I do not. I want to remain in Berlin, but I'm concerned about the Führer's generosity waning over time."

Anna looked away. "You needn't concern yourself with that."

"Why do you say that?"

Anna shrugged. "I believe that as long as you attend to your music, you'll be fine."

"Fine?"

"Yes. Fine."

Ursula examined Anna. "You've cut and dyed your hair."

"Do you like it?"

"Does he?"

"Who?"

Ursula narrowed her eyes.

"Yes, he likes it."

"You know, Anna, with your hair in that style you resemble Hitler's niece, Geli. You know who I mean? She committed suicide nine years ago."

"I know who she is. Was."

"Now that I think about it, she was about the same age as you are now when she started spending a lot of time with her uncle. *A lot* of time."

Anna rounded on her sister. "What is your point, Ursula? Speak plainly or not at all, as Papa is fond of saying."

"Alright." Ursula turned in her chair. "Are you in love with him, Anna? You spend every spare minute talking about him, drawing his likeness. Ever since you met him at the amphitheater two years ago, you and he have dined together on countless occasions. You attend his rallies and spew Nazi doctrine. I feel like I don't know who you are."

"You don't seem to mind dining on his food, Ursula. Besides, you don't understand him. He's kind and makes me feel special."

"You *are* special, Anna. That's why I don't want you to spend any more time with that man."

"He says that I'm a prodigy. A German prodigy."

"He is using you. Do you understand?"

Anna set her mouth.

Ursula sighed. "In the end, Anna, you are related to a Jew. Your relationship, or whatever you have with him, will end badly."

Anna smiled in triumph. "That's where you are wrong. The Führer says that I am Aryan, and I play the violin as only an Aryan could. My fingers are exceptionally long and shapely, as most Aryans' are. See?" She extended her hands and wiggled her well-manicured fingers.

"What does being Aryan *mean*, Anna?"

"I asked the same question, and the Führer told me that it's not enough to be blond and blue-eyed. One must be defined by the Reich as being a member of the master race in order to be considered Aryan. It is quite an honor, especially considering that you are—"

Ursula stood and put her face close to Anna's. "You're making me very uncomfortable because I'm starting to think that you believe Hitler's vile lies."

Anna tilted her head. "They're not lies. The Jews are truly ruining the fatherland. And not only Germany, but all of Europe. The United States government is run by money-grubbing, capitalist Jews."

Ursula grabbed Anna's shoulders. "Stop it, Anna! Do you hear yourself? You're no longer allowed to spend any time with that madman. I will speak to Papa and see to it, mark my words."

Anna smiled openly. "Papa doesn't mind, Ursula. He understands." Ursula thought back to Otto's comment about remaining close to Hitler. *I wonder how close he meant?*

A voice called through the door. "Ursula? It's Hilde. Are you ready for me?"

"We'll finish this conversation later, Anna. Come in, Hilde."

Hilde waltzed in with Ursula's costume and spread it across the chaise. "Anna, how lovely to see you! My, what a fine addition you have been to the symphony!"

"Thank you, Hilde. I must go, sister. But don't worry. I won't mention our discussion today to any of my friends. Nor will I mention that you are considering leaving the fatherland for England."

"What?" Hilde gasped.

Ursula glared at Anna. "I'm not leaving, Hilde."

"I should hope not," Hilde muttered as she organized her hair and makeup brushes.

Ursula said, "I'll be speaking with Papa later."

Anna opened the door and gave her a smug smile. "I'm sure you will."

After Anna left, Ursula glanced at Herr Ebert's letter, wondering if she should reconsider his offer. Hilde interrupted her thoughts. "Did you hear about Fritz Rosen?"

Ursula jerked her head up. "What about him?"

"He's no longer at the opera house. I was told that he was classified as being 'unwilling to work.'"

Ursula's mind floated back to her debut, when she'd become overwhelmed at the audience's positive response. Fritz had been at her side, offering support and kindness. "That doesn't make sense. He was always the first person here before a performance and the last to leave afterwards. He is a wonderful, kind man. The hardest worker I know."

"Yes. It's awful. Last I heard he was on a train heading east along with some others. Who knows? Perhaps he'll find some good work there."

12

As the final chord descended with a thunderous clap, the crowd was on its feet, cheering and crying. Ursula glanced at the maestro, who offered her a tight smile. Ursula responded in kind, as they both knew that tonight's performance had not been her best. Not even close. She had been so distracted by her conversation with Anna that she had forgotten her lines not once, but twice during the opera. She had muddled through, and the audience had been entertained, so she supposed she should be happy.

After taking two curtain calls, Ursula stood at the top of the staircase receiving well-wishers. Despite her concerns about the wartime economy affecting opera attendance, the line snaked down the stairs and out the door, reminding her that music knew no race, color, or creed, and how its universal language could permeate all socioeconomic and religious barriers. She observed the people waiting to greet her and realized that many—no, most—were either Nazi officers and their wives or the wealthy with swastika armbands advertising solidarity with the Reich.

With a jolt she realized that she was most likely the only Jew in the room.

Yet, people revered her. The reviews of her performances in the Nazi newspapers were always brimming with praise such as "exquisite tone quality" and "impeccable phrasing." She would often receive notes and gifts from up-and-coming officers who wanted to express their "undying affection" and desire to spend time with her. She would graciously accept the gifts—usually some hard-to-find food, coffee, or cigarettes—then readily give it away to Hilde or one of the other opera house staff. The officers either had no idea that she was Jewish or chose to ignore it given her celebrity, and she wondered how long she could continue taking advantage of their generosity. None of them knew about her relationship with Willy, as Hitler had mandated it remain a secret. Willy told her that if men thought she were available, their morale would remain high. But Ursula believed it was because she was a mischling. If it were known that Hitler paid homage to a Jewish diva, his Christlike status might be diminished. Either way, the gifts she received contributed to her community.

"Are you ill, dear?"

Ursula started and realized that she'd been daydreaming. A white-haired, matronly woman wearing a fox stole was smiling and holding her hand. Ursula glanced at the beady glass eyes of the unfortunate fox and felt a stab of camaraderie with the dead bauble.

"Please excuse me. I don't feel well." Ursula glanced at the new opera director, then slipped through a small door built into the wall. She returned to her dressing room to find Willy sitting in her makeup chair.

"There she is! My favorite—" Willy stopped short when he saw her face. "What is it, Ursula?"

"I'm the hired help."

"What do you mean?"

"I was standing on the staircase receiving patrons when I suddenly realized that I was the only Jew in the room." Willy looked away.

"You know it to be true!"

Willy tilted his head at her. "That fact does not diminish how the public feels about you, Ursula."

Her face crumpled. "Really, Willy? You don't think they would turn on me in an instant if they knew? I have half a mind to tell them myself!"

Willy sat up straighter. "You wouldn't do that. You'd be putting your family at risk."

Ursula rolled her eyes. "Anna would be fine. She's Aryan. Your uncle told her so."

Willy approached her and brushed some hair from her eyes. "Anna *is* safer with Uncle than without him. Wouldn't you agree?"

Ursula twisted her mouth, unable to bring herself to acknowledge it aloud.

"Ursula, Anna is not Aryan. She doesn't fit the requirements."

"But she told me—"

Willy shook his head, interrupting her. "My uncle made her Aryan."

"I don't understand."

Willy shrugged. "He had her papers altered. Her status is now listed as Aryan."

A sudden burst of anger shot through Ursula. "That horrendous fop has altered her brain! She seems to honestly believe the filth that your uncle and his cronies are spouting!" Ursula collapsed in the chair and buried her face in her hands. Willy knelt before her.

"Look at me, Ursula." Ursula lifted her head. "You are the most exquisite jewel, to me and to my uncle."

"Then why am I not deemed Aryan?"

Willy examined her face. "Would you like to be? I'm sure it could be arranged."

Ursula's eyebrows knitted in thought and then she blew out a frustrated mouthful of air. "No!"

"I didn't think so. There are many differences between you and your sister, but your honor and integrity are among the most obvious."

"So, it's that simple? I could request a reclassification and obtain it forthwith?"

"Only if you have special access. Or a lot of money."

Ursula's mouth dropped. "One can purchase Aryan status?"

"Of course. Everything is negotiable these days. The Weiss family just assured their freedom through reclassification. They are now considered Aryan."

"Do you mean the Weiss family that lives on Petersstrasse?"

"Yes."

"Herr Weiss is the brother of the rabbi who oversaw the temple on the same street, is he not?"

"He is."

Ursula shook her head and stood, then paced around the small dressing room. "This is lunacy."

"It's going to get worse, Ursula."

Ursula stopped pacing. "What do you mean?"

"I'm not supposed to talk about it, but the war is going well in France. Paris should fall any day."

Ursula winced. "Just like you said."

"His chess game continues. Soon Paris will be part of the Reich. Rumor has it that all anti-Semitic decrees will be enforced there as they have been here."

"Where will all of the Jews go? Many of the German Jews fled west and now they'll be displaced again? Where will they go?" she repeated.

"I don't know."

"What about the United States? Surely that country would authorize admittance?"

"Apparently, their Congress has not altered immigration laws, so at this point no more immigrants are allowed entry."

"Even if they are desperate and have nowhere else to go?"

"Sadly, yes."

"Willy, what does it mean when someone is labeled as unwilling to work?"

"Why do you ask?"

"Because Fritz Rosen, the wonderfully kind property custodian, was labeled as such, and now he's no longer employed here. Hilde said that he's taken a train east. Do you know anything about that?"

Willy sucked air quickly and then exhaled slowly.

"Willy?"

"Ursula, sit down."

"Why?"

"Just . . . sit down."

Willy's eyes traveled the room, searching for the right words. "There are camps that were created for political dissidents."

"Camps?"

"Yes. Places where political dissidents are housed. They're put to work there."

"Doing what?"

"All sorts of things."

"Who are these political dissidents?"

"People who have spoken out against the Führer and the Reich."

"And these camps . . . the guests are treated well?"

"They are fed and housed."

"Are they allowed to come and go as they please?"

"No."

"So, it's a prison."

"Of sorts."

"Have you seen one of these camps?"

"In photographs."

"I see." Ursula nodded and looked at her hands. One of her nails had broken, she noted absentmindedly. "And you're telling me this because you believe that Fritz was sent to one of these camps?"

"Perhaps."

"For what crime? He wasn't a political person, or even an outspoken man. My goodness, he had trouble looking in my eyes when we spoke."

"If he wasn't a political dissident, maybe he was sent to a ghetto."

"What's a ghetto?"

Willy's shoulders dropped. Ursula could tell that this information weighed heavily on his mind, but she had to know.

"A ghetto is a place where enemies of the Reich are sent to live."

"That doesn't sound so bad."

"Ursula, there's a ghetto in Poland that's about three-square kilometers but houses four hundred thousand people. They are confined to that small area. If they try to leave, they'll be killed."

Ursula shook her head. "That many people in such a small area is impossible. They would be on top of one another."

"Living conditions are very bad. Food and medicine are scarce."

Ursula's eyes narrowed. "Willy, Fritz was not the kind of person who would ever harm a fly. He is, in fact, the exact opposite of that. So, tell me,

Herr Hitler, how could my soft-spoken friend ever be considered an 'enemy of the Reich'?"

"He's Jewish."

Ursula burst out laughing. "You're joking! That is utterly ridiculous! I understand that the Nazis hate the Jews, and they want them out of Germany. But being Jewish is not a *crime* for which he should be imprisoned. Stealing is a crime. Murder is a crime. But being Jewish is not a crime."

Willy grabbed her shoulders. "Look at my face, Ursula. I have never been more serious in my life. People keep saying things will get better, that the restrictions on Jews will be lifted and everything will go back to normal. Honestly, I can't even remember what normal looks like."

"I can," Ursula whispered, suddenly sober. "Normal is a place where I could walk the streets without fear of seeing someone stomped to death. It's greeting my neighbors without fear of being reported. Normal is being able to speak my mind without fear of being killed, and being able to purchase goods from anyone, even if they're Jewish." Tears ran down her face, tracing crooked lines in her makeup. "I remember normal, Willy. It was a beautiful, warm, calm place that all of us took for granted."

"Oh, Ursula." Willy gathered her in his arms.

"You say that things will get worse. What is to become of me, the only Jew in this entire opera house?"

He didn't answer. He simply held her tightly against him. She wished that they could remain there, wrapped in the glorious color of their love, while the drab, gray outside world faded away.

"What if you weren't a Jew?"

She looked up at him, her eyes smudged black with mascara and eyeliner. "We already discussed this. I will not be reclassified on principle. So many people are worse off than I am. I shouldn't receive special treatment."

"That's not what I mean."

"How else could I become . . . not Jewish?"

Willy knelt and took her hands in his. "I was waiting for the right time to do this, but I don't believe that there will be a better time."

"What are you doing?"

"Ursula Estelle Becker, since the day I met you I have been hopelessly, desperately in love with you. It would be the greatest honor of my life to call you my wife. Will you marry me?"

13

Ursula stood frozen in place, her face a mosaic of smudged makeup and her mouth forming a small 'o.'

Words poured from Willy's mouth, as if pent up too long and finally finding release. "Ursula, I love you. I think about you all the time and when I sleep, you're in my dreams. We've been dating for two years and I cannot imagine spending my life with anyone else."

Ursula's mouth opened and closed several times before she found her voice. "Willy, my goodness. I was not expecting this. I must look a fright." She glanced in the mirror and was shocked to see her wig askew and colorful smears from her eyes to her chin. She grabbed a cloth and wiped her face, straightened her wig and then smiled. Willy remained on his knees awaiting a response.

"Willy, please stand."

He obliged. "Well?"

"You could not have chosen a more imperfect time to ask me the most perfect question in the world."

"I know."

"As you indicated, the situation in Germany is going to get worse."

"That is true."

"And you would be marrying a Jew. My marrying you would not alter the fact that I am Jewish."

Willy smiled. "You are correct."

"Even though you said that I would become 'not Jewish' if I married you."

Willy blushed. "I thought the idea of marrying me would be more appealing if you thought you were receiving a bonus."

Ursula playfully slapped his arm.

"Are you sure you want to marry a Jew? It won't be easy for you."

Willy wrapped his arms around her slender waist. "I am sure I want to marry the Jew standing in front of me."

"Our children will be mischlings of the third degree."

Willy drew back. "Our children?"

Ursula twisted a loose button on his coat.

He tilted his head, trying to catch her eyes. "Is that a yes?"

Ursula looked up at him and smiled. "That is a definite yes, Herr Hitler."

* * *

Ursula stole a glance at Willy, who stood stoically in front of a scowling Otto. "Tell me, Willy, is this the way betrothal is completed in England? Not requesting permission from the young lady's father for his daughter's hand in marriage? I must say, son, that I am not impressed." Otto rose from the kitchen chair and crossed his arms.

Willy stepped forward and Ursula followed suit. "My most sincere apologies, Herr Becker. I have the utmost respect for you and your daughter. Our situation is not typical, but nothing in Germany is typical at this moment. The fact is that I love Ursula and will do everything in my power to protect her and provide for her, sir."

The pleading tone in Willy's voice struck Ursula, and she felt a rush of love for him. Otto glared at Willy and then shifted his attention to Ursula. "And you, my daughter, accepting Herr Hitler's proposal without discussing it with me. I am disappointed."

Ursula smiled brightly. "I'm sorry, Papa."

Otto narrowed his eyes. "You don't look sorry."

Ursula's smile widened. A look of consternation crossed Otto's face, and then he broke into a lopsided grin. "Alright, enough, you two. I suppose a celebration is in order."

Ursula jumped up and down and clapped her hands. Willy blew out a mouthful of air and shook Otto's hand. Ursula crossed to the kitchen cabinet and removed three of their best glasses. She filled them with water and handed them out.

"So, you are to become Ursula Hitler?" Otto sputtered a laugh. "The irony cannot be denied. A Jew becoming part of the Führer's extended family!" Otto raised his glass. "To the health of Herr and Frau Hitler. L'chaim!" The three of them burst out laughing at Otto's little joke. "Prost!" Ursula announced as Willy simultaneously said, "Cheers!"

They drained their glasses. "We need to tell your sister the good news."

"No," Willy said, a little too quickly. "I think we should keep our wonderful secret among us three only, at least for a little while."

Otto's face fell. "Why?"

"Because some people might not be happy about our engagement, and I don't want to raise their ire." He glanced at Ursula, who smiled tightly. The silent implication momentarily dampened her enthusiasm, but Ursula was determined to continue the celebratory mood.

"It's alright, Papa. The three of us know, and that's enough for now. We'll find a way to tell Anna later."

Ursula squeezed Otto's hand and he nodded. A moment later a grin replaced his worried scowl. "I'm so happy for the two of you!" he gushed.

Willy laughed. "I must go now, Ursula, but I'll see you soon. Thank you for making me the happiest man in all of Germany. Maybe the world!" They hugged as a beaming Otto looked on. Otto walked Willy out of the apartment and closed the door behind them so they could speak privately in the hallway. Curious, Ursula tiptoed to the door and opened it a crack so she could observe. With tears in his eyes, Otto said, "I know that you're a good man, Willy. I trust you to take care of my Ursula. She and Anna are all I have."

"I know, Herr Becker, and I promise. Ursula is my world. I will do everything in my power to give her a good life." They shook hands, and Otto clapped Willy's shoulder.

Otto watched him descend the stairs, then turned to find Ursula standing in the doorway, grinning from ear to ear. She rushed forward and jumped into his arms, throwing her arms around his neck and kissing his face repeatedly. "Thank you, thank you, thank you, Papa! I know that you're not happy about Willy's family lineage, but you have made me the happiest girl in the world!" She kissed him again and then released his neck.

Otto looked suddenly sad. "It's a shame we can't share this wonderful news with Anna."

Ursula's elation evaporated as she recalled her conversation with her sister at the opera house. "About Anna, Papa."

They reentered the apartment. Otto gathered the three glasses and placed them on the sideboard. "What about her?"

"I'm worried."

Otto turned around, a confused look on his face.

"She's been spending too much time with the Führer. She's changed."

Otto shook his head. "You know that I have no love for the man or his leanings, but he does seem to care for our Anna."

Ursula was shocked. "His leanings? Papa, Jews are being shipped east!"

Otto waved his hand. "That is rumor, Ursula."

Ursula stared hard at Otto. "I'm not sure what's happening to you, Papa. The Otto Becker I know would balk at the news I just shared with you. Yet you stand here and rationalize everything I'm telling you."

Otto dropped his gaze. "I'm scared, Ursula. I believe that the scales are tipping in Hitler's favor and that he will become even more powerful. If that's true, then I want my daughters protected. And what better way to be protected than by remaining close to those in power? I may not like it, but that's the practical reality." He glanced at her. "Where did you hear about people being sent to the east?"

"Willy told me about places called ghettos that are being used to house Jews so that they remain away from Germany, unable to return."

"I have heard of them, but they are for political enemies of the Reich."

"You're talking about the camps, Papa. Those are different. These ghettos are small areas that house hundreds of thousands of Jews."

Otto looked at her, his countenance darkening. "You heard this from Willy?"

Ursula nodded. "He said that things will get worse for the Jews. Already you and I have seen people ridiculed and beaten in the streets, forced into humiliating situations. The Nazis want to break our spirits, Papa."

Ursula watched Otto process what she'd said. His face registered worry, then despair. When he spoke, the whispered words tumbled out of his mouth, jumbled on top of one another. "The Great War seems like yesterday and here we are again, embroiled in another major conflict. Hitler will not stop at ruling Europe. He will want to control Britain and maybe even America." Otto shook his head. He reached toward Ursula and she noticed that his hands trembled. "He will cause another great war, Ursula. A world war. We cannot have a world war. We *cannot*."

Ursula listened with a mixture of sadness, anger, loss, and fear. Her father, the rock she'd relied on her entire life, suddenly looked old and frail. His veiny hands shook with impotent frustration. He was not a young man who could take matters into his own hands. His fate, and that of his family, was at the mercy of a madman whose ego knew no bounds. But mostly it was the terror in Otto's voice that scared her. She ran forward and grabbed his outstretched hands. "Papa, it won't come to that. I know it won't. It will be alright. Besides, we have Willy to take care of us."

Otto's wild eyes darted around the small apartment. "And Anna has the Führer," he said in a shaky voice.

As much as it pained her, she could understand Otto's perspective. But that didn't mean that she would readily concede the point. "I suppose so, Papa."

Otto's eyes found Ursula and calmed somewhat. "He cares for her."

"Don't forget that he's a monster."

"Who holds great power and can protect my daughter. She is safe with him."

Ursula remained silent. She didn't want to trouble him further by disagreeing.

"Now that she is Aryan, she is safe," Otto mumbled more to himself than Ursula.

A powerful wave of anger brought redness to Ursula's face. "What a hypocrite Hitler is. Aryanizing her for his own amusement."

"He will protect her, but never marry her," Otto muttered.

Ursula threw up her hands. "I don't know if that makes the situation better or worse, Papa. How do you know that he will not marry her?"

"He told Anna that if he were to marry, he would not be able to give all of his attention to the Reich. He is already married . . . to Germany."

Ursula rolled her eyes. "How convenient for him."

"And for us, Ursula. As long as Anna is with the Führer, she will be protected. Again, ironic, but true." Otto was quiet a moment and then sighed heavily.

"What is it?" Ursula asked.

"I was thinking that if your mother and Anna's mother were alive, they would be . . ."

"Would be what?"

"I was going to say angry, but now I realize that they would be proud they each bore an independent, practical girl."

Ursula smiled.

"My two daughters are involved with Hitler men. Who would have predicted it?"

1941

14

Ursula returned from rehearsal to find Otto sitting in the middle of the living room floor, his long, spindly legs strewn awkwardly ahead of him. Surrounding him were neatly organized piles of sheets, towels, clothing, jewelry, dishes, utensils, and drinking glasses. As Ursula looked on, he counted aloud, then wrote something down. He was so involved in his work that he took no notice of Ursula's entrance.

"Papa, what are you doing?"

Otto looked up and smiled. "I am taking note of our possessions."

"Why?"

He removed his thick glasses, a recent gift from Willy that allowed him to see details he hadn't enjoyed for several years. He squinted at her. "Because Adolf Eichmann has decreed that Jews living within the Reich must declare all property."

"Papa, that decree was made in 1938."

Otto looked at her with sadness in his eyes. "An SS officer stopped by, Ursula, wondering why we had not yet listed our property. *Your* property."

Ursula dropped her gaze. "I see."

"You must be extremely careful."

Ursula looked at their frugal lives strewn across the threadbare, faded throw rug. "What is the purpose of listing our possessions?"

Otto shrugged. "I'm not sure. Perhaps the Reich wants to know our worth as the war rages on."

"Do you think that all of this will be sold to raise funds for the war?"

"I honestly don't know, Ursula. What I do know is that we will not defy Herr Eichmann, as I have seen what he does to those who defy him."

Ursula felt a pain in her chest as she considered the broken man before her. Once so physically and morally strong, over the last year Otto Becker had been reshaped into a reactive, obedient man. She pushed her poisonous thoughts aside. "Can I help you?"

"No. But thank you. I'm almost finished."

Suddenly the door to the small apartment burst open and Anna appeared, her violin case tucked under one arm. "Hello, Papa. Hello, Ursula." She walked past them and into the bedroom that she and Ursula shared and closed the door behind her.

Ursula looked at Otto. "Did you notice that Anna didn't ask what you're doing? Perhaps it's because she already knows and doesn't care."

Otto blinked twice, then continued his task. Ursula knew that his fragile ego didn't want to entertain her suggestion. She approached the bedroom door and paused at the threshold. Unsure why, she knocked before entering. Anna was packing a bag, humming a tune Ursula recognized as part of Bach's Brandenburg concertos.

"Why are you packing?"

Anna looked up and smiled. "You should be packing as well."

"Why? Where are we going?"

"To the Alps."

Ursula pulled a face. "I'm not going to the Alps. I have a performance this weekend."

Anna smiled brightly. "No, you don't. It's been cancelled."

Irked, Ursula crossed her arms. "Really? By whom?"

"The Führer."

Ice crackled through her. "I don't understand."

Ursula watched Anna pause and look at the ceiling, as if she were preparing to explain something to an obstinate child. Her silk skirt swished as she approached Ursula. "It's simple. The Führer wants you to attend a weekend retreat at the Berghof with him and some of his closest acquaintances. You are to sing." Anna nodded once to indicate that the discussion was complete, then resumed packing.

Ursula's stomach heaved but she forced her voice to remain neutral. "Anna, have you lost your senses? I'm going nowhere this weekend except for the theatre where I will perform *Der Rosenkavalier*.

Anna barely glanced at her as she spoke matter-of-factly. "You cannot perform the opera without your tenor, can you?"

"What are you talking about? Speak plainly or not at all." Ursula smirked.

Anna's smile dropped, and her tone became serious. "Max Schmidt, Germany's beloved tenor, has abandoned the fatherland for England, the coward."

Ursula's mouth dropped open. Max had confided to her that he'd received a letter from Carl Ebert requesting he join Glyndebourne Opera. He had told her that he had no intention of going, but that was obviously a lie meant to maintain his charade until he was ready to leave. Although Ursula could understand Max's secrecy, she felt betrayed.

"Yes, it's shocking that anyone would abandon the Führer just as Germany is reaching the pinnacle of greatness," Anna commented. She resumed packing. "Anyway, your talent is no longer required at the theatre this weekend, and the Führer requires your presence at his country estate."

"I will not be ordered about like some lackey, Anna. I determine where and when I sing. And for whom." Ursula turned on her heel and exited the room, slamming the door behind her. Her heart surged, and she struggled to catch her breath.

Otto removed his glasses and cleaned them on his shirt. "You must go, Ursula." Ursula rounded on her father. "I will not!"

Otto raised his glasses until the light from the window shone through them. Spotting a smudge he had missed, he resumed cleaning them. "You must. If for no other reason than to protect your sister."

A brilliant flare of indignant fury blazed brightly in her eyes. "Papa, she has made her choices and must live with them. I am not responsible for her bad decisions. She is a grown woman!"

"She is twenty-one, Ursula. Did you make good decisions at that age?"

Ursula dropped her head, remembering how little she knew of the world at that stage in her life. She wanted to protect the sister with whom she had shared a common musical dream. But this haughty, well-dressed woman who marched into the apartment making declarations did not automatically command Ursula's loyalty and respect. She sighed deeply. "I cannot save her, Papa. She must do that herself. You said she is safe with Hitler."

"I did say that, yes."

"So why must I go?"

Otto was silent for so long that Ursula finally sat down on the floor next to him. He carefully donned his glasses and then looked at her, his pleading eyes willing her to understand so that he need not verbalize his embarrassment.

"Papa, what is it?"

And then she realized with a start what his pride wouldn't allow him to voice.

"Oh, Papa, I'm sorry. You're correct. I must go."

Otto smiled weakly as a tear rolled down his cheek. "I'm sorry, Ursula, that you bear my weight on your shoulders. You and Anna are valuable to the Reich, but I am not, and I am afraid."

His eyes held such anguish that she scolded herself for not realizing the strain he'd been under. Ursula hugged him hard. "Of course I will go, Papa."

The door to the bedroom flung open. Anna emerged and examined the piles on the floor. "You know that you need not count my things, don't you, Papa?"

"I know, Anna."

"Because I am—"

"Aryan. Yes, we know," Ursula said.

"You could be Aryan too, Ursula."

"No, thank you." Then a thought struck. "But what about Papa? Could he be classified as Aryan to ensure his protection?"

Anna tilted her head in thought. "I suppose I could ask."

"Would you?" Ursula begged.

Anna smiled. "Of course. Ursula, Willy will be here soon to fetch you, so you should hurry and pack."

Ursula blinked. "Willy is coming to the Berghof with us?"

Anna stopped at the door and turned. "Yes. It was his idea that you sing this weekend. See you there."

Anna exited the apartment without closing the door behind her. Ursula stood, closed the door, then crossed to the window to see Anna enter a Mercedes Benz 770 convertible decorated in Nazi regalia. Onlookers gaped at the monstrosity, unused to seeing such opulence in their practical lives. The swastika flags waved proudly on either side of the doors, and Ursula felt her stomach tighten as she realized that she might be forced to ride in such a vehicle.

A knock at the door interrupted her thoughts. Otto answered it and smiled broadly. "Willy, so good to see you." Willy entered to find Ursula glaring at him, her arms crossed tightly over her chest.

"I understand that it was your idea that I sing this weekend at your uncle's mountain retreat."

"Listen, Ursula, I just thought—"

Ursula held her palm toward him. "Willy, I have not expressly stated my feelings on this matter, so let me do it now. My voice is mine. Not yours. It is a gift that I was bestowed, and I use it as I see fit. Do you understand?"

"Yes, but—"

"No buts, Willy. I need to know that you respect my wishes."

Willy nodded. "I understand. Now may I say something?"

"Of course."

"I was hoping that you might have a chance to get to know my uncle a little better this weekend."

"I have no desire to know your uncle better."

"That might be a problem."

The hairs on Ursula's arm became taut and a chill ran up her spine. "Why?"

"Because he's asked me to officially join the Nazi party as an officer. Of course, as my betrothed, you would become a member as well."

Otto's hand flew to his mouth and he excused himself from the room. Ursula's eyes followed her father as she processed what Willy had said.

Willy took the opportunity to press his case. "Before you say anything, can you please pack your bag? We need to be at the Berghof by four p.m. and—"

"It will take a lot longer than that to drive to Berchtesgaden."

"No. My uncle has a plane waiting for us."

Ursula gaped at him. "Willy, this is too much. I can't process it so quickly."

He approached her and took her face in his hands. "I know, my love. I know it's a lot, but I have two questions for you. Do you love me?"

Ursula glared at him as her anger wrestled with her strong love for him. "You know I do."

"Do you trust me?"

Ursula paused. She trusted Willy implicitly. Or thought she did. Until now. "Do you?" he repeated, his eyes more sincere and intense than she'd ever seen them.

She took a deep breath. "Yes."

"Then pack your bag and let's go. Bring a gown for this evening."

Ursula stared at him a moment longer, then dashed into her bedroom and packed a light wool jumper and a white, collared shirt. She added some stockings and a pair of low-heeled black shoes that buttoned on the side, as well as her pink, cotton pajamas, and her makeup bag and toiletries. Finally, she opened her wardrobe and perused her collection of recital gowns. She removed a blood-red silk, strapless dress and held it in front of her while looking in the mirror. The gown highlighted her delicate bone structure. She lifted her chin and smiled confidently. "Yes. This is definitely the correct choice." She placed some matching red high heels in the bag and exited her bedroom to find her father sitting at the kitchen table speaking quietly with Willy. Otto glanced in her direction, then patted Willy's hand and stood.

"What are the two of you discussing?"

In response, Otto approached, hugged her, and kissed the top of her head. He spoke quietly but quickly in her ear. "Listen to what Willy has to say, Ursula. Do not dismiss him out of hand."

She withdrew from her father and searched his tired eyes. She had neither the time nor the energy to question him further. After a beat, she nodded. "Alright, Papa. I promise."

Willy took Ursula's bag, and they exited the apartment and descended the stairs. After they were settled in the royal blue Opel Olympia that had been a gift from the Führer upon Willy's arrival in Germany, Willy started the engine and cleared his throat.

"I would like to tell you how we've come to this point with my uncle."

Ursula stared straight ahead as the streets of Berlin whizzed by. She noted that the sea of black Nazi uniforms seemed to have multiplied in the last few weeks. *Where are all of the regular people?* she wondered. *Maybe the Nazis are the regular people now.* Without looking at him, she stated, "*We* have not come to this point, Willy. *You* have come to this point."

Willy sighed. "What I mean to say is this. Six months ago, my uncle asked me to join the Party and I politely declined. Two months ago, I asked him for a promotion, and I was transferred from the bank to the automotive factory."

"I wondered how you came by that position but never asked," Ursula quipped as she watched an SS soldier drag a child by his hair. The boy's body was slack, and Ursula wondered if he'd been killed by the soldier or whether the soldier was simply clearing the street.

"After being in my new position for a little while, my uncle approached me again and asked me to join. I politely declined, and he informed me that my continued success and advancement was contingent on joining. So, I must join."

Ursula was silent for the rest of the journey. She had done what her father asked. She had listened to Willy. But that didn't mean she had to respond.

Willy pulled into the parking area of the airstrip and Ursula blanched as a large plane landed. A massive red and black swastika glared from the tail. Its grandeur drew the eye, causing her to rethink boarding the plane. Her gaze then traveled the length of the aircraft, stopping when she saw a machine gun turret. She closed her eyes and pictured her father. She had made a promise to him that she would go. She had to uphold it. After the plane taxied to a stop, a set of stairs was wheeled over and placed against the door, which opened quickly.

Willy glanced at his watch. "Leave it to Uncle Alf to ensure that his plane lands exactly on time. Ever efficient," he muttered.

Ursula turned to face him. "His *personal* plane?"

Willy nodded. "He wanted you to feel welcome."

A sudden, irrepressible urge to run away took hold of her. "Willy, let's not get on this plane. I believe in you! You don't need your uncle's approval or advancements to be successful. You can do it on your own."

Willy shook his head. "Ursula, you're one of the smartest girls I've ever known. Yet you seem to have a blind spot when it comes to Adolf Hitler.

He's ruling Germany with an iron fist, and I've heard his discussions with Himmler, Goebbels, Goering, and Hess. He aims to rule all of Europe, Britain, and America. If he allows me to be successful, I will be. But if he decides to stand in my way, to block my advancement, then I will be left with nothing. Do you understand?"

Ursula had stopped listening. Her head felt stuffed, as if her brain had ingested too much information and couldn't move. "But still, I'm sure that there are positions that you can attain—"

Willy took her left hand and shook it. "Ursula, look at me! We must do this if we want to survive, especially given your circumstances."

Ursula slowly turned toward him and pulled her hand away. Like droplets of water rolling off a raincoat, she felt her anger drain away. An unsettling calm nestled into her core. "*My* circumstances? A minute ago, they were *our* circumstances. You've finally spoken the truth. The inevitable Jewish connection. How long will this be held over my head? Forever?"

Willy sighed heavily. "We must board the plane, Ursula."

Ursula looked past him at a steward who stood at the top of the stairs. "Life is full of choices, Willy, even when we feel like there's not a choice to be made."

Willy stared at her long enough that she finally met his deep blue eyes. In them she saw two things she'd never seen before—fatigue and defeat. She had always felt safe and protected in Willy's presence. But now, for the first time, she felt fear and uncertainty stalking her. Her heart softened.

Willy looked at his hands and sighed deeply. "Alright. So, let me tell you a choice presented to me by my uncle, Ursula. Either you and I join the Nazi party, or you and your father become expendable."

15

Ursula climbed the stairs, where she was greeted by the uniformed steward. She paused at the entrance and glanced to her left. The steward followed her stare and smiled. "That's the Führer's cabin, Fräulein. Guests go this way." He ushered her into the back of the plane, where she found a well-appointed space that looked more like a small living room than a plane cabin. Thick curtains covered each window, and a dark, lush carpet dulled their footfalls. As Willy placed their belongings in the storage area, Ursula noted the seating layout. Two loveseats faced each other, separated by a stained oak table. Across the narrow aisle were two more chairs that faced each other, also separated by a table. Once Willy and Ursula were seated in one of the loveseats, another steward appeared and asked if they'd care for some refreshment. They both declined, and the steward vanished.

"Is it going to be just you and me on this large plane, Willy?"

As if answering her question, two women appeared in the cabin's doorway. The younger of the two smiled openly and nodded in acknowledgment. The other glowered and then dismissed them before seating herself across from her companion. The older woman's entire demeanor spoke of negativity, and Ursula decided that she didn't care for her. The steward materialized and placed a drink in front of each woman. That fact, along with the manner in which they carried themselves, made Ursula believe that they were accustomed to traveling on Hitler's private plane.

The massive engines roared to life, effectively ending all possibility of communication for the duration of the flight. Having never flown before, Ursula thought she might be nervous. But the adrenaline coursing through her veins overrode any nerves, and she found herself awed by the feeling of the wheels leaving the ground. She leaned back into the plaid, cushioned seat and lay her head on the pristine, white pillow. As the metal bird soared into the sky and leveled out at thirty-two-thousand feet, the sense of weightlessness and the drone of the engines lulled her into a fitful slumber.

Otto was being hauled away by three soldiers. He repeatedly screamed her name, and when she tried to yell out to him, she found that her voice had been stolen. She clawed at her throat in a vain attempt to retrieve it and turned to find the Führer standing next to her, holding a small golden box in his hand. His smug smile revolted her, and she realized that he was in possession of her voice box. She was mute. Powerless.

The plane landed with a hard *thwump*, and Ursula was jolted awake. The dream left her feeling despondent, caught between impossible choices: join the Nazi party and become complicit in the horrors it continued to inflict, or decline and never see Willy again. She pictured herself wearing the Party uniform that signified loyalty to the Reich. The vision left her nauseous. Then she shuddered as she remembered Otto's terror in her dream, so she closed her eyes and focused on her breath. She calmed her heart rate and tried to be logical.

On some level she had always understood that she'd eventually have to make a choice. She couldn't live as a mischling in an Aryan-dominated world forever. The choice, as unpalatable as it seemed, was becoming clear. Her eyes flew open. For the sake of her father, she would cast aside her ethical code. She would become Aryan and join the Party. Her lip curled as she realized that the decision had been made long before she'd even begun to argue it in her mind. Willy knew it, and so did Otto. That's why he had asked her to consider what Willy had to say. Otto knew that when presented with facts, eventually Ursula would make the safe choice. *But safe for whom? Not for the Jews*, she thought. *I'm one more sheep in a sea of decadent, amoral hypocrites. How fast and far I have fallen. Was it only a year ago I refused Willy's offer to become Aryan?* She shook her head as she remembered how she had clearly stated, from high atop her horse, that her conscience wouldn't allow such a travesty. So many thoughts swirled, and she couldn't pin them down. Or didn't want to.

She glanced out the window to see an impossibly tall granite mountain that reached into the clouds. Evergreens graced its lower two thirds, while the top was anointed with pure white snow. Her mind flitted back to the haunting dream, and the resolve she'd recently fostered continued to build. She'd made a decision. To turn back now might cause doubt. And doubt was dangerous. She turned to Willy and took his hand while her brain fully accepted the consequences of her decision. They sat like that until the engines powered down. Once she could be heard, she said, "Please forgive me, Willy. I know we're living in extraordinary times, so I must make decisions that I normally wouldn't make. For the sake of my family, and for you."

A wave of shock swept over Willy's features, and for a moment she hesitated. *He thought I'd choose differently. Have I made the wrong choice?* He leaned over and kissed her. "I know that wasn't an easy decision, Ursula. I'm grateful that you made the logical choice. You don't have to believe. You just need to . . ." His words trailed away when he noted the strained look on her face. "Thank you," he whispered.

Ursula turned toward the window, afraid Willy would see the truth. If she were completely honest, she felt as if a weight had been lifted. *How cheaply your ethics were sold,* a voice whispered. *Is this the new currency? Your soul in exchange for survival? Your conscience for food?* Seeing Willy's happiness and knowing that her family would be protected did little to dull the culpability she felt at having sacrificed her morality. She shook her head to clear it of the venomous self-doubt as Hitler's personal pilot, Hans Baur, entered the main cabin.

"Ladies and gentlemen, please gather your belongings and exit the plane via the stairs. There is a car waiting to escort you to the Berghof." Ursula stood and accidentally bumped into the angry woman, who pushed past her and exited the plane. Willy smiled at Ursula in encouragement and motioned for her to exit before him. A cool breeze greeted her as she evaluated the steep stairs, and she paused a moment to breathe the most refreshing air she could remember.

One of the stewards glanced at her and then looked away as he stood at attention.

"Fräulein, may I assist you? These steps are very steep."

Ursula lifted her chin. "No, thank you. I can manage." She took one step and stumbled. The steward materialized and caught her in his arms. Ursula cleared her throat and quickly righted herself.

"Thank you."

"My pleasure, Fräulein. Now . . . may I assist you?"

Ursula pursed her lips but acquiesced. As she placed her gloved hand in his, he stole a peek at her and smiled ever so slightly. "I am a fan, Fräulein. You appear . . . like your voice. Exquisite." His large brown eyes exuded warmth as they searched her face. *He's no older than eighteen. In many ways still a child, yet he works for a madman,* she thought. Then her stomach clenched as her mind returned to her recent decision. *I, too, will be working for a madman.*

She glanced at the SS insignia on his collar, then held his eyes for a moment, trying to rationalize the juxtaposition between his kindness and the uniform he was wearing. She wondered whether he truly believed the Nazi propaganda or whether he was simply trying to survive. *It doesn't matter. He is a cog in the Nazi war machine,* the voice whispered. *Just like you'll be soon,* it finished viciously.

"Thank you," she finally managed.

"Everything alright here?" Willy asked as he looked from Ursula to the steward. Ursula nodded and transferred her hand to Willy.

"Yes, sir. Heil Hitler!" the young man replied, his right arm outstretched in the perfunctory salute. Any warmth Ursula had perceived vanished as he morphed into the efficient automaton Hitler demanded. Willy tilted his head at Ursula, silently asking if she was alright. She nodded in return and fell into step with him as they descended the stairs. A car awaited them and, as she had feared, the large automobile was adorned with Nazi regalia. Her hands trembled, and the word *hypocrite* repeated continuously in her mind as she settled into the soft brown, buttery leather seats.

The two women from the plane now sat facing Willy and her. The friendly woman was about Ursula's age with a stylish pixie cut and a large nose. She openly evaluated Ursula and grinned when they made eye contact. The cranky, older woman simply stared out the window, a permanent frown etched into the corners of her ample mouth.

"Relax, my darling," Willy muttered.

Ursula looked deeply into his eyes, unable to express the dread that sat like a stone in her stomach as it spurted acid into her throat. Willy saw her anguish and squeezed her hand, the only solace he could offer in current company.

The younger woman cleared her throat. "Hello, Fräulein Becker. My name is Christa Schroeder. I think you are an exceptional singer. My mother was an opera singer, not to your caliber, of course, but she was wonderful."

Ursula smiled. "Thank you, Fräulein Schroeder. Where did your mother perform?"

"She sang in Berlin and Munich but stopped, of course, when I was born."

Ursula tilted her head. "Why do you say that she stopped, of course, when you were born?"

"Because a woman's role is in the home with her children. The Führer insists upon it. All women are the mothers of Germany."

Ursula opened her mouth to respond but Willy squeezed her hand. She cut her eyes toward him, then smiled sweetly. "Are you married, Fräulein Schroeder?"

The young woman chuckled. "Oh, my goodness, no. If I were to marry, then I could no longer work for the Führer."

"Why not?"

"Because just as he is married to Germany, I am married to his cause."

Willy's grip tightened. Ursula removed her hand and stole a glance at the older woman, who was staring directly at her, her narrowed green eyes taking in Ursula's clothing. Her colorless lips traced a thin line below her aquiline nose, and her auburn hair was pulled back tightly in a no-nonsense bun at the base of her skull. Fräulein Schroeder caught Ursula looking.

"This is Johanna Wolf. She is the Führer's chief secretary. She has been with him for some time."

Fräulein Wolf gave her colleague a withering look and spoke in a quiet, deep voice. "I am able to speak for myself, Christa. However, I choose not to speak." She returned her piercing gaze to the birch trees.

Ursula looked out the window and was startled to see that the landscape had changed dramatically in the short amount of time they'd been driving. The mountain that she'd observed from the plane was now directly in front of them as the spacious car started the winding trek upwards. Large evergreens lined the one-lane road as they wound around curve after curve. On a particularly sharp turn, she glanced down and involuntarily threw herself toward Willy. The car was dangerously close to an edge that dropped off into nothingness. Willy laughed and wrapped his right arm around her shoulders. "It's alright, Ursula. Erich knows how to negotiate this stretch. I believe that he could drive it while asleep." In response, the chauffeur smiled in the rearview mirror and said something Ursula couldn't hear.

Suddenly day turned into night. Before Ursula had time to react, Erich turned on the headlamps and the tunnel they'd entered was illuminated in white light. The inside of the car became an artist's palette of hued shadows that danced as the headlamps bounced off the moist stone walls. Ursula turned to face Willy but could discern only the whites of his eyes and the flash of his perfect teeth as they smiled in an effort to calm her. Just as she was about to ask how much longer they would remain in darkness, the car erupted into impossibly bright daylight.

"We have arrived."

Ursula's heart skipped a beat as the Mercedes climbed a final hill and there, before her, was the most glorious chalet she'd ever seen. A beautiful, expansive lawn climbed to a natural stone foundation that grew into whitewashed walls. Spacious balconies sported jaunty red and white flowers in neat window boxes. If it weren't for the Nazi flag waving proudly in front of the luxurious estate, Ursula would have fallen in love with the house and its location, high above the market town of Berchtesgaden.

The guards waved the car through a log and stone checkpoint, and then Erich rolled to a stop in front of a set of stone stairs. He exited the car, removed the luggage from the trunk, and then opened the door and held his hand toward Ursula, who exited and smoothed her skirt. Before she could retrieve her suitcase, two soldiers appeared and whisked away the luggage.

The two secretaries rushed up the stairs and disappeared as Ursula took Willy's arm. Halfway to the top, Ursula looked up to see a German shepherd panting and wagging its tail. As they drew closer, the dog turned in circles and barked. Ursula pulled back, unsure of the animal's intentions, but Willy laughed and called, "Blondi, come!" The dog bounded down the stairs and, as it approached, Ursula turned away, terrified. But it ignored her and jumped into Willy's outstretched arms, whining and licking his face.

Ursula stared at the dog and then Willy. "That is disgusting," she said.

Willy smiled through the tongue bath. "Ursula, meet Blondi, the best dog in the world."

A shrill whistle sounded. Blondi dropped to the stairs and bounded upwards, where Hitler stood smiling down on the ridiculous scene. "I see that Fräulein Becker has made the acquaintance of Blondi."

Ursula stood straighter and attempted a smile. "Yes. A lovely creature to be sure."

She and Willy finished the upward trek and were greeted with a warm handshake for Willy and a lingering kiss on the hand for Ursula. "How lovely to see you again, Fräulein. Welcome to my humble abode, Der Berghof."

"It is our sincere pleasure to be here, Uncle. Thank you for your kind invitation."

Hitler's eyes examined Ursula's face. "Are you quite alright, my dear? You look peaked. Perhaps it was the plane ride. Had you been on a plane before?"

"No."

Hitler smiled knowingly. "Well, you must be exhausted then. Gretchen will show you to your room, where you shall rest before your performance this evening. We do expect your best." He held her eyes. His words were benign. His tone was not.

Ursula realized with alarming clarity that her performance tonight was the most important audition in her life. *Der Berghof means the mountain court*, she thought. *He is a king holding court, and I am the jester, meant to entertain and distract.*

The mischling singing for her supper.

The Jew singing for her life.

16

Ursula was unpacking her suitcase when a light knock sounded, followed by her door opening slightly. "Ursula? It's Anna."

"Come in."

Anna entered the dark, oak-paneled bedroom and rushed forward to embrace Ursula. "I'm so glad that you're here!"

"Are you?" Ursula asked as she disentangled herself and resumed unpacking.

"But of course," Anna replied. "The Führer's house is breathtaking, but it doesn't seem like home unless those I love are here as well."

Ursula turned to face her. "What of Papa, Anna? Would he be welcomed here?"

Anna turned away and ran her fingers along the heavy silk, royal blue drapes that adorned each corner of the canopied bed. "Ursula, you sound cross, but why? This is a happy occasion. You are to sing for the Führer in this most glorious of spaces." Anna spread her arms wide. "You should be honored, nay, humbled, to perform here." The timbre and tone of her voice revealed the reverence in which she held the estate and its owner.

Ursula suppressed a shudder. "You astound me, Anna. Germany is crumbling around you, yet you act as if the world is perfect."

Anna smiled openly. "My world *is* perfect."

Ursula crossed her arms and looked at the floor. She considered how best to break through the Reich fog that clouded Anna's perspective. "Is it? You're in love with a man who will never marry you."

Anna narrowed her eyes and smirked. "Yet we have adjoining bedrooms. What do you think of that?"

"It disturbs me."

"I have my own pink tiled bathroom that boasts big, fluffy towels with my monogram on them."

"Bully for you," Ursula said in English. Willy had used the curious phrase after she had performed particularly well. Whereas he had said it borne of pride and happiness, Ursula spoke sarcastically, knowing that Anna wouldn't understand. She closed her empty suitcase and slid it under the bed. "Anna, did you speak to the Führer about Papa being classified as Aryan?"

Anna crossed to the window and drew back the blue and gold, brocaded drapes. "I did."

"Well? What did he say?"

"What do you think of Blondi?"

"Who?"

"The Führer's dog."

Ursula raised her eyebrows. "I think it's a dog."

Anna continued to stare out the window. "Oh no, Ursula. Do not be mistaken. She is much more than a dog. The Führer loves her. She is loyal only to him."

Ursula couldn't help but smile. "The Führer requires loyalty from all of his subjects, doesn't he?"

Anna turned and cut her eyes. Ursula could see that she'd struck a nerve. "You should be wary of your words, Ursula. You are no longer in Berlin. Although the Führer obsesses over you for reasons I cannot fathom ..." She paused and threw Ursula a supercilious glance. "You are still subject to the same requirements as all who are close to the Führer."

"Requirements?"

"Yes. To your point, those around him must project loyalty and humility."

"Like the dog."

Anna smiled thinly. "Yes, like Blondi."

"I didn't know that you were so fond of dogs, Anna."

Anna shook her head. "I don't care for Blondi. In fact, sometimes when we are dining, I kick her under the table."

"Why?"

"Because he adores her."

Ursula laughed. "Anna, you're jealous of a dog?"

"Don't be ridiculous."

Ursula approached her sister, placed her hands on her shoulders, and looked into her eyes. "Oh, my goodness. I was joking, but I see that you are truly jealous of the dog. Anna, what power does this man have over you? Help me understand."

Anna's face collapsed and she turned away. "I cannot explain it, Ursula. I know on the surface that Adolf does not seem like much of a man, but he is good and kind. He cares about me and my music."

"He believes in you."

Anna whirled around. "Yes! He believes in me. He sees what I can become."

"But, Anna, does he see who you are? Not who you can become, but who you are right now? Does he love *this* Anna?"

Anna's eyes became large and she stared through Ursula. After a moment, Ursula shook her head and turned away. "You're settling for less than you deserve, Anna."

"I disagree."

A soft knock sounded followed by a whisper. "Ursula, it's Willy."

"Come in."

As Willy entered, the smile dropped from his face. "Oh, I didn't know you had company."

"Willy, so good to see you!" Anna rushed over and embraced him. "I was just telling Ursula that she must mind her manners while here."

Willy cast a nervous glance toward Ursula. "I know better than to advise Ursula on etiquette."

"Nevertheless," Anna continued, "you may want to reinforce the importance of appropriate behavior. Well, I must go." Anna started toward the door.

"So suddenly, Anna?"

Anna turned and tilted her head. "Yes, Ursula. I must dress for dinner. Adolf enjoys when I look my best. It takes me at least an hour to prepare."

"Every evening?"

Anna looked at her with disdain. "But of course."

"You never answered my question, Anna."

"Which question?"

"What did the Führer say about Papa being classified as Aryan?"

"He said that he would consider it."

"That's all he said? Did he say when he might make a final decision?"

Anna shook her head.

"Anna, what do you do all day while you're here?"

"I walk or swim when it's warm, of course. I take photographs and practice violin as well."

"But you're really just biding time until you can be with him again, aren't you?"

Anna blushed. "You always knew me so well, Ursula. Yes. I am awaiting Adolf's return." She smiled, then exited the room.

Ursula's eyes lingered on where Anna had been standing. She sighed heavily. "Of course you are," she whispered.

* * *

Ursula descended the carpeted stairs dressed in her red silk gown. Her hair was swept into a twist that accentuated her high cheekbones and narrow chin. She had donned minimal makeup, except for the emerald green liner she had applied to accentuate her eyes. The overall effect was startling as she crossed through the dark-paneled entrance to the reception hall, where every head turned at her arrival. Although she was accustomed to being ogled, the sea of dark Nazi uniforms overwhelmed her, and she felt her breath come faster. Suddenly Willy appeared at her side, his right arm around her waist, and his left hand holding hers. He whispered, "You are radiant," and gently kissed her cheek. Reinforced, Ursula stood taller as she and Willy descended the three steps to the first level of the enormous, marble-floored room. To her right a roaring fire filled the large fireplace, and her eye was drawn to the man who stared into the flames. Hands clasped behind his back, he stood alone amidst a sea of muted activity, and it occurred to Ursula that he looked lonely and sad. As if sensing her scrutiny, Adolf Hitler turned. The look on his face was nothing short of awe as his eyes ran the length of her body, but he quickly recovered and donned a cordial mask as he approached.

"My dear, you are simply breathtaking. Literally. Like some glorious enchantress, you enter the room and time falls away, as does my breath."

He bowed and kissed her hand, and in that tiny span of time, Ursula understood how Anna could be so taken with him. His sincerity in the moment was undeniable, and his eyes were intense as they bored into hers, as if attempting to memorize her every detail. He was, in his way, intoxicating.

"I trust that you find your accommodations satisfactory?"

Ursula allowed herself a moment of emotional veracity. "Yes, Herr Hitler. They are more than adequate. Your home is lovely."

Willy chimed in. "Yes. Thank you, Uncle, for hosting us."

Hitler seemed pleased. He tilted his head in faux obeisance. "It is a pleasure, nephew." He returned his focus to Ursula. "Thank you for your kind words about the Berghof. This place is mine. I have built it with money I have earned from the sales of my book, *Mein Kampf.* I designed it and furnished it, along with its artwork, myself."

Ursula inspected the painting to her right. "Is that Cupid?"

The Führer's face lit up. "It is, my dear. *Cupid with Venus*, painted by Paris Bordone. You have a good eye."

Ursula's smile was genuine. "Thank you. It's beautiful."

"I dare say that you rival Venus's beauty this evening."

Ursula blushed and looked away. His attentions were making her feel uncomfortable. Her eyes came to rest on a painting on the other side of the room. Hitler followed her gaze and smiled. "Ah. Yes. My Geli."

Mesmerized, Ursula walked forward. She felt drawn toward the artwork, unable to stop herself. She examined the painting's subject.

It was her.

Hitler approached and stood so their arms were touching. She could feel heat radiating from his body. They stood like that, one lost in disbelief, the other lost in memory, until Hitler broke the silence.

"I commissioned Adolf Ziegler to paint this portrait."

Ursula remained silent. The detail in the painting lured her, defying her to discover what set her apart from the young woman on canvas.

"You are her twin, you know."

Ursula slowly shook her head. "It's difficult to believe that painting is not me."

"I agree. The first time I saw you in person I was astonished. The resemblance is nothing short of a miracle. Which is why I cannot find it in myself to dislike you, despite your obvious faults."

Ursula marveled at Geli's smile, so similar to her own. The playful glint in her eyes taunted, as if she knew a secret and would share it only with the chosen few. Ursula found herself smiling at her reflection. "She's beautiful."

Hitler turned toward her and spoke quickly. "She is you and you are her. You are everything that she could have been had she applied herself. You are the matured version of Geli." Ursula turned her head to face him. His eyes burned with feverish excitement; the whispered urgency in his tone scared her.

"I am not her."

"But you *could* be."

"I don't know what that means." Ursula searched for Willy. He remained on the other side of the room, deep in conversation with an SS officer she didn't recognize.

"It means that I have the power to make you anything you wish to be, to give you anything you desire."

Ursula's shock at the abruptness of his indecent proposal turned quickly to anger. "What of Anna?"

Hitler waved his hand as if swatting at a mosquito. "She is a fine specimen to be sure. But you, well . . ."

Ursula was astonished at his choice of words, and how easily he dismissed a woman who would lay down her life for him.

"And Willy?" she asked. "You know we are to be married." As soon as the words left her lips, she regretted them. She had spoken without considering the repercussions. She watched Hitler's eyes glaze over, then refocus, all in the span of one second.

The dinner chime sounded. He threw his shoulders back and smiled as if they'd just enjoyed a lighthearted conversation. "No matter, my dear. We shall pick up our subject later in the evening." He offered her his arm. Quickly reviewing her options and finding none, she slipped her arm through his. As they passed Anna, Ursula noted that her sister's eyes burned with jealousy. *Did she overhear the conversation?* Ursula wondered. She stared at Anna, trying to communicate her thoughts, but Anna set her mouth and marched away.

They entered the dining room paneled in cembra pine. A long, wooden table was decorated with vases of colorful flowers, ornate place settings, and silverware engraved with a swastika and a calligraphed *AH*. Hitler took his place at the head of table and gestured to the chair on his right. The familiarity with which he'd previously spoken vanished. "I would be honored if you would take the seat next to me, Fräulein Becker." Willy appeared on Ursula's right side, withdrew her chair and whispered, "I saw you two chatting. It seems that things are going well."

Ursula dreadfully wanted to scream at Willy, to drag him to another room to describe the disgust she'd felt at his uncle's advances. But she pictured Otto seated on their sagging couch, waiting for his dutiful, obedient daughter to return. She smiled weakly and remembered Otto's words. *You are now in the belly of the beast.*

The scrumptious meal of roasted rabbit, rosemary-roasted potatoes, and molasses-glazed carrots was wasted on Ursula, who nibbled at the feast. True to rumor, the Führer ingested only vegetables and abstained from the incredible pinot noir that most of the guests imbibed with relish. Anna sat directly across from Ursula, to the Führer's left, and Blondi settled on top of Ursula's feet, as if to take her rightful place next to her master.

Ursula kept replaying Hitler's declaration. "I have the power to make you anything you wish to be, to give you anything you desire." Her eyes traveled the luxurious dining room. Its parquet floors shone, and the view of the Alps was undeniably breathtaking. Surrounded by opulence and gaiety it was easy to forget that only kilometers away hungry, dislocated people wondered if they'd ever return to their homes. *Who am I to receive Hitler's grace because I resemble a dead girl?* The practical voice in her head instructed her to take advantage of every opportunity in order to survive. The other voice, the moral compass that had directed her until the recent insanity of war had ravaged it, urged her to resist, to fight. That voice spoke with integrity and honor, with strength and character. *Resist*, it whispered. *Resist.*

Willy squeezed her hand and she returned to the gathering. She remained silent as vibrant conversation played around her.

"Fräulein Becker, might you titillate us by sharing some behind-the-scenes drama from the opera world?" Hitler asked.

Ursula turned to face him, unsure of his intentions. He reminded her of a chameleon, able to change color with his varying moods. She could tell by the curious twinkle in his eyes that his inquiry was genuine. She hesitated but decided that obliging his request might earn some goodwill. Conversation ceased as guests became privy to the inner workings of rehearsals and the relationships that did (or didn't) blossom when forced into close quarters. After several juicy stories, Ursula decided she had disseminated enough gossip.

Hitler smiled broadly as he evaluated the rapt audience. "She is quite remarkable, isn't she? Not only a brilliant vocalist but a spellbinding story-teller as well!"

Ursula stole a glance at Anna. Her eyes were cold, sterile, expressionless. Ursula had seen Anna angry before, but this dead-eyed stare was new, and it frightened her. She smiled across the table. "Anna, perhaps after supper you and I might have a private moment?"

Anna held her gaze, unmoving. "I think not, dear sister. What's done is done."

Ursula shook her head. "What does that mean?"

Anna turned away as the pastry chef appeared pushing a cart that held the pièce de résistance—a concoction topped with white, fluffy crème. Flames licked the mixture, leaving brown, crispy tips on the sweet dessert. The crowd laughed and applauded as the chef placed the dessert in front of a beaming Hitler. With a flourish Hitler stood, then gently lowered a silver cover to extinguish the flames. He bowed to the crowd in mock appreciation, then retook his seat.

Under the table Willy took Ursula's hand. He leaned toward her and whispered, "I cannot tell you how grateful I am that you made the decision to join the Party. Our life will be secured. Together forever." Ursula turned to face him. Like two windswept waves crashing in the open ocean, guilt over her agreement to join the Party butted against the insistent whisper in her head to resist. The choice was awful, unthinkable. But she had to commit. She opened her mouth to speak when Hitler leaned toward her and whispered conspiratorially, "I was so dismayed to hear of Max Schmidt's defection."

The abrupt change in topic spiraled Ursula's already chaotic thoughts. She swallowed and took a moment to compose a response. Whatever her final decision, she wasn't going to declare it now. Certainly not in front of Hitler. "His timing was unfortunate."

"He left you very vulnerable, did he not?"

Ursula replaced her napkin, smoothing it across her lap. It was as if Hitler read her inner turmoil and was using it to force her hand. He was a shark circling a desperate seal. *No*, she thought, *he is a hyena, a scavenger taking advantage of the wounded.* "I'm not sure what you mean."

"Well, we all need to be useful to the Reich. If you're not singing, then how else will you make yourself useful?"

Ursula felt a chill in her core. His entire demeanor had changed so quickly, leaving her unsure how to respond. Then, suddenly, he broke into a grin. "I have figured it out. Perhaps you will bear a child who might one day become Führer. What do you think of that?"

Ursula's head swung to Willy. "Uncle, I think—"

Without removing his eyes from Ursula, Hitler raised his hand. The room fell silent.

"Look at me, Fräulein."

Ursula forced herself to look him in the eye. She gritted her teeth and breathed deeply to calm her galloping heart.

"Do you know what my name means?"

Again, Ursula was unprepared for the abrupt change in topic. "I do not."

"It is a combination of two words. Adal, which means noble, and wolf. Therefore, you see, Adolf means noble wolf. Why do you think I was named Adolf?"

Ursula struggled for a response as she listened to guests shift uncomfortably in their leather chairs. She willed herself to look away from his intense, piercing gaze, but the draw was irresistible. A moth to a burning candle. "I don't know."

Hitler smiled broadly and spread his arms wide. "Nothing occurs by chance, my dear. Every single thing that happens in our lives has meaning. It is our job to discover that meaning. That is the purpose of life." He paused and waggled his finger at her. "But I had a distinct advantage growing up, as my mother gave me a name that contained my destiny. The reason I am Führer is because I am of nobility, perhaps not by birth, but certainly by fate. I was destined to become a wolf, the pinnacle of wild animals, hunting and challenging my rivals until I become head of the pack."

Ursula had known that the Führer had an office that was colloquially referred to as the Wolf's Lair, but she hadn't understood the import of the name or what it represented. As if on cue, Blondi scuttled out from under the table and sat like a statue next to Hitler. The Führer's eyes softened as he patted her head. "You see, Blondi and I understand each other. She is similar to the wolf, which is why I value her so much. She is incredibly powerful yet knows that I am more so. She respects my control. In fact, she is nothing without it."

He turned to the enthralled faces seated at the long table. "It is much like the Jews, is it not, my friends? They value my authority over them. They are nothing without me. That is why they crave my leadership."

Ursula evaluated the guests, who nodded their heads in solemn unison. She then looked at Anna, whose eyes had narrowed as her lips flirted with a smile. Finally, she turned to Willy, who sat silently, staring at his hands as they wrung the cloth napkin in his lap.

Realizing that she would receive no assistance, she returned her attention to the Führer. Her brain was screaming at her to excuse herself, but her body would not obey. It was as if she were glued to the chair, watching the terrifying scene unfold as it happened to some other ill-fated young woman.

Hitler leaned back in his chair and snapped his fingers. Blondi whined, then reoriented herself so that her focus was riveted on Ursula. Ursula glanced fearfully at the shepherd and then looked at Hitler. His blue eyes had calmed and now held the horrifying confidence of complete and utter control. She had no doubt that Blondi would attack on command, and Ursula knew that Hitler wouldn't hesitate to watch her be mauled if it suited his sadism. As Hitler stared at her, the right side of his top lip rose slightly to form a barely discernable sneer.

Without warning, he clapped his hands loudly to break the spell. Blondi bounded away and the guests returned to life.

"Enough philosophical discussion! Who would like to hear Fräulein Becker sing?"

17

Ursula remained at the dining table after everyone else had exited the room. She felt as if she'd detached from her body and jumped when Willy touched her hand.

"Are you alright?"

Ursula looked at him. A torrent of fear and anger swamped her, and she rushed from the table.

She managed to quell the bile rising in her throat until she arrived in the bathroom, whereupon she unloaded the little she'd eaten into the toilet bowl. Grabbing a towel, she moistened it and sank to the floor, where she held the cool cotton against her sweating brow. Her breath was quick and shallow, so she placed her hand against her heart, willing it to calm.

Willy announced himself, then entered the bathroom and knelt next to her. "Ursula, I'm so sorry that he spoke to you that way. Are you alright?"

Staring straight ahead, she wrinkled her brow. "'Am I alright,' he asks. Am I alright?" She looked at him. "What do you think, Willy? No, I'm not alright! I'm the lone Jew in the home of a madman who openly compares Jews to pigs and honestly believes they crave his sadistic punishments. The worst part is that no one speaks against him, even though they all must know how insane he is. You included! He's like a child in his stubbornness and rancor!"

Willy sank to the floor and smoothed the hair from her eyes. "I'm sorry, Ursula, but I'm not going to place our safety at risk by speaking out."

"How can you live with that, Willy? I'm not sure I can."

Willy's hands stopped caressing her hair. "Ursula, you don't mean that."

She shook her head. "There are two Ursulas, Willy. The one that existed before the Nazi madness overtook logic, and one who wants to ensure that I do what it takes to survive. I don't know which voice to heed!" Her voice broke.

Willy embraced her. "Ursula, survival is paramount."

She noted his arms stiffen slightly as he spoke, and his tone sounded strained. She pulled away. "You know something you're not telling me."

"My uncle has been kind to you—"

"Right until he openly threatened me. It's all a façade. A ruse to pull me in before he takes me to slaughter. A corn cob for the pig on the way to being decapitated."

"I think you're being dramatic."

She straightened. "Don't tell me that I'm being dramatic, Willy. You have absolutely no idea what it's like for those not in his favor. Do you know that Papa was forced to report all of our possessions to the Reich?"

Willy looked away.

"So, you knew," Ursula said. "Tell me, why does the Reich need to know exactly how many sheets and glasses my family owns? What's happening, Willy?"

Willy threw his head back and closed his eyes, sighing deeply.

Ursula slapped her dress in frustration. "Tell me! I need to know!"

Willy looked at her. She could see that he was trying to decide something. After a few moments, he set his mouth. "You're right. You need to know. He's planning on closing all Jewish emigration from the Reich later this month."

"I don't understand."

"It means that Jews will no longer be able to leave Germany. The net is closing in. Escape will be impossible."

Ursula stared past him, her frazzled mind attempting to assimilate the new facts.

"Do you understand now, Ursula? Do you now appreciate why I can't disobey him?" She looked at Willy. His eyes were urgent, desperate. She'd been so self-absorbed, she hadn't realized what a tightrope he'd been walking, trying to keep his uncle at bay while simultaneously trying to appease her ego. Ursula admonished herself for being selfish and shortsighted. The war was so much bigger than her, yet she'd really examined it only through her narrow lens of life experience.

"Why does he hate the Jews so much, Willy? Was he wronged in his youth? Did he love a Jewish girl who didn't love him back? Help me understand."

Willy's shoulders sagged. "You're applying logic to an illogical man. He's brilliant in a twisted, egomaniacal way. He's a gifted orator who whipped discontented Germans into a frenzy and then took advantage of the chaos by stepping in to lead."

"Was he always like this? Controlling, domineering?"

Willy nodded. "From what I've heard from my mother and father, yes. He's always been this way, railing against perceived wrongs. He lived with my parents for a time in England, and my mother refers to him as being 'different.' But I'm told his behavior altered dramatically after Geli's death."

"How?"

"He's always felt incredible guilt at her suicide. You'd think he'd try to make amends for his role in the whole affair, but instead, the exact opposite of that occurred. It's as if her death untethered his leash to morality. No insidious act seems to be prohibited."

"And I look just like her. I'm his chance at redemption."

"What do you mean?"

Ursula looked at Willy and started to cry again. "He made a pass at me."

Willy drew back in surprise.

"I told him we're engaged."

"No," he breathed.

"I'm sorry but I didn't know what to do. He was so insistent."

Her distress was evident, and Willy softened. "It's alright, Ursula. We'll figure it out together. After all, there is precedent."

"What do you mean?"

Willy smirked. "Uncle's favorite tenor is Max Lorenz."

"Yes. I know him well and thoroughly enjoyed singing with him."

"He is a homosexual."

Ursula gasped. "No, he's not! He's married to Lotte Appel—"

"Who is Jewish," Willy finished. "Uncle tolerates her because he loves Max's voice. You might be placed in that same category if you don't anger him."

Ursula blinked quickly as she digested the astonishing information. Her gaze landed on the monogramed towels, *AH.* "Will his need for dominance never be quenched?"

Willy looked away. "No. He will never be satisfied. It will never be enough. How can one fill a bottomless hole?"

Someone knocked on the bathroom door. "Fräulein Becker, are you alright? We are waiting for you."

Ursula took a deep breath. "I'll be right there."

Willy quickly turned back to her and grabbed her shoulders. "Ursula, you need to remain valuable to him, which is why you need to gather yourself and sing like you've never sung before. Understand?"

Ursula slumped, defeated. "I'm not sure that I can."

The despondent look in Willy's eyes pained her. "Do it for your father, Ursula."

Fat tears formed at the corners of her eyes, then trailed down her face in green streaks as her eyeliner washed away. Willy quickly removed a handkerchief from his breast pocket and offered it to her. She accepted it with a weak smile, wiped her eyes, and stood.

"Alright," she whispered. "I'll sing."

* * *

Ursula returned downstairs and consulted with the accompanist, Walter Gieseking. Although she hadn't worked with him before, his skill and dexterity were renowned, and she knew that he was one of Hitler's favorite pianists. She suggested two songs, "Bist du bei mir," an aria from the opera *Diomedes*, and "Die stille Nacht entweicht," from *Faust*. When she proposed the two pieces, Walter smiled. "Fräulein, your choices of two German masterpieces are impeccable."

Ursula took her place in the crook of the Steinway grand piano as the excited crowd quieted in anticipation. She lowered her gaze and inhaled deeply, calming her nerves. When she raised her head, Gieseking began. As he played the unmistakable introduction to "Bist du bei mir," she saw the Führer lean back in his chair and close his eyes. Willy had told her that "Bist" was one of Hitler's favorites because it describes unconditional love, a woman expressing her willingness to die as long as her lover remains with her. Ursula caressed the melody as it undulated in unison with the exceptional accompaniment. When she had completed the first verse, she glanced at Gieseking and was shocked to see that he was weeping as he negotiated the bridge into the second stanza.

Willy stood and approached her. Confused, she paused, but he motioned her to continue singing. To her amazement, he began singing with her. She had no idea that he could carry a tune, much less harmonize. He wrapped his arms around her waist and leaned his cheek against her head. She closed her eyes. The audience faded to the background and she focused only on their blended voices. After the recent stress, the moment felt timeless and her love for him boundless. Echoes of the last piano chords faded, and Willy whispered in her ear. "I love you, Ursula Becker." Ursula smiled and opened her eyes to see the Führer staring at her as a tear ran down his cheek. Silence descended on the room until he leapt to his feet. "Brava! Brava! Encore, Fräulein. Encore!"

Ursula, swept up in the moment, forgot her earlier concerns and kissed Willy deeply in front of the appreciative crowd, who responded with applause and joyous laughter. For a brief moment she was not a mischling whose future depended on her voice. She was simply Ursula Becker, adored diva, who happened to be in love with an Englishman named Willy Hitler. It was glorious.

As the audience quieted, Willy retook his seat and smiled at her, silently urging her to continue the goodwill that had grown. Ursula met Gieseking's eyes. The connection they'd made through performance was palpable. "Please play the next piece, my friend." Gieseking raised his fingers above the keyboard and launched into the introductory chords of the German aria. Ursula closed her eyes and allowed herself to metamorphose into the character Kuneg- ilde. Gieseking played majestically, keeping perfect time and matching her dynamics as she expressed the character's roiling emotions. The result was a performance that left the audience weeping as she wove Kunegilde's tale of being held prisoner, only to be rescued by a man who attempts to steal her love away from her fiancé.

Ursula glanced at Willy. His face was ashen as he gaped at her. She took note of it, but her years of experience on the stage overtook her curiosity, and she forged ahead. It was only when she transferred her gaze to the Führer that she faltered. His countenance had darkened, and his eyes blazed. Standing quickly, he held up his hand. Silence descended as Hitler walked slowly forward and stood directly in front of Ursula. Terrified, she stole a glance at Gieseking, who sat hunched at the piano, his hands balled together as if to protect them.

Hitler said nothing for several moments. He simply stared at her as spittle gathered in the corners of his mouth. He was livid, and she had absolutely no idea why. Ursula watched his eyes narrow as his body trembled. He was so angry that she wondered if he'd have her killed on the spot. For what she didn't know. She dropped her eyes.

"Why did you choose this song, Fräulein?"

Gaze still downcast, Ursula answered. "Because it's a beautiful aria from an early German Romantic opera. I know that you enjoy music written during that time period."

He nodded once. "That is true. But why did you choose this *particular* early Romantic piece?"

Ursula took a chance and met his eyes. She didn't know why she had chosen it and frantically searched for an answer that would appease him.

"I . . . I don't know."

He stepped closer. "I think you do know."

Ursula glanced at Willy again. He shook his head. She didn't understand what he was trying to communicate to her. He obviously knew something that she didn't.

Suddenly Hitler turned to Gieseking. "Would you be so kind as to play some Beethoven while Fräulein Becker and I take a stroll?" Ursula turned to Willy. She was terrified that if she left with Hitler, she may not return. Hitler's gaze followed. "Willy will remain here. We shan't be long." Ursula saw the anxiety in Willy's eyes and knew that he was helpless to intervene. She swallowed and steeled herself for what was to come.

Hitler offered his arm, and she saw no choice but to take it. His anger had abated, and his body no longer trembled. But Ursula knew better than to think her transgression, whatever it was, had been forgotten. Together they walked out of the room, through the hallway and into the cold evening air. A light snow was falling, and she shivered. She peered into the darkness and wondered if Blondi was out there, waiting for her. She turned back to see Hitler nod to four armed SS soldiers, who disappeared from the expansive front porch. They were now completely alone.

Hitler stepped to the top of the stairs, where he'd greeted them only hours earlier. "Come here, Fräulein." She briefly wondered if he planned to throw her down the stone steps. It would be easy to tell Willy that she'd slipped, lost her footing on the slick stone. She thought about running away but quickly realized how futile that feeble attempt would be. She joined him.

"Tell me the storyline of Spohr's opera *Faust*."

Ursula analyzed his question for traps but saw none. She cleared her throat. "A young maiden named Kunegilde is held captive and rescued by Faust, who falls in love with her and gives her a potion on her wedding night so that she will be drawn to him and not her husband, Hugo."

"Very good. Now, tell me about the aria you chose to sing this evening."

Ursula paused, then said, "Kunegilde has had a bad dream in which Hugo is killed. She awakens and professes her undying love for him. She describes how he will come and rescue her from her captor, who is kind to her, then alternatively cruel in an effort to control and—" She stopped speaking when she realized that she'd unconsciously chosen an aria that reflected her current situation.

"Tell me, Fräulein, when Kunegilde sings, is she trying to anger her captor? To betray him? Taunt him?"

Ursula's mouth dropped open. Hitler approached her so that their lips were almost touching. "I think you knew *exactly* what you were doing when you chose that song."

"No, I didn't. I promise," she babbled. "I would never show you disrespect!" Her body shook from comingled cold and fear.

Hitler burst out laughing, walked away, then turned. "My God, but you *are* Geli! We used to have screaming rows and then, hours later, she would apologize, and all would be well. We would enjoy dinner and then . . ." He raised his eyebrows and stared at her. *He's enjoying this*, she marveled. His blazing blue eyes locked onto hers, and she noted how his pupils quickly dilated and then shrank to a pinpoint. "I just had a wonderful idea. How about we return inside, and you sing 'Der Tod und das Mädchen'? I love that piece. Remember, Fräulein, in the end, death always wins."

Ursula shivered uncontrollably. Through her terror, a tiny piece of her applauded his cleverness. Whereas her choice of song had been by chance, his was deliberate, sending her an unmistakable message. When she spoke, her voice trembled. "An excellent choice, Herr Hitler. 'Death and the Maiden' by Franz Schubert. Of course."

18

After the concert Willy excused himself and retired for the evening. Ursula had attempted to catch his eye before he left, but he had avoided her as she chatted with grateful listeners. After her private chat with the Führer, Ursula had sung at least ten more lieder, or German art songs, as Hitler would announce the next piece as she was completing the previous one. Gieseking had been eager to avoid confrontation and had played each piece with gusto and dexterity, obviously relieved to be negotiating safe music once more. By the time Ursula had finished chatting with the final officer, it was well past one a.m., and she fell into bed without even washing her face or brushing her teeth.

She awoke the next morning with the sun streaming through her window and someone banging loudly on her door. "Fräulein, please wake up. Your plane is leaving shortly. Wake up!"

Ursula sat up quickly. "What do you mean? I'm to leave tomorrow. Not today."

"There has been a change of plans and your plane is leaving within the hour. Make yourself ready. A small breakfast is awaiting you downstairs."

Ursula crossed to the bathroom and washed quickly, wondering if a brewing storm was causing the premature exodus. As she repacked her suitcase, she decided that it didn't matter why they were leaving early. She was simply happy to have performed her duty and was eager to return home.

She entered the dining room to find the table strewn with plates of half-eaten breakfast. The door to the kitchen opened, and a server bustled toward her holding a platter filled with cheeses, fruits, and schweineohr, or pig's ear danish.

"Fräulein, this is for you. Please eat quickly as Herr Hitler is waiting for you in the car."

Panic gripped Ursula as she stared at the buxom woman who seemed about her age. "Which Herr Hitler?"

The young woman smiled shyly. "The Führer left very early this morning. He said that he had urgent business in Berlin. The younger Herr Hitler is awaiting you. *Your* Herr Hitler, Fräulein." The woman smiled, curtsied, and cleared the table of dishes while Ursula rapidly consumed a small chunk of cheese and some strawberries. She wiped her mouth, thanked the servant, and walked quickly to the idling Mercedes. Willy was seated inside.

"Hello, my darling. I hope that I haven't kept you waiting too long." She leaned toward Willy to buss his cheek, but he pulled away. "What's wrong?"

Willy gazed out the window.

"Willy? What is it? Why are you angry at me?"

"I'm not angry."

"Then why is the vein in your forehead throbbing?"

He turned to her, his eyes ablaze. "Do you think this is some sort of game, Ursula?"

"What? No, I—"

"Do you believe that you're untouchable? That perhaps my uncle will not harm you because I'm in love with you? I believe that it might be the opposite."

"Willy—"

He shook his head and returned his gaze out the window. Ursula looked toward the driver. His eyes flitted toward her before resuming their task of negotiating the dangerous mountain road.

She watched Willy process emotions that accompanied the conversation that was clearly occurring in his head. Finally, he barked out a laugh. Without looking at her, he said, "You truly don't understand. I actually blame myself because I've protected you. I haven't worked hard enough to help you conceive the destruction that my uncle is capable of. So, let me remedy that error." He faced her fully and fixed his hard eyes on hers. "The camps that I told you about, the ones in the east? They're called concentration camps. They're for human extermination."

Ursula's eyebrows came together in confusion. "I don't understand."

Willy laughed derisively. "How could you, Ursula? Trust me, no one can fathom what's happening there." He took her face in his hands. "My uncle is planning something that will extinguish millions of Jews."

"What are you talking about?"

"It's called Operation Reinhard. The plan is to send people to the camps and then murder them."

Ursula's eyes grew large. "You must be mistaken."

Willy shook his head. "I'm not. Most of the Jews will be from Poland, but if he's acting with such disregard for human life in that country, then it'll be only a matter of time before he brings that horror to Germany."

"He's practicing on the Poles," Ursula whispered, horrified. "He's perfecting his killing machine before bringing it home."

"There's more," Willy said.

Ursula looked at him with tears streaming down her face. "No," she said. "I cannot bear it."

"People are being worked to death, starved, gassed."

"I don't—"

"Women are raped, and children are taken from their parents. Their possessions are confiscated. They're told that they will return home, but none of them do."

Ursula blinked several times. *That's why Papa was taking note of our belongings. When we're exterminated, the Reich will collect our things. One less Jew and Jew harborer in the fatherland.* Ursula knew that Willy wouldn't lie to her, but her brain found his words untenable. How could she possibly accept the horrid picture he was painting?

"It's not just criminals, Ursula. It started that way, sending political dissidents and the like, but it's expanded quickly to anyone who is not Aryan. Jews, homosexuals, dark-skinned, frail, or touched in the head."

Crimson rushed to Ursula's cheeks. *What a fool I've been!* Guilt sat lodged in her throat, leaving her unable to speak. She had been rationalizing events when, in reality, the situation was so much worse than she could have imagined. She covered her face, embarrassed at her own ignorance.

Willy took a deep breath and then blew it out. "Your friend Fritz Rosen?"

Ursula looked out the window, her breath uneven. "Yes, Hilde told me that he was on a train heading east to find work—" She stopped as the pieces fell together. "Oh, no. Not Fritz."

Willy's voice softened as he took her hands in his. "I paid a friend to check on Herr Rosen's whereabouts and well-being. He was sent to a camp called Dachau. He's still alive."

Ursula drew a sharp breath, and her hand flew to her mouth. "Fritz was sent to this place, this Dachau camp because—"

"He's Jewish."

"Oh, my God." Ursula covered her face with her hands and wept openly. Willy placed his hand on her thigh to calm her. "Ursula, the stunt you pulled last evening was beyond risky. You sang the *Faust* aria knowing that Uncle would explode. It was selfish and stupid."

A wave of anger surged, and Ursula rounded on him. "I didn't choose it on purpose, Willy! It was an accident! I apologized to your uncle. When we went out on the terrace, he told me again how I reminded him of Geli, how he and she used to argue and then make up . . ." She shuddered, then glanced at the driver, who gave no indication he was listening. But she knew better. She leaned toward Willy, so her lips were touching his ear when she whispered. "He scares me, Willy. The way he looks at me."

Willy whispered back. "He scares me too, but, Ursula, you're headstrong. Please understand that we are well past the time that you can play sophomoric games and expect no retribution. He can control us if he likes. And he will if we're not more careful."

"I wasn't playing a game!" Ursula's gaze switched frantically from one of Willy's eyes to the other, but Willy remained motionless. He allowed her the time to accept the truth. After a full minute, she leaned into the soft leather seat and sighed heavily. "Is that why we were made to leave early? As a punishment for my singing an aria that angered your uncle?"

Willy leaned against her. "Yes, and we were fortunate to escape with such a mild penalty."

Ursula raised her eyebrows, regaining some of her haughtiness. "Well, I'm happy we're being disciplined. That way we don't have to spend one more night kowtowing to that man!"

The chauffeur stifled a laugh and Willy allowed himself a small grin. "Normally I wouldn't speak so openly in front of a driver, but Erich and I have had many conversations about Uncle. Like us, Erich is loyal to him, but understands how . . . challenging he can be. We keep each other's confidences. Isn't that right, Erich?"

In response, Erich nodded once and returned to his task. Ursula wrung her hands. "Poor Fritz. He's such a kind man."

"Do you now understand how seriously we must take our situation?"

Ursula turned to Willy, noting his use of the pronoun "we." Although he wasn't Jewish, his fate was inexorably entwined with hers, and she loved him all the more for it. "Yes. I do, and I apologize that I put us in a precarious position, albeit by accident. I will not do it again. Do you forgive me?"

He caressed her cheek. "Of course I forgive you." He stared into her eyes, red from crying. "Did you enjoy singing with me last evening?"

Ursula drew away from him. "Yes! I had no idea you could sing! Why had you not told me?"

Willy shrugged. "Our little family needs only one celebrity. Besides, I wouldn't want to eclipse you with my talent."

A slow smile spread across her face and Willy leaned in to kiss her. When he withdrew, she whispered, "I love you, William Patrick Hitler. How did I get so lucky to have met you?"

"It was fate," he whispered back.

Ursula smiled playfully. "Fate can be very fickle, you know."

Willy leaned in. "She wouldn't dare challenge our happiness."

They arrived at the airstrip and boarded the plane without incident. Holding hands through the flight, they landed and returned safely to Ursula's apartment building, where Willy said, "I shall escort you upstairs, Fräulein Becker, to ensure your safety."

Ursula grinned and replied in kind. "Why, thank you, Herr Hitler. Your gallantry is much appreciated."

They climbed the stairs and entered the apartment to find a kitchen chair broken in half. Pieces of broken glass littered the floor and crunched under their feet as they took in the scene.

"What happened?" Willy asked.

Ursula looked around and shook her head. As she bent to retrieve the head of a broken figurine that her mother had cherished, she noticed droplets of blood on the wood floor. They led in a straight line to the—

A small grunt from her bedroom. She whipped her head up. Her entire body tensed as she considered the possibility that the perpetrator was still in the apartment.

"Who's there?" she called out. In response, she heard a raspy cough and gasp. She turned to Willy, who gently pushed her behind him and approached the bedroom door. On the way, he plucked a heavy candlestick from a side table and held it aloft as he crept closer to the bedroom. "I have a weapon," he stated as he pushed the door open quickly.

Otto Becker lay faceup on Ursula's bed, his head turned away from them. It struck Ursula as odd that he would be resting on her bed. "Papa, what are you doing?" Her eyes traveled from her father to the lily-white bedspread that was sprinkled with crumbs. "Were you eating bread and jam in my room?" She stepped closer to brush the crumbs away but stopped when she processed what she was seeing. Otto turned his head toward her, and her hands flew to her mouth. In slow motion her eyes traveled from Otto's mutilated face to the bone fragments and drops of blood that littered the bedspread.

"Oh my God, Papa!" He turned away and covered his face with one hand while using the other to rise. His efforts were fruitless, however, as he fell back onto the bed, his good eye rolling backward with the effort.

Ursula stood fixed with fear, mouth agape, a scream trapped in her throat. Willy rushed forward and knelt by Otto.

"Don't rise, Herr Becker! Stay down. I'll get help. Ursula, get some water and bandages."

Ursula couldn't move. Time had stopped.

"Ursula! Get water and bandages. Now!" he ordered.

But still, Ursula remained motionless.

Willy patted Otto's arm. "Don't move. I'll be right back." He exited the bedroom and Ursula heard water tinkle from the faucet.

Otto groaned. The sound awakened her, and she asked without moving, "Who did this to you, Papa?"

Otto shook his head, unable to speak through his broken jaw. She repeated her question. "Who, Papa? Who did this to you?" Willy returned to the bedroom with towels and water. Otto looked from Ursula to Willy and gestured with his chin toward Willy. "Him," he managed.

Ursula followed his eyes. "Papa, you're confused. Willy didn't hurt you."

Otto looked imploringly at Willy. "Him, him!" he repeated urgently.

Ursula followed his eyes, and the hair on her neck rose. The breakfast servant had said that Hitler left the Berghof early because he had "urgent business in Berlin." That meant that his generals had also left early. Her blood turned to ice. She could feel it running through her veins and she lost sensation in her arms. "You're nodding at Willy, Papa. Why?" Ursula was breathless. She had to know, to be sure.

What was left of Otto's face fell and he started to sob, choking on his spit and coughing up phlegm. A bizarre calm overtook Ursula as she crossed to her father and fell to her knees. She leaned forward so Otto could look directly at her with his good eye. "Papa, did Hitler's thugs do this to you?" Otto grunted. "Was someone else here as well? Someone of great importance?" Otto's eyes bulged.

Ursula swallowed slowly, deliberately. She rose to face Willy, who stood motionless, not understanding. Her body trembled but her voice was low and even as she spoke. "Your uncle left the Berghof early. He returned to Berlin on urgent business." She pointed at Otto. "*This* was his urgent business. He had to ensure that the sentence for my transgression last evening was carried out to his satisfaction, so he ordered a high-ranking officer to oversee my father's beating. Papa wasn't saying 'him.' He was trying to say Himmler."

Ursula watched Willy's mouth silently open and close several times. She felt devoid of emotion as she walked toward the bedroom door. A welcome darkness enveloped her as she fully digested the impact caused by her infraction from the previous night. She turned back to Willy, who was gently wiping Otto's face. The soaked white towel was streaked with bright red blood that mingled with the water to create light pink droplets that fell to the floor. They reminded her of flower petals.

"You were right, Willy. I wasn't aware what your uncle is capable of." She tore her eyes from the bloody petals and glanced at her broken father. "But I am now."

19

A hard rap on the door drew their collective attention. Ursula and Willy glanced at each other, both silently wondering if the Gestapo was returning to finish the job they'd started earlier.

"I don't think they'd knock, do you?" Willy asked.

In response Ursula started toward the door, only to feel Willy's hand on her arm. "No. You remain here with your father. I'll deal with whomever is on the other side of the door."

Ursula glanced at Otto, who lay on his right side, facing away from her. His breath was even and whistled as he exhaled. He had either passed out or fallen asleep. She nodded. "Be careful."

Willy set his mouth, grabbed the candlestick and placed it behind his back, hidden but ready for use. He tiptoed to the front door, inhaled, and then quickly opened it. The visitor looked up, surprised at the abrupt reception. Both men stood staring, shocked at the other's presence. Willy was the first to gather his wits, and with them, his manners.

"Dr. Morell, how good to see you. What brings you here?"

Dr. Theodor Morell, one of Hitler's private physicians, lifted his multiple chins. His thin hair was combed across his large head in the aging man's perennial effort to hide a balding pate, and his round, black glasses seemed too small on his rotund face.

"Willy. I should be asking you the same question."

Willy smiled tightly. "I'm engaged to Fräulein Becker. The *elder* Fräulein Becker," he hastened to add.

Morell smiled. His beady blue eyes were all but erased as his fleshy cheeks rose. "You were smart to clarify, young man. It would not bode well for you if you were to be involved in any capacity with the younger Fräulein Becker. Would it?"

Willy ignored the implied threat. "What can I do for you, doctor?"

Dr. Morell stood straighter. "It is what I can do for you, Herr Hitler. I have been sent by the Führer to check on Herr Becker. I understand that he has encountered an unfortunate accident."

Willy glanced at the closed bedroom door. "Herr Becker is not in need of your services, doctor. We appreciate your coming, but—"

Morell shook his head. "Willy, we both know that I will be entering the apartment and treating the broken man inside. We can stand here and play this game, or you can let me do my job without incident. Of course, you know that I will report back to the Führer about my experience here, so let us make haste, for our sakes and for the sake of the man lying somewhere, perhaps bleeding to death." Morell stared at Willy with no rancor in his gaze, just determination and the secure knowledge that he wouldn't leave until his task was complete.

Willy's shoulders fell and he withdrew the candlestick from behind his back. Morell glanced at it and smirked.

"What did you plan on doing with that?"

"I thought I might have to use it if someone dangerous came through the door."

"Makes perfect sense. Good thing I am not dangerous." He looked directly at Willy.

Willy held his stare. "Let me take you to Herr Becker." Willy opened the bedroom door to find Ursula seated on the bloody bedspread, Otto's head laying in her lap. She had cleaned his face of blood and was stroking his arm as she sang Brahms' lullaby. A loud, raspy snore erupted from Otto's open mouth each time he inhaled.

Ursula looked up and froze. Although she hadn't met the man standing before her, he wore a Nazi uniform and oozed the sickening smugness that accompanied people in power. Without thinking, she said, "Get out of my father's house. Right now."

Willy stepped between them. "Ursula, this is Dr. Theodor Morell, my uncle's private physician whom he trusts implicitly. On more than one occasion Dr. Morell has cured my uncle of various maladies that plague him intermittently. If it were my life in question, I would want him to treat me."

Willy's eyes implored her to accept the circumstances without making a scene. She glared past Willy to the fat man who smelled of garlic and body odor. "Did the Führer send you to clean up his mess?" she asked.

Dr. Morell cleared his throat and glanced at Willy. "Our beloved leader has graciously asked that I call upon Herr Becker, as he came to understand that your father had fallen ill under bizarre conditions."

Ursula choked out a laugh. "They are bizarre conditions, to be sure." She glanced at her father, who roused as she spoke. "Papa," she whispered. "There's a doctor here to see you." Otto turned his head and released a guttural sound as he struggled to rise. "No, Papa, don't get up!" Ursula ordered. "I promise that Dr. Morell is here to help you. Not hurt you." As she spoke, she glared at Morell, who inspected Otto as if he were a frog to be dissected. "I find it odd, doctor, that my father is frightened. Could it be your uniform?"

Dr. Morell glanced at his jacket. "I cannot imagine why my uniform would cause your father consternation. Now, shall we get started?"

Dr. Morell took one step toward the bed, and Ursula instinctively pulled Otto's head closer to her breast. Otto groaned. Willy placed his hand on Ursula's shoulder, silently willing her to give the physician access. Ursula looked at Otto's ravaged face and choked back a sob, then gingerly placed his head on the bed. She stood, but stayed close to Otto, ready to defend him if the doctor's intention was to cause further pain . . . or worse.

Morell approached and opened his large, black leather bag. He withdrew a stethoscope and listened to Otto's heart and lungs, then used a small light to examine his eyes, mouth, and nose. Otto was silent during the examination except for an occasional gasp or moan. Dr. Morell frowned as he palpated various parts of Otto's body. Ursula cringed each time Otto winced and finally averted her gaze to avoid witnessing her father's pain. Upon completion, Morell stood. "Your father will make a full recovery, Fräulein. He is a lucky man. It could have been so much worse."

Ursula looked from Morell to Willy, who had retreated to a corner. "That's all? You haven't told us what's broken, or what we must do to aid his healing."

The physician began packing his bag. "Your father has a broken nose and a broken jaw. He will not be able to eat solid foods for at least six weeks, so you will have to prepare him meals that can slide down his throat. His nose will heal in about the same period of time and will be crooked. I could straighten it, but that would cause him considerable pain. He may have trouble breathing when laying down, as blood and mucous will drip into the back of his throat, causing him to cough, which will be extremely painful due to his broken ribs."

Ursula gaped at the man standing before her. "How many ribs are broken?"

"At least four, which will also make breathing difficult. He has lost two teeth and the left side of his skull is fractured, but it will heal on its own. The good news is that I don't believe he has any damage to his brain or any internal bleeding."

Tears trickled down Ursula's face as she listened to Morell list her father's injuries, damage that had been inflicted because she had inadvertently angered the Führer. *How stupid!* she thought. *Never again. I need to pay more attention. I need to appreciate that my decisions have consequences beyond myself.*

Willy stepped forward. "Thank you, Dr. Morell. What shall we do to ease Herr Becker's pain?"

The doctor withdrew a glass vial from his bag, as well as a roll of cotton gauze. "Use these bandages to wrap his head and give him one pill every six hours as needed for pain."

Ursula took the bottle and shook it. "What is this medicine?"

Dr. Morell shook his head. "I could explain it, my dear, but I don't believe you would understand. It will ease his pain. That's all you need to know."

Ursula saw red at his condescension. She swallowed her anger and smiled at Otto, whose one working eye held a blank expression. She said, "I will return soon, Papa" and motioned for the men to follow her. Once outside the bedroom door, she spoke sternly but politely to Morell. "I am a mature woman with a fine brain. Please tell me what is in these pills."

Morell sneered at her and then faced Willy, ignoring Ursula completely. "If you must know, those pills are a concoction that I have created specifically for the Führer, to dull his pain and help him wake in the morning." His red face turned to Ursula. "Or, if you like, *Fräulein*, I could take the pills with me, and your father can heal from his numerous wounds without the aid of a painkiller." His voice was whiny, reminding her of a spoiled toddler throwing a tantrum.

Ursula glared at the pompous man. "We will take the pills. If they're good enough for the Führer, then my father might benefit from them. Thank you and good day."

Ursula turned on her heel and marched back to the bedroom, slamming the door behind her. Willy grimaced.

Dr. Morell looked at him. "She is quite a handful."

Willy raised his eyebrows and stuffed his hands into his trouser pockets. "Yes. That she is."

Morell's eyes lingered on the bedroom door. "She is quite lovely. Quite."

Willy paused and lifted his chin. "Yes, she is. We are to be married."

Morell tore his gaze from the door and smiled. He raised an eyebrow. "You might want to marry her soon, lest someone else snatch her up. Her exquisite eyes burn holes when she is angry. She is . . . truly breathtaking."

20

Weeks had passed since Otto's attack, and during that time Ursula had rarely left her father's side. His ribs were slowly healing; he was now able to inhale without significant pain. Ursula had propped him on the living room's small, bedraggled couch and had spoon-fed him each meal. When she couldn't mash up the food in advance, she would chew each bite before gingerly removing it from her own mouth and slipping it through Otto's parted lips. Otto remarked through gritted teeth that he was like a baby bird who relied on its mother for sustenance.

"Stop fussing, Papa. You're healing and I suppose we should be grateful that the injuries weren't worse. If I hadn't—" She broke off when Otto placed his hand on her arm and shook his head. He patted her arm as his eyes crinkled at the corners, his new version of a smile.

"You're remarkable," she said as she examined his gaunt frame. He had lost weight since the attack, not only from consuming less calories, but also from worry. "Papa, you're becoming so thin. I'm concerned."

Otto shook his head. "Fine. More."

Ursula dipped the spoon into the bowl and lifted it to her father's mouth. He tilted his head back and swallowed, but a little dribbled down his chin. "We're becoming quite a team, you and I," she joked. "Only a small amount wasted this time." Ursula gently wiped Otto's chin with a cloth and showed him the bowl. "You ate the entire bowl. Excellent!"

She rose and crossed to the kitchen as the door flew open. She didn't need to turn around to know who it was. Anna had come to entering her former home in this manner, throwing open the door as if she owned the room and everyone in it. As was usually the case, she walked to the bedroom she shared with Ursula and closed the door, leaving the front door ajar. Ursula sighed and looked at her father, who shrugged and then winced from the effort. Ursula closed the front door and returned to the kitchen to wash the spoon and bowl. Anna emerged from the bedroom, her hands on her hips.

"Ursula, where is my black shawl?"

"What black shawl?"

"The one with the embroidery on it."

"Oh. I borrowed it because I was chilly in the opera house. I didn't want to catch a cold."

Anna threw her arms wide. "So . . . where is it?"

"I'm sorry, Anna. I must have left it in my dressing room. I'll retrieve it after my next rehearsal."

Anna rolled her eyes. "Which will be when?"

Ursula smiled. "You tell me, Anna. Since Max Schmidt left the country, it seems that rehearsals are on hold. Besides, I've been busy with Papa."

Anna noticed Otto for the first time. "Oh, Papa. How are you?"

Otto's eyes smiled and he bobbed his head from side to side.

"Well, I'm glad you're feeling better."

Ursula's eyes widened. "That's all you have to say to Papa, Anna? You haven't visited him since the attack. Is it because you feel guilty?"

Anna drew back in surprise, her hand drawn to her chest. "Why should *I* feel guilty?"

"Because you're closely associated with the man—no, the *animal*, that did this."

Anna glanced at her father. "Ursula, don't be ridiculous. Adolf didn't hurt Papa."

Ursula felt her face flush as frustration swelled. She stepped forward and spoke through clenched teeth. "How can you be so blind? Himmler was carrying out orders directly from Hitler!"

"You don't know that for a fact. Adolf told me that he had nothing to do with it."

"So, you think that Himmler and the Gestapo acted on their own?"

"Yes. That's what Adolf told me."

Ursula threw up her hands. "So that's it, then? He said it so it must be true?"

"Yes."

"Even if logic dictates otherwise."

Anna crossed her arms, her stony blue eyes boring into Ursula.

Ursula shook her head in disgust. "Anna, I don't understand what has happened to you. You were such a bright, kind child. Yet you've grown into an egotistical, selfish woman who chooses to believe the vile lies of a dictator instead of the truths of family members."

Anna rounded on her sister. "*I* am selfish? It is you, not I, who has caused Papa such pain. Who are you to lecture me on being selfish? If you hadn't sung that ridiculous aria, none of this would have happened!"

They glared at each other, their noses inches apart, until a small groan caught Ursula's attention. She turned to find Otto's large eyes riveted on the two most important people in his world as they verbally tore each other apart. A single tear tracked down his cheek and clear mucous ran from his nose. Ursula threw a nasty look to Anna, then kneeled next to Otto.

"Papa, I'm sorry. I'm so sorry I did this to you." Otto hung his head as his body shook with grief. Ursula carefully gathered him in her arms. When he had calmed, she stood and turned to Anna. "For Papa's sake, you and I need to find a way to get along. We have so much shared history, and we shouldn't let one man get in the way of that." Ursula opened her arms, inviting Anna to hug her. Anna paused, but then walked forward and returned Ursula's embrace. Ursula felt her anger fall away as she enjoyed Anna's closeness. She allowed her mind to fly back to happier times and, after a moment, realized that she was smiling.

"What of Papa being classified as Aryan, Anna? Has the Führer made a decision?"

Anna pulled away. "He had made a decision that Papa could be classified as Aryan."

"That's wonderful!" Ursula clapped her hands together and looked at her father, whose face bore no expression. "Isn't that wonderful, Papa?" Otto slowly shook his head and stared at Anna. It was then that Ursula realized the verbiage that Anna had used. "You said that the Führer *had* made the decision that Papa could be classified as Aryan. Why do you say it like that?"

Anna sighed, seemingly older than her twenty-one years. She looked at Ursula, and for the first time in months, Ursula saw her sister. Not Hitler's toy whom he strung along for his own amusement, but the girl with whom she'd shared the dream of one day performing in the finest performance halls in Germany. "Anna, what is it?"

Anna took Ursula's hands. "Your performance at the Berghof had several consequences, Ursula. Papa is no longer allowed to be classified as Aryan. I'm truly sorry."

Ursula stopped breathing. Although her choice of aria was unintentional, her rebuffs to Hitler's advances were not. She was certain that current circumstances, Otto's beating and Hitler's refusal to classify Otto as Aryan, were retribution not only for her choice of song, but also for rejecting Hitler's overtures. She couldn't tell Anna what had happened on the terrace. Anna wouldn't believe her and nothing good would come of it. Anna would simply blame her.

Ursula shook her head and started babbling. "No, no, no. Anna, you must do something. You must speak to him. Willy told me that circumstances will get worse for the Jews, and certainly that extends to anyone related to a Jew. You must make Hitler see reason. You must make him change his mind!"

Anna laughed mirthlessly and turned away. "Ursula, you and I both know that one cannot *make* the Führer do anything he doesn't want to do."

Ursula's eyes were wild as she searched for a solution. "Then we must somehow make Papa valuable to the Reich."

Anna shook her head. "It's far too late for that, Ursula. You've severed any goodwill that existed."

Ursula turned away from Anna, her brain reeling. "Then I must marry Willy immediately and be classified as Aryan. I will join the Party and protect Papa that way."

"Ursula, marrying Willy will change nothing, and I'm not sure that given recent events you're considered valuable enough to classify."

"What are you saying? If I join the Nazi party, surely that would—"

Anna shook her head.

Ursula's panic twisted itself into anger. "Who are you to come into an apartment that you no longer call home and inform me of my value to the Reich? I know you're jealous of the way the Führer feels about me. Are you trying to destroy me, Anna? To destroy Papa?"

Anna sighed heavily. "I'm not trying to destroy anyone, Ursula. I'm telling you what is realistic given the circumstances."

Ursula's eyes searched Anna's, desperate to find a solution to her insolvable problem. "You can do nothing to help us? Truly?"

Anna's eyes dropped to the ground. "I cannot. I have tried. Honestly."

Ursula sat heavily on a kitchen chair and stared out the window. Two SS officers stood on the pavement, smoking and leering at passing women. "You would choose that madman over your own father and sister?"

"It's an impossible choice, Ursula. But I'm choosing life over—" Anna paused.

Ursula's head swiveled back to Anna. "Over what, Anna? Death? Is that the word for which you were searching?"

Anna's eyes hardened. "Adolf is a decent, kind man who loves me."

"He doesn't love you."

"He does!"

"He's using trains to ship Jews and dissidents to camps where they're worked to death. Does that sound kind and decent, Anna?"

"That's not true."

"It is."

"Well, then . . . they deserve it."

Ursula gaped at her sister. "These men and women have done nothing illegal, Anna. They are Jews. That's all. Please tell me that you think sending people to their deaths simply because they are Jewish is wrong. *Please*." Ursula was begging, desperate to find her sister once more among the aloof attitude, stylish clothes, and dyed hair that stood haughtily before her. But Anna turned away. She had been re-absorbed into Hitler's brainwashed, clandestine concubine.

"I must go. Papa, I hope your health continues to improve. I'm not sure when I'll be able to return, so I'll hug you and take my leave." She approached Otto and hugged him gently. "I love you," she whispered before running out the front door.

Ursula chased her down the stairs, yelling, "You're a coward, Anna! A coward!" Arriving at the bottom of the stairwell, she was stopped by the arm of a young man smoking in the doorway.

"You're in my way," Ursula said as she tugged at his arm.

"Are you Ursula Becker?"

"Yes."

"The opera singer?"

"Yes."

The man bowed formally. "I love your singing, Fräulein Becker, and I'm happy to make your acquaintance. I wish it were under better circumstances."

"What do you mean?"

The man handed Ursula an envelope, then took a step back, clicked his heels and announced, "Heil, Hitler!" He turned and walked briskly down the pavement.

Ursula stared after him, then slowly climbed the stairs to the apartment. She entered to find her father staring at her, his look of sadness quickly replaced by curiosity as he spotted the envelope. Ursula tore it open and quickly scanned the page. She returned to the top of the letter to reread it, believing that she has misconstrued the letter's intent.

```
Fräulein Becker,
    It has come to the attention of the National
Socialist German Workers' Party that you have
undertaken actions that are contrary to its
tenets. Additionally, you have not offered an
Aryan certificate in order to become a member
of the Chamber of Culture and are considered a
mischling of the second degree.
    Therefore, under article 3, section 17, you are
hereby banned from rehearsing and/or performing
in any capacity within the Reich.
    Be assured that violation of this decree will
result in immediate corporal punishment up to and
including death, if deemed appropriate.

Signed this day, November 9, 1941
Joseph Goebbels
Reich Minister of Chamber of Culture
```

"What . . .?" Otto managed.

Ursula looked through Otto. "They have banned me from singing."

Otto's eyes bulged and he attempted to rise. Ursula watched him stagger and fall to the floor, groaning. She knew that she should go to him, but her legs felt leaden.

"He may as well kill me," she whispered. She gathered herself and knelt by Otto, who gazed at her with the openness of a child.

"How . . . live?" he asked.

Ursula stroked his head. "How will we live? Is that what you asked, Papa?"

Otto nodded.

Ursula's mind had already moved to what must be done next. "Don't worry, Papa. I have a plan."

21

Ursula sat at the kitchen table and traced a scratch with her fingernail. She stared at Goebbels' letter as she listened to Otto snore quietly on the couch. She glanced at the clock and realized that Willy would arrive any minute for their evening stroll. Such had become their new routine, Willy stopping by after Ursula had ensured that Otto was safely tucked away for the evening. They would steal away for a walk along the Spree River, hands entwined as they discussed Willy's day at the car factory or Otto's improvement. During one of these walks Willy had suggested that they wait no longer, that they marry the following week. Ursula had hugged him and smiled, reminding him that they had committed to wait until the political situation had cooled. After all, Ursula said, "Wasn't it you who said that people wouldn't support a Hitler marrying a Jew, even if she is only a mischling of the second degree?" She had spoken in jest, but the reality was that she feared for Willy's safety if he married her. She had almost lost her father. She wasn't prepared to lose Willy as well if his insane uncle decided on retribution against him for marrying her.

A gentle knock jostled her from her reverie. She rushed to the door, threw it open, and launched herself into Willy's arms.

"Whoa, whoa. What's happening?"

Ursula glanced at her father who lay on the couch, his breathing deep and even. Satisfied that he was asleep for the night, she grabbed her coat from the hook on the wall and closed the door gently, motioning for Willy to follow her downstairs. As they stepped into the cold night, Ursula buttoned her coat and took Willy's arm. She inhaled deeply and coughed as the frigid air hit her lungs. Willy looked at her.

"Care to tell me why you're so upset?"

Ursula shook her head and continued walking until they reached the river. She sat on a bench and removed the letter from her pocket. Without speaking, Willy took it and sat next to her, tilting it so the light from a nearby streetlamp shone on it. As he read, Ursula watched his facial expression change from curiosity to confusion to anger. When he was done reading, he stared in the direction of the Chancellery.

"This will not stand. I'll speak to my uncle first thing in the morning, Ursula. You have my word."

Ursula took the letter and refolded it, then placed it in her pocket. She took Willy's hand as they stood and resumed walking along the river. "Ursula, did you hear what I said? I'll speak to Uncle Alf and you'll be singing by the end of the week."

Ursula smiled sadly. "No, Willy. I've given up the fantasy that I have control over my fate. The world is on fire. I can feel the change happening. It was swirling around me, but I was unable or unwilling to see it. But now I do."

"This doesn't sound like the Ursula that I know and love. Where has she gone?"

"She's still in here." Ursula pointed to her heart. "But unfortunately, my head must take over now." She sighed heavily. "Willy, I can no longer remain in Germany. It breaks my heart, but I fear if I stay, life for Papa and me will become only more complicated."

"I don't understand."

She stopped and took his hands. "Anna told me that Papa will not be classified as Aryan and I'm no longer able to join the Party. My value to the Reich is gone. I know that emigration has been halted for German Jews, but I must find a way to leave."

"No, Ursula. I can speak to my uncle. He will allow you to be Aryanized."

Ursula shook her head. "Even if that were true, Papa would still be vulnerable. I cannot abide him being bullied. Or worse." She shuddered. "He's been through enough."

Willy shook his head, refusing to concede. "You'll see. When I speak to uncle Alf—"

Ursula placed her hand on his arm. "Enough, Willy. Our entire relationship has occurred in the shadow of your uncle. We've never once been simply Willy and Ursula. We never will be, not while he's in power."

Willy's eyes became suddenly intense. "Then come with me."

"Where?"

"England."

"England?"

"Yes. You told me that the former opera director was working there and invited you to join him. You could even sing with Max Schmidt once more."

"But how?"

"I know people who can forge the necessary documents."

Ursula narrowed her eyes. "You've obviously been thinking about this for some time."

"I always hope for the best but prepare for the worst."

Even in the depths of resignation, she felt a surge of love for Willy as she considered his determination to ensure her safety and happiness. She couldn't imagine a more wonderful life companion. She squeezed his arm and regarded the dark water of the Spree as it traveled its winding path to the ocean. Just as a stick gets swept away by the current, so had her career and family become collateral damage in the tide of anti-Semitism. She finally understood that she must find a way to successfully negotiate the current or drown. "When I said I was leaving, I meant to go elsewhere in Europe. I'm not sure that Papa could survive a trip across the ocean. It's so far."

"It's not that far, Ursula, and you would have a strong partner in me."

Despite the circumstances, Ursula smiled. "But I don't speak the language."

Willy pulled back. "You, of all people, will be able to master English in less than a year. You sing in multiple languages already. English will be the final feather in your operatic cap. Repeat after me." Willy cleared his throat and switched from German to English. "My name is Ursula." Willy spoke slowly and deliberately and then motioned for Ursula to try the English phrase.

Ursula stared at him. "This isn't a game, Willy."

"I know. But I'm trying to make you understand that coming with me to England will be good for you and your father."

Ursula turned away.

"Is there something else?" Willy asked.

"I'm not sure that I can leave Anna."

Willy's eyebrows shot up. "You must be joking. She left you and your father a long time ago. You emigrating to England will not affect her in any way."

"That's not true. Whatever relationship we still enjoy will be demolished in an instant."

"You're kidding yourself if you still believe that she cares for you and Otto."

"And you are an only child who can come and go as he pleases, with very little regard for those around him and how they're affected."

Willy physically withdrew. In their years together, they had fought only once, and that was in regard to Ursula's belief that Willy was working too many hours. The issue had been resolved in compromise and their relationship had been strengthened from the experience. But this was new territory.

"Excuse me?" Willy asked.

Ursula closed her eyes and sighed. "I apologize, Willy. I shouldn't have expressed my feelings in those words. It was hurtful."

"But you're not apologizing for what you said, Ursula, only the way in which you said it."

Ursula nodded. "That's true."

"Do you really think me that selfish?"

"You are not selfish, per se. It's just that you've not had to worry about how your actions directly impact those around you like I have, like anyone who has a larger family does."

Willy ran his hands through his hair and walked several steps before turning to face her. "Ursula, I grew up in England with a mother and no father. Why? Because my father came to Europe for a gambling tour and apparently got trapped in Germany after the Great War, or so I was told. All I know is that he abandoned my mother and me. So, when I was old enough, I crossed the ocean to visit him here in Germany and ended up falling in love with you. It wasn't enough that I worried about you, given your . . . circumstances, but I willingly took on the responsibility of your father and sister, before she decided to fall in love with my uncle. Your family became the family I never had. I love all of you. But I've been denied promotions because of my engagement to you, and I've saved your father from persecution on many occasions of which you have no knowledge. So please don't stand there and tell me I don't have to worry about how my actions affect others. I live with it, literally, each and every day, just as you do."

Ursula gazed at the blackness of the water so Willy wouldn't see the blood staining her cheeks. The rushing river provided a soothing respite as she gathered her thoughts.

"I'm sorry, Willy. I had no idea."

"I know. I wanted to keep it that way."

Ursula stole a glance at him. "Thank you for protecting us."

"It was my pleasure."

Ursula twisted her mouth and cut her eyes. "Was it? Truly your pleasure?"

Willy caught her insinuation and shrugged. "Sometimes."

She turned and unbuttoned his coat, then slipped her arms around his waist. She gazed up at him. "Like when?"

He stared into her warm eyes. "Like when I do this." He leaned down and kissed her neck, then transferred his attention to her lips. "I love you," he mumbled into her mouth.

Ursula giggled. "I love you too, Willy Hitler. Perhaps when we go to England you might consider changing your name."

Willy pulled her away from him. "You said 'when,' not 'if.' Does that mean you'll come with me?"

Ursula grinned.

Willy hugged her hard until she squirmed out of his embrace. "I was serious. Would you consider changing your name?"

He tilted his head and frowned. "Why? I like the name Willy."

22

Ursula burst out laughing and shook her head. "Not your first name! Your surname." Willy linked his arm through hers and they continued walking, taking a right onto Friedrichstrasse.

"I knew what you meant. Yes, I have considered it."

"What would you call yourself?"

He raised his chin and mimicked an announcer's voice. "William Patrick Stuart-Houston."

Ursula laughed. "I'm not sure I can pronounce that very long name!"

"Well, you should practice, my dear, as you could be Ursula Estelle Becker Stuart-Houston."

"That's a mouthful, to be sure."

A shrill scream pierced the air. The shriek was followed by the sound of glass shattering and muted cries of terror. They arrived at a busy thoroughfare to find the entire street littered with debris. Broken windows lay in jagged shards on the cobblestone. Terrified bodies huddled in shadowed, recessed doorways.

A woman carrying a small child wrapped in a blue blanket sprinted toward them as a blast erupted, hurtling her several meters to land with a grotesque thud. At the same moment, an explosion shattered a building's lead glass windows. Orange, red, and blue flames licked its granite walls. Ursula screamed and covered her eyes as a man broke through the front door and zigzagged down the street, his clothes on fire. His shrieks echoed against the buildings, magnifying as he ran blindly, streaks of flames following him.

"Willy!" Ursula screamed.

"Get down!" Willy yelled and pushed her to the pavement. Ursula raked her nails against Willy's coat, her futile effort to stop him as he raced toward the burning man. She watched in horror as he tore off the man's coat and tackled him, both of them entwined as Willy rolled to extinguish the flames. After a minute they both stopped moving and Willy pushed himself away from the man as Ursula rushed over.

Willy lay on his back, his heaving breath coming in waves. His hair was singed, and he was covered in dirt and soot, but otherwise he seemed unscathed. The other man lay in the fetal position, unmoving, his long gray beard burnt away and still smoking. His clothes had melted to his body, yet his yarmulke remained pristine and intact. Ursula couldn't take her eyes from his charred corpse. She covered her nose and mouth to stifle the stench.

"He's a rabbi," Willy whispered.

"He *was* a rabbi," Ursula corrected him. Her eyes wandered to the building that was being consumed by fire. "That was his temple."

The woman who had been thrown by the blast wandered past them, a bloody blue blanket clutched to her chest. Her vacant eyes wandered over Ursula and Willy, then rested on the rabbi. "He is dead?" she asked. Willy nodded. She hummed and rocked her unmoving baby. After a few moments, she gently tucked her child against the rabbi's chest. Ursula stifled a sob. The broken mother couldn't save her son's life, but she could ensure his soul's deliverance in death.

"He is safe now, my son." The woman's face was streaked with dirt, but she smiled and walked away, her body swaying as if she were drunk.

"My God," Ursula breathed. "What is happening?"

A truck bearing multiple swastikas turned the corner and accelerated quickly toward them. It showed no sign of stopping, so Willy grabbed Ursula's coat and pulled her to safety just as the large military vehicle ran over the smoking corpse. The truck slammed to a halt when the driver caught sight of Ursula.

"Well, well. What do we have here?" He put the truck in park and exited, as several more soldiers leapt out of the back. "A pretty Jew perhaps?"

"Is there such a thing?" another jeered.

"I have seen and enjoyed several," a third offered. They laughed.

Willy stepped in front of Ursula and lifted his chin. A cruel smile crawled up the driver's cheeks. "Relax, friend. We only want to have a little fun."

"Then please get back in your truck and search for fun elsewhere."

The driver squinted in the darkness. "You look familiar. Show me your papers. Both of you." His eyes lingered on Ursula's breasts. Both Willy and Ursula reached into their pockets and produced their kennkarten. The driver took Ursula's first, his fingers brushing against hers as he continued to grope her with his eyes. He glanced at the cover of the folded document and laughed as he tapped the red J that was stamped there. "You *are* a Jew!"

Turning to Willy, he extended his hand, and Willy gave him his papers. The driver took note of the swastika and sniffed. "What are you doing cavorting with *her*, Herr . . ." The driver trailed off as he opened the card and searched for Willy's surname. The man inhaled sharply. "You are the Führer's nephew?" The driver stood at attention and offered Willy a stern "Heil, Hitler!" before returning the document to Willy with an apology.

"You should get off the streets, Herr Hitler." The driver looked at Ursula and then at Willy. "I do not know, nor do I want to know what your relationship is to this woman, but if I were you, I would cut my losses. She will be dead soon if she remains in Germany."

Otto's beating, her disagreement with Anna, Goebbels' letter, and the rabbi's death jumbled together in Ursula's mind. Desperation and frustration twisted within her, gaining momentum as they joined forces. She willed herself to remain calm, knowing that an outburst would be detrimental.

"Perhaps when you're finished, we might enjoy her company too?" The soldiers laughed. Ursula's entire body trembled with anger she could contain no longer. She launched herself toward the soldier, her flailing fists desperate to find a target. Willy grabbed her from behind and pulled her away. The soldier laughed. "What are you going to do, Jewess? Rip out my eyes? Are you going to hurt me?" His smile morphed into a sneer, and his eyes became cruel. "Not if I hurt you first." They locked eyes, and Ursula felt as if she were seeing the devil, pure evil encapsulated in human form. "You are fortunate to be with Herr Hitler. Otherwise, who knows what fate might have befallen you." He smiled viciously, then yelled to his colleagues. "Load up, boys! Let us go and have fun somewhere else."

As they pulled away, the driver tossed Ursula's kennkarte, which struck her face before falling to the ground. Still breathing heavily, she leaned down to retrieve it and realized that her life would never be the same. *How did I not see it before now? How could I have been so blind?* As if clairvoyant, her new reality come into stark focus. She would never again grace the stage in Berlin, perhaps all of Germany. She would never again walk, speak, or act freely. She could no longer provide for her family and had become completely dependent on Willy for her survival. Her desire to leave suddenly became all-consuming. She shook with impotent rage as she stared at the rabbi's mangled, burnt corpse and imagined her near-rape or worse, near-death encounter with Hitler's animals.

"Are you alright?" Willy asked softly as he touched her shoulder.

She flinched unconsciously. Willy quickly removed his hand and held it aloft. "I'm sorry, Ursula."

She looked through him. "You shouldn't be with me. It's not safe."

"I will not allow you to apologize for who you are. I love you, and I'll defend you until my last dying breath."

Ursula started crying and found that she couldn't stop. "And then what?"
"What?"

Ursula took heaving breaths in between her sobs. "What happens if you're no longer able to defend me?"

Willy's eyes hardened. "It will never come to that, Ursula."

"You don't know what the future holds, Willy. For the first time in my life, I'm scared. I'm old enough to understand the value of life, yet young enough to know that I have much more to do before I die." Her knees buckled, and she sank to the ground.

Willy knelt next to her. "Ursula, look at me. You're the strongest person I know. You'll get through this. *We* will get through this. You have my word. Alright?"

She held his eyes, desperate to believe his empty promise.

"We can be in England by next month. I can get the necessary documents in a week or so. That will give you time to write a letter to Carl Ebert accepting your new position at Glyndebourne. Imagine it, Ursula, singing French and Italian music for people who appreciate their beauty!"

She smiled through her tears. "I thought you didn't like opera."

"I don't. But I care very much for one of its finest sopranos. Now, let me help you." He stood and offered his hand, which she accepted. Brushing dirt off her coat, she glanced at the rabbi and the baby. She closed her eyes to block out the image, then forced herself to reopen them. She needed to be an active witness to the horror. "What shall we do with them?"

Willy shook his head. "I know that you want to help him, but I believe that our earlier encounter has consumed our good luck for the evening."

Willy's argument held reason, but Ursula averted her eyes, ashamed that they were leaving a man's body in the street. As they walked away, a stunned child gawked at them from a nearby doorway. No more than four years old, his haunted eyes seemed too big in his tiny round face. Ursula briefly wondered what his future held, then turned her gaze to her own future.

1942

23

"I can't believe that we're scheduled to leave this evening!" Ursula gushed as she repacked her large suitcase for the third time.

"I can't believe that you have so many clothes," Otto responded.

Ursula paused, hands on her hips. "Papa, Willy told me that in England people dress for dinner. Apparently, his mother wears a beautiful dress each evening. How am I to choose?" she asked, exasperated. She covered her face in her hands. "It's impossible!"

Otto smiled. He hadn't seen Ursula happy in some time and enjoyed the spectacle. Since witnessing the horror of the rabbi, Ursula had rarely ventured from the apartment. The one time she'd taken a stroll with Willy, she was stopped by an SS officer, who informed her that she was in violation of the decree stating that all Jews affix a yellow star of David to their clothing. Indeed, if Willy hadn't been with her, she surely would have been killed on the spot. She had promptly returned to the apartment, sewn the star onto her coat, and slipped into an emotional sinkhole.

The weeks slid by with no possibility of escape on the horizon. Although Willy had said he'd have identity papers within a week, it took months to procure forged documents. As her hope dwindled, she ate little and spoke even less. Worried, Otto spoke privately with Willy. The next day Willy returned with some lamb stew and suggested a practical distraction—English lessons in preparation for their voyage.

Ursula had been reluctant at first, but Willy balanced the challenging lessons with well-timed presents that ensured her continued interest. Over time she amassed many new dresses and even a bright pink tube of lipstick, a treasured item given recent rationing. She'd come to look forward to her lessons and worked hard to perfect the new language. Last week Willy announced he had finally obtained the documents, and Ursula's mood had gone from hopeless to elated in a matter of seconds.

Otto smiled as she curtsied and said in heavily accented English, "Good evening, Mr. Becker. It is a pleasure to make your acquaintance."

Although Otto had been attending the same English lessons with Willy, his progress had been slower, and he struggled to understand what Ursula said. Nevertheless, he clapped his hands in delight. Ursula curtsied once more in appreciation. As she rose, she suddenly realized how much she missed the stage.

Otto sensed her mood shift. "Ursula? Are you alright?"

She silently chastised herself for the moment of self-pity. "Of course I am, Papa. I have the two best men in the world taking care of me. I love you so much." She hugged him gently, careful not to squeeze too hard.

"But?"

Ursula smiled sadly. "But my heart weeps for the broken, missing, and maimed, Papa. I know I'm fortunate, but I grieve my personal losses—Anna and singing."

Otto nodded. "I know. I miss her too. She's always with the Führer now. I can't even remember when we saw her last."

"Hello?" someone called out in English.

"Willy!" Ursula rushed out of the bedroom and covered him in kisses. "Good evening, Herr, um, Mr. Hitler. How lovely to feel you."

Willy burst out laughing and responded in English. "Good evening, Miss Becker. It is lovely to *see* you as well." Ursula laughed at her gaffe. Willy embraced her and returned to German. "Your English is excellent, Fräulein."

"Danke, Herr Hitler."

Otto cleared his throat. "I'm sorry to interrupt, but do we not have an appointment to keep this evening?"

Willy shook Otto's hand. "Of course, you are right, Herr Becker." Willy glanced at his wristwatch. "We shall leave the apartment in twenty minutes."

"Twenty minutes!" Ursula exclaimed. "I have so much to do!" She rushed back into her bedroom and slammed the door.

Willy took a seat at the kitchen table. "What will happen to your apartment, Herr Becker?"

Otto looked around. "Well, most of our belongings, at least the ones of value, have been confiscated. And the furniture? I think it will be taken after we leave. In fact, I plan on leaving the door ajar as we exit. No use making people work to steal our things." He smirked.

"You have a wonderful attitude. It will serve you well in England."

Otto bowed his head in appreciation of the compliment and turned serious. "Do you think we'll have any trouble getting on the ship?"

Willy paused. Otto's question was fraught with perilous possibilities. He decided to be direct in his answer. "We'll be traveling on a Swedish ship. Sweden's neutrality will allow the vessel safe passage, especially because this particular ship is used for repatriation between the United States, England, and Germany. I've spoken with my uncle and told him that I'm going to England to check on my mother, which is true. And that I'll return within one month, which is, of course, not true."

Since Otto's beating, Hitler had been busy running the war. While he was preoccupied with opening new concentration camps and defending his conquests, Japan had attacked the United States, drawing it into the world conflict. In response, Germany and Italy had declared war on the United States. Hitler was so busy strategizing his next move and protecting his ever-growing empire, that his obsession with Ursula had been relegated to periodic check-ins via telephone calls with Willy. Through the communication, Willy had rebuilt trust and once again enjoyed a jovial relationship with his uncle.

"Having said that, I don't foresee any problems. Your passports are in order, as are your additional identification papers. Our ship tickets are right here." Willy removed three folded documents from his suit pocket and placed them on the table. "I believe that we're ready to go." He glanced at Ursula's door. "Does she understand that she may carry only two suitcases aboard the ship?"

Otto shook his head. "I've told her that, but who knows?" He threw up his hands. "She's just like her mother. Stubborn, beautiful, and more stubborn." Willy laughed as Ursula exited her room with two suitcases in tow.

"Ah, so you did follow the instructions. Excellent!" Ursula returned to her room and withdrew another two bags. Willy stood and crossed his arms. "Ursula, I told you that the ship allows only two bags per person."

"But I can't decide."

"You must."

Ursula pouted and considered her options. "Fine, but when I'm wearing the same dresses day after day, I don't want to hear a word from you."

Willy smiled. "I'll buy you one hundred new dresses once we're settled."

Ursula narrowed her eyes. "One hundred?"

He nodded.

"Then we have a deal," she said as she returned two bags to her room.

"Just like her mother," Otto muttered. "The ultimate negotiator."

* * *

The ship was scheduled to leave from the port of Hamburg. The ride from Berlin would normally take approximately five hours, but given the frequent checkpoints, it was taking longer. Ursula was subdued as she considered the possibility of never returning to Germany. Given recent events, she no longer questioned Willy's political acumen, so when he warned her that the situation would worsen, she took him seriously. Her only regret was leaving Anna behind, but she was certain that her sister would never leave the Führer. Although she would miss seeing Anna, she now understood that she'd lost her the day she'd met Hitler.

Ursula looked out the window and watched the fallow fields fall away as the car sped from persecution and bigotry. The last few months had taught her to value the moment, to act quickly and decisively in favor of those she cherished. She was excited to begin anew in England with Willy by her side, and the opportunity to sing again with Carl Ebert and Max Schmidt was simply icing on the proverbial cake. She fell asleep dreaming of performing in English at Glyndebourne.

* * *

She awakened to find Willy entering the parking lot at the Hamburg dockyard. Nazi uniforms were everywhere, and her anxiety spiked. Willy had assured her that no one in Hamburg would recognize her, and that even if they did, he was confident that he could talk his way out of any situation that might arise. As if sensing her unease, he said, "My uncle is far too busy to worry about us, Ursula. Not everyone knows that you're Jewish, even though it might feel that way. Remember, your papers indicate otherwise." He smiled reassuringly and she relaxed.

Willy withdrew their six suitcases, paid a valet to carry them aboard, and dropped his keys in the front seat.

"What are you doing?" she asked.

Willy smiled. "We can't take it with us."

"So, you're just leaving it here?"

"Someone will steal it before day's end. I thought I'd make it easier for the thief by leaving the keys."

Ursula turned her attention to the massive ships that crisscrossed the Elbe River, some carrying cargo while others carried people. Tugboats chugged alongside of the larger ships, urging their charges to move faster in order to make way for incoming vessels. Willy had informed her that Hamburg boasted the third busiest port in the world, but she had had no idea how active the harbor would be. On the shore, the Bismarck monument towered over the crowds of people jockeying for position as queues formed to buy tickets and board ships. Nazi officers observed the controlled chaos with an air of detachment as boys dressed in khaki, miniature Nazi uniforms played tag. The girls, dressed in strapped leather shoes, white ankle socks, and short dresses, looked on enviously, giggling when a boy was tagged.

"Well, what do you think?" Willy asked.

"It is . . . it is . . ."

"Amazing," Otto breathed.

Willy placed his hand on Otto's shoulder. "Our ship is called the *Drottningholm*."

"I see," she said as she examined the roiling water of the Elbe River.

Willy followed her gaze. "You'll be fine, Ursula. I've purchased tickets that allow us each a cabin of our own, so you'll have a porthole and space in which to relax during the voyage. Besides, when you're aboard, you won't feel the movement of the water."

Ursula raised her eyebrows, unsure whether to believe him. Otto, ever logical, offered, "Ursula, it doesn't matter whether or not you feel the churn of the waves, as we're boarding that ship!"

They made their way among the throngs of people and found the gangway. Once they had joined the queue, Ursula took a moment to observe the family directly in front of them. A tall, regal woman wearing a mink stole and pearls clutched the arm of her well-dressed spouse, who smoked a hand-rolled cigarette and smiled as if he hadn't a care in the world. The woman turned to Ursula and smiled primly, her apprehension evident as she glanced nervously at the ship and then at the raucous river. Their two children stood in front of them, and Ursula focused on the boy, who poked his sister until she collapsed in tears halfway up the gangway. The embarrassed woman turned to Ursula, apologized for her son's disobedience, and grabbed the child's ear to drag him the rest of the way.

"That could be you someday," Willy whispered.

"I certainly hope not," she sniffed.

"You don't want children?"

"Perhaps. But not a child like that."

Willy laughed. "Boys are different than girls, Ursula. You have no experience with taking care of boys."

Ursula made a show of considering his words. "Then I believe that I shall give birth only to girls."

Otto barked out a guffaw, the lighthearted mood infecting all three of them. "Just like her mother," he muttered, shaking his head and smiling.

24

Once aboard the vessel, a valet ushered them to their staterooms, which were situated next to one another. The young man handed Willy the keys before accepting a tip, bowing slightly toward Ursula, and retreating. Willy unlocked Ursula's door and stepped aside. Ursula crossed the threshold and inhaled sharply.

"What is it?"

Receiving no response, Willy stepped inside the stateroom and dipped his head so that he could see Ursula's face. Her mouth hung open as her eyes scanned the spacious room.

"Do you not like it?" he asked.

Ursula shook her head. "It's beautiful, Willy, and so big. Surely all of this space is not just for me!"

Willy smiled. "It's for you only. Your father has the stateroom immediately next door. See?" He approached a narrow door in the wall and placed his hand upon the knob. "You can access your father's room through this door." He knocked twice and then swung the door open to find Otto on the other side with a surprised smile on his face.

Ursula shook her head. "I've never seen such a beautiful room, Willy."

Willy winked at Otto, gently closed the door, and gathered Ursula in his arms. "You will have a home in England where each room is as exquisite as its mistress." He leaned in for a long, lingering kiss. She withdrew slowly, a little breathless.

"Now," Willy said, all business once more, "the ship will depart in twenty-five minutes. I assume that you want to freshen up before meeting me on the Lido deck for a cocktail?"

"I don't know what a Lido deck is."

Willy smiled. "It's the top deck. The passengers meet there as the ship pulls away and wave good-bye."

Ursula looked at him askew. "This is a tradition?"

Willy made an "x" over his heart. "Cross my heart. It's true."

"I'll meet you there in twenty-five minutes."

He took her hands. "This is the beginning of the next chapter of our lives, Ursula. I cannot wait to spend the rest of my life with you, making memories . . . and babies." He waggled his eyebrows at her and she slapped his arm. He ran away playfully and snuck out the door before she could do any real damage.

Closing the door behind him, Ursula turned and drank in the luxurious stateroom. The walls were a light yellow with coordinating honey-colored wainscoting. The bed was large enough to fit three people and was covered in a corn-yellow chenille spread. A six-foot-tall, round mirror was attached to the wall directly across from the bed, and it had the effect of exaggerating the room's size. Next to the bed was a Mediterranean blue nightstand, and diagonally across from that was a loveseat upholstered in the same color, and a glass coffee table that held a vase of fresh daffodils. Above the sitting area was not just one porthole, but three, allowing the stateroom a breezy, open feel. A retractable curtain divided the sleeping area from the sitting area, giving the room a completed, designer look.

Ursula walked past the couch and stopped. She'd been so taken with the grandeur of the sleeping area that she'd not yet noticed a beautifully appointed bathroom, complete with a spacious bathtub for soaking after a long day of—*what?* she wondered. *What did one do all day aboard a large ship such as the* Drottningholm*?* She glanced at the coffee table and noted, through its glass top, a backgammon set and a deck of playing cards. Ursula smiled as she envisioned an entire day of doing nothing but playing games and relaxing.

"I could definitely get used to this lifestyle," she said aloud as she placed her dresses in the closet, carefully smoothing any wrinkles. She had managed to stuff ten dresses into her two suitcases, along with her toiletries and three pictures. The first was of her mother, smiling as she basked in the love and strong arms of Otto. The second was of Anna and her, taken immediately after Frau Bergmann's memorial service. The third was of Willy and her at a picnic. She placed them delicately on the nightstand, then withdrew her toiletry bag and retreated to the bathroom to wash her face and reapply her makeup. Afterwards, she donned her favorite dress—the one she had worn on her first date with Willy—and examined her reflection. The stress of the last few years had melted off too much weight. But as she smiled at her reflection, she assured herself that the food aboard the ship would remedy the situation.

She turned to her open suitcase and saw a small white box that sat atop her pajamas. Curious, she removed the box, sat on the bed, and opened the lid to find a folded piece of paper. Ursula set the box aside to read the note.

```
My Beloved Ursula,
    I cannot express to you the joy—no, the elation
that I felt when you agreed to accompany me to
England. My mother will adore you (as I do), and I
know that you will become fast friends.
    My life was a dull gray until you sang your
way into my heart. I'm proud to say that a
plethora of colors now fills my emotional palette.
I am rapt by your beauty, passion, and fortitude.
You're an exceptional woman whom I am proud to
call my fiancée—soon, wife.
    And, I dare say, I have become a fan of the most
dreaded of all art forms, opera.
    Your humble servant and most loyal love,
    Willy
```

Ursula smiled as a happy tear traced her cheek. When she'd met Willy, time had seemed to stand still, then sped up uncontrollably until this moment. As she reflected on their four short years together, she realized how fate had played a hand in their impromptu meeting. She appreciated how fortunate she was and had learned to take nothing for granted. Her heart ached when she thought of Anna, but then hardened when her mind wandered to the burnt rabbi. She felt firm in her resolve to leave Germany. Once Hitler had been defeated, perhaps she might rejoin Anna. Maybe there was a chance they could enjoy each other's company as sisters once more. But for now, she must focus on her father and Willy, the two most important people in her life.

Ursula sighed and refolded the note, then tucked it gently into the frame of her picture of Willy.

She picked up the small box and gently removed the cotton. Inside lay a gold, oval locket at the end of a thin, box-link chain. A single rose surrounded by leaves was carved into the face of the locket, and her breath caught in her throat as she remembered Willy showing her this necklace. His father had given it to his mother before leaving for Europe, a keepsake for her to cherish until his return. He hadn't returned, however, so Willy's mother had given it to Willy to bestow upon his one true love.

"It's beautiful," she whispered aloud as she opened the locket. Inside rested a tiny picture of Willy and Ursula, taken on the day he'd first expressed his love for her. Ursula smiled as her finger traced the photograph, remembering her reaction when Willy had first said the words "I love you." She had thrown her arms around his neck and kissed his entire face before responding, "Well, of course I love you too!" She stood and donned the locket, silently vowing never to remove it.

A knock sounded. She glanced at the bedside clock and realized she was running late. Willy must have returned to gather his wayward fiancée. She ran to the door and quickly opened it, ready to embrace him. A surprised steward took a step backward, then regained his composure when she dropped her outstretched arms.

Speaking in German, she said, "Please excuse me. I thought you were someone else."

Confusion contorted the young man's features before he responded in English. "You have a telephone call—" Ursula stared at him, uncomprehending. He blinked several times and then said, "Telephone," as he mimicked holding a phone receiver, then pointed at Ursula. "A woman. For you."

"Ah." Ursula smiled, understanding. Then she frowned. *Who would be phoning me on this ship? I told no one I was leaving.*

Ursula nodded and held up her finger to ask him to wait. She reviewed her reflection once more, smoothed some unruly strands of hair, and motioned him to lead the way. She closed the door behind her and decided that she would surprise Willy after taking the telephone call. She would sneak up behind him and cover his eyes, then show him her exquisite necklace. *How clever of him to slip it into my bag when I wasn't looking.* She followed the steward, musing as to when Willy might have hidden the gift, when the young man stopped before a closed door marked "Telephones." He nodded curtly and left, leaving Ursula alone.

She opened the heavy door to find a bank of four telephones. The small, rectangular room was empty, and one receiver lay on its side, awaiting her. She picked it up. "Hello?"

"Yes. Hello, Ursula. I was calling to say good-bye and safe travels."

The door to the room opened and two well-dressed gentlemen entered, arguing loudly in German. Ursula turned away from them and placed her left hand over her ear in an attempt to muffle the noise, but they raised their voices even more.

"Who is this? I can barely hear you." She cast an annoyed glance at the men, but they were too involved in their disagreement to pay her any attention.

"It's Anna. I was just calling to say good-bye and I'm sorry."

A frisson of fear pricked Ursula. "How did you know where I am, Anna?"

The men abruptly ceased speaking, and a quiet stillness permeated the air. Before her brain could register what was happening, she felt pressure against her back. A hand grabbed the receiver she was holding and wrapped the cord around her neck, pulling her backwards into the body of her attacker. Choking, she clawed at her throat and managed to get her fingers under the cord but still couldn't breathe. As her vision narrowed, the man released the cord just enough to allow a full breath. She heaved and coughed before he tightened it once more, renewing her paroxysms. She thought of Anna listening on the telephone line, then ceased struggling as bright lights appeared at the edges of her visual field. As she faded into oblivion, hot, uneven breath on her cheek roused her and a deep, raspy voice whispered in her ear.

"Hello, Fräulein Becker. You are to come with us. Listen carefully. You have a choice. You can quietly follow me, and your father will sail happily to England with Willy, or I can inject you with this drug and then kill your father. Which would you prefer? Hmmm?"

Ursula made a small choking sound and the cord relaxed. She threw herself against the wall as she doubled over coughing. Anna's tinny voice came across the line.

"Ursula? What's happening? Are you alright? Ursula?"

The man with the raspy voice picked up the receiver, listened for a moment, and then gently replaced it in its cradle. "It was thoughtful that your sister called to say good-bye."

Terrified, Ursula stood up and massaged her neck. When she spoke, her damaged larynx created a hoarse tone that sounded eerily similar to her assailant's. "Who are you?"

The man glanced at his companion and waved his small hand as if swatting at a fly. "It is of no consequence who we are."

Ursula's eyes darted from one man to the other, and then to the door. Her attackers stood between her and freedom, but she calculated that if she could just—

"I know what you are thinking, Fräulein, but please understand that the action you are entertaining will end with not only your death, but Otto's as well."

Hearing this disgusting man say her father's name enraged and emboldened her. "I do not know who you think you are, but when my fiancé discovers what you have done, you can rest assured that you will lose not only your jobs, but perhaps your lives as well!" Her outburst provoked a new round of coughing.

The men exchanged amused looks. "Well, I must say, you are living up to your reputation as a spitfire." His smile faded slowly, and his eyes darkened. "Make your decision, Fräulein. If you come quietly, your father lives. If you do not . . ." The man let the unspoken threat hang in the air between them. "The ship leaves in . . ." He consulted his wristwatch. "Four minutes."

Ursula panicked and lunged for the door. The man with the raspy voice moved quickly and in one efficient movement grabbed her wrist and twisted her arm behind her, slamming her face against the wall. She cried out but was silenced as a needle slid into her carotid artery. She melted to the floor, unconscious.

SWAN SONG

* * *

    Willy stood at the railing on the Lido deck, two glasses of champagne in his hands. He searched the crowd for Ursula as Otto stood beside him, waving wildly at the well-wishers who lined the dock. As the huge ship commenced the laborious process of detaching itself from its berth, Willy took no heed of two well-dressed men walking down the gangplank with a large bundle slung between them.

II

2 5

"Anna, if you don't stop banging your violin against the bed it will break!" Ursula ordered.

The rhythmic thumping continued. "Anna, did you hear what I said? Willy gave you that beautiful instrument. If you don't have respect for the violin, think of how sad Willy will be when he discovers your irreverence towards his generous gift." Still, the measured strikes persisted. Ursula sighed heavily. "Anna, my head is exploding with the noise. Please stop—"

A rush of cool air startled Ursula awake. She opened her eyes, and blurry objects swam in her vision. She blinked several times and tried to lift her head, only to be rewarded with a stabbing pain in her neck and shoulders. Raising her hand to her face, she was shocked to feel swollen eyes. Slowly she traced a finger along the bone of her nose and grimaced. It was no longer straight.

"Looks like you were in a nasty altercation, if I might say so."

With great effort Ursula turned her gaze slightly to the left. Her vision cleared enough to see a woman of about sixty seated diagonally across from her. She clutched an embroidered bag tightly against her chest. "I'm no doctor, but I believe your nose might be broken."

Ursula nodded and retched, catching her vomit in her hands. The woman quickly unfastened her bag and withdrew a cotton towel, then reached across the narrow space between them and placed the towel in Ursula's hands. When Ursula didn't move, the woman tutted and crossed to sit next to her. She wiped Ursula's hands, gently but efficiently restoring her cleanliness. Ursula examined her. She was well dressed and carried herself with dignity. The woman stopped rubbing. "It's not polite to stare, young lady. Didn't your mother teach you that?"

Ursula gazed out the window. Streaks of green, yellow, and brown hurtled by. She remembered traveling at a fast speed recently, but she couldn't remember where she'd been traveling, when, or with whom. A thumping sound permeated her consciousness and her muddled brain slowly grasped that she was on a train. The rhythmic thwacks of the wheels against the tracks echoed the thumping of Anna's violin in her dream. "My mother died years ago."

The woman removed the cloth and sat still. "I'm sorry to hear that." She paused, then resumed rubbing Ursula's hands. "I had a daughter. She was about your age." The woman stole a glance at Ursula's face. "She was beautiful, like you were before recent events I would imagine."

Ursula stared dumbly, unable to process an appropriate response.

"My name is Marika. And yours?"

"Ursula."

The woman physically withdrew. "Mein Gott. That was my daughter's name. What a coincidence."

Ursula's eyebrows knitted and a wave of nausea followed. She swallowed hard. "What happened to your daughter?"

Marika's lips formed a thin line as she balled up the soiled cotton towel and placed it gently on the wood floor at her feet. "She was mauled by the SS. The animals raped her to death." Marika's stare turned cold. "As long as I live, I will fight in her memory and honor." The last words caught in the grieving mother's throat, and she brought her hand to her mouth. "Please forgive me. It happened some weeks ago and I'm not accustomed to speaking so plainly. The wound is so raw, so—"

Ursula placed her hand on Marika's arm, silencing her. "You don't need to explain," she whispered. "We've all seen unspeakable horrors. I'm so sorry about your daughter." The two women sat quietly for a moment in an immediate kinship borne of tragedy.

Ursula asked, "Is that why you're on this train? To get away from your daughter's killers? I'm afraid the SS is everywhere these days. I'm no longer sure you can outrun them by train."

Marika tilted her head and stared at Ursula. "My dear, I'm not escaping. On the contrary. I never would have chosen to leave the town in which I was born, grew up, married, and raised my daughter. I was ordered to appear at the Hamburg train station. My number was thirty-nine. There are about fifty of us here."

Ursula's jumbled thoughts started to clear as she stared at the yellow, six-pointed star on Marika's overcoat. *I have a star on my coat too.* She looked at her clothes. Her dress was streaked with dried blood. *Where is my coat?* she wondered. Marika noted her scrutiny and pointed to the star. "This is what caused my Ursula's trouble. She refused to wear it and was singled out as an example." Marika breathed deeply, then cleared her throat. "I see that you don't wear a yellow badge. You're not Jewish. So, why are you on this train?"

Ursula stared in confusion. "Yes," she mumbled. "Why am I on this train?"

Marika patted Ursula's hand. "You're not feeling well. Your uncle carried you onto the train in Berlin. He said that you'd been in a car accident, and that you were heavily medicated. But that if you awoke before your stop, to tell you that your father is safe, and Willy will be waiting for you in England. Does that make you feel better, dear?"

Ursula's eyes welled up and a look of concern swept Marika's features. "No, no, Ursula. Your uncle said that your father is safe. That's a good thing. And Willy will meet you in England."

Recent events hurtled back and sent her imagination into a tailspin. She touched her neck where she'd been choked with the phone cord. Her skin was raw. She closed her eyes and could feel her assailant's hot breath as he promised to kill Otto if she didn't cooperate. That had been immediately before she'd lunged for the door. She hadn't cooperated. "I have to get off this train." She stood, and vertigo returned her to her seat.

Marika shook her head. "It won't stop until we get there."

"Where?"

"East."

"*Where* in the east?"

A cloud crossed the older woman's features. "I was told that we're being sent to a new town for our own safety. It's referred to as a spa town. Can you imagine? My husband was part of a transport that left a while ago in order to prepare for our arrival. He's a carpenter, you see. I'm anxious to see him again." She glanced about the train car. "All of us in this car are Jews. All except for you, at least. We were told that the move is temporary until a suitable place for us can be found. Although I didn't want to leave my home, the choice was clear. The conditions for the Jews in Berlin were very bad. We were confined to a small living area, and food was becoming scarce. None of us were allowed to work anymore, so as much as I didn't want to leave, perhaps the new living conditions will be better. We met at a synagogue on Levetzow Street and then walked to the railway station. I was allowed to bring fifty kilos of personal items."

Ursula glanced at Marika's embroidered bag. The woman smiled. "Of course, I couldn't carry fifty kilos of anything, so I packed as much as I could into this bag, and the rest of my things will be shipped to me."

Ursula's stomach dropped. "Who told you that?"

"The officers who delivered the notice of my transport."

"Do you trust what they said?"

Marika looked away. "I've heard about other trains, Ursula. Ones that are packed with the living dead, who arrive at camps where people are beaten, starved, and gassed. You and I are on a regular railway car traveling to a spa town. We're fortunate. Don't you agree?"

Ursula was torn between disgust and resignation. Marika seemed intelligent. Surely, she understood that their destination fell far afield from what she'd been told. But the unfortunate woman didn't really have a choice. Like her, Marika was merely a puppet to be manipulated for Hitler's enjoyment.

Ursula's head felt as if it were stuffed with cotton. The aftereffects of the drug she'd been given made her lethargic and nauseous. Her stomach seized as details of the attack flashed intermittently through her mind, and she wondered if Willy had realized that she'd been kidnapped and was searching for her. If the situation were reversed, she would explore the ship first, which would take at least a day, and then expand the search from there. A rush of adrenaline surged as she considered her father. Despite what Marika had been told, had her attacker made good on his commitment to kill Otto?

"Ursula, you look concerned. Everything will be alright. I just know it." Marika pressed her hand against Ursula's knee as she spoke. "Besides, if you're thinking about Willy and your father, they're safe. Please try to relax."

Avoiding her throbbing nose, Ursula gently wiped tears from her eyes and sat up straighter to examine the train car and its passengers. The spacious, comfortable seats were upholstered in brown leather, and each window had its own set of gold-colored curtains. The floor was covered in a patterned, wool runner that ran the length of the car. Most passengers were over the age of sixty and were dressed in upper middle-class attire, many coats sporting a star identical to the one Marika wore. Many women wore ornate jewelry and openly stared at her wounds, their faces displaying extreme distaste. Ursula made eye contact with a man who looked away after his wife slapped his hand. "Best not to get involved," Ursula heard his wife whisper.

"So, Ursula, why did your uncle put you on this train?"

Ursula shifted in her seat. She attempted a laugh but ended up coughing up phlegm and blood. Marika shook her head and admonished, "Be still, child!" as she grabbed the towel and gingerly wiped Ursula's face.

"You wouldn't believe me if I told you the truth."

Her companion seemed unmoved. "You'd be surprised what I can believe."

Ursula sighed. "That man wasn't my uncle, and I was placed on this train because I angered the Führer so badly that he wanted me to disappear."

Marika narrowed her eyes. "You mean that you angered an SS man, or you didn't follow an order, perhaps like my daughter?"

Ursula shook her head but quickly stopped as her nausea threatened once more. "No. I mean that I angered Adolf Hitler."

"How?"

Ursula stared out the window. She didn't know how to answer. There were so many reasons, but none of them seemed rational. "By deigning to sing a song he didn't like. By not agreeing to join the Party. By not falling prey to his advances. By looking exactly like a woman he once knew and loved. By falling in love with his nephew, who asked me to marry him and planned on taking me to England, where I could live and sing freely."

Marika's confusion was evident. "I don't understand, dear."

"Do you attend the opera?"

"Of course."

"Have you heard of a singer named Ursula Becker?"

Marika nodded. "Oh, yes. She is marvelous. I had the opportunity to see her when my husband and I—"

Ursula watched her make the connection. She leaned in, examining Ursula's puffy, altered face. "You are Ursula Becker! Oh, my goodness! What an honor! Why have you not been singing? It was as if you disappeared. One day a star and the next, poof! You were gone. Oh!" She caught herself as her recollections collided with the facts in Ursula's story. "Oh, Ursula. I'm sorry." Marika looked down, continuing to draw the puzzle pieces together. "So . . . your fiancé is . . .?"

"Willy Hitler, the Führer's nephew."

"Oh, my."

"Yes. Oh, my."

"And this Willy is—"

"According to the man who hit me, drugged me, and put me on this train, Willy is on his way to England with my father, who supposedly is safe."

"And you are here on this train," Marika added quietly.

"Yes. I am here," Ursula said as she watched the desolate landscape fall away. "Wherever 'here' is."

26

Willy downed his champagne and searched the deck for Ursula. It had been twenty minutes since they'd agreed to meet, and he was beginning to wonder if she'd lost track of time. He turned to Otto and noted the vigor with which the old man waved to people on shore. Willy had never seen him so lighthearted and didn't want to spoil his mood, so he decided he would find Ursula himself.

"Herr Becker, I will return shortly."

"What?" Otto shouted over the din.

Willy patted his back and yelled, "Back soon!" Otto nodded and continued to wave.

Willy placed the glasses on a waiter's tray and returned to Ursula's stateroom. He knocked three times. Receiving no response, he found a steward and asked the young man to unlock the door.

Willy entered her room to find it empty. As he turned to leave, he saw a small white box lying open on the bed. His eyes found the pictures on the nightstand and went to the folded piece of paper tucked in one of the frames. Smiling, he picked it up and reread the note he had penned that morning. All of his words had been heartfelt. He had been so worried that something might go wrong along their journey—that their documents might be confiscated at a checkpoint, or that once aboard the ship, their tickets might not be honored, or that his uncle might intervene in some way—that he had written the letter just in case he wasn't able to express his thoughts directly.

But everything had gone smoothly, much better than he'd expected, and now they were on their way to a better life without chaos or persecution. Sure, Willy didn't have the fortune he'd planned on amassing during his tenure in Germany, but he had Ursula. He was certain that with her by his side, anything was possible. He grinned as he imagined the first interaction between his beloved mother and her. Bridget Dowling Hitler, an Irishwoman by birth, would embrace her future daughter-in-law, immediately accepting her into their family without question. Ursula, a German to the core, would take a moment to warm to Bridget. But once she did, Willy knew that the bond would remain unbroken.

Willy picked up the empty white box and smiled. Ursula must be wearing the necklace. He reflected on his mother's words the day she'd entrusted him with it. "Place it around the neck of the person your soul chooses to be your mate for life. If she accepts it, then be confident that you've chosen wisely."

"I've chosen wisely, Mum," Willy murmured as he pocketed the letter and exited the room, determined to find his love. He passed the steward in the hallway.

"Ms. Becker had some trouble understanding me earlier, but we worked it out. I can't speak German, so I acted it out."

"What are you talking about?"

The young man waved his hand. "It's okay, sir. It happens all the time. I've learned to pantomime quite well." He brought his hand to his ear with his middle fingers closed and pinky and thumb extended, mimicking a phone call.

"Are you telling me that Miss Becker received a telephone call?"

"Yes, sir."

"From whom?"

The steward shrugged. "I don't know, sir, but she seemed eager to take the call."

Willy felt a surge of relief. He had been concerned that Ursula might be frantically searching for him in the throngs of people on the Lido deck, but she was most likely still talking on the telephone. "Where's the telephone room?"

"This way, sir. Follow me." The steward led the way up some stairs, weaved his way through a small crowd of slightly inebriated passengers, then stopped before a door marked "Telephones."

"Here we are."

"Thanks."

Willy entered, and the door automatically closed behind him. The small room felt sterile. The walls were painted pristine white, and four black telephones sat on a green marble counter. There were no chairs or stools. Clearly the room was meant for brief telephone communication. He turned to leave and noted a reddish-brown streak on the wall behind the door. He removed a handkerchief, swiped it across the substance, then raised it to his nose. The unmistakable aroma of copper filled his nostrils, and Willy knew, without a doubt, that the smear on the wall was blood. He leaned forward to examine the area more closely and drew a sharp breath. The hair on the back of his neck stood at attention as he stared at the bright pink blotch under the blood. He heard himself mumbling, "No, no, no, no," as he remembered how excited Ursula had been when he'd given her a tube of lipstick several weeks ago.

Given the rationing, it was next to impossible to obtain such a frivolous item, even on the black market. Only Nazi wives enjoyed such luxuries. But he had traded fourteen packs of cigarettes and a large sack of flour for Ursula's prized, hot pink lipstick, and she had been ecstatic.

Willy threw open the heavy door and sprinted down the stairs. He found the steward who had guided him to the telephone room and commanded him to unlock Ursula's stateroom. The surprised steward obliged, then watched in confusion as Willy rushed into Ursula's bathroom and rummaged through her toiletries. He emerged gripping a lipstick tube.

"Follow me," Willy said, as he ran past the steward. The young man sprinted to keep up with Willy as he remounted the staircase and burst through the telephone room door. Panting, Willy removed the lipstick cap, twisted the tube until the lipstick appeared, and drew a line on the wall directly under-neath the bright pink smudge. He dropped his head when he realized that the colors were identical, an exact match.

"God damn it!" he screamed. "I knew it was too good to be true! Ahhhh!" he raged as he picked up phones and slammed them against the wall. The horrified steward gawked in helpless confusion, unable to imagine what might cause such fury.

"Sir! Please. The telephones. You're destroying them."

Willy doubled over, desperately trying to regain control over his anger. Breathing heavily, he rasped, "Who originally accepted the phone call for Miss Becker?"

"I did."

"But you're assigned to our stateroom hallway, are you not?"

"Yes."

"Then how is it that you took the phone call?" Willy's eyes became accusatory.

The steward unconsciously took a step backward. "I . . . I . . ."

"Spit it out, boy!" Willy's fury was barely contained as he jammed the steward against the door.

"I happened to be walking by and the telephone was ringing, so I answered it."

Willy glared at the frightened young man and suddenly realized that his anger was misdirected. He felt foolish as he turned away and raked his hands through his hair. Thoughts were flying through his mind. He closed his eyes in an effort to harness them.

"Was there anyone else in this room when you answered the phone?"

"No, sir."

"But someone might have come in between the time you answered the phone and the time you retrieved Miss Becker from her stateroom."

"Um, yes. Maybe."

Willy's mind was racing. "You said that a woman phoned Miss Becker. Are you certain?"

"Absolutely."

Willy quickly reviewed the small group of people Ursula called friends and came up with only one person who might have phoned the ship. Anna. *But how would she have known Ursula was here?*

"Listen, I'm sorry that I scared you. I didn't mean to. It's just that. . . well. . . can you please make a ship-to-shore call for me? Right now?"

Relieved to no longer be the hapless target of Willy's animosity, the steward picked up the receiver and requested an operator. An excruciating minute later Willy heard a nasal voice come on the line. The steward handed the receiver to Willy.

"I need to be connected with the Chancellery in Berlin."

"I'm sorry, sir, but I can't—"

"It's a matter of life and death. Literally. Please," he begged, his voice cracking.

A long pause ensued, followed by an exasperated sigh. "Hold please."

Several minutes passed before a young woman's voice came on the line. She sounded tinny and far away.

"Hello?"

"This is Willy Hitler. I need to speak to Anna Becker. Is she there? And if she's not there, do you know—"

"She is here. Hold the line."

Willy breathed a sigh of relief. A minute later Anna said, "Hello?"

"Thank God! Anna, it's Willy."

"Willy, why are you phoning? Are you not on the ship with Ursula?"

"That's the problem, Anna. I can't find Ursula and there's blood on the wall in the telephone room."

"Oh, my goodness!"

"There's more. A smear of Ursula's lipstick is underneath the blood. Did you phone her earlier?"

"Yes. To wish her well. But—"

"How did you know we were on the ship?"

"Adolf told me. Why?"

Willy took a shuddering breath. *I should have realized that Uncle Alf would know our plans. It seemed too easy.* "Tell me, Anna, and *do not* lie to me! Did my uncle harm Ursula?"

"Willy, what are you talking about? Of course not!"

"Stop it, Anna! You and I both know the ill will he harbored. And now, when we were so close to happiness, did he steal her from me? Tell me, please." Willy felt like he was being strangled. "I couldn't bear it."

"Willy, you're being ridiculous. I'm not aware of any plan to harm her."

"Is Uncle Alf with you?"

"No. He's at the Berghof. I'm to join him later this afternoon."

"You tell him that I need to speak to him immediately. Do you understand? *Immediately!*"

"I understand."

Willy's eyes found the bloodstain on the wall and he squeezed them shut. "Tell him that he needs to contact me on the ship. Right away!"

"Willy, you already said that. I'll relay your message. But you need to calm down. I'm sure that Ursula is fine. She's probably elsewhere on the ship searching for you."

"What about the blood and lipstick?"

"Willy, the blood could be from someone else. And what shade was Ursula's lipstick? Pink? She always favored pink. Do you know how many women wear pink lipstick?"

Willy opened his eyes. He hadn't thought of that. "How many?"

Anna huffed. "I'm not sure exactly how many, but my point is that you're being rash in your judgment of Adolf. He loves you and he's a good man. What you're suggesting he's done is outside of his moral compass."

Willy's eyes went wide. "His moral compass? Anna, do you hear yourself? Uncle Alf has no moral compass. He wouldn't hesitate to harm Ursula, or me or you, for that matter, if we stood in the way of the Reich. Don't fool yourself. You're sleeping with a madman."

Anna drew a quick breath, and Willy knew he had stumbled. "How dare you say such a thing to me!"

Willy pinched the bridge of his nose, instantly regretting his antagonistic attitude toward Anna. His harsh words had been accurate, but he might have found a kinder manner in which to express them.

"I must get off the line now, as I need to search for Ursula. I desperately hope that she's still on the ship, as you suggest. But listen closely to me. I'm not mistaken in my perception of my uncle, and I pray that you realize your naïveté before it's too late. You're useful to him now, but someday, maybe not too far into the future, if you become a liability, you will be discarded like the Jews."

Silence buzzed across the miles. "I am not a Jew."

"You're not Aryan either, no matter what the paperwork says. The fact is that if you become an inconvenience, you will be cast aside."

Willy wasn't sure if he heard a sniffle on the other end of the line, or whether it was simply static.

"Just give Uncle Alf the message, alright? Anna?"

A harsh buzz came across the line. She had already disconnected.

27

Several hours later Ursula awakened when her head collided with the window. "Ouch!"

Marika winced. "Oh, Ursula, you poor thing. You fell asleep again after we spoke. But look! The train is slowing down."

Ursula rubbed her eyes, careful not to jostle her damaged nose, then pressed her forehead against the glass. Outside she saw a small gray building with a dilapidated roof. In front of the small structure stood a tall, dark-haired SS officer with a long, sharp nose and eyebrows that formed a shelf above his glacial blue eyes. His gaze met hers, then moved past as he stood perfectly still, hands clasped behind his back. He reminded her of an eagle appraising the most efficient way to attack its prey. She shuddered involuntarily.

As the train slowed, he jumped aboard and walked slowly down the aisle, openly examining the mute travelers who had long ago learned to stare at their feet when in the presence of Nazi officers. Ursula stole a glance and her pulse quickened. The tall officer stood ramrod straight and puffed out his chest, proudly exhibiting the swastikas on his crisp uniform as his black boots landed heavily with each step. He would nod intermittently or utter an indistinguishable sound, and Marika and Ursula would exchange worried glances. Ursula listened as he reached the end of the car, his thick leather boots squeaking as he turned. He returned along the length of the car, back toward the open door through which fresh air rushed, then turned quickly and announced in a clipped baritone voice, "I am seeking Ursula Becker. She was to be on this transport. Yet she is not here. Has anyone seen or spoken to Ursula Becker?"

Before Ursula could react, a man several rows behind her spoke. "Do you mean the opera singer?"

The SS guard smiled, his white, straight teeth dramatically altering his visage. His tone become jovial, and he seemed kind and youthful. It wasn't difficult to see who he might have been prior to coming under Hitler's evil spell. "Yes. That Ursula Becker."

A boy no older than sixteen answered. "We would know if we had seen such a beautiful creature, sir. We are not fools."

Ursula cringed. Flippant words from an ignorant child could get them all killed. She noted tension etched in passengers' faces as they awaited the officer's reaction. To everyone's relief, he smiled and nodded. "You're not fools." Ursula felt her shoulders relax. "But you *are* Jews. What is your name?" he asked the boy.

"Markus Appel." The boy's tone was relaxed. *He's either stupid or has been shielded from Nazi horror*, Ursula thought.

Her jaw clenched. She wanted to look away but couldn't, drawn by irrepressible human curiosity. The officer had accepted the insubordinate comment too easily. She held her breath as he sauntered toward Markus, then leaned toward the boy. "She is beautiful, is she not?"

Do something! Ursula's mind screamed. She started to raise her hand, but Marika grabbed it and forced it back to her lap. Marika shook her head almost imperceptibly as her eyes commanded silence. Ursula struggled against her grip, but the older woman was stronger than she appeared.

Markus' boyish audacity smothered good sense. "Yes, she is, sir."

With her hands pinned against her lap, Ursula opened her mouth to speak. Marika hissed, "Don't make a sound! Let's see the guard's intentions before you make your identity known."

"Why?" Ursula whispered. "The boy might—" Marika's blazing eyes held hers as she shook her head again. *Do. Not. Speak*, she mouthed. The knuckles of her trembling hands had turned snowy white.

"Tell me, Markus. If you were to meet Fräulein Becker, what would you say to her?"

The sixteen-year-old looked around, suddenly embarrassed. "Um, I suppose that I would say—"

Bang! Screams erupted, and she looked up to find Markus' body slumped against the seat, a small hole in the center of his forehead. Somehow the officer had drawn his gun and fired, all in the span of a breath. Another SS guard appeared and held the car's door shut from the outside as terrified passengers scrambled over seats and each other in an effort to escape the mayhem. The crowd piled against the door trying to force it open, but there was nowhere to go. A stunned Ursula stood and glared at the guard while Marika sat stoically, her arms wrapped tightly around her embroidered bag, her eyes riveted to the floor.

The officer observed the chaos with irritation. Ten seconds after firing the fatal shot, he holstered his gun. "Silence!" In response, the crowd quieted somewhat, then stilled as they noticed that he no longer brandished his weapon. He motioned for them to return to their seats, but no one moved. Placing his right hand on his gun, he yelled, "Sit, Jews! Sit! Unless you want someone else to die today!" Reluctantly they returned to their seats, all of them clutching their few belongings as they stared at the eagle watching them. His back was to Ursula as he spoke calmly and evenly, the tone of a schoolteacher admonishing his class. "That unpleasantness could have been avoided. Now, I ask again, where is Ursula Becker?"

"I am Ursula Becker."

The guard's head swiveled quickly. Starting at her feet, his eyes scanned the length of her body, taking in her disheveled clothes, her rat's nest of tangled hair, and her ravaged face with its blood-caked, crooked nose and black eyes. "But of course you are!" He threw his head back and roared with laughter. Ursula marshaled her inner diva and drew herself up to her full height. He took note of the change. "Sit down. You are not the person I seek."

Ursula stood her ground, then took a step forward, determined to avoid another calamity. Without warning he rushed forward, simultaneously removing his revolver. He moved so quickly that she had no time to react before she felt pressure against her forehead. "I should shoot you for lying."

Ursula didn't blink or move. Her hands balled into fists. Her anger replaced her pain and public humiliation . . . and logic. Similar to Markus, she spoke without considering the repercussions. "Do it. But know that you would be shooting Ursula Becker."

They stared at each other while the guard attempted to see through her injuries. Over a very long minute, Ursula watched realization dawn in his eyes. He slowly lowered his weapon and nodded. "It is you. I was not informed that you had been . . . that you were . . . I was only told that you'd be on this transport."

Ursula quietly blew out the breath she'd been holding when, to her complete astonishment, the guard bowed slightly and offered his beautiful smile. "It is truly my pleasure to make your acquaintance, Fräulein Becker. I was lucky enough to see one of your performances several years ago and was astounded at your depth of character, not to mention your breathtaking voice."

Once again, Ursula found herself at a loss for words as she contemplated the duplicity of the human spirit. This child killer had turned on a dime and spoken passionately about the pure beauty of art. It was astounding and rendered her speechless. She found herself wondering about Nazism. *Is it a way of life? Does a person wedge it into his soul, where it festers? Or is it simply a coat one dons that anesthetizes the wearer against the burdensome weight of a conscience?* She glanced at Marika, whose pleading eyes spoke for everyone in the train car. *Make this better for us*, they begged. *Or, if you can't make it better, please don't make it worse.*

Still staring at the guard, she said, "Thank you, Herr . . ."

"Seidl. Siegfried Seidl. It is my honor." He bowed deeply this time, holding the revolver against his chest as he leaned forward. When he rose, his face had morphed into stone. He turned away from her to face the car's occupants. "Disembark! Take all of your belongings with you. Upon exiting the train, queue up, and place your bags in front of you. Do not speak unless spoken to. Is that clear?"

Ursula glanced at the frightened passengers, who nodded in unison. Seidl turned back to her and smiled. He leaned toward her and whispered, "I know that you are Jewish, but I find myself wanting to pretend that you are not."

Ursula stared at the floor, not wanting to cause any more trouble. She remained silent as passengers filed past, throwing various looks her way— anger, jealousy, disgust, sympathy. When the car was empty, Seidl's large blue eyes took on a look of deep concern. "They really hurt you. The men on the ship."

Ursula looked away. *He knows about the men on the ship.* "I'm fine."

Seidl cupped her face in his left hand. "Let us see the doctor about your nose. Perhaps he can straighten it, at the very least. You must be in a lot of pain."

Ursula quickly shook her head, the effort causing her to lose her balance. She fell against Seidl but immediately pulled away. "I'm fine."

"Where are your bags?" Seidl examined the area where Ursula had been sitting.

Ursula arched a brow and immediately regretted it as pain shot through her swollen eye. "The men who attacked me didn't allow me time to pack a bag."

Seidl acknowledged her sarcastic comment with a half smile. "I had been warned that you are a lot to handle, but you should know, Fräulein Becker, that I want your stay in Terezín to be a good one. You could have been sent elsewhere. You've been given a gift by being sent here instead of Birkenau, for example. Plus, there are several other musicians already in the ghetto, and I know more will be arriving in the coming weeks." He became suddenly serious. "But your happiness depends on how well you obey the rules. You saw what happened when the boy spoke out of turn, so please pay attention and don't take risks, especially with other people's lives."

Ursula's eyes filled with tears at the reminder of her role in Markus Appel's death. She glanced at his young body, slumped against the seat, a perfectly round hole in the center of his smooth forehead. A blond cowlick sprouted atop the wound, as if the force of the impact had blown the boy's hair aloft. A lone drop of blood creeped slowly toward his vacant green eyes as they stared past her. His mouth lay slack and open. *You did this,* he whispered in her mind.

"Did you hear me? Do you understand?"

Ursula found herself nodding dumbly, realizing that she had crossed the invisible line from physical freedom to prisoner. When the Nazis had imposed increasingly strict sanctions on the Jews in Berlin, she had felt stifled and cheated out of what should have rightfully been hers. But this was a different matter altogether.

"Good. I was also told that you are extremely bright. I see that to be true."

A guard stepped onto the train and saluted. "Heil Hitler, Commandant!"

"Heil Hitler. Clean up this mess," Seidl said, waving dismissively towards Markus' body.

"Right away, sir!" The young man vanished.

"So, you are in charge here?" Ursula asked.

"I am."

Ursula glanced out the window at the mass of people awaiting instructions. "What is this place?"

"This is our last stop before Theresienstadt, or Terezín for short. It is a spa town."

Before she could stop herself, Ursula rolled her eyes. Seidl caught the gesture and shook his head. She dropped her gaze. "That is exactly what you must avoid, Fräulein, if you want to remain happy here."

"Forgive me. I'm tired."

"As I was saying, Terezín is home to a number of older Czech Jews and German Jews who served their country with honor in the Great War. We also offer respite to Jews who hold artistic places of honor in the Reich, such as yourself."

"Artistic places of honor?"

"Yes. In addition to you, we house several musicians and artists. Viktor Ullmann, Bedrich Fritta, Leo Haas. There are more, but that should give you an idea of the company you will be keeping. Shall we?" Commandant Seidl stepped aside and swept his arm forward, indicating Ursula should exit the train.

Lifting her chin, she folded her arms across her chest and climbed down the four steps onto the packed earth. She was still dressed in the outfit she'd been wearing when she was kidnapped. The air had changed dramatically during their long voyage. The sun was setting and with it came a wind that seeped through her thin dress. Within seconds she was shivering.

Seidl took no notice as he stood in front of the crowd.

"You will walk the rest of the way. Take only what you can carry for two and a half kilometers."

Sharp intakes of breath were followed by murmurs. Clearly the travelers hadn't been informed of the long trek ahead of time.

"Forgive me, sir," an elderly man said, "but I cannot walk that far, and certainly not with my suitcase."

Seidl shook his head. "You will walk that far or die along the way. It comes down to how much you value your life. As for carrying your belongings, that is your decision."

Another woman spoke. "We had been told that our luggage would be sent from our homes. If I leave my suitcase here, will it arrive later as well?"

Seidl smiled. "Absolutely."

The woman nodded. Ursula wondered how she could believe a man who belittled them as he spoke, a man who had just murdered a boy in cold blood. She also wondered if the woman's suitcase contained an overcoat that she might borrow for their walk.

Seidl winked at Ursula, then turned to the crowd. "Everyone form a queue and start walking. Anyone who falls behind will be shot."

28

Ursula took her place at the end of the line.

"No, Fräulein, you will drive with me. My car is there." Seidl pointed to a black sedan with Nazi flags on the front fenders.

The crowd turned to her and she blushed, embarrassed to be singled out for special treatment. "Thank you, but I prefer to walk."

He closed the distance between them in three strides. His face was impassive, but his eyes burned. She wondered if he was going to strike her. She forced a smile and spoke earnestly. "If you would graciously permit me to walk."

He held her eyes, gauging her sincerity. His consternation, which had spiked so rapidly, abated just as quickly. "I will allow it." He turned and marched to his car while the stunned crowd started the long walk.

One kilometer into their trek the sun gave up and fell behind the horizon, throwing shadows on ash trees that lined the narrow dirt road. If it weren't for the chill and Ursula's blistered feet, she might have been able to better enjoy the serene beauty of the stark landscape. The budding limbs of deciduous trees jutted from their trunks at complicated angles and appeared to Ursula as exquisite pieces of art yet to be captured on canvas. Such had her brain decided to attend to the current situation, heretofore simply unimaginable, in order to maintain some semblance of normalcy and order. "Find beauty in chaos," her mother had instructed when she was stymied by a particularly challenging piece of music. *And this*, Ursula thought as she evaluated the bedraggled walking group, *is chaos*.

Early into their walk, Ursula had offered to carry a woman's luggage in return for borrowing an overcoat. She had flatly denied Ursula's request. Marika had come to the rescue and had negotiated with the woman on Ursula's behalf. In exchange for the coat, Marika had offered a knitted scarf. The woman had begrudgingly agreed but remained close to Ursula throughout the journey, perhaps afraid that she would abscond with her jacket.

Ursula turned up the collar and pulled the coat tighter as she evaluated the confined path on which they walked. The road, if one could call it that, was wide enough for only one car to travel, leading her to believe that it had originally been a horse path. The forest on either side was vast, but the trees were diffuse, thereby disallowing any thought of escape and concealment.

Besides, she had no idea where they were and no way to return to Hamburg. Even if she were successful in returning, Willy and Otto were on a ship to England and may not even realize that she's missing. Ursula's heart galloped as she imagined her father's concern for her safety. She briefly closed her eyes and sent him a mental message that she was alive.

A conversation between two prisoners discussing the history of their destination caught her attention. She opened her eyes and decided to focus on the two men. The more she knew in advance of their arrival, the better. Plus, distraction was a blessing when one felt powerless.

"In the late eighteenth century, a fortress named Theresienstadt was constructed that ended up being used as a prison in the Great War. After the war, a town called Terezín sprouted within the fort's walls in which ethnic Germans and Czechs successfully cohabitated. But when the Great Depression occurred and German rhetoric became more patriotic, some Germans wanted Terezín returned to Germany. When Terezín and its surrounding land came under German rule once more in the Munich Agreement, ethnic Germans wasted no time in welcoming the Nazis. Even after the Nazi invasion, however, German-speaking Czechs continued to live in Terezín, thereby furthering the rumors that living there would be enjoyable."

"So, we will be safe?" a woman asked the historian.

"We should be. I understand there are many Jews from the Protectorate of Bohemia and Moravia already living there, people of considerable means who live in housing commensurate to what they left behind. Otherwise, why would the Nazis have asked us for so much money in advance?"

Ursula shook her head, angered by the desperation that had caused rational, reasonable people to abandon their homes and offer their life savings in a hopeless quid pro quo for their lives. She didn't fault them. Just the opposite. She applauded their pluckiness. What infuriated her is she knew that their efforts would probably be fruitless. What sickened her was the power that Hitler held over people whose only crime was having been born into a Jewish family.

"How are you doing?" Marika asked.

Unwilling to burden Marika with her mental musings, Ursula focused on her most glaring physical impairment. "My feet feel as if they will disintegrate into nothing."

Marika glanced at her high-heeled shoes. "Probably not the best choice for walking, my dear."

"Yes, well, I certainly didn't know I would be walking so far, did I?" Ursula shot back.

"It could be worse, Ursula."

Ursula cut her eyes toward Marika, a sharp retort at the ready, but noted the sadness in her new friend's gaze. She surmised that Marika was thinking about her daughter, so she put her arm around Marika's shoulders and pulled her close. "You're correct, Marika. It could be much worse. Thank you for your kindness, for taking care of me when I was completely alone."

Marika smiled and waved her hand. "It was nothing."

A man ahead of them stumbled. He attempted to rise but fell again. One of the two soldiers accompanying them appeared at his side. "What is it?" he asked.

"My ankle."

"Can you walk?"

"I'm sure that I can." He managed to stand but dropped when he put weight on his right leg. The man sighed deeply. "I cannot walk."

The soldier's mouth twitched. "What's your name?"

The elderly man straightened and lifted his chin. He looked to be about seventy years old, and he carried himself with pride and authority. His voice was strong and resonant. "Leo Baeck."

The soldier turned to his colleague. "Check the list." The second guard opened a small black notebook and perused its contents, then nodded. The main guard examined the tired group and pointed to two prisoners who looked to be about fifty. "You two. Get over here and carry this man. We have approximately one kilometer remaining." The guards walked away briskly, returning to their positions amidst the queue.

"What just happened?" Ursula asked.

"That's Leo Baeck, a well-known rabbi and hero from the Great War. His name must have been in that notebook. Perhaps it's a list of Jews who shouldn't be killed."

Ursula looked disbelievingly at Marika.

"I bet your name is in that notebook, Ursula."

Before Ursula could respond, Marika continued. "I bet that my name is not."

"Don't say that. Your husband has been invaluable, has he not? You told me that he came several weeks ahead of you to prepare the housing for us."

Marika's eyes glistened. "That's true."

"Don't worry, Marika. You and I will take care of each other."

Marika turned to face her. "And your Willy will speak to his uncle and return from England to fetch you and whisk you away to live happily ever after."

Marika's words saddened Ursula to her core. *How could Willy possibly find me in this wilderness?* But she knew Marika was trying to lighten the mood, so she smiled to appease her worry.

They continued to walk in silence until, forty excruciating minutes later, Terezín came into view. Anticipating warmth and an end to their trek, the group moved faster and started chatting excitedly. The guards didn't discourage the banter and even engaged in small talk with the first in line, a relatively young man Ursula recognized as a famous artist from Berlin.

Ursula looked up as they approached the main gate. She read the words etched in iron.

ARBEIT MACHT FREI

"What do you suppose that means?"

Marika glanced up. "Work sets you free."

"I know what it says, but what does it *mean?*"

Marika shrugged. "As long as there's a hot meal and a comfortable bed, I don't care what it means."

They passed through the gate, and the group slowed its pace. Tension crept into Ursula's shoulders as she examined her new home. Sidewalks lined the cobblestone street, which was wide enough to accommodate two cars. Large, beige buildings with tall windows stood on either side, and as she scanned the second floor of the building on her left, a woman with a haunted visage stared back at her. Ursula couldn't pull her gaze away from the gaunt woman whose vacant eyes reflected the ghetto's lack of color. She whirled around to see ten armed SS men block the path they'd just taken, and she was overwhelmed with a sudden, ridiculous urge to run. Tossing aside all logic, she quickly searched the area for a hiding place, but everywhere she looked she saw guards with guns. Panicking, she turned to Marika, but her companion, like everyone else in their convoy, had sunk to the sidewalk to rest as they leaned against their meager possessions. With an anguish she hadn't known possible, the weight of a thousand empty souls bore down on Ursula, and she realized with dismal certainty that she'd entered Hell. *They're sheep being led to slaughter, and they're so grateful for a rest that they ignore the captivity that stares them in the face.*

"Fräulein?" Ursula spun around to find Commandant Seidl at her side, his hand on her elbow. "Did you enjoy your stroll?"

Ursula remained silent.

"It's this way to the physician's office. I shall escort you."

Ursula stared at his hand on her arm. She wanted to strike him. She wanted to steal his gun and shoot him. "No thank you, Herr Commandant."

Seidl's eyes became hard and he leaned toward her. "Now what kind of gentleman would I be if I allowed a beautiful woman to be scarred by the barbaric actions of some thugs. Follow me." He walked away, obviously expecting Ursula to follow him. Desperate, she glanced at Marika, who nodded and inclined her head in the direction he had taken.

Ursula closed her fingers around Willy's locket and envisioned him: his smile, his embrace, his laughter, his warm eyes. A voice in her head whispered so quietly that she strained to hear it.

Survive. Live to see another day.

Pushing all unproductive thoughts aside, she took a deep breath and followed Seidl, who had disappeared around a corner. As she hurried to catch up, a woman in a mink coat mumbled something. Ursula stopped. "Were you speaking to me?"

The elderly woman smiled sadly. "He's doing you a favor."

Ursula shook her head. "Who?"

The woman glanced toward Seidl, whose pace had not slowed. "He's doing you a favor and will expect something in return. They always do." Ursula's mind wandered to her father's similar warning. Although he had been describing Hitler, Otto's words mimicked the woman's perilous prediction. *"A man like that always expects something in return for a favor. He will want loyalty. And loyalty can be deadly."*

29

Willy alerted the captain that Ursula was missing, and the *Drottningholm*'s small security team performed a thorough inspection of the ship. They found no sign of Ursula, save the blood smear and lipstick smudge that Willy had originally discovered. Believing that someone might have heard a commotion, Willy requested that they question passengers whose cabins bordered the telephone room, but the captain reiterated the points that Anna had made. How was Willy sure that the bloody smear was Ursula's? And, as luck would have it, the captain's wife wore the same shade of lipstick as the smudge. Just for good measure, the captain added, how did Willy know that Ursula had not changed her mind and walked off the ship of her own volition? At that point, Willy had explained who Ursula was and how she'd angered the Führer, then pleaded with the captain to return the ship to Hamburg. By the end of the tale, the captain agreed that Ursula had most likely been kidnapped but had informed Willy that by law he was not allowed to return the ship to its port of embarkation.

"So, what are my options?" Willy asked, exasperated.

"When we arrive in England, use every possible connection you have to put pressure on your uncle to return Miss Becker."

Willy had stormed off in frustration and had spent the rest of the voyage awaiting contact from his uncle and calming Otto, neither of which had been successful. Otto, initially ecstatic about the voyage, had turned morose upon hearing of Ursula's disappearance. He kept to his stateroom and resisted any attempt to draw him out. Willy never heard from Hitler and questioned whether Anna had actually delivered the message. Two more ship-to-shore telephone calls had been equally as unsuccessful, one of them failing to go through and the other resulting in another unreturned message.

Willy and Otto arrived in Southampton, England, and presented their landing cards at the custom house, where—due to his surname—Willy received an icy stare from the clerk as he stamped his documents. The clerk then questioned Otto as to why he was traveling with Willy, and Otto broke down sobbing. Otto's emotional breakdown, combined with Willy's last name, led to them being detained for questioning.

The Southampton police ushered them into a small, gray room where they peppered Otto with questions that Willy translated into German. Otto answered in fits and starts, vacillating between grief and anger. As the officers gained an understanding of what had transpired, they became sympathetic and ended the interview by wishing Otto "all the luck in the world" in finding his daughter. The men exchanged sad glances with Willy and told him that if he ever needed anything, to call and ask for them personally.

"That Hitler is a real pisser, isn't he? No offense, sir. I know he's your uncle and all."

Willy waved the comment away. "No offense taken, my good man. I hate my uncle. In fact, when all of this is said and done, I believe that I'll write a book about why I detest him so much."

The men had a chuckle at that, then walked Willy and Otto to the Southampton train station, where they purchased two one-way tickets to London. Several hours later Willy yawned and stretched, then shook Otto awake as the train pulled into the station. Otto looked out the window and blinked several times while Willy collected their belongings.

"It is so large," Otto marveled.

"What? The train station? Wait until you see the city, Herr Becker."

Otto stood and placed his hand on Willy's shoulder. "Willy, I believe that the time has come for you to call me Otto." The older man became teary and then gathered Willy for a hug. Willy returned the embrace and whispered, "Upon my honor, Otto, I *will* find Ursula and return her to both of us."

When Otto withdrew, he was crying openly. "I am afraid it might be too late, Willy. Both of my daughters are lost to me. They might be alive, but I cannot access either of them. It's enough to break an old man's heart."

Willy leaned close and gripped Otto's arms. "Listen to me! I will find Ursula and bring her home."

Otto's beseeching look was so desperate, so needy, that Willy had to turn away. "Follow me, Otto."

The two men exited the dark train station to discover a brilliant summer day. Cars, buses, and taxicabs whizzed past, crammed with businessmen rushing to meetings and women carrying colorful shopping bags. Otto started to cross the street but stopped when he spotted a red, double-decker bus. He stared, open-mouthed.

"What is that?"

Willy smiled. "It's a bus with two levels."

"Why?" Otto asked as his eyes traced its path down the road.

Willy placed his hand on Otto's back to keep him walking. "Because some of our streets are so narrow that a longer bus cannot negotiate the turns. So, a Parisian came up with the idea of a shorter bus that has two levels."

"Miraculous," Otto breathed.

Willy's pulse quickened as they approached his mother's house. He had been gone for several years and was excited to see her. "Two more blocks, Otto. Can you make it?"

Otto looked offended. "Of course I can."

Willy glanced at Otto's red face. "How about I take your suitcases?" Without waiting for a reply, Willy took the bags and continued walking. As they rounded the final corner, Willy smiled broadly. "Here we are!"

They stopped in front of a smart, brick house that boasted window boxes filled with brilliant flowers. A gardenia wreath graced the front door, which burst open with such gusto it banged against the inside wall. Bridget Hitler stood there beaming, an apron tied around her ample waist. Her hands flew to her rosy cheeks. "I was staring out the window, waiting, when I saw a striking young man round the bend. As I live and breathe. William!" She rushed down the stairs and wrapped her arms around her only child. "Let me look at you!" She held Willy at arm's length and evaluated him. "You look very thin, young man. Very thin. Oh! Who might this handsome devil be?"

Otto removed his hat and smoothed his sparse hair. He spoke in broken and heavily accented English. "Hello, Madame Hitler. I am Otto Becker. I am pleased of make to my acquaintance."

Bridget drew herself up to her full five-foot-three frame and smiled up at Otto. "Hello, Mr. Becker. I am Bridget Hitler and I, too, am pleased to make your acquaintance." Otto grinned, incredibly proud that he had made himself understood in a language so foreign to his tongue.

"Let's get you inside for a good meal and some rest."

Bridget and Willy led Otto to his bedroom and then showed him the bathroom in the upstairs hallway. A buzzer sounded and Bridget excused herself to finish preparing tea. When she had gone, Otto spoke in German. "Only one person lives in such a large home, Willy?"

Willy reminded him that there used to be three people living there. "But then my father went to Europe on business and remained in Germany during the Great War. Initially he couldn't get out of the country and then, when he finally could, he no longer wanted to. So, it's been Mum and me for some time. That's why I went to Germany, Otto, to see my father and his brother, Uncle Alf. Unfortunately, neither relationship worked out."

"Your mother must have missed you while you were away."

"She did, but she was so pleased when she heard that I'd met Ursula. And she was so excited to meet her—" Willy's voice failed him, caught off guard by a rush of emotion.

"Boys, tea!" Bridget called from downstairs.

Otto squeezed Willy's shoulder and set his mouth. "As you said, Willy, you will bring her home."

They returned downstairs to find the dining room table covered in tasty tidbits: cream cheese and cucumber sandwiches, butter pecan crumpets, deviled eggs and Battenberg cake, scones with raspberry cream, and, of course, tea. Otto clapped his hands together and laughed. "Danke, Frau Hitler!"

After the men had eaten their fill, Bridget held Willy's gaze. "Now, son, tell me what on God's green Earth has happened."

Willy had sent Bridget a telegram ahead of their arrival that outlined the gist of Ursula's kidnapping, but as he filled in the details, Bridget removed a hankie from her sleeve and wiped her eyes. Willy paused every so often and translated for Otto, whose eyes glazed over as Willy spoke.

"So, what will you do now?"

"I've been thinking about that." Willy's eyes darted from his mother to the floor and back again.

"What is it? William?" Bridget grabbed Willy's chin and forced him to look at her. "Tell me."

"Well, I was wondering if we might ask Da to intervene on Ursula's behalf."

Bridget released Willy's chin and leaned back in her chair. Her lips became a thin line. Sensing tension, Otto stopped eating and folded his hands in his lap.

"We?" she asked.

"Well . . . you."

Bridget crossed her arms. "Why can't you ask? Why does it have to be me?"

Willy leaned forward. "You know why, Mum. When I went to Germany seeking a relationship with Da he told me, in no uncertain terms, that he didn't want to know me . . . in any capacity. Given that, you can't expect me to ask him for help."

Bridget's consternation was evident as she sought a flaw in his logic. "What do you think your Da could do to help?"

"I'm not sure, but we have to try."

"Son, I know that Adolf and your Da are close, but—"

"Mum, please."

Bridget leaned forward and took Willy's hand. "You were only three years old when he left us to marry and raise another family in Germany. He's your father in name only."

"Yes, I know. He made that very clear when I was in Germany, which is another reason that the request can't come from me. But you had a relationship with him. You loved him once, and from what you've told me, he loved you too."

Bridget nodded her head and smiled sadly. "You're not wrong, but ... do you know why I didn't accompany him to Germany in 1914?"

Willy blinked. "You told me it was because you didn't want to leave your parents."

Bridget nodded her head. "That's what I said, but it wasn't true." She sighed deeply. "I adored your father, but it turns out he'd been lying to me since the first day I met him. I refused to go with him to Germany because it was a chance for us to escape."

Willy's eyebrows knitted. "What are you talking about, Mum? What do you mean?"

Bridget removed her hand and picked at a thumbnail. She licked her lips and then swallowed. "He was beating us, Willy. Do you not remember?" She shook her head. "You were so little. How could you remember? Perhaps it's better that you don't." She started to cry and stood, then turned away from him. "He hit you so badly that you had a bruise on your cheek for three weeks. I lied to neighbors and said that you'd fallen down the stairs." She wiped her eyes and turned around to face him. Her tone hardened as she continued. "Based on the craziness that's happening now in Germany, I'm convinced that insanity and abuse runs in the Hitler blood." She retook her seat and put her hands on either side of his face. "Except for you, my dear, sweet boy. I don't know what I did to deserve such a blessing, but every night I get on my knees and thank the Lord for giving me such a kind, intelligent child. You love Ursula, I know that, and you're desperate to find her." Bridget paused, tears running down her face. "But please don't make me contact that animal of a man."

Willy took hold of his mother's hands and gently removed them from his face. He kissed each one and then held them to his chest. "You know how much I love you, Mum, and how incredibly grateful I am for everything you've done for me. But I have to find her. I'll do whatever it takes to make that happen. Do you understand?"

Bridget examined her son's eyes. "I wonder ..."

"What?"

She smiled through her tears. "I wonder what my life might have been like if I had married someone of your character, someone whose soul was linked so completely to mine. That's the way you feel about Ursula, isn't it?"

"It is. I would die for her."

Bridget traced Willy's cheek with her thumb. "Please don't say that, Willy. It's bad luck."

"But I mean it—"

She held up her hand. "I know, son. I know you mean it." She sighed heavily. "Give me some time. I'll think about contacting your father."

January 1943

3 0

The promise of a spa town had shriveled when the women and men were separated shortly after their arrival. Though they'd protested, husbands and wives quickly acquiesced when SS guards wielded their weapons. The men were led away to another building while the women were herded into Dresden barracks and told to find sleeping accommodations among already overcrowded conditions. Every time Ursula tried to stake a claim, someone would appear and say, "taken" loudly enough that she didn't challenge her. She finally secured a spot under a window and placed her thin burlap mattress on the floor. Since she'd arrived seven months ago, new train tracks had been erected by prisoners, allowing direct access to the ghetto. Many more transports had appeared, making a crowded situation even worse.

In her first week of confinement, she had expected Willy to use his relationship to the Führer to rescue her from Terezín. But when that hadn't happened, she decided that he was probably negotiating with his uncle in order to free her. As more time passed, she had come to terms with the fact that, if Willy *had* tried to negotiate, he had failed. She was on her own. On more than one occasion she had become overwhelmed at the notion and blamed him for not saving her. But in other moments she was honest with herself and acknowledged with humble embarrassment that her own foolish actions had caused her current predicament.

The days turned to weeks, then months, and Ursula began to let go of the notion that Willy could free her. She settled into a routine in which some days flew by while others crawled. Her attitude was always linked to the weather and the guards' moods. She had been assigned to work in the kitchen and looked forward to it on frigid days like today.

Despite the bone-chilling temperature, Ursula stepped outside Dresden. She reached under her layers of clothing and fondled Willy's locket that lay against her skin. The gold had absorbed her body heat and warmed her fingers. She imagined Willy standing next to her, gathering her in his arms and hugging her tightly. She closed her eyes and pictured his handsome face. She felt the brush of his lips against her ear as he whispered, "I love you." If she focused hard enough, she could actually conjure his sincere blue eyes. Willy was never far from her mind, even though her chest physically ached each time she thought of him.

Ursula breathed deeply. Glacial air rushed into her nasal cavity and leeched moisture from the membranes, causing burning pain and a headache. Her nose had healed well after having been set, but the bridge now sported a bump, a result of the bone not melding together precisely. The doctor had patronizingly referred to her healed nose as a "Jewish beak." She didn't mind, however, as it resembled Otto's, and the thought made her feel connected to him.

"Ursula, what are you doing out here? It's freezing."

Ursula turned to find Marika standing next to her. "It's almost as cold inside the barracks, Marika."

"Well, at least wear your scarf!" Marika huffed as she bundled Ursula in the gray, handmade scarf she'd knitted for her. Ursula smiled and snuggled her chin and nose into the wool. Because Ursula had arrived without a suitcase or additional clothing, Marika had rallied the women in Dresden to clothe her for the winter. They had balked at first, unwilling to give away the meager possessions they'd been allowed to keep, but as Marika continued to press Ursula's case, calling her contribution to the arts a "bright light in an otherwise dark landscape," the women had relented and begrudgingly handed over some items.

"You know that I couldn't survive here without you," Ursula commented. Marika leaned into her friend. "You're my new Ursula. I know that my daughter is gone, but God sent you to me. Not to replace my daughter, but to remind me that I still matter."

Ursula turned to face her. "You will *always* matter, Marika. No matter what happens, *you matter*."

Marika nodded, her face a mask of sadness. "Did you hear what happened to Herr Abendroth?"

Ursula stomped her clogged feet to keep warm. "No."

"Seidl told him to shine his boots and he refused."

Ursula shook her head. "What was he thinking?"

Marika cupped her hands and blew into them. "I don't know."

"So, what happened to him?"

"Seidl ordered him again to shine his boots and he spat on them, so he's now in the Little Fortress. A small cell with no heat, no light, no toilet. If there are others in there, then he might survive. Otherwise, he'll freeze to death."

Ursula considered why someone would risk his life over something as trivial as shining a pair of boots. "Perhaps it was not his boots Seidl wanted shined, Marika."

The older woman turned quickly. "You don't mean . . ." Her words fell away with the light snow that drifted lazily to the ground.

Ursula shrugged. "Who knows what the commandant likes to do in his spare time."

Marika blushed at the implication.

"Marika, I'm kidding. But I find it difficult to believe that someone would risk his life over a pair of boots."

Marika was quiet a moment. "What would you have done, Ursula?"

"I would have shined his boots."

"No. I mean the other thing. If you were faced with that choice, what would you do?"

Ursula scratched her head and shook out her long hair. "I don't know. Is my life worth . . . shining an arrogant man's boots?" She thought a moment and watched a guard in the distance. He was hassling an inmate who carried a large, iron pot toward the kitchen. She scratched her head again. "I believe I've contracted lice, Marika. The itching is intolerable."

"Don't let the guards know or they'll shave your head."

A woman named Eva appeared next to them, her coat bundled tightly against the cold. She held out her hand to Ursula. "Take this," she said.

An exquisite, ivory, carved comb with very narrow teeth lay on Eva's palm. "It was my mother's, but I want you to have it."

Ursula looked at the young woman, whom she knew had recently miscarried a child. The doctors had refused to treat her, and she had almost bled to death. "Oh, no, Eva. Thank you but I couldn't take it."

Eva smiled and placed the comb in the pocket of Ursula's coat. "I saw you scratching from the window. You need it more than I do."

Ursula felt a surge of warmth for Eva's kindness. She had never before had to rely on the generosity of others and initially had felt ashamed to accept charity. But as time passed, she had come to realize that her survival was linked to those around her, and theirs to her. She had kept to herself for the most part, but as stories spread about her antagonistic relationship with Hitler, people started treating her with respect and admiration. She had become a sort of folk hero in the ghetto.

In return for their gracious generosity, Ursula offered imaginary escape through storytelling. She would plant herself atop the wooden bunks, surrounded by women and children who huddled in ragged blankets, and recite the storylines of operas, often bursting into quiet song to emphasize the emotion the character was feeling.

Before coming to Terezín, she thought she understood the impact her performances had on people, but to perform in close proximity to her listeners, to see their immediate reactions, made her giddy. She reveled in transporting her audience to another place where the beds were soft and food plentiful, where they could be warm and surrounded by loved ones, if only for a few moments. She was able to momentarily forget that her food intake that day had been a bowl of turnip soup, and that she had not washed properly since her arrival. Her stories were all she had to offer, and she gained as much joy from it as her audience did, if not more.

"Thank you, Eva. That's very kind. I'll cherish it."

Ursula exhaled, watching her warm breath cloud in the wintry air. She bounced up and down to stay warm as a Czech guard named Edvard Svoboda approached them.

"What are you doing? You three know that you shouldn't be out here alone. You could be punished."

Ursula smiled. "Hello, Captain. We needed a respite from the stench and the bedbugs."

He looked around to ensure that they were not being watched, then whispered, "Get inside, Ursula, before you get in trouble!"

"Fine. We'll go. But first, tell me, did you enjoy the story last evening?"

The gendarme blushed.

"I saw you there, Edvard Svoboda. Right outside the door of our cramped quarters. You are captain of the guards, but you are not a Nazi. You are a simple Czech policeman who was recruited into this nightmare. You are also, I now know, a lover of opera and good stories. I shall remember that."

Svoboda suppressed a smile, then stood straighter, filling out his uniform. He became serious. "I am also, as you stated, captain of the guards, in charge of ensuring that prisoners are following the rules, and right now you are not. Get inside before I do something that I don't want to do."

Ursula held his gaze a moment longer. "As you wish."

The three women reentered the building, where the temperature was only slightly warmer. Ursula had never been so cold in her life and wondered if she should offer to start cooking detail early. Not only did the work break up the monotony of interminable gray winter days, but in the kitchen she could huddle over a steaming kettle while stirring the seemingly unending supply of tasteless beet and turnip soup.

She passed the bunkroom on the second floor and saw a group of young girls listening to a woman read aloud. Ursula stopped and leaned against the doorway, drawn in by the reader's melodious voice. She glanced at the book's cover, *Mendel Rosenbusch: Tales for Jewish Children* by Ilse Weber, and smiled as the young audience laughed and squealed. The woman finished the story, closed the book, and stared at Ursula, causing all heads to swivel towards her.

Ursula stepped into the room. "Hello. I enjoyed your reading."

"Thank you."

Ursula smiled. "I am—"

"I know who you are. It's my pleasure. My name is Ilse Weber."

Ursula paused and glanced at the book. "You're the author of this book?"

"Yes. It's about an old man named Mendel who lives behind the synagogue and his positive interactions with the town's children."

"You must be very talented."

"As are you."

"It strikes me that there are many talented people in Terezín."

"That's true."

"I suppose we're the fortunate ones."

Ilse tilted her head. "How so?"

"My understanding is the camps farther east are much worse than this," Ursula stated matter-of-factly.

Ilse quickly turned to the children. "Girls, please chat among yourselves while Fräulein Becker and I step outside."

As soon as the two women retired to the hallway, Ilse faced Ursula. "You mustn't speak like that in front of the children, Ursula. Their spirits have not yet broken and it's our job to keep them aloft as long as we can. They are our future."

Ursula felt her cheeks get hot. She glanced at the children, who reenacted a scene from Ilse's book. "Of course. My apologies."

Ilse stared hard at Ursula and then shifted her gaze. "I'm sorry if I spoke harshly. It's just that I haven't seen my husband or son since our arrival. I worry about them."

"I'm sorry. They're in the ghetto?"

"My husband is in the men's barracks and works in the sluice, organizing luggage from new arrivals, but I haven't seen him."

"Why not?"

"I work at the hospital in the evenings, and that's usually when trains arrive. I only know about his work because a note was smuggled to me from another man who stayed behind to clean."

"And your son?"

"He's in the children's house."

"How is it that we've not met before?"

"I stay across the compound in Hamburg barracks. I convinced Edvard Svoboda to let me entertain the children."

Ursula's mouth dropped. "He allows you to read a Jewish book?"

Ilse laughed. "Of course not. I told him that I was making up stories for the children. I hid the book in my undergarments."

"You took a big risk, Ilse."

"I had to. The children must learn about their heritage."

Ursula's eyes flitted toward the girls.

"Are you Jewish, Ursula?"

Ursula shook her head quickly. "No. I'm here because I angered the Führer."

Ilse pulled away, a look of confusion on her face. "Oh. I had heard that you're Jewish."

"Well, I'm not."

Ilse considered her.

Ursula rolled her eyes. "On paper I'm Jewish. I'm a mischling of the second degree."

Ilse nodded knowingly. "Ah. I see." She smiled. "It's not a disease, you know."

"What?"

"Being Jewish. It's not a disease. In fact, it's wonderful. You should try it sometime." She squeezed Ursula's hand and reentered the room to excited squeals from the children.

Ursula observed from the doorway as Ilse gathered the girls around her once more. In this freezing room, with crumbling walls and wooden planks for beds, Ilse had created a sense of family when hers had gone missing. She had created an atmosphere of celebration for children who were growing very thin from lack of food. As she watched, Ursula saw the girls huddle together, arms around each other's waists, ensuring that each person was as warm as possible.

She marveled at their ability to find joy where there should be nothing but fear and mistrust. She realized how much time she had wasted in waiting for Willy to save her when all the while she'd been surrounded by people who wanted to help. She had accepted charity from others but had not reached out to truly befriend anyone except Marika. Even her storytelling was more about herself than anyone to whom she was speaking. A true sense of community existed within the prison that could potentially provide solace, if only she opened her heart and mind to it.

Movement in the far-right corner of the room caught her eye. Curious, Ursula approached the bunk and noted only a pile of threadbare blankets. Thinking it must have been a rat, she turned to leave when the pile moved again. She glanced at the children as they laughed at something Ilse had said. She didn't want the girls sleeping with a rat, so she rustled the covers to scare the rodent into exiting. Instead, it was Ursula who was startled as a small body popped out from the tangle of dirty blankets.

31

Months had passed and Bridget had not yet agreed to contact Willy's father, Alois. Willy had approached her several times asking if she'd come to a decision, but each time she would hold up her hand to silence him. He was coming to understand how complicated his parents' relationship was and how it had damaged his mother. He scolded himself for being so impatient, but Ursula remained foremost in his mind, especially at night when she was stomped to death by SS guards in his nightmares. At times his impatience boiled over and anger burst forth, demolishing everything in its path. Otto would appear and speak soothingly in German, reminding him that Ursula was a fighter. She would never give up on herself or him. His words calmed Willy yet added to the guilt he felt at his helplessness.

He had tried to contact his uncle directly several more times. Telephone calls to Germany were unthinkable because of the war, and his letters returned to him, never having made it out of England. He had reached out to the prime minister's office seeking diplomatic assistance. His calls went unreturned. He had even contacted the American Embassy in London. They had, at least, spoken with him, but had declined to aid his efforts to find Ursula. After seven months of desperate attempts to obtain help, he was no closer to finding her.

One evening Willy came downstairs to find Bridget on her knees in front of the fire grate, her fingers worrying her rosary. Willy paused on the stairs, watching his mother pray. He had been raised Catholic but hadn't been to church in several years.

Bridget turned. "Hello, William."

"Hi, Mum. I didn't mean to interrupt. Here, let me help you up."

He crossed to her, took her hand, and hoisted her from the floor. She sat heavily on the overstuffed couch and tucked her rosary in her apron pocket. They sat quietly, staring into the flames of the fire that warmed the small parlor.

"You might want to try it, Willy."

"Praying? I don't think so, Mum."

"He hears you."

Willy continued to gaze into the flames. "I hope I don't offend you, Mum, but I gave up on God a long time ago."

"He'll never give up on you, son," she stated quietly.

Willy shook his head. "What kind of god allows men to mutilate and kill? What type of god allows children to be kicked to death in the streets?"

Bridget nodded. A stern frown was etched in the lines around her mouth. "Free will is a powerful force, Willy. If men choose badly, there will be consequences."

"Really, Mum? Because I don't see Uncle Alf being held accountable."

"There will be a reckoning. Count on it."

Willy faced his mother. "What happens if this 'reckoning' doesn't come before Ursula is killed?"

"Actually, I—"

"You're not going to contact him, are you?" Willy demanded.

"I'm praying because—"

"Mum, Ursula is fighting for her life, if she's even still alive! She could be starving or freezing to death, and you're going to let a man like Alois Hitler bring you to your knees? Literally, bring you to your knees?" Willy pointed to the spot where Bridget had been kneeling.

"William, you need to understand—"

Willy grimaced and shook his head. "You raised me on your own. You were my rock growing up. You taught me right from wrong. Where's the mother who taught me never to look the other way, always to help a neighbor, to fight for what's right, despite the challenges?"

"She's right here, William! Listen, I sent—"

Willy stood quickly and shook his head. "I thought you were stronger than that. I'm disappointed." He grabbed his coat and ran out of the house, slamming the door behind him. He heard Bridget open the door as he sprinted down the sidewalk.

"William, come back! I need to tell you something!"

He ignored her and continued running, his hands jammed deeply in the pockets of his overcoat. He pace was manic, and he saw mothers pull their children close as he passed. He was so lost in thought that he'd covered several kilometers before stopping suddenly and looking around, not understanding how he'd arrived in front of Queen Victoria's Memorial in St. James Park. The sun hugged the horizon, and he popped his collar and tightened his coat against a light wind that had kicked up. Very few people milled about as he caught his breath and allowed his eyes to travel the length of the twenty-five-meter monument that celebrated England's beloved queen. A golden, winged Victory perched atop a globe stood at the highest point of the glorious marble structure. Directly underneath were personifications of Constancy and Courage. He turned his attention to a throned Queen Victoria flanked by Motherhood, Justice, and Truth. Willy looked past the memorial toward Buckingham Palace and realized how much he had missed England, its pomp and circumstance, its formality and long tradition of loyalty, the way the royals interacted with the national government to form a solid social foundation that assured care of its citizens. Decisions, for the most part, were fairly negotiated and benefited the people.

His troubled mind then turned to Germany and the autocracy his uncle had created. The people had allowed it to happen. *No*, he thought. They had *invited* it. Inch by excruciating inch they had offered Hitler unchecked power. And why? Because they were despondent. *Desperate people make rash decisions that might benefit them in the short term, but in the end, it's they who pay the highest price*, Willy thought.

Without realizing it, his feet started moving again. Before he understood where his mind had led his body, he was standing in front of Britain's seat of power—10 Downing Street.

Winston Churchill had been prime minister for two and a half years, voted into office after Neville Chamberlain failed to deliver on his promise of "peace in our time." Less than a year after Chamberlain negotiated the Munich Agreement with Germany, Hitler invaded Poland, drawing England into war. Then, after British forces failed to stop the Nazis from invading France, England's citizens decided that Chamberlain didn't exhibit the characteristics required of a wartime leader. Since taking office, Churchill had created a coalition consisting of various government factions whose united goal was to defeat Hitler. He had shown himself to be a true statesman, granting authority to his underlings, but never so arrogant as to ignore important details. He was proving himself to be the leader England required during this most dire period in its enduring history.

Willy felt pressure on his lower leg and looked down to find a tiger-striped cat negotiating a figure eight through his legs. It rubbed its head against his pants, and, despite his mood, he smiled. He leaned down and scooped up the cat, who donned a jaunty Union Jack bow tie around its neck.

"Well, don't you look sporting." In response, the cat rubbed its face against Willy's stubbled chin.

"I see you've found Munich Mouser."

Willy turned to find a fashionably dressed woman of about twenty-five gazing at him, her light eyes shaded by heavy lids. She wore a black fedora with mesh that cascaded over her right eye. Her head was tilted to the left, and Willy noted that she wore a half smile that played all the way into her eyes.

"More to the point, I believe that he's found me."

She walked forward slowly, a confident gait that landed her directly in front of him. Her height rivaled his own, and her meticulously styled, brunette hair curled gracefully around the hat's brim. Her half smile extended to a full grin as she stroked the feline's head. "He has a tendency to do that. Find people, I mean. You should know that he's an exceptional judge of character. Count yourself blessed to have been anointed by the prime minister's cat."

"This cat belongs to the prime minister?"

She tilted her head back and forth. "Well, technically he belongs to the former PM, but Mr. Churchill keeps him around."

"Why?"

She smiled. "Because not only does this little guy catch vermin, but the PM thinks that he helps to keep Nelson in check."

Willy chuckled. "And Nelson is . . ."

"Mr. Churchill's cat. The two have quite a rivalry going."

"Ah. I see. You seem to know a lot about it."

The woman's gloved hand found the pearl choker at her throat. "Well, I should hope so. I've worked as Mr. Churchill's secretary for almost two years. My name is Elizabeth Layton."

Willy stepped forward and took her hand in his. "William Patrick Hitler."

Willy felt the slightest change in her grip. But being the secretary of a politician, she was practiced in the art of public diplomacy and quickly regained her measured gaze and steady smile.

"Any relation?"

Willy swallowed. "He's my uncle."

Before she could respond, words poured forth from his mouth with an urgency that surprised him. "I hate him. You should know that. He's taken my fiancée and is holding her somewhere. It's a long story, but the gist of it is that she's Jewish and she angered my uncle." Willy looked at the number "10" on the shiny black door. "I'm not sure why I'm here but . . . I am." His shoulders sagged. "I'm sorry, Ms. Layton. I phoned but no one returned my calls. I suppose I was hoping that, if I showed up in person, I couldn't be ignored. You see, despite my surname, I'm one hundred percent English in spirit."

"I'm not ignoring you." She smiled. "Mr. Hitler, your surname is no fault of yours. You shouldn't act as such."

Willy felt a rush of gratitude for her benevolence.

"Now, as for your fiancée, Mr. Churchill isn't here. He's in French Morocco. Casablanca actually, meeting with President Roosevelt in an effort to map out future military strategy. He won't return until the twenty-fourth. I'm very sorry."

What did you really expect? he asked himself. "I understand."

"What's her name? Your fiancée?"

Willy came alive at her question. "Ursula Becker. I don't know where she's being held, but when the prime minister returns, perhaps he might—"

"Intervene?" She shook her head. "I don't mean to be indelicate, but do you know how many requests the PM's office receives on a daily basis related to finding loved ones who are missing? Hundreds. Literally hundreds. I'm sorry, but—"

"*Please*, Ms. Layton!" Willy rushed forward and gripped her hands. Her eyes widened. He released his hold and lowered his gaze, embarrassed at his outburst. "I'm so sorry. I didn't mean to scare you. I just don't know what else to do." He raked his fingers through his hair. "I feel like I'm losing my mind."

"You feel powerless."

"Yes."

"Then do something."

He looked up, confused. "I am doing something."

She looked at him with patient kindness. "It seems to me that you're going in circles and placing your faith in people with whom you have no relationship or control."

Willy didn't understand where she was going.

"Enlist."

"What?"

"Join the armed forces, Mr. Hitler. Fight for your fiancée's freedom, and for the freedom of the other victims who are being held captive by the Nazis. You *will* make a difference."

Willy blinked, then stared into the distance. *She's correct*, he thought. *I'm doing no good wallowing in self-pity. At least if I were fighting, I'd be closer to Ursula. I'd be shoulder to shoulder with people who hate Uncle Alf as much as I do.*

Willy's head started nodding so vigorously that he thought it might roll off his shoulders. "Yes! That's what I'll do. Right then . . . thanks so much!" Without thinking, he rushed forward and impulsively pulled Ms. Layton into an embrace. Realizing his gaffe, he immediately released her and apologized, but she laughed and said, "Oh, my!" as he sprinted away.

He felt exuberant, filled with renewed purpose as he ran through St. James Park. He stopped abruptly at Queen Victoria's statue and stared at the gold Winged Victory. Her majesty and dignity reminded him of Ursula. "Hold on, my darling. Help is coming," he whispered before continuing through Green Park. He marveled at the beauty of the Buckingham Palace Gardens, even in the dead of winter, then continued winding his way back to South Kensington, stopping only to purchase a bottle of champagne. He returned home forty-five minutes later and burst through the front door to find Bridget and Otto seated quietly together on the settee, drinking tea.

They both stood at his entrance. He breathed heavily and waved the bottle of champagne. "Good news!" Willy managed between ragged breaths. "I've decided to join the—"

Bridget held up an envelope.

"What's that?"

"I tried to tell you, but you ran out of here so quickly . . . I wrote Alois a letter several months ago. I didn't think it would make it through to him, but somehow it did."

"Why didn't you tell me you'd written him?"

Bridget grimaced. "Perhaps I should have, William, but I was afraid you'd be disappointed if he didn't respond."

Willy's eyes went to the envelope. "Is that his reply?"

Bridget nodded. "A man just dropped it off. There's no way it could have arrived via regular post, given the war."

"It must have been smuggled out of Germany," Otto added.

"What does it say?"

"I don't know. We were waiting for you."

Bridget repeatedly bit her upper lip with her lower teeth. The last time Willy remembered her doing that was when his father had left them the second time, for good. He had been only eight years old, but the memory was as vivid as if it had happened yesterday. He took the letter, then met Bridget's eyes.

"Well, let's open it then."

32

"I'm sorry I startled you," the girl said through a yawn. Although she looked to be about twelve years old, early in her stay Ursula had learned not to assume children's ages. Many had been in the ghetto for a while, and the lack of food and proper hygiene led to slower growth and development.

"It is I who should apologize for waking you. I thought you were a rat scuttling under the blankets."

The girl smirked. "If there were a rat under here with me you needn't have worried. I would have killed it myself."

Mature words from such a small mouth shocked Ursula. "How would you have done that?"

The girl held up her hands and wiggled her fingers. "With these."

Ursula's eyebrows shot up.

"Don't tell me that you've never killed a rat," the girl said.

"I have not."

"Well—" The girl swung her legs over the edge of the roughly hewn board that served as a makeshift bed. "You don't know what you're missing." She jumped down hard, the thump of her landing reverberating throughout the large, sparsely furnished room. Where her black boots landed, a puff of dust exploded. She stretched and yawned, then bent her neck left and right, causing cracking sounds.

"I'm Ursula. What's your name?"

The girl smiled, revealing a mouthful of crooked teeth. "I'm Addi Lutz."

"Do you stay here in Dresden?"

"I do, but on the first floor."

"So, what are you doing up here?"

Addi gestured to the blanket. "Sleeping."

"Yes. I see that. But why?"

Addi tilted her head and squinted. "Do you sleep well here?"

"Of course not. My mattress, if you can call it that, lies on the floor and I have no pillow."

"I sleep on the floor as well and use my jacket as a blanket. So, if I'm given an opportunity to take a nap in a proper bunk, if you can call it that, then I'll take it."

"Aren't you worried that the guards will catch you sleeping?"

She snorted. "How old do you think I am?"

Ursula paused. "Twelve."

Addi grinned. "I'm sixteen. If the guards knew my true age, then I would be put to work. But since they believe I'm only twelve, I'm allowed to remain with the younger children." She gestured to the eager group listening to Ilse reading from her book. "While they listen and learn, I rest."

"Where are you from?"

"Prague."

Ursula smiled and spoke in Czech. "I'm from Berlin but I learned to speak Czech from my mother. I'm probably a little out of practice though."

Addi responded in kind. "Your accent is horrendous, but at least I can understand you. There are many of us here from Czechoslovakia, so you'll get a lot of practice if you want."

"I see that you wear a pink triangle on your coat."

Addi glanced at the badge. "Yes, I like girls."

Ursula had known several male operatic performers who preferred the company of other men, but she had never met a woman who favored the same sex.

"Is that why you were sent here?"

Addi nodded. "The Nazis believe that I am immoral. I was to be sent to another camp, but Edvard Svoboda intervened and had me sent here instead. I'm an artist, you see. Well known in Prague, especially for my age. I knew Edvard before all of this." She gestured with her hand. "Our families were friends before."

"So, he knows your true age but doesn't reveal it?"

"Correct."

"Why not?"

Addi averted her eyes.

Ursula pointed to the pink triangle. "And he doesn't mind that?"

Addi drew her lips in and shrugged.

Ursula thought back to her conversation with Marika. If she could gain the protection of a guard by sleeping with him, would she do it? What if it meant extra food? Or blankets? *No*, she decided. She would not. Inwardly, she cringed. She had been in Terezín only seven months, yet she was contemplating trading her virginity for what? Food? She was hungry, but she wasn't yet starving.

She changed the subject. "You said you're an artist. What's your medium?"

"Pastels."

"Are you able to draw much here?"

Chaos erupted outside in the form of barked commands in Czech and German. The sound of gunfire drew the girls to the windows just in time to see a guard take careful aim at a boy who was running down the street. A bullet found its mark and the child fell to the ground, jerking convulsively before rolling over and using his arms to pull his useless legs forward. The same guard who had wounded him let him crawl a few meters, then sauntered over and completed the kill with a precisely placed bullet in the back of the head. The boy's forehead bounced off the cobblestones.

Ursula shifted her attention to the girls. Several of them watched quietly, their faces expressionless. Others gasped and burst into tears as they slid to the floor. A girl of no older than eight stared unblinkingly at the unmoving body and mumbled in Czech, "That was my brother. That was my brother."

Ursula followed the stunned girl's gaze to the mayhem outside. Several guards approached the boy's body and pushed it with their boots to ensure that he was actually dead. One of them grabbed the child's arm and dragged him across the courtyard while another turned and issued orders to the remaining guards. As the officer spoke, his eyes swept past Ursula and then darted back to her. It was Siegfried Seidl. Ursula had rarely interacted with him since she'd arrived and was surprised by the trepidation his presence created. She backed away from the window, but she knew that he'd seen her. Marika's earlier story of Herr Abendroth going to the Little Fortress for not shining Seidl's boots replayed in her mind, and she found that her hands had balled into fists.

"Ilse, I believe the commandant is on his way."

Ilse had been trying to calm the girls, but in response to Ursula's statement, she snapped her fingers and whispered, "Girls, focus on me. You must sit in neat rows and recite multiplication tables to one another. We shall have a visitor shortly." The girls, ranging in age from four to fifteen, sprang into action. Within seconds they'd put on dull countenances and quiet voices, blending into their dismal surroundings. Addi positioned herself among the twelve-year-olds and slumped her shoulders to appear smaller. After ensuring that the girls were organized, Ilse stuffed the book into her undergarments.

The commandant appeared at the door. He paused at the threshold and stomped snow from his boots as his penetrating eyes swept the room. Finding nothing out of the ordinary, he entered and settled his gaze on Ursula.

"Fräulein Becker, how are you?"

"Cold . . . and hungry."

Seidl cut his eyes toward her as he waggled his pointer finger and spoke loudly, ensuring everyone could hear. "To think that I have ordered extra rations for you, and this is how you repay me? With insolence? No, that will not do."

Ursula reddened. She hadn't known she'd been provided more food than her fellow inmates. She glanced at Ilse whose stoic expression gave away nothing.

"I wasn't aware that you had done that, Commandant. Although I'm grateful, I respectfully request that I be given the same amount of food as the others."

Seidl made a show of considering her appeal. "Which others, Fräulein?"

"I beg your pardon?"

"Do you want the same rations as the elderly? Or the children? Or perhaps you would like the same amount of food as the Council of Jewish Elders?"

Ursula blinked.

"I see that you don't understand. Nor do you need to, silly girl. Just know that I'm looking out for you." He leaned in. "You should be *thankful*, Fräulein." His eyes bore through her. She wondered if he actually saw her at all.

He turned suddenly to the collection of girls and clapped loudly three times. "Up! Follow me!"

Ilse and Ursula exchanged glances. The fleeting look contained their concern that Seidl might focus revenge for Ursula's insubordination on the girls. "Where?" Ilse asked.

Seidl's eyes hardened and he stomped toward her. "Do not question me, Jew!" he screamed into her face.

Ursula rushed over to stand by Ilse. "She didn't mean to offend, Commandant. Please forgive her outburst."

Seidl's heavy breathing slowed as he continued to glare at Ilse. After a tension-filled minute, he turned his gaze to Ursula, who managed a tentative smile. She watched the muscles in his face relax. He removed his cap and smoothed his hair, then straightened his jacket and replaced his cap. In a more rational state, he turned to the girls.

"Follow me."

The girls started to rise from the floor when a voice asked, "Where?"

Believing that it was Ilse who had spoken, Seidl whirled around and raised his right arm across his chest. Ursula saw what was happening and threw herself in front of Ilse, absorbing the blow from the back of Seidl's right hand. The force of the impact threw her to the floor and sent the girls scrambling to the bunks.

"Mein Gott, Fräulein! Look what you made me do!" Siegfried yelled, his head shaking back and forth as he stepped backwards towards the door. "Look what you made me do! You did this! Up! Get up! All of you!" His ire was palpable as his wild eyes scanned the people in the room.

Without warning his petulant demeanor changed dramatically. Singling out Ursula, his furious eyes burned as he repeated, "You did this. You did this." He lunged forward and grabbed her wrist, forced her to stand, then dragged her out of the room, down the stairs and out into the snowy street. Ursula remained silent and ran to keep up with his long strides as visions of being shot or hanged ran rampant through her fertile mind. She knew better than to ask where he was taking her, and she steeled herself for what was to come.

Each time she stumbled he would drag her until she managed to stand again. By the time they reached a building three blocks away from Dresden, she was out of breath and struggling to see out of her swollen eye. Seidl slowed and walked her toward the Eger River. As they neared the edge of the bridge that crossed the river, Seidl stopped, stepped behind her and grabbed her shoulders. *This is the end*, she thought. *He's going to shoot me and throw me in the river.* She closed her eyes and pictured Willy and Otto, allowing the wonderful images to wash over her like the water rushing below her feet. Her trembling body calmed as she spoke to Otto in her mind, silently saying good-bye. Willy whispered sweetness in her ear, reminding her who she is, and urging her to maintain her dignity and composure.

After several moments of silence, however, Ursula realized that Seidl hadn't drawn his weapon. She opened her eyes and found that she was facing a building on the other side of the bridge. The Little Fortress. *He's going to imprison me*, she realized. *Like Herr Abendroth, I am to be jailed. But I will not die today.* "Resist. Survive," Willy whispered in her ear. A euphoric relief shuddered through her, and she sent a silent prayer upwards.

Seidl gripped her shoulders. "Do you see that building, Fräulein?"

Before she could answer, he shook her so hard she was concerned her neck might break. His lips brushed her ear. "It's as if you *want* to go there. Do you?"

Afraid to respond, Ursula remained mute.

He whipped her around to face him. "Do you?" he screamed in her face.

Ursula cringed and whispered, "No."

"Then *stop* defying me! This will be your *last* warning!"

He shoved her away from him and raked his fingers through his hair, upending his cap, which fell to the snowy earth. "I don't understand this hold you have on me!" He walked in circles as puffy, white snowflakes settled on his dark hair. After several moments he retrieved his cap, brushed it off, and replaced it on his head. Abruptly he turned to her and looked suddenly sad. "You came to me with special instructions."

What does that mean? she wondered.

"I shouldn't tell you that, lest it embolden you, but I can't help myself. I had heard that you were a siren, but you are not. You are so much more than that. Even now . . ."

Ursula stared at the ground.

"You are so beautiful." He walked forward slowly and gingerly touched her face. Her stomach heaved, but she stood motionless as he outlined her bruised eye. She watched him remove a glove and wondered if he would strike her again. Instead, he gently wound a lock of raven hair around his fingers before tucking it behind her ear. She closed her eyes, afraid if she didn't, she would lash out and cause herself more physical harm. He touched her lips with his thumb before placing his forehead against hers and closing his eyes. Ursula clenched her teeth, terrified to move. She listened to his steady breathing as she considered whether it would be worse to go to the Little Fortress or be raped by the sociopath before her.

"Come." He took her hand and turned away, but she didn't move. Without knowing it, she had made a decision. She wouldn't willingly let him violate her. If he was intent on doing so, then she was going to fight, to the death if necessary. She steeled herself for the altercation.

"It's alright. I'm no longer angry."

His abrupt emotional change startled her. "I won't hurt you. Come." Unsure, she reluctantly allowed herself to be led inside the building they'd passed earlier. A man stood behind a chair, his face a blank mask. Ursula recognized him as Elias, a German Jew who had been on the same transport as her. Confused, she stared at him, silently asking for an explanation. His face betrayed nothing.

"Sit," Seidl ordered.

Ursula's eyes flew around the small room. This building was used for laundry and occasional washing, so she couldn't imagine what was about to happen. Until this moment she had thought that the greatest stressor in the ghetto was lack of food and medical care. But she now understood that those were simply physical challenges. It was the psychological torture that was the biggest threat. Uncertainty and unpredictability gnawed at her resolve and strength. Not only had she been stripped of her identity, but her fate was now at the whim of an emotionally unstable man. If she knew what was coming, she could prepare herself, but the volatility cultivated by the SS was the mental torment that kept her constantly on edge. As she stared at Elias, he gave her an almost imperceptible nod of assurance. That was enough to force her feet forward toward the wooden chair.

She lowered herself into the seat, and Seidl placed his hand on her shoulder. "Fräulein Becker, it has come to my attention that you have lice. Unfortunately, Elias will be shaving your head. It's the only way to rid yourself of the vermin."

Ursula stared straight ahead, unable to move or speak. Her mind had created so many horrible scenarios, but this had not been one of them. She struggled to reconcile the reality with what she thought might happen.

"Your loss will not be in vain, however. Your hair will be cured and combined with other human hair to create various items that will aid the Führer in growing the Reich."

Ursula heard a click, then a buzzing sound. She felt pressure on the back of her head as Elias gently pushed her head forward and lifted a handful of her hair. The razor made contact with her scalp and sheared away long, ebony strands that fell to the floor. A mere three minutes later, Elias stepped away and disengaged the electric razor. He wound the cord around the device and left the room, all the while staring at the floor.

Ursula dug her fingernails into her palms so she wouldn't cry. She stared at her hands, her back erect and her body trembling uncontrollably. Seidl opened a nearby drawer and removed a hand mirror. He stood in front of her and held it up, then leaned forward and lifted her chin until she was staring at her reflection.

A gaunt stranger with a swollen eye gazed back at her. Her raggedly shorn head bled from multiple cuts caused by the razor, and the tears that perched on her dark lower lashes only enhanced the depth of her brown eyes. Ursula's imagination soared away to a safe, happy place where Willy's hands caressed her undamaged face and swept through her long hair. His laughter echoed in her mind and, for a moment, she was transported back to her apartment in Berlin, seated at the kitchen table as she and Willy played cards with Otto.

Seidl cleared his throat, shattering her reverie. Her eyes met her broken doppelgänger in the mirror, and the tear that had sat idly on the ledge of her eyelid spilled down her pale cheek.

Seidl leaned forward and frowned, then wiped away the tear. "Perhaps now you will not be so appealing to me."

33

Willy's plan to join the armed forces was all but forgotten as he stared at the letter and sank into a chair.

Bridget fidgeted. "No matter what Alois says in the letter, I want you to know that I'm proud of you, William. You're an exceptional person."

Her strained smile gave away her anxiety. Willy felt for her as he reviewed what she'd told him about Alois. "When your father moved back to Germany, I didn't hear from him for over a year. When I finally received a telegram in November 1919, it said that he had remarried and was expecting a child. I pointed out to him that he had married bigamously, a crime that might interest the German police. That was our last communication. I didn't follow through on my threat because I felt embarrassed to have been abandoned."

Willy winced as he remembered the anguish on her face as she'd spoken. But he was determined to find Ursula.

"Aren't you going to open it?" Otto urged.

Willy's hands shook as he tore open the envelope. The entire letter was in German, so he translated as he read aloud.

> Dear Bridget,
> What a surprise to receive your letter. It's been some time since we've spoken.

Bridget sniffed and Willy looked up. Her lips were pinched into a small pucker.

> I trust that you are well and happy. I, too, am very happy, as my son Heinz is growing up to be an extraordinary young man.

"Hah!" Bridget stood.

"Mum, please."

"Sorry, William. But you're exceptional too, no thanks to—" Willy threw her a pleading look. She sat again. "Go on."

> I received your letter seeking my help in
> finding Willy's fiancée. You should know that
> Adolf wasn't pleased with their engagement. You
> said that she was abducted, and that you believe
> Adolf was involved. Quite frankly, I find that
> highly unlikely. I believe you're being emotional.
> That was an issue in our marriage, if I remember
> correctly.

Willy glanced at his mother. Her cheeks burned crimson, and her knuckles were lily white as they wrung her apron. "Shall I read silently?"

Bridget shook her head.

> Additionally, my understanding is that the
> young woman is a Jew. You stated in your letter
> that she was partly a Jew, but I need to be clear
> on this point, Bridget. One is not partly a Jew.
> One is simply a Jew.
> Nevertheless, in considering your request, I
> have recalled enough fond memories of our time
> together to—

Bridget jumped to her feet. "How dare he! Our time together? We were married for eight years! We're still married, for Christ's sake! On paper anyway." She collapsed on the settee.

Willy looked to Otto, who shook his head.

Willy continued reading aloud but switched to German so Bridget would be spared.

> I have recalled enough fond memories of our
> time together to help you. I will ask Adolf about
> the young Jew and will follow up with another
> letter when I can. As you know, I certainly can't
> predict when that will be.
> I mentioned my son earlier. He is a guard in a
> Polish camp, working each day for the greatness of
> the Reich. Perhaps that's where the Jew was sent to
> work until she is no longer useful.

Willy paused and Bridget noted the silence. "What is it?"

"He says that Ursula might have been sent to a work camp in Poland."

"Is he giving us a clue?" Otto asked.

"I'm not sure."

"What kind of camp?" Bridget asked.

"A work camp where Jews are sent until they are no longer useful."

"Then where do they go?"

Willy didn't answer.

"William, where do they go?"

Otto placed his large hand over Bridget's. "Alois will speak to his brother, Bridget. If she's in a camp, then she may still be alive." Otto's desperation was heartbreaking.

"Who knows when he'll get back to us? It might be too late, even if Uncle decides to relent."

"Does he say anything else?" Otto asked.

Willy read the rest of the letter. "Nothing important."

"I'm sorry, son. I did the best I could."

Willy looked at his defeated mother. "Don't be sorry, Mum. I appreciate how hard that was for you. Thank you."

"Where are the Jews sent when they're no longer useful, William?"

Willy swallowed hard and gazed evenly at Bridget. "They're probably killed."

"But there must be hundreds of thousands."

"Millions, actually."

Willy watched Bridget struggle to grasp the enormity of his words. "Ursula will be fine because of her voice."

"But for how long, Mum?" Willy slumped in the chair and rubbed his eyes.

"When you were six years old you taught yourself to ride a bike. Do you remember, William?"

Willy looked at her with a mixture of confusion and annoyance. "What does this have to do with—"

Bridget crossed to stand in front of him. "Just listen. You fell off repeatedly, yet jumped up and remounted every time, determined to please your absent father. Despite my efforts to convince you otherwise, you believed that if you worked hard enough at being a good boy, Alois would return." She smiled sadly at the memory and brushed some bangs away from Willy's forehead, revealing a small scar. "You received this scar on your last bike attempt before giving up for the day."

His fingers found the scar.

"Do you remember what happened the next day?"

Willy shook his head.

"You awakened and mastered the bike on your first effort, as if the previous day's failures had congealed during sleep into a hard core of bike-riding knowledge." She caressed his cheek. "You, William Patrick Hitler, are full of integrity and honor. I wish more than anything that I could take away your pain. But I can't. Just like I couldn't when you were that six-year-old boy waiting for his father. You dealt with that loss in your own way, by conquering the bike. And you'll figure out a way to deal with this as well, on your own terms."

Willy felt her words seep deeply into him, binding together into an actionable plan. Helplessness disintegrated within him, then reconvened as determination.

"I know what I must do." He kissed Bridget's cheek and took her hands. "Is it alright if Otto remains here while I take a trip?"

"What? Where?"

"Germany."

"Are you daft, Willy? You can't return to Germany!"

He smiled broadly. "I can if I'm a soldier."

Bridget blanched and pulled her hand to her heart. "No, no, no. Please, Willy, don't go." She reached out and grasped his sleeve. "I lost one love to a war. I can't lose you as well."

Willy took her hands. "I've tried everything in my power to find Ursula, and nothing's worked. Furthermore, I'm not convinced that Da will speak to Uncle Alf." He stood quickly. "Mum, you were right. I've been allowing others to act on my behalf when I should have been taking action myself. For the first time since Ursula was taken, I have a purpose. I no longer have to sit idly by while I wait for a miracle."

Her terrified eyes searched his face. "I don't understand."

"I'm going to enlist in Britain's armed forces to fight Uncle Alf and his Nazis. Once he's defeated, I'll return home with Ursula on my arm."

He spoke with the brash confidence of a young man who is hopelessly in love, and who's not yet lived long enough to appreciate the fickleness with which fate can hand down punishment. As Bridget observed the strong, confident young man standing proudly before her, she knew, without a doubt, that her words no longer mattered.

Her only son had already slipped from her grasp.

34

Ursula closed her eyes and leaned over the contents of the large black pot, allowing herself a brief, warm respite from the biting cold that seeped through the cracked kitchen windows. The ersatz soup smelled of boiled potatoes and rutabaga, and Ursula's stomach protested against its emptiness. She crossed to the oven and used a wad of cloth to protect her hand as she checked on the black bread. The aroma made her mouth water, even as she considered that the "flour" she had used to fashion the dough had been equal parts milled grain and sawdust.

She adjusted her purple, knitted hat. When she'd returned to the barracks with a bald head, women had crowded around her asking what happened. She had refused to speak about either her black eye or shaven head, repeating, "It's nothing. Don't worry," over and over, until people had eventually given up trying to talk to her. It was only when she was alone with Marika that she had shared her terror. Marika had listened intently and said little, occasionally nodding in solidarity. When Ursula's words were spent, Marika had crossed to her bunk, lifted the pallet, and removed a purple, knitted cap. "I used the last of my yarn on this hat." She had placed it gently on Ursula's bleeding scalp. "There. You look lovely. Shall we go to work?" They had walked quickly to the kitchen, arms linked, and huddled together against the cold.

Ursula appreciated Marika's kind ear, her willingness to listen without reproach or judgment. In Marika Ursula had found a mother figure she hadn't realized she needed or wanted. And although she didn't want to admit it to herself, Marika's ability to move forward in the face of adversity was becoming critical to her survival.

"Ursula," Marika whispered.

Ursula turned to her friend.

Marika ensured that the kitchen guard was facing away from her before removing something from the waistband of her skirt.

Ursula stared at the small can of sardines and then motioned with her head toward the pantry, indicating that Marika should put it back.

Marika shook her head and replaced the tin in its hiding place.

Ursula glanced at the guard, who yawned and rubbed his eyes. She whispered, "You'll be shot, Marika."

"They won't know."

Ursula angrily rolled her eyes and gritted her teeth. "They always know. I've seen the kitchen guards count and recount the supplies. They'll know!"

Marika peeked at the guard, who was leaning against the doorjamb with his eyes closed. "Do you know what I can get for this?"

"From whom? No one has anything left to barter."

"That's not true. Anissa Wagner has some yarn she would trade."

"How do you know?"

"Because her husband's birthday is tomorrow, and she would like to give him something special." Marika raised her eyebrows and smiled.

Ursula glanced at the guard, who seemed to be asleep. "You would trade your life for some yarn, Marika?"

Marika crossed to the oven and removed the bread. "I believe this is done, and yes, I would. Knitting reminds me of my life before, much as singing must remind you. Speaking of which, have you met Karel Ancerl or Rafael Schächter yet?"

The guard snorted, waking himself up and drawing their attention. He glanced at them, then left his post to walk down the hallway. Ursula knew he would return in under a minute. She stopped stirring and faced Marika. "I'd heard they were here, but I haven't met them."

"They're organizing a choir."

"A choir?"

"Apparently there's a piano in the basement of Magdeburg barracks, and they've been meeting there to rehearse."

"The SS allows this?"

"They ordered it."

"Really?"

"Yes. Rafael Schächter was ordered to perform Verdi's *Requiem*."

Ursula reflected on the number of times she had sung Verdi's masterpiece, the work he'd completed in honor of Alessandro Manzoni, an Italian poet and humanist. She had soloed in the *Requiem* a half-dozen times, but never in dire circumstances and never in response to an edict. She wasn't some circus animal who would sing on command. As she had told Willy, her voice was her gift, and she would use it when and where she chose. On the other hand, she desperately missed singing, and she found herself humming the *Libera me* section of the work.

Marika cut the steaming black bread into fifty-gram slices, exact in her measurement lest she incur punishment. "You need to stop thinking so much about death, Ursula, and begin focusing on life."

"How can I when we're constantly reminded of how precarious our situation is? Look at me, Marika! My nose is broken, and I can't see out of my right eye. My scalp is bare and covered in blood! Don't tell me not to think about death. It stalks me in my sleep."

Marika continued to slice. "I don't need to look at you, Ursula. Your damaged face is burned into my memory. But that doesn't mean that you should focus on death."

Ursula shook her head. Marika's perseverance was admirable . . . and sometimes irritating. "Some say that another transport to the east will be leaving tonight."

Marika shrugged. "I've heard that rumor as well, but what of it? We must enjoy today because there may not be a tomorrow."

The guard appeared and loomed over the bread. "The old woman is correct. There may not be a tomorrow." He grabbed three slices and stuffed them into his mouth, chewing loudly. "Yech! This tastes like shit. Perfect for the dogs who will eat it." He spat the half-chewed remnants on the floor. "Clean up this mess!" he ordered as he resumed his post outside the door.

A silent look of understanding passed between the two women.

"I shall mix more dough," Ursula announced loudly as she removed the flour and yeast from the pantry. While she pounded the heavy bag of flour onto the wooden table and made a show of dragging down a bowl from a high shelf, Marika knelt, scooped up the semi-masticated bread into a towel and stuffed a large wad into her mouth. After she had eaten half of the mound, she turned to Ursula and said, "Let me help you with that. We'll swap positions."

"Thank you," Ursula said as she kept her back to the guard and took several bites from the towel. Marika mixed the bread ingredients and kneaded the dough with gusto as Ursula finished her meal. She couldn't remember when her stomach had felt so full.

She returned to the soup and considered Marika's suggestion that she concentrate on living instead of dying. The two men Marika had mentioned were fine musicians and conductors. Karel Ancerl hailed from Prague and led that city's symphony, and Rafael Schächter was an acclaimed Czech composer and choral conductor.

"Perhaps I'll find a way to contact Herr Schächter to see if he's in need of a soprano," Ursula whispered.

Marika smiled knowingly. "No need, my dear. He'll be seeking you out this evening when he works the transport. As you know, the collection point is directly in front of Dresden, so look for him."

Ursula shook her head in amazement. Marika had planned the entire conversation so that Ursula would come to her own conclusion about taking up singing again. She smiled, wondering if it were possible that Marika had been sent by her deceased mother to protect her.

The rest of the afternoon passed without incident. It was well past six p.m. when Ursula and Marika finished cooking. After cleaning up, they returned to Dresden to find the entire building empty except for two little girls playing with a handmade doll on the second floor. The girls glanced at them before resuming their game, their bald heads seeming too large for their wasting bodies.

"Where is everyone?" Ursula asked.

The older girl shrugged and rubbed her head. "They're getting their hair cut like we did."

"Like you did too!" the smaller girl squealed, a black spot gaping where she'd recently lost a baby tooth. Ursula removed her cap and ran her hand over her prickly scalp. Although she missed the warmth of her longer hair, she was surprised to find that once the initial shock had passed, she didn't mind that much. Besides, she knew her hair would grow back and once it did, she had already resolved to cut it only when necessary. She would have a long, thick, raven mane again. She was sure of it.

"You're the singer," the gap-toothed girl said.

"Yes. My name is Ursula."

"I'm Anna and this is Sophia," the older girl said.

Ursula smiled. "My sister's name is Anna."

"Is she here?" Sophia asked.

Ursula shook her head.

"Did she die?" Sophia asked, her little face scrunched up in concern.

"No. She's alive."

"That's good to hear," Sophia announced, sounding older than her years. "Would you like to play with us? My mother made this doll for me before she was sent away."

Ursula's heart seized. The girl spoke so matter-of-factly about her mother's departure, probably assuming that she would return. The older of the girls, Anna, stared resolutely at Ursula. Stories about the transports' destinations flew like wildfire around the camp. Although it wasn't known exactly where the trains went, everyone appreciated the fact that no one had ever returned after heading east.

"No thank you, Sophia, but I appreciate the offer."

The sound of multiple footfalls on the stairs drew their attention. A group of about fifty women and girls entered the room and collapsed onto their bunks or on the floor, all of their heads roughly shorn. Addi trailed the pack and grimaced at Ursula as she deposited herself on the floor.

Ursula crossed over to her. "You'll find that you don't miss your hair as much as you think you would."

"Actually, I believe that this look suits me," Addi said, striking a pose.

Ursula marveled at Addi's gaiety amidst chaos and filth. She started to say so when she heard the unmistakable sound of SS boots clomping up the old, wood stairs. The women knew what was coming and hugged the little ones close as a guard appeared at their door and removed a sheet of paper from his coat pocket.

"You will stand!" he ordered.

They gathered quickly and quietly. A girl of about ten years whimpered and her mother whispered, "They wouldn't have taken our hair if . . . we'll be alright, sweetheart."

The guard scrutinized his paper. "Numbers forty-nine through seventy-five, step forward!"

The prisoners obeyed. Ursula's heart sank as she realized that the ten-year-old and her mother were among the chosen ones. The girl started hyperventilating and her mother knelt to calm her as others looked on.

"You will go immediately downstairs and enter the train. You need take nothing with you," the guard clipped.

The despondent group said their brief good-byes and walked slowly out of the room as the rest of the women returned to their bunks.

"I'm not finished!" the guard yelled. "On your feet!"

Panicked glances were exchanged. Normally there was only one announcement. The remaining inmates formed a line.

"Numbers nineteen through thirty-five, downstairs!"

Ursula's mouth dropped. For some ridiculous reason she had thought that she'd remain inoculated from a transport. She looked at Marika, whose ashen face betrayed her surprise.

"What are you waiting for! Go!" the guard ordered.

Ursula took a halting step forward, still disbelieving that she'd been chosen. She turned toward Marika with a desperate look.

"May I walk with her?" Marika asked the guard. He glared at Ursula but nodded curtly to Marika.

Ursula trudged with heavy feet, wondering what awaited her. Terrible visions assaulted her imagination, and she wondered if she might collapse. But Marika held her elbow, assuring her with empty platitudes that they would see each other again. Ursula comforted herself with mental pictures of Willy and Otto, but reality took hold when she descended the stairs and saw the look on Jakob Edelstein's face.

Although the SS set the laws and the Czech guards enforced them, the Council of Jewish Elders was responsible for daily administration within the camp. One of the council's duties was to assign prisoners to various transports, and as chairman of the council, Jakob Edelstein supervised the loading of each transport.

Edelstein's face looked pained, as if he had eaten something that didn't agree with him. Ursula caught his eye, and he shook his head. She stopped, thinking that perhaps a mistake had been made, that she shouldn't enter the car. But he inclined his head toward the train, indicating that she should board. Confused, she continued to look to him for guidance, but he had turned his attention elsewhere. She reluctantly turned to Marika and hugged her tightly while fighting back tears. She didn't want Marika's last memory of her to be a blubbering mess.

"Thank you for everything you've done for me. You're a true friend, Marika."

The older woman cupped Ursula's face in her hands. "I'll miss you," she whispered as tears flowed openly down her lined face. "You will always be my beautiful girl." Ursula wasn't sure if Marika was speaking to her or to the daughter she'd already lost. Either way, she'd spoken from her heart.

She gently removed Marika's hands from her face and stepped onto the train. She turned to walk to a seat and came face-to-face with the guard from the kitchen.

"Well, look who it is. The thieving Jew."

Ursula knew better than to respond. She cast her eyes downward.

"Where is the can of sardines you stole?"

She looked at him with a blank expression. Without warning he raised the butt of his pistol and whipped her with it. The skin on her cheekbone under her bruised eye split open and she crumpled to the floor. She curled into a ball, her arms wrapped protectively around her head, and awaited the inevitable kicks from the guard's heavy boots.

Marika leapt onto the train and screamed, "It was me! I stole the sardines!"

A grotesque smirk worked its way across the guard's face. He ignored Marika and continued to speak to Ursula. "You thought I was sleeping, but I wasn't."

Ursula peeked past the guard and saw Jakob Edelstein's sorrowful face. She now understood why he'd shaken his head. He'd been attempting to warn her. *But what could I have done?* She sat up slowly and looked at the other inmates on the train. Emaciated, dirty bodies with vacant eyes stared at her. *What kind of life is this? Maybe I should let it happen. Maybe I should let them kill me.* She suddenly felt incredibly tired. She looked at Marika, whose wild eyes radiated desperation. Ursula didn't want to see her friend die, nor did she want her to witness the cold-blooded murder of her second chance at a daughter. Faced with another impossible choice, Ursula swallowed her despondency and dragged herself to her feet. "She's lying. I stole the sardines."

Marika turned on Ursula, her eyes ablaze. "No, Ursula! Don't lie to protect me."

The guard laughed and turned to the prisoners in the train, some of whom watched the horrific scene unfolding while others stared at their hands. "You Jews are all the same. Liars and thieves."

The guard's black eyes bored into Ursula. "Maybe next time you won't steal from the Reich."

For the second time in one day, Ursula closed her eyes and waited for the bullet. She had taken action. She had made the decision to end her life. She was sad, but in the end, it had been *her* choice. She released all the tension in her body and breathed deeply, enjoying the cold air as it hit her lungs. She smiled and pictured Willy, secure in her belief that they would meet again someday.

Taking precise aim, the guard leveled his Luger and fired.

35

Willy gazed upwards at the War Office building that stood at the corner of Horse Guards Avenue and Whitehall. A relatively low structure with four domed turrets that erupted from each corner, Willy thought it looked more like a museum than a place where generals had strategized the Great War. Brushing some lint from his overcoat, he climbed the steps and greeted the bored young man seated behind a tall, oak desk.

"Hello . . ." Willy leaned forward and squinted at his name tag. "Private Washburn. I'm hoping to speak to someone about enlisting in the armed services."

The young soldier examined Willy's expensive, wool overcoat and necktie before answering. "It's Sergeant, and go through that door, sir. Take a right and it will be the first door on your left."

Willy tilted his fedora in thanks. He followed Sergeant Washburn's directions and found himself standing in front of a glass door labeled "Recruitment Officer." He opened the door to find a corpulent, bald man blowing on a cup of steaming tea. "Sorry to interrupt, sir, but I was hoping to enlist in the army."

The man glanced at Willy and pointed to the chair opposite him. Although Willy felt confident in his decision to enlist, this man made him nervous with his large frame and hooded, heavy brow. He continued to blow on his tea and then took a huge, loud gulp.

"Ahhhh. Too hot," he said as he sucked in air.

Willy took a seat and evaluated the small space. The walls were bare save for a framed commendation for bravery and a picture of the man and a woman Willy presumed to be his wife. "Are you sure about enlisting, son? It's a lot of paperwork."

Willy looked at him in confusion. The man's light blue eyes crinkled at the corners. "I'm joking, son. Relax." He stood and held out his hand. "The name is Captain Stephen Hicks." Willy stood and took his hand. "I'm Willy." Hicks retook his seat and leaned forward, his chin in his hand. "So, tell me why you want to enlist."

Willy paused. He had decided that he would divulge as little information as possible. "I want to serve my country, sir. It's that simple."

Still maintaining eye contact, Hicks picked up his tea, blew on it, and took another sip. He sighed and replaced it on the blotter. "I remember being enthusiastic like you, son. That was many years ago. Back when I earned that thing." He nodded his head toward the commendation hanging on the wall.

"I noticed that, sir. Impressive."

Hicks smiled ruefully. "It's not so remarkable when you hear how I earned it. I got shot in my ass trying to retrieve my superior's wedding ring, believe it or not. The damned thing slipped off in the mud during a skirmish, and I was the idiot private sent to retrieve it. Got hit and sent home. That's how I ended up here." Hicks took another sip. "Worked out for the best, though. The wife is happy with my situation."

Willy wasn't sure what to say, so he smiled.

Hicks observed him. "You haven't really answered my question. *Why* do you want to serve your country?"

Willy felt the situation slipping away from him. He hadn't thought he'd have to explain himself. He'd believed he could walk in, sign on the dotted line, and receive a uniform. Apparently, the military had become more selective. He decided to offer some of the truth. "My father left when I was young, sir. To Germany. You see, he was German by birth, so I'm fluent in the language. I thought the army could use soldiers who speak German."

Hicks' eyebrows shot up. "Well, well. That changes things, son. We do need people who speak German. Hold on." Hicks held up a finger toward Willy and lifted his phone receiver. "Come in here, Nigel."

Ten seconds later the sergeant from the front desk entered the office. "Yes, sir?"

"Nigel, Willy says he knows German. Say something to him."

"Of course, sir." Nigel turned to Willy. "Sie sehen nicht aus wie der normale Rekrut, der durch die Tür geht."

Nigel's German was passable, but his accent was horrendous, the result of learning in the classroom but never having spent any time in a German-speaking country.

"Ich kenne. Ich konnte es an deinem Gesichtsausdruck erkennen."

Nigel laughed and nodded.

Hicks' forehead furrowed in concentration as his eyes darted between the two younger men. He leaned forward with his heavy arms on the desktop. "Well, what did you two talk about?"

Nigel became serious. "I told him that he didn't look like a normal army recruit. He responded that I looked at him funny when he entered the building."

Hicks tilted an eyebrow toward Willy. "Alright. You can speak German, but what makes you think the army will need you to speak German on its behalf?"

Willy sat up straighter. "I'm sure you're familiar with the history between Germany and the USSR?"

"I know that Germany signed a non-aggression pact with the USSR in 1939 that resulted in the two countries dividing Poland."

"That's right. Then the USSR went on to invade Finland and the Baltic states."

"And eventually Germany took note and began Operation Barbarossa, during which it attacked Italy, Romania, and eventually, the USSR."

"Yes. And in 1941 the siege of Leningrad began, which has been waging ever since. When Germany eventually gave up trying to take Moscow, the USSR fought back with brute force."

Hicks leaned back in his chair and evaluated Willy. "Well, I'll give you this, you certainly know your recent military history."

Willy smiled. "Anyone who's following the political happenings would be aware of what we discussed."

"Alright. So, what does all of this have to do with you speaking German on behalf of Britain?"

"It's my firm belief that the Leningrad battle might well result in Germans surrendering to the Soviets in the coming months."

Hicks' already stern countenance darkened, and his eyes flitted in Nigel's direction. "You're dismissed."

"Yes, sir." Nigel saluted and left the small room.

Hicks glared at Willy, evaluating him more seriously than three minutes previously.

"What makes you say that?"

"Because Hitler is now fighting wars on both fronts and his resources are dwindling."

Hicks' face went from concentration to suspicion in a matter of seconds. "You sound very confident in your analysis."

Willy held his gaze. "I am, sir."

"Have you studied the history of war, son?"

"Not in school, sir."

Hicks lifted his chin. A long moment passed before he spoke again. "You seem sane and quite frankly, credible. Although I can't exactly say why." He sighed heavily and leaned back in his chair, his cup of tea forgotten. He tented his fingers and placed his chin atop them. "Based on recent reports, I happen to agree with your assessment. This Hitler is insane. I've even heard rumors of work camps where he sends people who disagree with him."

Willy's heart hammered in his chest. He swallowed to quell his nerves, afraid his voice would give him away. "I've heard those same rumors, sir."

"By God, we just got through one world war. I can't believe we're doing it again." He breathed heavily and shook his head. "But if the rumors are true ..."

"They're true, sir. I'm sure of it."

Hicks paused, looking Willy up and down. "You're motivated. I'll say that for you. Looks like you're going to be the army's newest recruit."

Relieved, Willy stood quickly. "Thank you, sir. You won't regret it. I promise."

Hicks waved his hand. "Well, well, let's not be too eager. There's paperwork to complete, son. Sit down." He removed a manila folder from a drawer and slid it across the desk. "Fill these out and then we'll talk about next steps. A physical exam will be required. Assuming you pass that, you'll be issued a uniform and we'll figure out whether you'll be housed in a barracks or if you can remain at home and report daily."

Willy could barely contain himself. His hands were shaking as he opened the file and completed the application. He kept thinking of Ursula, willing her to remain strong as the wheels turned to get him closer to her. It might take some time, but his plan was moving forward.

36

Ursula touched the hollow in her neck where Willy's locket used to be. She couldn't get used to the empty space. Her fingers kept returning to twirl the chain that was no longer there.

After Marika had been shot on the train, the guard had pistol-whipped Ursula again before ripping the locket from her neck. Bloodied and battered, Ursula had looked on helplessly as he had pocketed the necklace and dragged Marika's still twitching body from the train. Her muddled brain wrestled to understand why Marika had been killed instead of her. The only logical explanation was that the guard had known the truth and was toying with Ursula when he aimed the gun at her. Ursula had been directed to carry her friend's body almost a mile to the Little Fortress. Once there, she'd been forced to dig a shallow grave while several SS men verbally and physically threatened her.

The ground was almost frozen. Each time the metal shovel hit the earth it sent a jolt up the wooden handle into her hands. She didn't mind the pain, however. It was small price to pay for surviving. The guilt surrounding Marika's death started as a niggling in the back of her mind but burst to the forefront as she shoveled, numbing her to the cold. She was certain that as soon as she completed the hole she would be shot and tossed in next to her friend. She shoveled with gusto, even as the blisters on her hands burst. The sooner she completed the hole, she reasoned, the sooner she'd be free. She welcomed the notion, as she was certain that she couldn't survive knowing the part she'd played in Marika's murder. After digging the shallow hole, Ursula stood sweating and breathless, waiting for the shot that would end it all.

"Put the body in," the larger of the two guards said.

Of course, Ursula thought. *Get Marika in the hole and then shoot me. Less work for them.* With great effort, she dragged Marika's body into the grave, then carefully arranged her limbs. She stood, fully expecting a bullet in her back. When the shot didn't come, she turned around to find the guards smiling.

"Fill in the hole." The guard gestured with his gun.

Ursula was confused. *Are they going to let me live? Why?* She felt miserable but climbed out of the grave and shoveled dirt on top of the body. Starting at Marika's feet and working upward, Ursula held her breath as she poured dirt over her friend's mouth. "I'm sorry," she mouthed. When the burial was complete, the guards ordered her to recite a prayer in Hebrew.

She faced them and blinked several times. "I can't do that."

The smaller guard raised his pistol and took careful aim at her chest. "Do it," he said quietly.

Ursula felt an exhaustion she'd never known. She glanced at her freezing hands, covered in drying blood. *Blood on my hands. Literally and figuratively.* She touched her cheekbone and felt the gash. Blood had clotted and frozen, creating a makeshift bandage. Hopelessness and fatigue overwhelmed her, and she swayed on her feet.

I should join Marika in sleep. I should step toward the guard.

But then her mind turned to Willy and Otto.

She closed her eyes. "I don't know Hebrew."

The guards laughed. "But you are a Jew."

Her eyes flew open. She shook her head, then stopped herself, acutely aware that any opposition would fuel their anger. "Yes, but I don't know Hebrew."

The guards snickered at her perceived ineptitude and called her condescending names as they pushed her back and forth between them. She allowed herself to be shoved and showed no reaction to their taunts. It wasn't a challenge to remain silent. Her mind escaped the torment, leaving the shell of her freezing body behind as it soared to the warmth of Willy's embrace.

Receiving no reaction from Ursula, the guards quickly tired of their game. "You will go there." The smaller guard gestured toward the Little Fortress.

So, I am to be killed, she thought. *But very slowly.* She entered the stone structure and was shoved into the first cell on the right. Inside were four other people who barely acknowledged her entrance, too cold or despondent to care. No one spoke as night fell and they came together for warmth. In the morning they were given a liter of water but no food. The day passed slowly. When not dozing, Ursula spent her time leaning against the frigid stone wall, staring at Marika's resting place, wondering if her friend's soul was at peace and questioning if she'd made the correct decision in not forcing the guard's hand to end her own life. Early into the second day, a light snow began to fall. Ursula watched the fat flakes float down and lay a soft, white blanket over her friend, as if nature had found a way to tuck Marika in for her last, long sleep.

On the third day Ursula awoke to find a man curled around her. She struggled to lift his arm and realized that he was frozen solid. She managed to disengage from him, then scuttled away from the body as fast as her cold, aching limbs would allow. When the other inmates realized he was dead, they fell on the body like hyenas. Frozen hands clawed at the buttons on his coat as they stripped him of his clothing. Despairing, she turned her attention outside. The snow had completely obscured Marika's grave. She was truly gone. As if she had never existed.

Ursula was alone.

Terror enveloped her in a black shroud. Her breath came quickly until she thought she'd faint. But she remembered her conversation with Marika about concentrating on life, and she forced herself to focus. She slowed her breathing and made a silent promise to Marika that she would honor her legacy. As she considered the best manner in which to do that, her attention shifted to two guards walking quickly toward the prison. Ever efficient, they dragged her back to Dresden barracks, where they dumped her on the threshold. Her knees shook as she stood and surveyed the stairs she would need to climb to get to her pallet. All at once Addi appeared, put Ursula's arm around her tiny shoulders and helped her up the stairs. They were both breathing heavily when they arrived on the third floor. Ursula collapsed and immediately fell into a deep slumber.

"Ursula, wake up," Addi said. "You must eat. I've saved half of my rations for you." Ursula swam up from the depths of exhaustion. She desperately wanted to sleep but knew that Addi was correct. Her body needed sustenance. She opened her eyes, and Addi placed a small piece of stale bread in her mouth. Her tongue rolled the bread around to soften it before she swallowed. The effect was instantaneous. Her salivary glands reacted, and she felt ravenous. She sat up, took the chunk of bread from Addi and shoved it in her mouth.

"Slowly, Ursula." Ursula nodded but added the potato peels Addi had scrounged to the mélange in her stuffed mouth.

"Take care you don't choke, Ursula," Addi admonished as she looked on worriedly.

Ursula washed down her meal with a cup of water and then sighed. "Thank you, Addi."

"You're welcome. I was worried about you."

Ursula shook her head. "Poor Marika . . . I had to . . ." Her mouth wouldn't form the words.

"I know. I'm so sorry." Addi gathered her in her arms and rocked her. Ursula couldn't believe that a sixteen-year-old possessed such grace and maturity. She was so thankful to have found another true friend.

* * *

Over the ensuing months Ursula's physical wounds healed, but her spirits remained dampened, matched only by the dreary weather that continued into the Spring. Addi encouraged her to attend drawing classes that she offered to the children, but Ursula always begged off, claiming fatigue.

Concerned about Ursula's waning morale, Addi furthered Marika's plan by speaking secretly with composer/conductor Rafael Schächter, who suggested that Ursula become the soprano soloist in his fledgling choir.

Under the guise of attending a Council of Jewish Elders meeting, Addi dragged Ursula to the basement of Magdeburg barracks. Once her eyes had adjusted to the relative darkness of the underground space, Ursula had at first stared, and then shaken her head in disbelief as she processed the scene before her.

A legless, Wurlitzer piano rested on the packed earth, and in front of the keyboard sat a very focused young man pouring over a tattered, dog-eared music score. His brown hair flopped over his eyes as he hummed to himself. He was so engrossed in his task that he didn't notice the two onlookers until Addi cleared her throat.

Rafael Schächter looked up quickly, his soulful brown eyes registering panic. When he realized that his visitors were friendly, he visibly relaxed.

"Forgive me. I was in the middle of reviewing music." He stood suddenly and broke into a lopsided grin. "Ah, my goodness. If I had not been taken to this terrible place, I might never have had the pleasure of making your acquaintance, Fräulein Becker."

His graceful bow stood at odds with the dismal surroundings, but Ursula responded in kind with a curtsy. "The pleasure is mine, Herr Schächter. Your wonderful reputation precedes you."

"You are too kind." His glanced about the subterranean space and spread his hands. She examined his long, slender fingers that moved with strength and grace. A pianist's hands. She smiled as he continued. "Alas, I have no seat to offer you."

Ursula waved away his concern and looked past him at the musical score that sat atop the broken piano. "What is that score?"

Schächter grinned again, and his entire face came alive. "It's Verdi's *Requiem*. Have you sung it?"

Ursula pulled back, her hand at her heart. "But of course! I performed it several times when studying Italian repertoire in Vienna."

"Dare I ask that you become my soprano soloist?"

Ursula looked uncertain. "Certainly, you don't mean to lead a choir in a performance of this magnificent work?"

"I do."

Ursula scanned the dank basement. "Here?"

"Yes." His earnest eyes bolstered her confidence and filled her with hope. If she'd learned one important lesson since arriving in Terezín, it was that hope could be simultaneously inspiring and dangerous. Hope implied a future.

"How will you muster the bodies to compose a choir?"

"Well, I have about fifty members, but if you agree to sing, I'm certain that I can rally others to the cause."

Ursula examined his open, triangular face. He was a natural leader, a practical, logical dreamer. She liked him. But she harbored doubts about the reality of executing such an enormous work with so few resources.

"How can we perform such a majestic piece in this desolate place?"

"It is precisely because of our surroundings that we *must* perform such a masterpiece. Music allows the soul to soar. During that flight, bleakness vanishes, like so much dust on a windy day. You know that. You're an artist, like me. Like Addi. Time stills when you're creating. You're transported to another world, another time." He stepped forward and locked eyes with her. "Art is not what we do. It is who we are."

Ursula gasped. *Did I not say those exact words to Willy on our first date?* Schächter's statement seeped into her mind and warmed her wounded soul. In the depths of despair, unsure how she would carry on after Marika's murder, a lifeline had been thrown to her.

She reached for Willy's locket, and once more was disappointed when her fingers found it gone. Willy would want her to accept Schächter's generous offer to sing, as would Marika, who had set this in motion prior to her death. After a beat, Ursula nodded as her eyes danced between Schächter and Addi. She hadn't been this happy since Willy asked her to marry him. "It would be my honor to be your soprano soloist, Herr Schächter."

Schächter turned to Addi. "My apologies, Addi. Would you care to join the choir as well?"

"Me? Oh, no. My artistic talent doesn't extend to singing."

The composer smiled. "Then we're agreed. Choir rehearsals begin in September."

The summer passed in a blur of work and personal rehearsal. Ursula would complete her required duties and then report to the Magdeburg basement, where she and Schächter would rehearse the soprano solo until the curfew horn sounded. She would rush back to Dresden and fall asleep humming, only to awaken and do the same thing all over again. The weather had turned sunny and warm, matching her disposition perfectly. If it weren't for missing Willy and the constant hunger pangs that punctuated her day, she would have said she was content. She hadn't even noticed that every woman and child in Dresden, to a person, had been shipped east within the last few months until Addi pointed it out to her.

"You really didn't notice, Ursula?"

Ursula gawked at the strange faces surrounding her. There were far more people in their bunkroom than she remembered ever seeing. She recognized none of them. "I really didn't."

Addi shook her head. "Well, I'm glad you're happy, all things considered."

September finally arrived. The day of the first rehearsal lasted forever as Ursula completed her kitchen duties and attended an art class with Addi. She kept glancing out the window to determine the time, and when the sun finally fell prey to darkness, she could no longer contain her excitement. Addi had to remind her to maintain her composure lest the guards become angry.

Later that evening, after the children had fallen asleep and most of the guards had withdrawn to the outside walls of the ghetto, Addi and Ursula crossed the compound to Magdeburg barracks. They slipped through the open door and down the stone stairs to the basement, where they found a large group quietly performing vocal warm-ups. Ursula's heart raced as she scanned the crowd, noting only a few familiar faces. As she joined in, she found that she couldn't stop smiling.

Schächter waved his hands as he conducted and then suddenly closed his fists. The group ceased singing and the maestro smiled.

"Ah. A group that is already well-trained. I appreciate that. Now to business. We have only one copy of the music, so we must all memorize our parts via rote repetition. As the *Requiem* is sung in four parts—soprano, alto, tenor, and bass—we will divide and conquer. Basses, please come to the piano to review your part with me while the other three sections rehearse as best you can."

Ursula walked to the corner of the room closest to the stairs. She turned around and was shocked to see a group of women approach and stare expectantly at her.

"Fräulein Becker, will you please lead us in the opening of the piece?" someone asked.

Ursula opened her mouth to protest when someone else added, "Please, Fräulein?"

Not knowing how she could gracefully decline the request, she nodded with much more confidence than she felt. Singing required a certain skill. But conducting was a different animal altogether. However, Ursula's insecurity fell away as she led the sopranos through the beginning of the *Requiem*. Like a steady flow of water gracefully wends its way around bends in the riverbed, voices swelled and lowered as the music demanded.

By the end of the first movement, tears of joy streamed down her face. She smiled, proud of her talented group, and noted tearful faces grinning back at her. The maestro had been correct in pushing forward in this endeavor. *Oh, but how I have* missed *music!* she thought gleefully. As she glanced at the undernourished, unwashed prisoners in the other vocal groups, she felt herself coming alive again. Embers of hope were stoked, motivating her to promise herself that she would persevere, survive, and find Willy, no matter the odds. She had forgotten what it felt like to be happy, to be lost in the music. She had forgotten the joy of working with others to create a work of art that was so much bigger than herself. "*Persist*," she heard Marika whisper. Ursula smiled. "I will," she whispered back.

A hacking sound in the tenor section drew her attention. All eyes turned to see a man sink to the floor, wheezing and coughing up blood. His brown, burlap shirt hung on his wasted frame and his pants were held up with a tightly knotted rope. He turned toward her as he coughed, and she noted that he was missing two teeth and had crepe paper arms. She walked over to him even as the others were backing away, putting distance between themselves and the ill man. As she knelt next to him, his rheumy eyes focused and came to life.

"Fräulein, it's nice to see you again," he wheezed.

Ursula's breath caught. "Fritz?"

"Ja." His smile was interrupted by a new round of coughing that left the area around him stained red. Onlookers stepped back farther.

Ursula's expression betrayed the dismay she felt at seeing his unhealthy state. Willy had told her that Fritz was in Dachau. She wondered if he'd been mistaken or whether Fritz had been moved. In the end, it didn't matter. He was here now.

"I know that I look a fright." A shaky hand reached atop his head to smooth what remained of his wiry, unkempt hair.

Ursula shook her head. "No, Fritz. You look ever the man you always were."

"Danke, Fräulein."

Ursula smiled as a tear ran down her cheek. "I asked you to call me Ursula, remember?"

Fritz started coughing again. When the fit had subsided, Ursula stood and faced the crowd.

"This man is one of the most important people in the Berlin opera world. He single-handedly ensured that the opera house was impeccably clean and that the productions were carried out to his high standards. Ladies and gentlemen, for those of you who don't know him, this is Herr Fritz Rosen, and he is my friend." She leaned down and wrapped her arm around his wasted body, then hoisted him to his feet. "I will walk you back to your barracks, Fritz."

The gratitude in the old man's eyes pained her as she maneuvered him up the narrow stairs. As they exited the building, he staggered and fell to the ground. She leaned down to retrieve him but stopped when she saw the look on his face. Following his gaze, she looked upwards, directly into the face of Commandant Siegfried Seidl.

37

Willy completed the first document in the enlistment packet and slid it to the side. In his peripheral vision, he saw the captain pick it up. He was so intent on his task that he didn't notice Hicks' expression as he reviewed it.

Hicks stood suddenly. "Is this some sort of joke?"

Willy looked up. "Excuse me?"

Hicks slapped the paper with the back of his right hand. "Hitler? Your last name is Hitler?"

Willy held his stare. "That's right, sir."

From Hicks' disgusted expression, Willy could tell that he'd truly believed it was a bad joke.

"You're serious. Please tell me that you're not related to him."

Willy remained silent.

"Oh, my God. Is he your father?"

Willy stood. "No, no, sir. He's my uncle, and I've just spent several years with him in Germany—"

Hicks' entire body tensed, and he raised his hand. Willy thought he might strike him, but Hicks pointed to the door. "Get out."

Willy was speechless. "But sir, I'm serious about serving my country. You see, my fiancée is being held in one of the camps you mentioned, and I need to get to her—"

"Get. Out."

Willy stopped speaking and gently placed the pen on the desk. "You're making a mistake, sir. I could really help England in the war."

"Yes. About that. How is it that you're so certain about Hitler's battle plans? Are you some sort of spy that plans to work both sides?" Hicks crossed from behind his desk and approached Willy.

Willy unconsciously stepped backwards to create more space between them. The office was so small that his back touched the wall. "No, sir. Of course not. I've spent a lot of time with my uncle over the last few years and I can be of service in terms of intelligence."

"I bet you can. Why didn't you tell me your surname in the beginning? Why did you hide it?"

"I didn't hide it."

"But you didn't say it either. Why not?"

Willy laughed bitterly. "Because I was concerned that I'd be received exactly like this."

"Well, maybe if you'd been more forthcoming, I might have seen things differently."

"But you need soldiers, sir, and I can fight. I *want* to fight!"

Willy's chest heaved with suppressed frustration. Hicks glared at him for a moment, then suddenly his posture relaxed, and his eyes softened. He sat on the edge of the desk, crossed his arms over his chest, and sighed heavily. "Listen to me, son. The fact is that even if I approved your enlistment, my superiors wouldn't. You'd be hounded by your fellow soldiers. Everyone would constantly question your loyalty. Can you imagine the field day the papers would have with the headline 'Führer's nephew joins the British army'? It just wouldn't work."

Willy's shoulders sagged. His brain struggled to find words that would convince Hicks he was wrong, that Willy would be a strong asset to his fellow soldiers. But in the end, he simply held out his hand. Hicks took it. "I wish you the best. I really do."

Willy nodded dejectedly and exited the office. He entered the cavernous foyer, and Nigel called out from the reception desk, "See you soon!" Willy didn't look at him. He didn't want the sergeant to see his tears. He held up his hand in good-bye and remained silent as he trudged slowly home.

He entered the empty house and collapsed on the settee. He sat hunched over, his head in his hands. Months had passed, and he was no closer to discovering Ursula's whereabouts, much less being able to rescue her. Hicks' comments about the work camps floated through his mind. *Was Ursula scared? Was she being fed and clothed properly? Was she still alive?* The final thought sent him reeling, and he raked his hands through his hair.

The jarring ring of the telephone jolted him from his nightmarish reverie. He stared at it, then reluctantly picked up the receiver.

"Hello?"

Silence. Crackling.

"Hello?"

Breathing came across the line.

"Who is this?"

"Meet me in ten minutes at the Rusty Scupper."

"What? Who is this?"

"You want answers? Meet me there."

"I don't know what you're talking about. I think you have the wrong—"

A growl came through the phone. "Stop playing around! Meet me if you want to learn anything about Ursula."

The call disconnected. Willy sat frozen, the receiver against his ear. He wasn't sure he'd heard correctly. Then his mental fog shattered, and he was on his feet. He grabbed his coat and ran out the door, down the street, and across the small common. As he ran, he wondered how he would recognize the man on the phone. His voice had been unfamiliar, with an East London accent.

He arrived at the Rusty Scupper, threw open the door, and stepped down two stairs to the stone floor. The abrupt change from light to dark momentarily blinded him. In that moment, the voice from the phone mumbled, "Follow me." As Willy's eyes adjusted, the man turned away and walked to a small, sticky booth. Willy took a seat in front of a mug of warm ale. The man pointed to it, then took a swig of his own, half-drunk glass. Willy scanned the pub's patrons. Overweight, middle-aged men circled the bar, glued to a football match on the tele. The dingy atmosphere reflected Willy's sour, dark mood.

"Thank you for coming."

Willy focused on the man seated opposite him. He was about Willy's age but was prematurely balding and had a scar that severed his left eyebrow. "It's not like I had a choice. If you have information about Ursula, I need to know."

"You've been busy, that's for sure. You must really love this girl."

Willy's eyebrows came together. "You've been following me?"

"For some time. Sorry about the enlistment. Rough one, that."

Willy looked away. "How did you know?"

The man shrugged. "You don't have to be a brain surgeon to know that the army wouldn't accept a lad with your surname." He finished his beer and pointed to Willy's. "Are you going to drink that?"

Willy shook his head and slid it across the table.

"You need to stop searching for her, Willy."

Willy's anguish instantaneously dried up and became a solid nugget of anger. "Never."

The man shook his head. He struck Willy as being genuinely sad. "It won't end well for you."

"Is that a threat?"

"No. It's a fact."

"Where is she?"

The man's eyes became hard. "This isn't a game, yet you treat it like one, attempting to outsmart the Führer like you did. You shouldn't have defied him, Willy. No one defies him and lives to talk about it."

"Another threat." The man held his gaze. "Tell me, how do you sleep at night knowing that you're a traitor to your country?"

"My country betrayed me a long time ago. Besides, Hitler pays better." They locked eyes. "If he hurt her—"

The man chuckled. "You are so naïve, Willy. He is the Führer. He can do anything. Literally. How do you think the letter from Alois arrived? He has people everywhere. Watching. Waiting. He obviously knows your address. He knows that Otto lives with you. He knows . . . everything."

Willy's vision narrowed. He refused to be baited when Ursula's life was at stake. "What did he do with her?"

The man suddenly leaned forward and spoke quickly. "I've been kind and patient but hear me when I say this: Every word of this exchange will make its way back to him, so I strongly suggest that you rethink your tone." He leaned back, seemingly spent, and finished his ale in one massive gulp.

Anger twisted into terror that gripped Willy's head in a vise. His voice sounded desperate to his own ears. "Did he hurt her?"

The man's eyes settled on the football match. "Did you really think he would let you waltz away from the Reich with Ursula on your arm? Your actions gave him no choice. Did you honestly believe that he knew nothing about the false documents you obtained, or the plan to relocate?"

Willy fought the urge to cry. He pictured his uncle, seated in the Berghof by a roaring fire, caressing Blondi's head. Then he pictured him at the height of anger, breathing heavily with spittle covering his lips. Willy had seen his fury many times but had never been its recipient. Understanding Hitler's capacity for ruthlessness, terror for Ursula's safety engulfed him.

The man removed a piece of paper from his pocket, then leaned forward again, his voice calm and quiet. "These next words are directly from your uncle, Willy. Listen carefully. 'You came to Germany with nothing but my surname, and I opened my home and my heart to you, nephew. You have repaid me with disloyalty and treachery.'"

"I have not—"

"*Silence!*" the man ordered. "You have turned your back on me and the Reich. Therefore, you are no longer welcome. Ever."

Willy's entire body became numb. He was being excommunicated. The evidence lay in the finality of Hitler's declaration and his curt manner of speech. Excommunication meant that his chances of finding Ursula dropped almost to zero.

"What of Ursula?" Willy whispered.

The man sighed deeply. "You're single-minded, aren't you? Here's the rest of your uncle's letter. 'Like Geli, Ursula belongs to me now. Forever. You won't see her again.'"

Like Geli. Willy's head felt like it would explode, and he choked back a sob. When he spoke, his voice sounded otherworldly. "Is she alive?"

Seconds ticked by as the man stared at Willy. His face was expressionless. A cheer went up from the bar as the favored team scored. The man's eyes fell to the letter. He spoke so quietly that Willy strained to hear. "Ursula is dead."

38

In a matter of seconds, Seidl's face registered shock, happiness, then confusion upon recognizing Ursula.

"Fräulein, you are out past curfew."

Being found outside after dark had resulted in several fatalities in the last few weeks. Ursula fought the panic that rose in her chest and offered her best smile. "Yes, Commandant. You see, we were downstairs rehearsing the *Requiem*, when I realized that my friend is ill and needs care."

"Ah, yes. Verdi. A beautiful piece of work. I'm glad that you're singing with the group. It thrills me actually."

Ursula glanced at Fritz. Seidl's lip curled upwards as he examined the ill man, who lay on the ground wheezing unevenly. Ursula wasn't sure he was even conscious, as his glazed eyes were open but exhibited no fear given their current predicament.

"You can't expect him to be taken to the medical facilities here. You know that medical care is for the guards only."

"Yet I was seen for my nose upon arriving in the ghetto. You saw to it personally if I recall." She smiled again and touched her healed nose for emphasis.

Seidl narrowed his eyes at her. "You are a clever one." His gaze traveled along the lines of her body before settling on Fritz. "What's wrong with this man?"

"I'm not sure, but he coughs blood, and his breathing is labored, as you can hear."

Seidl stepped back, withdrew a handkerchief from his pocket, and held it against his nose and mouth. "We have had many cases of illness such as this. It's probably acute pneumonia or tuberculosis. Either way, it's usually fatal."

"Not if he receives treatment."

Seidl's eyes moved slowly from Fritz's emaciated frame to Ursula's hopeful face. She felt the hair on her arms stiffen.

"You are correct, Fräulein. Not if he receives treatment. But what are we to do? What kind of agreement might we strike in order to aid your dying friend?" He withdrew the handkerchief from his nose and wiped the corners of his mouth before meticulously folding the hanky and replacing it in his breast pocket.

Ursula started trembling. She glanced at Fritz and knew that Seidl was correct. Fritz would die without medical intervention.

"Do not ponder your friend's situation too long, Fräulein. He doesn't seem to have much time left."

Ursula's eyes darted between Seidl and Fritz.

"Ah. I see. You're calculating if he would survive if he received treatment."

Ursula was shocked at Seidl's insight. He was not only intelligent. He was also cunning. A malignant combination.

"The answer is that I'm not sure. But what I do know is that he will die without treatment. We have already sent hundreds of prisoners east due to illness."

The veiled threat hit home, and Ursula closed her eyes. Her conscience wouldn't abide Fritz being sent to his death, especially when she could have prevented it.

Seidl leaned in close. "Fräulein, we both know I could demand what I want, but I am a gentleman. I offer you a choice."

"It's not a choice!" she hissed.

Seidl was unfazed. "Oh, but it is. The choice may not be a palatable one, but it's still a choice. I leave the decision to you. Please hurry." He glanced at his wristwatch. "My wife will wonder where I am if I don't return home soon."

Ursula gaped at him. "You have a wife?"

"Yes, and two beautiful children."

Ursula shook her head. "You would betray her?"

He laughed. "Our transaction has nothing to do with my wife."

Suddenly Fritz sat up and vomited. The sour aroma wafted up from the frozen ground. Despite the frigid temperature, sweat ran down his face. He looked around, found Ursula's eyes, and collapsed again.

A wave of nausea swept through Ursula. Without making eye contact with Seidl, she nodded. Silently, he led her into a small room that was used as an office for guards on duty. He closed the door behind them and caressed her face, then leaned down to kiss her. At the last second, she turned her head, so his lips landed on her cheek. She cringed, expecting to be slapped for her noncompliance, but instead he shrugged. "Pull down your undergarments." She reached under her skirt and lowered her underwear so that it fell around her ankles. He leaned into her so that she could feel his erection on her abdomen. She fought the urge to strike him and focused instead on Fritz, laying outside on the frozen earth. "Turn around," he whispered. Relieved to not look at him, she turned and felt his hands on her back rubbing gently. "You are so beautiful." She felt his hands bunch up her skirt until it was hoisted above her hips, then pressure on her upper back as he bent her over the small wooden desk. She gasped as his cold fingers entered her while he fumbled to unlatch his heavy black belt. "You feel so good," he moaned.

She heard the belt thump to the floor. His breath came more quickly as he unzipped his pants. She steeled herself by digging her nails into the wood and clenching her teeth as he repeatedly tried to enter her. He cursed under his breath. For a moment she thought that he might give up, but his hands gripped her hips in a vise. Suddenly he was inside her, thrusting violently. She stifled a scream by stuffing her fist into her mouth and tried to ignore the pain as he climaxed. She squeezed her eyes shut, silently apologizing to her father and Willy, willing them to understand the sacrifice she was making for a friend.

As Seidl withdrew, her mind turned to the conversation with Marika about shining Seidl's boots. At the time, she'd been adamant that she would never exchange sex for a favor. But as she thought of Fritz, she realized that no one knew how they'd react until presented with an ultimatum. She couldn't allow Fritz to perish knowing that she could have helped him. She decided that Marika would forgive her. She prayed that Willy and Otto would.

Seidl lowered her skirt and smoothed it against her buttocks. "I was not aware that you were a virgin. I must admit that I'm shocked, but it made the experience even more pleasant than I had imagined. Definitely worth the wait. You may dress now." Ursula pulled up her underwear. Her shame was complete as a warm wetness filled her undergarments, and she wondered if Willy would still desire her once he discovered her transgression.

She became aware that music was carrying up from the basement. Had the group just started singing again, or had they been singing the entire time and she'd simply not heard it?

She glanced at Seidl as he buckled his belt. "How is rehearsal going?" he asked.

Ursula stared, unsure how to respond.

"Verdi's *Requiem* is beautiful," he continued. "Shall we go and watch?"

"Your wife will worry if you don't—"

Seidl raised his eyebrows. "How kind of you to concern yourself with my well-being. My wife can wait. Come. Let's go together."

Ursula thought quickly. "What of Fritz?"

"Who?"

Ursula suppressed an urge to kick him in the testicles. "My friend outside."

"Ah, yes. We will attend to him immediately following. Come."

He opened the door and started toward the stairs, seemingly unconcerned if she followed. Ursula glanced at the door that led outside. She had to choose between returning to Fritz or following Seidl. *If I disregard his order, he might refuse to help Fritz at all.* She rushed down the stairs and caught up with Seidl as he stepped off the last stair into the basement.

The four voice parts had come together and were singing through the second movement. For a moment time stopped as the vocalists, unaware of their visitors, sang harmonies that vacillated between melancholic and soaringly triumphant. Ursula watched Seidl for any sign of impulsive violence as he listened, seemingly transfixed. But after several moments, he closed his eyes and swayed as the musical tension built. One of the altos noticed him and stopped singing, followed quickly by others in her section. Schächter took notice and ceased conducting, which caused a straggling effect as the voice of one singer after another decrescendoed to silence.

Seidl opened his eyes and smiled, then brought his hands together and applauded as more than one hundred haunted eyes looked from him to Ursula. With dread she realized that they must think she had purposely brought him there. Although the commandant had ordered them to learn the work, everyone knew the volatile nature of Seidl's moods. If he were in a room with an inmate, there was a fifty percent chance that the prisoner might die.

"Marvelous! Simply wonderful! Keep going," he called out.

The singers turned their collective gaze to Schächter, who nodded dumbly. Fearing that Seidl might shoot them when they resumed singing, the conductor snaked his way through the crowd so that his back was to the commandant and the singers were facing him. Ursula realized that, even in this stressful moment, Schächter was protecting his choir. If anyone were going to be shot in the back, it would be him. If Seidl removed the pistol from his holster, the choir would see it and have time to flee. At least some of them might escape up the narrow staircase before they were executed. Ursula marveled at his leadership. His plan was severely flawed, of course, but hope has a way of turning logical thoughts into fairy tale.

Her eyes flitted to the stairs. She pictured Fritz lying on the cold, hard ground. "Do not even think of attending to your friend until I say so," Seidl muttered. She glared at him, but he ignored her. "Take your spot, Fräulein. You are a soloist, are you not?" Reluctantly, Ursula found her place among the sopranos.

The maestro made eye contact with each person as he raised his arms to start the movement. The terrified vocalists, some of whom shook uncontrollably, were completely focused, fearing that if they didn't deliver a stellar performance, they might be killed on the spot.

The group managed a private concert that left Seidl openly weeping, and when Schächter ended the movement with a dramatic hand flourish, a heavy silence descended. With collective breath held, they observed Seidl remove his handkerchief and wipe his eyes.

"Despite the fact that you are all Juden, I am pleased. Very pleased actually. We shall continue these friendly evenings and you shall perform for all of the officers. Who knows, if you are exceptional, perhaps the Führer himself may pay us a visit!"

Hysterical twitters erupted as people realized that they would live through the night. Ursula was saddened at how desperate they had become, when news of the Führer coming would bring joy. But of course, each choir member now held value and, therefore, would be spared another day.

"What of Fritz, Herr Commandant?" Ursula defiantly raised her chin. "He awaits your promise."

Seidl's good humor evaporated. "Ah, yes, Fräulein. We had an *arrangement*, did we not?" His lewd innuendo was not lost on some members of the choir, who openly stared at Ursula. She ignored their scrutiny and stepped forward.

"Shall we see to him now?"

Seidl stepped aside and swept his arm forward, indicating that Ursula should lead the way. As they climbed the stairs, he called out, "Keep rehearsing. I don't want to be embarrassed if the Führer comes."

Ursula stepped outside and was almost blown over by a blast of arctic air. She removed her coat and ran to Fritz, whose body shook uncontrollably. She knelt and placed it over him, chastising herself for not thinking of doing it earlier. "Come, Fritz. Let's see the doctor."

He opened his eyes and whispered through blue lips. "You should not have sacrificed yourself, Fräulein Becker. Not for me."

She shifted her eyes to avoid his knowing gaze. "Let's get you up now."

Seidl looked on, arms folded across his chest.

Fritz moaned as she attempted to lift his frail frame. "I am done."

"No, Fritz. You must fight. You must!"

She felt his body relax. He had ceased shivering. "I am tired."

"I know but . . ." Her voice trailed off as he slowly shook his head.

"It is your turn to fight."

Staring into his glassy eyes, she whispered, "I don't know if I have the strength, Fritz."

He closed his eyes and exhaled a ragged breath. "You are stronger than you know, Ursula." His body went limp in her arms.

Ursula stared at his kind, weathered face for several moments before looking to the dark sky. She followed a delicate snowflake as it descended, gracefully floating this way and that before settling softly on Fritz's eyelashes, as if God were anointing Fritz for his ascension. She stared at the snowflake and remembered learning that no two flakes are exactly alike. Each is unique. Her heart felt as if it were being squeezed. The hope she'd enjoyed earlier shriveled, and she felt the burden of life return. *Survive.* She closed her eyes, wondering if she possessed the strength to carry on. *Resist.* She stroked Fritz's cheek. "Thank you for calling me Ursula, Fritz. Be at peace, my friend."

39

"Willy!" Bridget called up the stairs. "Dinner!" When Willy didn't appear, she set her mouth and returned to the kitchen.

"He's not coming. Let's eat, Otto."

Seeing the concern on Bridget's face, Otto placed his hand on her shoulder. "Let me speak with him."

Bridget sighed. "Alright. But don't be too long. I don't want your dinner to become cold."

Following the Rusty Scupper meeting, Willy had settled into a depression that lasted months. He ate little, bathed infrequently, and drank too much. Bridget did her best to entice him by preparing his favorite meals, and even went so far as to invite childhood friends over for tea. But Willy had begged off, informing her that she had no right to interfere with his affairs, and remained in his room while the gatherings proceeded without him.

For his part, Otto had grieved in his own way upon learning the outcome of Willy's meeting. He desperately wanted to believe that Ursula was still alive, but reports coming out of Europe were dire and spoke of thousands of Jews dying in concentration camps in Eastern Germany and Poland. He had attempted to contact Anna through letters, all of which returned to sender within days. With both daughters absent from his life, Otto felt as if his limbs had been severed one at a time, leaving him a shadow of the man he once was. Additionally, being German, he was unable to find any type of work in England, which contributed to his feelings of listlessness and inadequacy. The only bright spot in his life was Bridget. They had discovered a kinship in their shared losses and relied on each other for companionship in these darkest of days.

Otto climbed the stairs and knocked on Willy's door before entering. The room smelled of unwashed clothes and body odor. He crossed to the window and threw it open, then pulled the covers from Willy's bed.

"Hey!" Willy groaned. He squinted at Otto, then assumed the fetal position, his back to his visitor.

Otto spoke in German to ensure his meaning was understood. "Is this the kind of man my daughter is supposed to marry? A man who breaks into a thousand pieces when faced with adversity? You should be ashamed of yourself, Willy."

Willy didn't face him and responded in English. "She's dead, Otto! Hitler's man told me. He said the words! How can you not accept that?"

Otto stared out the window at Bridget's small, tidy garden. The zinnias stood proudly amidst the other flowers and herbs in the well-tended ground. "Because I choose hope, Willy. Because as long as there is no body for me to bury, then I can pray that she is still alive."

Willy sat up. Otto noticed that his unshaven face wore a thick layer of stubble and his eyes were dull. "Hope is a four-letter word, Otto."

"So is love," Otto said quietly in English. "You told me that you loved Ursula. You told me that you'd move heaven and Earth to find her. You promised me, Willy. What happened to that man? The one who loved my Ursula so completely that he was willing to die for her?" Otto would have been crying, but anger had sapped his well of sadness.

Willy's shoulders sagged. "I don't know what else to do, Otto. My father won't help. Uncle has disowned me. The British army won't allow me entry. Tell me. Please. What should I do?" His voice was thick with desperation and helplessness.

Otto sighed deeply and glanced at Willy's desk. On it lay several pieces of writing paper. Otto picked them up and read the top line. "'Why I hate my uncle.' Willy, what is this?"

Willy shrugged. "It started as a diatribe against Uncle Alf, but then it changed into an article that outlines why it was good that America entered the war and why they should continue to fight. It's going to be published in an American magazine called *LOOK*."

Otto read some of the captions underneath the family photographs included with the article. His breath caught in his throat. "You cannot print this, Willy."

"Why not? I hate him."

"It will enrage him. If Ursula is still alive, he will kill her. Besides, all of this cannot be true."

"It is," Willy insisted.

Otto continued reading the article and shook his head. "Surely you are mistaken. You say here that Hitler had an intimate affair with his niece named Geli, and that she was pregnant when she committed suicide. That cannot be true."

Willy stood. "Which part, Otto? That my uncle slept with his niece, or that she was pregnant? Ursula looked just like her, by the way. Uncle even compared Ursula to Geli in his letter. I think he might be losing his mind." Willy paused. "Or perhaps he lost it when Geli died, but no one noticed."

Otto looked hopeful. "If Ursula resembles this Geli, maybe that's a good thing."

Willy shook his head. "She doesn't *resemble* her, Otto. She's her twin. At one point I would have agreed with you, but not now. I think he vented his frustration on Ursula as his quest for world domination became more challenging." Willy looked out the window, unable to continue his thoughts.

Otto's eyebrows knitted. "This Geli was pregnant when she committed suicide?"

Willy nodded. "The whole family knew about it. Uncle was furious when she told him about the baby. I'm not sure she killed herself, by the way. She might have been murdered. His gun was found next to her body."

Otto stared open-mouthed.

"I know. It's beyond comprehension. But it's all true, and I'm going to print it."

"You cannot."

"I need to get his attention, Otto."

"But not this way, Willy. He'll kill her."

Willy jumped up and grabbed Otto's shoulders. "She's already dead, Otto! He told me! I feel it. I know it. Now it's time for revenge." He turned away. "Besides, it's done. I've spoken with the editor of the magazine, and the article will run in the July fourth edition. All of America will know what a sick bastard my uncle is."

"You're going to the United States then?"

Willy shook his head. "Their state department has issued quotas for immigrants and England is already past its quota for this year. I'm unable to obtain a visa."

"So, it seems that you've not been wallowing in sadness and filth this entire time. You've been scheming."

Willy rolled his eyes. "There was a lot of wallowing in the beginning, but as my melancholy turned to anger, I started writing, and that's what surfaced." He pointed to the pages in Otto's hands. "I mailed the final draft to *LOOK* magazine, and they responded that they wanted to print it."

"Willy, what if Ursula is alive? You'll be signing her death warrant if the Führer finds out."

"Otto, if I thought for one second that Ursula were still alive, I wouldn't have sent the article. The only way my uncle will be stopped is if a powerhouse like the United States continues to intervene, and the only way to make the Americans listen is to have them come face-to-face with the devastation he's causing. In the article I describe Uncle Alf's world-domination aspirations. If the Americans think he's coming for them and their way of life, they'll continue to fight. Otherwise, we'll all be dead in a matter of months anyway."

The papers fluttered in Otto's hands and fell to the ground. Otto clutched his chest and collapsed, his breathing labored. Willy flew to his side, turned him on his back, and unfastened the top buttons on his shirt. "Otto, try to breathe. I'll get help." He ran to the top of the stairs. "Mum! Otto collapsed! Call the doctor!" Willy heard a plate shatter on the kitchen floor, then his mother's thick-heeled shoes running to the telephone. Her voice sounded frantic as she spoke with Dr. Morgan, who lived two houses away.

Willy ran back to Otto. "The doctor will be here soon, Otto. Hang on." Otto's ashen face became beet red as a jolt of pain shot through him. His entire body tensed and then relaxed as the spasm passed. "It's my heart."

He had reverted to German again and Willy responded in kind. "I know. Help is coming."

Moments later Willy heard Dr. Morgan's heavy footfalls on the stairs, and then he was in the room, black bag in hand. Bridget stood behind him in the doorway, her arms crossed protectively across her chest and her face a mask of worry. The doctor knelt by Otto and calmly smiled down at him. "Well, well, Otto. What have we here?"

Otto groaned. "My heart."

Dr. Morgan removed a stethoscope from his bag and listened to Otto's heart and lungs, then placed a small white aspirin under his tongue. He leaned back and sat on his heels. "How long have you had heart palpitations, Otto?"

Normal color was returning to Otto's cheeks. "For years."

"Have you been under any undue stress recently?" A knowing glance passed between Willy and Bridget. Dr. Morgan didn't know Otto's history. No one did. The neighbors had been told that Otto was a distant relative visiting from Austria.

Otto blinked rapidly before answering. "No."

Dr. Morgan nodded. "Well, keep it that way. I could take you to hospital and run some tests if you like, but I think you had significant heart palpitations. Although it most likely wasn't a heart attack, these symptoms should be taken seriously because they can lead to complications, including a heart attack. Do you understand?"

Otto nodded and slowly sat up.

"You need to avoid stress and walk daily to maintain good blood flow." Dr. Morgan stood and smiled at Bridget, who fussed with her hair and tried not to cry.

"Thank you for coming so quickly, doctor. I'll see you to the door," Willy said as he escorted him back downstairs.

When Willy returned to his room, Bridget was seated on the floor next to Otto. His head leaned on her shoulder, and her arm was draped around him. Her hand gently stroked his cheek and they spoke in hushed, intimate tones. Willy stopped on the threshold, transfixed. He had been so focused on himself that he hadn't noticed the relationship that had blossomed. He realized that he was smiling at seeing them together. Both had lost so much, and they were entitled to happiness.

Then his thoughts turned to Ursula, and his smile faded.

There would be no happy ending for Ursula and him.

There would be only revenge.

And that would have to be enough.

40

Months of rigorous rehearsals had ensured that the choir had mastered the *Requiem*. Despite having only one score, the 150 inmates had memorized the words, practicing until Schächter's exacting diction and dynamics requirements had been exceeded. The last rehearsal prior to the performance had been held the previous evening. The month of November had been unseasonably warm, and there was an electricity in the air as people gathered in the basement.

Schächter clapped his hands to draw everyone's attention.

"Have you seen them? The flowers?" He made eye contact with each member of the group, some of whom had trouble standing due to illness or undernourishment. "Even in the cold, in this most desolate of places, I saw a bloom, ignorant of the horrors that surround it. The flowers reappear, year after year, despite the chaos and ugliness into which they are born. And why?"

He walked among the singers, touching them lightly on backs and shoulders as he passed. Reminding them that they were humans who required touch, love, and beauty.

"Because life always vanquishes death. Because there is always a chance to be reborn, no matter the circumstances." He crossed to stand in front of the group. He radiated serene, passionate intensity.

"Verdi has allowed us the unique opportunity to be transported into his exquisite musical world. You will be warm, and your bellies will be full. Pain will cease, replaced by a euphoria that will bring you closer to God. Are you with me?"

Ursula reflected on the fact that there are people in the world who draw others toward them. They have an irresistible pull that cannot be denied. Hitler had this quality, and he used it to destroy. Rafael Schächter used it to create.

She pulled her eyes from the maestro and scanned the choir. Every single person was nodding reverently. He had captured the hearts and minds of souls whose bodies were already imprisoned. The silent crowd waited expectantly.

"You are the flowers. Do you understand? The flowers that refuse to yield in the face of overwhelming adversity. You continue to rise from the ground and bloom, even though others seek to crush your souls. It will not be so! You will rise. Physically, emotionally, spiritually, and musically. You. . . will. . . rise." He lifted his hands and the choir burst into grateful applause, many weeping openly. After a moment, he held out his arms, palms down, indicating the group should settle. When it was silent, he smiled.

"Tonight we have the opportunity to show how capable we are, that we are worth more than we have been given. I've had the pleasure of working with you, some of the brightest and most talented musicians in the world, and I look forward to exhibiting our skill to Adolf Hitler when he arrives."

Ursula's legs gave way beneath her, and she fell to the packed earth. Although there had been rumor about Hitler potentially attending the performance, she hadn't believed that he would actually lower himself to enter a prison camp. Like all bullies, at heart he was a coward and didn't like to witness the devastation he caused.

Addi knelt next to her. "Ursula, are you alright?"

Ursula started hyperventilating and Addi forced her head between her knees. "Slow your breathing, Ursula. Breathe with me." Addi inhaled and exhaled, her hand on the back of Ursula's neck. Eventually, Ursula's inhalations returned to normal, and she noted with embarrassment that a circle had formed around her. She briefly wondered if they were concerned for her, or for themselves if the soprano soloist wasn't able to perform.

The maestro broke through the line and grinned. "No need to worry, Ursula. Your melodious voice will carry from here to Berlin. You will sing to the Nazis what we, as Jews, cannot say." He held out his hand. She took it and he pulled her from the ground. He turned to the choir. "Remember, whatever we do here is just a rehearsal for when we will play Verdi in a grand concert hall in Prague in freedom." He turned back to Ursula and nodded, and she felt strengthened by his confidence.

He strode back to the front of the room. "I understand that you have a warm meal waiting for you and washed clothes in your barracks. Please eat and dress, then go to the Town Hall, where I will meet you at seven p.m. We begin singing promptly at eight." He clapped his hands twice in dismissal, and immediately tongues started wagging about the meal and fresh clothing.

Ursula and Addi rushed to the dining building, where they took their place in queue. Aromas of boiled potatoes, cabbage, and meat wafted from the kitchen. Ursula's mouth started watering, and she found she couldn't control her saliva. By the time she and Addi collected their food and sat at a table, she was wiping her mouth with the back of her hand. They were silent as they ate, and Ursula reminded Addi several times not to eat too quickly, lest she regurgitate her food before her body had a chance to digest it. Ursula ingested half of her food, then wrapped the rest in a handkerchief and stuffed it into her pocket. Their energy levels increased almost immediately after eating, and they ran to Magdeburg, where Ursula found a large, rectangular box lying on her mattress. As the other choristers ejected squeals of delight upon seeing freshly washed shirts and dresses, Ursula approached the box cautiously, wondering why her outfit was not laid out like the others.

Moments later Addi appeared at her side. "Look, Ursula!" Addi turned in a circle, her skirt rising and falling as she spun. Ursula was reminded of the day she had twirled in front of her dressing room mirror, the day Willy asked her to marry him. That had been seventeen months, nine kilos, and one headful of lustrous hair ago. It may as well have been a lifetime.

"Open the box, Ursula!" Addi ordered. Ursula looked at her, resplendent in her full stomach and warm clothes. She didn't want to spoil Addi's mood but couldn't shake the feeling that she'd just ingested her last supper. She evaluated her peers preening for one another. Their fresh clothes weren't a reward for a job well done. They were designed to hide the true state of the prisoners' physical malnutrition and degradation.

"Ursula!" Addi stomped her foot and crossed her arms, looking very much like the teenage girl she was. Ursula slowly unfastened the raffia string that surrounded the box, then removed the lid.

A deep-green silk gown lay gracefully within pristine, white paper. Ursula's heart skipped a beat as she withdrew it from its paper cocoon. She held it up and stared at its full length, then held it against her body. "It's exquisite," Addi breathed. Ursula glanced at the box. A pair of matching green, silk shoes lay in the box, along with an envelope addressed to her. She picked it up and read silently.

Dearest Ursula,
I had this dress fashioned specifically for you. Commandant Seidl was kind enough to provide me with your dimensions. My intention was for the green to highlight your fiery, feline eyes. I looked forward to seeing you wearing it when you perform for me, but alas I am unable to attend this evening's performance. Duty calls. After the performance, however, I have a surprise for you, and you alone.
Yours truly and always,
Adolf

Ursula ran her fingers through her short hair and clenched her teeth. Hitler's comment about Seidl was surely meant to belittle her by reminding her of the devil's deal she'd made regarding Fritz. She threw the dress and the note on her pallet. Addi picked up the paper and read it aloud.

"Wow," she breathed. "'When you perform for me' and 'Yours truly and always'? Is there more to this story, Ursula? The Führer writes as if he knows you intimately."

Ursula whirled around. "He does not!"

Addi held up her hands in surrender. "I believe you, but I'm not sure they do."

Ursula turned to find the other inmates staring at her. One woman spoke for the group. "I had heard that you knew the Führer, but for him to have a dress designed for you . . ." The woman left the thought unfinished as she and several others whispered.

Ursula sat heavily, her head in her hands. "I can't do it," she moaned.

Addi sat next to her. "You can do it. The question is, will you? It's your voice, so it's your choice. But you must recognize that the fate of the choir lay in your decision."

Ursula laughed derisively. "Why are we constantly surrounded by terrible choices, Addi? Watch someone be shot or intervene and risk dying ourselves. Offer food to a starving man and risk starvation ourselves. Give succor to a diseased person and risk acquiring the illness." She glanced out the window. "I remember a time, not too long ago, that my hardest choice was where to dine with Willy or which skirt to wear. Oh, how I yearn for those mindless, easy decisions." She turned back to Addi whose glassy eyes were far away. "What is it, Addi?"

Still staring into the distance, Addi spoke quietly. "I had to make a difficult choice."

Ursula waited, knowing that she would speak when she was ready. The pain in her eyes was almost unbearable. "When the brownshirts came to arrest me, they asked if either of my sisters preferred women like I do. I assured the soldiers that my older sisters were pure as the driven snow. But they didn't believe me, so they had me—" She stopped abruptly and broke down. Loud bursts of emotion broke through her carefully constructed façade.

Ursula rubbed her back. "Take your time," she whispered.

Addi's sobs subsided and became gulps of air. She wiped her nose. "They made me choose a sister to be killed as a reminder to follow the rules."

Ursula had imagined several scenarios, but not this. Even now, her imagination struggled against such cruelty. "What did you do?" she whispered.

Addi's unblinking eyes filled with tears. "I did nothing. How could I possibly decide? It was an impossible choice. So, I didn't choose. I did nothing." Tears spilled down her cheeks.

Ursula's eyebrows knitted. "What happened?"

Addi's eyes darted back and forth as they relived the past. "They shot both of them, right there in our apartment, before dragging me away. My parents were left childless in a matter of seconds."

Ursula couldn't speak. There simply weren't words to express her feelings. She squeezed Addi's hands and glanced at the group of women clustered in the corner. Her eyes traveled to the beautiful gown that lay crumpled on her filthy pallet. Addi's earlier words played through her mind—"the fate of the choir lay in your decision." Her mind wandered to the death of Markus Appel in the train car many months ago. Her indecision had directly caused his murder, and his vacant eyes still haunted her nightmares. If she chose not to sing tonight, she knew that the choir would most likely be killed. Like so many other instances in the ghetto, the outcomes of each choice were clear.

Sing and live. Or refuse to sing and cause the deaths of more than one hundred people.

She stood, undressed quickly, and slipped the dress over her head. Although it was too large, the effect was immediate. Standing erect, she felt the diva awaken inside her. The women sensed the change and congregated around her, her confidence luring them to her light. She lifted her chin and held out her hand to Addi, who wiped her eyes and stood. Ursula gave Addi a reassuring nod and smiled proudly as she addressed the women.

"Herr Schächter is correct. Tonight, it's our turn to shine. Let's show our captors that our voices will never be silenced. Let us sing the words that we cannot speak. Remember the words of the *Requiem*: 'Deliver me ... whatever is hidden will be revealed . . . nothing shall remain unavenged . . . from the ashes, the guilty man to be judged . . . how great will be the terror, when the Judge comes.' It's only a matter of time before our captors are judged, if not by other men, then certainly by a higher power. Let us lose ourselves in music while simultaneously making a statement." The women cheered, then chatted excitedly as they rushed downstairs.

"Are you coming?" Addi asked.

"Just give me a moment." Ursula watched from the window as the animated group walked down the street. The choir had worked so hard, and she wanted to look forward to the concert. But the dread she'd felt earlier sat like a stone in her stomach. She picked up Hitler's note and re-read it.

```
After the performance, however, I have a
surprise for you, and you alone.
```

The first time Hitler had surprised her was when he'd had Otto beaten and left him for dead. The second time was her kidnapping. Bile rose in her throat. She wasn't certain her sanity could handle any more of his surprises.

III

4 1

"It's not a very flattering picture of me," Bridget sniffed.

Willy wrapped his arms around her waist. "What do you mean? I think you look stunning. Otto, what do you think?"

Otto took the magazine from Willy and perused the article, "Why I Hate My Uncle," before focusing on the pictures that accompanied the story. When he spoke, he was blushing. "I believe you appear strong and beautiful, Bridget."

Bridget twisted her mouth in an effort not to smile. She waved her hand toward Otto and stomped to the kitchen, muttering about dinner. Otto glanced at Willy and shrugged. "Sometimes I don't understand your mother."

Willy rolled his eyes. "Welcome to the club," he joked.

"What are you going to do about the telegram?"

Willy held his finger to his lips. "Shh! Mum doesn't know yet."

Otto's eyebrows shot up. "She doesn't know you're traveling to America?"

A look of consternation crossed Willy's features. "Again, hush!"

"What do I not know?" Bridget appeared, wiping her hands on her apron. "Dinner is ready. What do I not know?" Her stern gaze swept between Willy and Otto. Willy remained silent and glared at Otto, willing him to hold his tongue.

"Willy is going to America!" Otto blurted. Willy dropped his head and sighed.

"What?" Bridget threw up her hands. "The armed services won't take you so now you're rushing off to America? When were you going to tell me? When you were on the ship?"

Willy looked at his mother. She meant business. Her hands were on her hips and dinner had been forgotten. "Mum, listen. I received a telegram from a man named William Randolph Hearst."

"Who in the bloody hell is he?" she fumed. Willy hadn't heard his mother swear in years. If he were honest, he'd admit that the curse word struck a wee bit of fear into him.

"He's a businessman in the United States. Very powerful. He read my article and wants me to come to the States for a speaking tour."

Bridget drew back. "Speaking tour? What would you talk about?"

"Why I hate Uncle Alf."

Bridget looked at Otto and then back at Willy. "You're joking."

"I'm not."

Bridget's mouth hung open. Finally, she said, "But ... can you get a visa? I thought that all of the UK visas are spoken for this year."

"Mr. Hearst has offered to sponsor me."

"What does that mean?"

"It means that he'll be responsible for me, financially and personally."

"He'll pay you for speaking?"

"Handsomely."

"He's certain that people want to hear you discuss why you hate your uncle?"

Willy approached his mother and put his hands on her shoulders. "Mum, magazines sold out within two hours of hitting newsstands. Americans are concerned that Uncle Alf might try to jump the pond, so they want to better understand what they're up against from someone who knows him."

Bridget shook her head quickly, as if to rid herself of an idea. "Why are Americans so bloody curious? Why can't they just let things be?"

"There's another benefit to my going, Mum. I'm certain that knowing people like Mr. Hearst will get me closer to finding Ursula. I've hit only dead ends here in England. My hope is that the clout of wealthy people like him will aid in my search. Who knows? Maybe the American president will get involved."

Willy could see that Bridget was trying to find fault in his argument. He decided to press his point. "There's something else you should know."

Bridget threw up her hands. "What could be more important than the fact that my only son is leaving me. *Again.*"

Willy smiled and glanced at Otto. Bridget noted the look and narrowed her eyes. "What have you two schemed?"

"You and Otto are coming with me. I've already negotiated it."

Bridget slowly turned to Otto, who was smiling from ear to ear. She crossed her arms. "You knew about this and didn't say anything to me?"

Willy pulled her into an embrace. "Mum, don't blame Otto. I told him just this morning. This is a good thing. We'll be welcomed in the States. You'll have a beautiful home—"

"I have a beautiful home."

"You'll have an automobile."

"My legs work just fine, thank you."

"But most of all, Mum—" Willy withdrew and held her at arm's length. "You'll have me."

Bridget glared at him, pursed her lips, and then shook her head. She huffed, then turned to Otto. "Well, don't just stand there. We need to start packing for America."

* * *

Willy walked down the gangplank first, followed by Bridget and Otto. A man dressed in a black suit and cap awaited them holding a handwritten sign that said "William Patrick." Following the treatment he'd received in England, Willy had requested that his surname not be listed anywhere other than the speaking circuit. He approached the man. "I'm William Patrick."

The man tilted his cap. "Hello, sir. My name is Matthew. I'll be driving you to your hotel. Your luggage will arrive in a separate car and be delivered to your rooms. Please follow me." Matthew led them to a black Cadillac limousine. He opened the door for Bridget, who peeked inside, then withdrew. "How many other people will be traveling with us?"

Matthew's eyebrows knitted in confusion. "No one, ma'am."

Bridget shook her head. "Surely this enormous car is not just for the three of us?"

"It is, ma'am."

Willy laughed. "Mr. Hearst sent it for us. Get in, Mum."

They rode in silence, Otto running his hands over the velvety leather while Bridget's nose remained glued to the window. As they traveled past Central Park, Bridget commented on the lush greenery in the middle of the city.

"Yes. It's beautiful, Mum, and our hotel is up ahead on the right."

Matthew pulled up in front of the Ritz Carlton. Valets approached and opened the car doors, then escorted them into the hotel, where they checked in. When the three of them were finally alone, Bridget breathed out a heavy sigh. "My goodness, William! This Mr. Hearst must value you greatly."

A knock sounded. Willy crossed to the door and opened it to find a tall, blue-eyed, elderly man who wore a colorful tie and a wide smile. He lifted his fedora in greeting. "Willy, I presume?"

Willy returned the smile. "Mr. Hearst, I presume?"

They shook hands and Willy made introductions. Bridget was uncharacteristically quiet, leading Willy to assume that she was overwhelmed by the opulence and overt "Americanism" of it all. Mr. Hearst wasted no time in getting to the point.

"Willy, your tour starts tonight here at the Ritz. My people have booked the ballroom, the large one, and it's already sold out. As word spreads, they'll book larger venues in various cities around the country. By the time I'm done with you, the name Hitler will have a new, better connotation, and you'll be a wealthy man." His hand landed heavily on Willy's back.

Willy smiled. "Thank you, Mr. Hearst. That sounds wonderful, and I'm hoping that shining a light on my uncle's motivations will aid America in fighting the war."

Otto cleared his throat. Willy glanced at him and nodded. "There's one more thing, Mr. Hearst. Do you remember I told you about my fiancée, Ursula Becker?"

Hearst's face became stern and he pinched his lower lip. "Yes, yes. I remember. A bad business, that."

"Well, I'm hoping that this speaking tour will highlight her situation and put pressure on my uncle to release her if she's still alive."

Hearst nodded in thought. "Based on what I've heard about Adolf Hitler, I don't think your speeches will have an impact. But, by all means, feel free to mention her in your talk and we'll see what happens. See you downstairs at seven p.m."

* * *

Bridget peeked behind her at the hundreds of people who packed the ballroom. She straightened Willy's tie. "You're very brave, William. I would faint if I had to speak in front of this crowd."

"Mum, if Ursula is still alive, she's the brave one. For all we know, as we eat caviar and enjoy luxurious beds, she's sleeping outside and starving. Every move I make is with the intention of finding her." Willy looked at Otto. His pained expression captured the immense sadness in Willy's heart.

Bridget squeezed his hand. "Good luck, son."

Willy took the podium to muted applause. Perusing the sea of expectant faces, he realized that all he wanted to do was talk about Ursula and his desperation to find her. But the audience had paid a tidy sum to hear the Führer's nephew speak, so he gathered his thoughts and began.

"Ladies and Gentlemen, thank you so much for attending this evening. My name is William Patrick Hitler, and I am the nephew of Germany's leader, Adolf Hitler. I would imagine you're here because you read my piece in *LOOK* magazine. I believe it's clear in the article that I detest my uncle. So, now that we've addressed the elephant in the room, let me open by saying thank you. On behalf of all those who resist, thank you for stepping in to aid the fight against my uncle and all he stands for. I know your country has made a sacrifice in entering the war, and I know many men will die, but I'd like to tell you what the German people are thinking at this most crucial point in German history. Imagine for a moment that you have become crippled. Through no fault of your own, you lost your leg in an accident. You are now unable to work and over time, become destitute. Your children turn to you, their father, and say, 'Dad, why don't we have food on the table and fresh clothes on our backs?' What's your response? Would it be enough to answer, 'I have no leg, child, and therefore cannot work?' Of course not. Just because you've lost your leg doesn't make you any less responsible for taking care of your family. It simply means that you need to find another way to put food on the table. Such it was with Germany after the Great War. After losing badly and signing the Treaty of Versailles, the people of Germany were ashamed and destitute. They turned to their government for help but received nothing because it, too, was broken and destitute.

"Now, I know what you're thinking. 'We cannot compare Germany to the father in my story because the father lost his leg through no fault of his own. But I submit to you that the people of Germany, like the children in my story, are not at fault. It was the kaiser who was greedy, but the children of Germany, its citizens, ended up losing everything. They became desperate and despondent." Willy paused and made eye contact with people in the front rows. He had their complete, undivided attention. It felt good to be taking action. He stood straighter.

"The fact is . . . when people feel hopeless, they turn to the man who offers them the most promising chance of a bright future, even if it seems implausible. In fact, I would argue that the actual idea one proposes is less important than the person who is delivering the message, and the manner in which it is delivered. My uncle, Adolf Hitler, arrived on the scene with strong optimism of once again delivering to Germany a respected place in the world. His initial message of hope was like a balm to a burn victim or a job for the crippled father. Citizens thronged to his ideas, and to him. His success become synonymous with Germany's success. Over time, he *became* Germany. As he grew in stature and power, so did the country. Suddenly food was on the table and men were back at work, able to hold their heads high, as they were providing for their families.

"What did it matter that first one group, and then another group's liberties were constrained? It didn't affect average Germans, so they looked the other way as their neighbor's shop was destroyed or as books were burned. What did it matter that soldiers patrolled the streets, killing those who spoke out?"

Willy stopped again. Eyes were riveted to him, some disbelieving, but most intrigued. "I'm sure that you've heard stories, rumors. I'm here to tell you ... they are true. Every single one of them. For each rumor you've heard, there are fifty other truths that have yet to be revealed about the horrors perpetrated against those who don't agree with my uncle. He is abhorrently cruel and will not stop until he's taken over the world." Willy drew away from the microphone and took a sip of water. "I don't need to lecture you on how we've arrived at this point in history, and you already know that the wolf is on your doorstep. Many of you think you understand my uncle, his ruthlessness, his insatiable desire for control. I'm here to tell you that the situation is far more dire than the newspapers have reported, and that any promise Adolf Hitler makes will be broken if it aids his quest for greatness. Thank you. Any questions?"

Hands shot up around the room. Willy pointed to an elderly man in the second row. "Yes, sir?"

The man stood. "We've all heard rumors that Jews are being persecuted, sent away to work in camps. Is that true?"

Willy nodded. "Yes. They're sent by train to camps in Germany and Poland where they're worked to death in many cases." Murmurs rippled through the audience.

A voice called out from the back of the room. "Why didn't the Jews just leave?" Heads bobbed up and down. The nods of agreement surprised Willy. He supposed it was a fair question for a person who had not lived through it. Yet it was difficult to hear without becoming angry. How easy it was for these well-to-do men, safe in their powerful country, tucked away from the chaos across the ocean, to toss out callous comments. Willy swallowed and reminded himself that he had an opportunity to educate the people sitting before him. *They're here because they want to learn, to be informed. Perhaps, even to help.*

"I would invite you to put yourself in the shoes of a Jewish family. Can you imagine leaving everything you've ever known, including extended family, to start life anew somewhere else, where you might not even know the language?" His eyes swept the crowd, driving his point home. Someone said, "I would leave if my life depended on it. I certainly wouldn't assume that countries like the U.S. would swoop in save me. Why didn't they leave?"

Willy smiled so that he wouldn't scream. "Because they didn't know their lives were at risk. Not in the beginning, at least. By the time many realized that they might be killed, it was too late to leave. Many countries, including the United States, closed their borders to refugees. By the time people realized that they should get out, there was no place left to go."

Again, Willy paused and took a sip of water. "Don't you see? I'm here to warn you. It's not too late for you like it is for the Germans. Some Germans are committed Nazis, but others support Hitler out of fear. They don't know about the atrocities. And if they do, they turn a blind eye because they'd rather be an unwilling participant than dead. But you don't have to be like the Germans. By informing yourselves and continuing to fight, you choose to stand up against Adolf Hitler."

Someone called out, "We just finished a world war. I say we pull our boys out and let the Krauts deal with their own mess!" Assent trickled across the room.

Willy shook his head. "Forgive me for hiding behind stories and niceties. I now see that the time has passed for all of that. So, let me state the issue clearly and unequivocally. People are being murdered by the thousands at the hands of amoral, power-hungry zealots who will stop at nothing to dominate the world. *Nothing*! If you choose to remove your support, Hitler *will* attack the United States. It's only a matter of time. And that time, gentlemen, is shrinking by the day."

Chaos erupted in the large room as men stood and shouted at him and at each other. Willy glanced at Mr. Hearst, who was drawing his hand across his throat. *End it!* he signaled.

Willy cleared his throat, then leaned into the mic. "Her name is Ursula Becker." The brief, confusing statement stunned the raucous crowd into silence. Willy glanced to his right and nodded. Otto emerged and placed a large photo of Ursula on a pre-positioned easel.

Willy stared at the photograph and swallowed the lump in his throat. "Her name is Ursula Becker, and she is my fiancée. Not only is she exquisitely beautiful, but her voice is angelic. My uncle kidnapped her. She may already be dead, or she may be locked away in one of the work camps I mentioned." Willy choked back a sob before continuing. "I requested the help of the British government, to no avail. I tried to enlist in the British military but was denied because of my surname. That's why I originally wrote the article that brought me here today. I implore you to continue aiding the Allies, to protect your country and its democracy. Otherwise, like me, before you know it, you might find yourself searching for your Ursula. Thank you." Willy stepped away from the podium and removed a handkerchief. He turned away and wiped his eyes.

Otto approached and patted him on the back. "Well done, Willy."

"Thanks, Otto. Let's hope that my speech made an impact."

"Excuse me," a voice said.

Willy turned to find a tall, balding man staring at him. His clear, blue eyes were warm, and he carried himself with an air of competence and authority.

"May I help you?" Willy asked.

"My name is Raoul Wallenburg. I enjoyed your talk, Mr. Hitler. I'm sorry about your fiancée."

Willy shook his hand. "It's a pleasure to meet you, Mr. Wallenburg."

"I'll get right to the point. The United States has created a War Refugee Board, WRB for short. It's working with the Swedish government to save as many Jews as possible from persecution. To that end, I've been tasked to work with my fellow Swedish countrymen to rescue Jewish victims in Budapest."

"That's wonderful."

Wallenburg shook his head quickly. "No, no, you're misunderstanding me."

"Alright."

He leaned closer to Willy. "I know about the camps to which you referred in your speech."

Willy stared at him, waiting. Finally, he said, "Yes? And?"

"How would you like to become my assistant, Mr. Hitler?"

Willy shook his head. "I appreciate your kind offer, but I'm touring the country speaking like I did here this evening."

"The International Red Cross is slated to visit one of the camps you mentioned."

"Really? Why?"

"Some six hundred Danish Jews have recently been sent to the camp and the king of Denmark insists that the Red Cross visit to ensure they're being treated well."

"I see."

"As a delegate of the WRB, I might be able to arrange accompanying the Red Cross during its visit. If you were my assistant, you would, of course, come along as well. You would enjoy diplomatic protection not normally afforded to foreign citizens on Nazi soil. Do you understand?"

Willy's arms tingled as he processed Wallenburg's implication. "Will you be visiting other camps as well?"

"The Red Cross has been given access to only one camp this June. But if things go well there, who knows? Perhaps Hitler might allow us to visit other camps. It would be a start in your search for Ursula."

"Which camp are you visiting?"

"It's called Theresienstadt, or Terezín for short. I'm told that many artists are housed there."

42

Ursula rushed to catch up with the rest of the women but stopped short when she saw a large black car parked in front of the Town Hall. It looked exactly like the one she and Willy had taken from the airstrip to the Berghof so long ago. She breathed deeply and continued up the stairs to join the rest of the choir. The side door opened, and laughter spilled out. She glanced inside and saw rows of chairs filled with inmates.

In the front two rows sat guards and SS officers. Looking more closely she recognized Heinrich Himmler, the SS animal who'd overseen Otto's beating. Next to him sat a woman dressed in a calf-length, periwinkle, silk dress with matching shoes. *What a lovely profile his wife has*, she thought. The woman's pixie short hair curled around her pearl-studded ears, and she laughed gaily. Ursula cocked her head. The lilt of laughter sounded familiar, and she squinted to get a better look.

She was staring at her sister. Her breath caught and she was transported back to the last time they'd performed together in Berlin. A surge of love overwhelmed her. She felt drawn to Anna, desperate to touch her, to speak to her, to apologize for all of the slights over the years. She wanted to reverse time, to undo the anger and hurtful words. She wanted to return to the period when they shared more than they differed, when all that mattered was the fact that they were sisters.

Without thinking, she rushed over and stopped abruptly, suddenly self-conscious. Anna's confused eyes looked her up and down. As recognition slowly dawned, Anna's mouth dropped open. "What has happened to you, Ursula?"

Ursula drank in Anna's lovely outfit, her rosy cheeks and styled hair. Her fingers flew to her own hair, unwashed and barely combed. She hadn't seen herself in a mirror since her hair had been shaved, and she realized with embarrassment how horrendous she must appear with her sallow skin and disfigured nose. She felt foolish in her gown and realized with alarm that the dress had been a twisted joke. Hitler had planned for her to stand out among the choir members dressed in everyday clothes. He had designed her dress to be too large in order to draw attention to the diva she used to be by highlighting the pathetic waif she had become.

Humiliation crawled up her back like the lice that continued to plague her once-beautiful hair. She fought the intense urge to cry and run from the room. Instead, she lifted her chin and opened her wasted arms, silently inviting Anna to hug her.

Anna's eyes went wide, and she looked to Himmler for guidance . . . or permission. Ursula's arms dropped to her sides as her eyes followed Anna's. Himmler wore a curious look, somewhere between fascination and disgust as he gazed evenly at Ursula.

"Fräulein Becker. How lovely to see you. You are looking . . . well." He dipped his head as he finished speaking, yet his eyes remained riveted to Ursula's. "The Führer wanted to come this evening, but duty compelled him to be elsewhere, thereby allowing me to escort Anna."

Hitler didn't come because he couldn't bear to see the devastation he's caused, Ursula thought.

"I see you received the Führer's kind gift. It's befitting your current stature. Wouldn't you agree?"

But he definitely wanted to make sure that I was embarrassed when I saw my sister. He's a bully and a coward!

Ursula desperately wanted to voice her thoughts but didn't want to anger Himmler. However, her conscience struggled against his smugness. She glanced behind her and saw the maestro observing her interaction. His intense eyes met hers and held a caution that stopped the barbed retort sitting on her tongue. She forced a smile. "I'm grateful for the Führer's generosity."

Himmler turned to Anna. "You see, Anna? Your sister is faring well in this community of Jews."

Ursula looked at Anna again. It was clear she hadn't been made aware of Ursula's true circumstances. She wondered what Anna was thinking, and how she would eventually reconcile what she'd been told with what she'd seen. "Ursula, I. . ." Anna's mouth hung open as if her voice box had suddenly stopped working.

"I'm happy to see you, Anna," Ursula offered. "You seem well. Have you spoken to Papa?"

Himmler stood. "She has not, but he is alive and well."

Ursula continued to look at Anna and wondered if Himmler was lying.

"Any news of Willy?" Ursula tried to sound lighthearted, but her voice rose towards the end of the question.

Himmler stepped forward, quickly closing the distance between them and blocking Ursula's view of Anna. "None, Fräulein. Absolutely none. He has not reached out regarding your whereabouts or condition. One might assume that he has moved on."

His words stung like individual darts puncturing her compromised soul. Her body trembled. "You're lying," she seethed.

Unbothered, Himmler shook his head while puckering his lips into a small moue. "I assure you that I am not. Willy continued to England after you left the ship. He has not returned to Germany. What does that tell you?"

Ursula fought the tears that flooded her eyes, but they broke through her stony façade and spilled down her cheeks. She wiped them away and stepped backward in order to look at Anna, who was nervously twisting her necklace chain. Anna averted her eyes, but Ursula could see that she, too, was crying. Ursula had never wanted anything more than to embrace Anna, the only remaining link to her previous life. But she knew that she shouldn't, or couldn't.

She dropped her gaze to her green shoes and was struck with the ridiculousness of her situation. She pictured her withering frame dressed in the glorious gown, hair askew, and realized how absurd she must appear. Color rushed to her cheeks.

"Ursula." Schächter's soft voice carried over the chatter of the crowd. "Shall we begin?"

Ursula turned to him and nodded. His kind eyes betrayed his empathy, and she choked back a sob.

"Anna, I would like to hug you."

Anna glanced at Himmler whose eyes remained on Ursula as he nodded. Anna stood and approached her sister, paused, and then wrapped her arms around her. She gasped. "You're so thin, Ursula."

"I'm fine," Ursula whispered back. "No matter what happens, know that I love you. Please take care of Papa. Make sure that he is alive and well. Do not forsake him because of something over which he has no control. You're better than that." Anna was crying openly, both of them silently acknowledging that they may never see each other again. As they separated, Ursula's eyes dropped to Anna's throat. "Where did you get that?"

Anna stroked the gold locket that sat at the end of a thin, box-link chain. "Adolf gave it to me. Why?"

Ursula stared at the oval locket with a rose intricately carved on it. She lost feeling in her arms and realized she was holding her breath. "It's mine."

Anna twittered nervously. "You're mistaken, Ursula. Adolf said that he purchased it in Berlin."

"When did he give it to you, Anna?"

Anna blinked several times. "Right before I came here." Ursula glanced at Himmler, who wore a blank expression. *He doesn't know*, she thought.

"He gave it to you because he knew that I'd see it."

"Ursula!" the maestro called more urgently. "Please. We should begin."

Ursula felt the blood coursing through her veins. At that moment she didn't care whether she was shot or dragged away to the Little Fortress. Willy had given her the locket, and she wouldn't have the memory of their commitment to each other flaunted in front of her.

She stared hard at Anna. "Willy gave that locket to me, Anna, when we got on the ship to go to England. I was on my way to meet him when I was told that I had a telephone call. I was speaking to you when I was abducted."

Anna's hand flew to her mouth. "I heard it," she whispered. She turned to Himmler. "Did you know about this?" Her voice was breathy, disbelieving.

Himmler's eyes hardened. "Don't be stupid, girl. She's a Jew who openly defied the Führer. If it had been up to me, she'd be lying dead in a pit. But the Führer is more generous than I and refuses to listen to reason when it comes to *her*." He smoothed his coat and calmed himself. "She is thriving here, along with all of the other Jews. Now, sit down and be quiet." His eyes blazed as he whirled to face Ursula. "I suggest you obey your maestro and perform."

As they faced off, Ursula finally accepted a fact that she'd been too stupid or stubborn to acknowledge—she would most likely not survive Terezín. Even if she managed to avoid illness, starvation, or freezing to death, she understood with startling certainty that Hitler would never stop finding ways to break her. Her resemblance to Geli wouldn't allow his conscience the luxury of killing her. Instead, he hid her away, suspending her somewhere between life and death. He was God and he had sentenced her to eternal purgatory. His obsession to control and intimidate was monstrous, and she feared her soul couldn't survive it. His guilt couldn't justify overtly murdering her, but he might very well kill her through a broken spirit.

The awareness left her feeling exhausted and liberated as she glared at Himmler. "Open the locket, Anna. You'll find a picture of Willy and me inside."

Himmler's eyes darted to the necklace. "Don't open it, Anna," he growled. Anna sat frozen in place, terrified and unsure, a trapped animal too scared to attempt an escape. Ursula's lips curled into a cruel smile as she noted Himmler's eye twitching. Without breaking eye contact, she said, "No need to open it, Anna. I'll chat with you after the concert." She turned her back and walked away, leaving Himmler seething in her stead.

Ursula found her place among the choir. Schächter caught her eye and raised his eyebrows, asking if she was alright. She smiled, surprised at how calm she felt. Perhaps it was the fact that she'd finally stood up to a Nazi and lived to tell about it. Or, maybe it was the opposite. Maybe she understood that her days were truly numbered, and she would no longer spend time worrying about things over which she held no control. Either way, she allowed her soul to be whisked away by the music. She felt the melodies flow through her as she sang with a lightness and clarity she didn't know she possessed. Her voice had changed since arriving in Terezín. Although her body was undernourished, her voice felt full and more rounded, as if it had matured. Perhaps it was her altered mind and soul that allowed her the freedom to fully enjoy her performance. She was simply the conduit through which the glory of Verdi's brilliant musical mind was passed. Afterwards, her body seemed weightless. As if from far away, she observed the rapt audience applaud. Himmler led a standing ovation, his gaze focused completely on her. *How ironic*, she thought, *that he wants to murder me yet is drawn to his feet by my performance.*

Ursula watched him whisper to Jakob Edelstein. Edelstein turned away quickly and slipped outside as Himmler returned his gaze to Ursula. He inclined his head in appreciation. She nodded once in return. Apparently, she would live one more day. Her vocal currency had paid her fare yet again.

Commandant Seidl burst through the door, his weapon drawn and pointed toward the choir. A panicked Edelstein followed him, accompanied by at least twenty more SS officers.

Seidl announced, "The choir will board the train that awaits outside!"

Schächter stepped forward. "Commandant, if I may, we've just performed the most wonderful—"

"Silence!" Seidl ordered. "To the train!"

Ursula's euphoria evaporated like morning dew under a hot sun. The terrified choir stood frozen in place. "I said move!" Seidl roared.

The maestro faced his loyal choir. His face wore a mixture of resignation and sadness. "Thank you for your remarkable performance tonight, my friends. I will remember each and every one of you and your commitment to the music." He bowed deeply before exiting the room. Now leaderless, the choir members exchanged glances, then slowly followed him outside.

Ursula's lips trembled as she walked past Anna, paralyzed and impotent, a beautiful puppet in Hitler's perverted sideshow. Ursula looked down at her dress and thought back to the note from Hitler. *The surprise. He sent my sister to see me off to my death.*

As she was herded toward the train, she recalled Himmler's words regarding Willy. "He hasn't reached out regarding your whereabouts or condition. One might assume that he has moved on."

Could that be true? she wondered. *If it is, I'll happily board the train.*

"Ursula!" She turned to find Anna walking behind her and almost laughed out loud. With her styled hair and healthy complexion, she could no more blend in with the emaciated, haggard group than if she'd donned similar clothing and adapted her erect stature to their rounded-back shuffle. They fell in step together, and Anna grabbed her hand. "Where will the train go?"

"Probably to another camp."

"But what does that mean?" Anna pressed.

Ursula stopped walking and faced her. The people behind continued around them.

"I'm not sure what you want to hear, Anna. We're told that the eastern camps are far worse than here. That's the reality, created by the man whom you claim to love."

"Anna!" They turned to find Himmler walking quickly toward them. "We're leaving, but don't worry. Your sister and Rafael Schächter are not traveling with the rest of the choir." He smiled wickedly at Ursula. "Once again, your earlier insolence has resulted in others being punished. How utterly selfish."

"No. Not this time. I *want* to get on the train." Ursula was shocked as the words escaped her lips. She hadn't planned them, nor had she known she felt that strongly about the choir. *Or am I committing suicide out of spite?* Either way, she had stated her choice. *And it was*, she thought, *my choice*.

Himmler's entire body hardened. "You will remain in this camp for as long as the Führer deems appropriate."

Anna interjected. "Ursula, don't be foolish! Listen to Heinrich. He's giving you a gift."

Ursula scoffed. "Anna, living here isn't a gift. Perhaps it would be more bearable if you were to remain here with me. Would you care for that?"

Anna dropped her head.

"I didn't think so."

Himmler seemed to be enjoying the sisters' exchange. "Well, we must be going. Ursula, it was lovely to hear you sing again. Your voice has blossomed here. Come, Anna." Without waiting he turned on his heel and walked away. Anna watched him go and turned to Ursula, stared at her a long time, then hugged her. As they separated, Anna placed something into her hand. She opened her palm to find the locket, unlatched to reveal the picture of Willy and her.

"Anna!" Himmler called. "Come!" He patted the side of his leg, and Ursula was reminded of the Führer's dog.

Anna leaned in and whispered, "You should know that Willy has been searching for you since you were taken. Adolf has people watching him, and he has never stopped looking for you."

Ursula's heart skipped a beat. "Truly?" she whispered, scarcely able to contain her excitement.

Anna looked deeply into Ursula's eyes. "Truly. I know that he won't stop until he finds you. Don't give up, Ursula. Do you understand?"

"Anna!" Himmler bellowed. *"Now!"*

Anna bit her lip. "I wish I were as strong as you, Ursula, but I'm not. You're the woman I will never be. I love you." She hugged her once more and then scuttled away.

Ursula's eyes fell to the locket in her palm. Her heart surged, then plummeted, as the sound of the full train car pulling away entered her consciousness. She looked up and met the gaze of the young tenor soloist. His eyes were hard, accusatory. They said, 'This is your fault.' She forced herself to meet the eyes of every person who stared at her. She understood their anger. She welcomed it. Their blame fed her guilt, and she *should* feel guilty. What broke her heart was the resignation she saw in so many people's vacant eyes as the train lurched forward. They knew what awaited them. They could no more change their fate than a zebra could change its stripes. She examined the details of the faces; she wanted to memorize every aspect and commit them to memory so she would never forget her role in their demise. As the train passed through the gate, a weighted knowledge settled into her soul. The world had dwindled down to basic, moment-by-moment choices.

Light or dark.

Good or evil.

Life or death.

Ursula stared at the locket in her hand, then reattached it around her neck. No matter what it took, she decided, she would choose life. For herself, as well as for the people who had died so she could live.

43

Once Willy understood that Raoul Wallenburg was offering him a chance to locate Ursula, he wanted to forget about the speaking tour and start his new position as Wallenburg's assistant. Ever practical, Otto urged him to complete the national tour.

"You will have earned a great deal of money by the time this tour is over, Willy. Ursula will be pleased when you bring her to her new home in the States. Besides," Otto had continued, "you have a contract with Mr. Hearst, and I believe that he'll sue you if you don't honor it."

"None of that matters to me. The most important thing is finding Ursula."

"Didn't Mr. Wallenburg say that the International Red Cross wouldn't be visiting the camp until June of next year?" Bridget asked.

"Yes."

"Even if you were to start right now, you wouldn't be any closer to finding Ursula until the June visit. Why don't you continue speaking through May and then start with Mr. Wallenburg after that? You will have fulfilled your contractual commitment to Mr. Hearst and can start your new job immediately prior to going to the camp."

As usual, Bridget's cool head prevailed, and Willy earned a tidy sum while motivating the American elite to continue supporting the international movement against Naziism. By the time Willy's first day at the War Refugee Board rolled around at the end of May, he had spoken in twenty-five cities and had saved enough money to buy a house.

He waited in Wallenburg's office, seated in the only chair that wasn't overrun with piles of paper that threatened to overtake the small space. He ran his fedora through his moist fingers as his busy mind imagined all the ways he might find Ursula. He fought to keep his imagination from succumbing to the unending rumors of vicious atrocities camp inmates endured. His worst fear was that Ursula was dead, that she had died long ago, alone and afraid. His troubled subconscious played out every imaginable horror as he slept, leaving him exhausted and anxious upon awakening. He looked forward to finally taking action after planning for so long.

Wallenburg rushed in and slammed a portfolio on the desk in front of Willy, interrupting his reverie. Willy stood and proffered his hand.

"Sorry, Willy. Sorry to be so late. I was in a meeting with the president and, obviously, I couldn't just leave. Coffee?" Wallenburg glanced at Willy's outstretched hand. "Oh, sorry." He shook Willy's hand.

"You were with the president?" Willy asked. He had known that Wallenburg was important, but he hadn't known he was *important*.

"Yes. Coffee?"

"Um, I'm—"

"Sarah?" Wallenburg yelled past Willy. "Two coffees with cream please." And then to Willy. "Oh, do you take cream, sugar?"

"Cream is fine."

"Great." Wallenburg sat and moved a pile from one side of his desk to the other, then placed his folded hands in the center of his desk blotter. Willy was shell-shocked. After their initial meeting months ago, Willy had created a version of Raoul Wallenburg that didn't match the harried man sitting before him. Willy had assumed that Wallenburg would be organized and meticulous, but he seemed scattered and impulsive. He questioned whether he'd made a wise decision in trusting Ursula's fate to this man. Wallenburg noted his skepticism.

"Your expression betrays your thoughts, Willy. You should know that some of the greatest minds of our time have offices that resemble mine. My strengths are negotiation and organization."

Willy's eyes fell to the paper piles. Wallenburg's gaze followed and he laughed. "I should be more precise. My organizational strength pertains to people, not paper. Trust me, you're in the right place. Besides, think of it this way, if I spent more time organizing my office, I'd have less time to coordinate rescues." He smiled warmly and Willy relaxed.

Sarah breezed in and placed a tray on the blotter.

"Two danishes. I hope you like raspberry, Mr. Hitler. Two coffees with cream. Raoul, your mother called and requested . . . actually, demanded that you be at her house by five-thirty for dinner." Sarah smiled sweetly, winked at Willy, and then exited the office, closing the door quietly behind her.

"Sorry about that." Wallenburg shook his head. "My poor mother. She and my grandmother raised me after my father died. Now that my grandmother has also passed, my mother is alone. She's here in the United States with me but doesn't speak much English. So—" He shrugged. "I'm her only companionship."

Willy chuckled. "It would seem that you and I share similar circumstances. My mother also raised me on her own after my father abandoned us, and she's also with me here in the States. I understand your plight as a loyal son."

Wallenburg gestured to the plate of danishes, but Willy demurred. Wallenburg cleared his throat. "Now, to business. You remember I told you that King Christian X of Denmark is concerned about approximately six hundred Danish Jews who have been sent to Terezín?"

"Yes."

"Well, you and I will be flying to Denmark, where we'll meet with a delegation appointed by the king before continuing on to the camp in Czechoslovakia. President Roosevelt wants to hear from the . . . what's the expression? He wants to hear the king's concerns from the horse's mouth."

Willy smiled. "I understand. And the International Red Cross?"

"We'll meet their people at the camp itself."

"How is it that the War Refugee Board gained access to a camp? I can understand the Red Cross being allowed access, but the WRB?"

"Hitler is under enormous pressure right now. He's waging war on two fronts and is being squeezed. Rumor is that Himmler has considered meeting, or has already met with, an emissary from the United States to discuss German surrender and what that might entail."

Willy's eyes went wide. "That's wonderful!"

Wallenburg held up his hand. "First, these are rumors, and secondly, according to my sources Himmler is fanatically loyal to the Aryan ideals. Perhaps not to Hitler, but to the 'cleansing,' as he describes it. In other words, even if Hitler were gone and Germany were to surrender in some capacity, Himmler would surely negotiate a fine deal for himself. Additionally, he wouldn't go away. He might disappear, but he'd continue working behind the scenes to finish what he's started."

Willy took a sip of coffee as he reflected on Wallenburg's words. "Forgive me, but I still don't understand how it is that the WRB has access to Terezín?"

"Yes, sorry. The chessboard is broad, and its players are complex. Those two factors make for complicated negotiations and, therefore, often intricate descriptions. As I said, Hitler is being squeezed, so is willing to make some compromises in order to show the world his magnanimity. He's allowed some Jews to live if their survival serves his larger purpose. He's aware of the WRB's work and hasn't blocked us as much as he could. When the Red Cross received this opportunity to visit Terezín, of course the WRB wanted to be involved. After agreeing to allowing the Red Cross into the camp, the master of manipulation couldn't very well decline entrance to the WRB. It would look to the world as if he were hiding something. He's crafty, that's for sure."

That's one word to describe him, Willy thought. *Evil is another.* "How many prisoners reside in Terezín?"

Wallenburg shook his head. "It's hard to know because we're not sure we can believe the propaganda coming out of Berlin."

"Trust me. You *can't* believe it."

"Alright, well, Berlin has told us that there are approximately seven thousand people in Terezín and that they're being treated well. Apparently, there are weekly lectures, performances, and artistic exhibitions."

Willy's heart surged. If his uncle wanted to hide Ursula, this camp would be the perfect place. If the rumors were true, if the inmates were being treated fairly, then perhaps Ursula was alive and well!

"When do we leave?"

"Three weeks from today, on June eighteenth. You'll spend the next few weeks understanding your role as my assistant and getting your affairs in order. Sound good?"

Willy nodded eagerly. "I would leave today if we could."

"I know you would, but you have a lot to learn about what we do here at the WRB, and I need to prepare for an upcoming relief and rescue effort in Budapest. I'm going there immediately following the Terezín tour. That's what I was discussing with the president. That, and you, of course."

Willy was shocked. "Me?"

"Yes. He was rather impressed with your article and how you're standing up to your uncle. Your commitment reinforced his own convictions." Willy felt proud that his words had made such an impact. That had been his goal, of course, and he was grateful to know that his time and energy hadn't been wasted.

Wallenburg stood abruptly. "Now, Sarah will show you to your new office. I need to call my mother and tell her that I won't be home until seven. That should go well." He grimaced.

Willy stood and shook his hand. "Good luck."

"Thanks. I'll need it."

44

In the months following the Verdi concert, the ghetto saw many changes. Commandant Seidl was replaced by a sociopath named Anton Burger, who took joy in having the inmates stand outside for hours in the freezing cold. Lieutenant Burger lasted only seven months before he, too, was replaced by the current commandant named Lieutenant Karl Rahm. The sadist liked to beat inmates but could be bribed, according to rumor. Not many prisoners had any valuables left, but trains arrived often, and they deposited new inmates who carried useful items. The train that had brought Ursula to the camp was luxurious compared to the more recent deposits. Cattle cars crowded with stinking, cramped bodies unloaded their exhausted, terrified cargo, often leaving onboard the bodies of people who didn't survive the trip. Current inmates were ordered to empty the cars, then hose them out so the train could reverse course and retrieve more hapless victims.

Each time a train arrived, Ursula would marvel at the sheer numbers of people who disembarked. *Where will they all sleep?* she'd wonder. Originally built to house approximately seven thousand people, the ghetto now contained more than fifty thousand.

Despite the increasing number of inmates, food supplies remained the same. This meant that rations, already meager, were halved. Then halved again. Typhus had raged through the ghetto, leaving thousands dead in its horrifying wake. Intelligent and opportunistic rats swarmed the barracks, their eyes glowing yellow in the moonlight as they scurried over sleeping bodies. Although Ursula often felt their sharp nails on her face, it was only when they decided to take a bite of her ear or nose that she would snatch them and throw them against a wall.

She had watched the frail and elderly fall in the streets, their sticklike legs no longer able to support them. Other inmates walked past without noticing, too busy with their own survival to be bothered. The bodies would lay where they fell until the guards were sure they were dead, at which point they would be thrown onto a makeshift hearse and transported to the camp's crematorium, which now ran twenty-four hours a day, seven days a week.

Since the *Requiem* performance, Ursula had worked through the crushing guilt she felt at the deaths of her choral friends. She and Rafael Schächter had decided they would honor their memories by creating a new choir. The evening of the first rehearsal only four people had appeared in the basement of Magdeburg barracks. They told her that many people wanted to sing but were afraid due to the outcome of the previous performance. Undeterred, she and Schächter had recruited people and sung the *Requiem* many more times. As they had feared, following each performance much of the choir would be loaded onto a train, leaving them fewer voices from which to choose and less motivated to perform.

Ursula, however, always remained behind, destined to bear the burden of the dead.

One day as they worked the sluice, Ilse Weber suggested that Ursula lift her mood by changing her artistic focus.

"What do you mean?"

"You can't keep repeating the *Requiem*, only to have your choir be sent away. You wear your guilt like a yoke around your neck, Ursula."

Ursula threw a red, leather suitcase on a wagon. "I'm fine, Ilse."

"You're not. Look at me."

Ursula turned.

"You've always worked only with adults, but there are so many talented younger voices in the camp."

Ursula straightened and rubbed her lower back. "I've never thought of that."

"Do you know Hans Krása?"

"No."

"He's a Czech composer who wrote a children's opera called *Brundibár*. He was just telling me that he wanted to work with his cast to improve their voices. Perhaps you should offer to help."

"I'm not a voice teacher, Ilse."

"True, but I don't think Herr Krása would be that picky, and you speak Czech."

Ursula rolled the idea around. "What if the children don't like me?"

Ilse crossed her arms. "Ursula, children are easy to work with because they're honest. If you treat them with respect and kindness, they'll return the favor. If you treat them as lesser or inferior, they'll act out. The children here are more mature. They've had to be in order to survive. Besides, the children in this production have performed together before. Many of them came from an orphanage where *Brundibár* was premiered. Don't worry. You'll be giving them the gift of better voices. They won't squander the opportunity to learn."

Ilse was correct. When Ursula approached Hans Krása and offered to coach the children, he jumped at the chance. Ursula spent the next two weeks working with Rafael Schächter to learn the *Brundibár* music, then met the cast in an attic on a warm afternoon in early April. Rafael Schächter had begged off conducting and had offered the honor to Rudi Freudenfeld, who graciously accepted.

Ursula asked the pianist named Gideon Klein to play some light music while she spoke to the group. He composed a carefree ditty on the spot, and the effect was immediate. The children smiled and gave her their full attention. She stood in front of the young group, whose expectant faces filled her simultaneously with joy and fear. "Hello, children. I understand that you have performed *Brundibár* many times. Herr Krása has graciously entrusted me to work with you on vocal technique. It's a serious responsibility, but I know that you're up to the task." She paused, humbled by the fact that several of the young people sitting cross-legged on the dirt floor had not yet been born when she first took the operatic stage. "My name is Ursula, and I am your vocal teacher. For some of you, this is the first time you will be performing. Although I have sung in many operas, this is my debut as an instructor, so we must practice great patience with one another." Light laughter rippled through the older children while the younger ones simply smiled, content to be distracted from their empty stomachs. A spindly arm waved in the air.

"Yes?" Ursula asked.

"Will we have makeup?"

Ursula looked to Addi, who stepped forward and smiled. "I'll be doing your makeup, and Ilse will be making some costumes."

The older children looked at Ilse skeptically. Resources were scarce, and Ursula wondered how Ilse would cobble together enough material. Ilse noticed their reactions. "You leave the worrying to me. Have faith, friends, that you will be costumed appropriately."

Her confidence set the children at ease, and Ursula took advantage of the good humor. "Alright. To work! Please stand." She ran the children through some vocalizations and was pleased to find that most of them not only could keep good rhythm, but also were able to sing on pitch. She grouped the children by vocal ability and worked with each group throughout the afternoon. By the end of the session, Gideon Klein pulled her aside to congratulate her and Hans Krása was beaming. The children walked down the stairs with a spring in their steps, and Ursula was once again reminded how powerful music could be, especially when combined with hope.

"You're doing a good thing here, Ursula." She turned to find Ilse gazing evenly at her. "An unselfish thing."

"I'm not sure what you mean."

"Forgive me for being blunt, but your primary concern since you came to Terezín has been yourself."

In another world, in another time, Ursula might have been offended by such a statement, but those days had long passed. "Isn't that the case for all of us?"

Ilse smiled knowingly. "You tell me."

Ursula reflected on Markus, the boy on the train who had been shot because she didn't speak up. Then her mind wandered to Marika, who mothered her and never asked for anything in return. She thought of Fritz, who offered her supportive words as he lay dying in the snow. And finally the choirs, who had perished because of her. In every circumstance she had taken more than she'd given. "Your words have reason, Ilse."

"Please don't misunderstand me, Ursula. You were always kind, but you've matured. You're now nurturing as you reach beyond yourself to create a legacy."

Ursula laughed. "You're making my involvement in this children's opera more than it is, Ilse."

"Am I?" She raised an eyebrow. "We're a part of history. Right now. This war will end and when it does, people will write about this camp. Historians will pass judgment." She smiled broadly. "They will write about your greatest role, voice teacher to the children in Terezín."

Ursula crinkled her nose. "You think so?"

"I know it. So do your best and continue to focus on the children. The rest will fall into place."

Ursula carefully considered Ilse's words. Was Willy somewhere out there looking for her as Anna had said? Would she ever see him or her father again? Darkness scratched at her mind. *What if I die here? How will I be remembered?* She decided to focus on the present while keeping a hopeful eye on the future. "I believe that you're correct, Ilse. I'll do as you suggest and focus on the children."

Addi rushed so quickly up the stairs that she stumbled on the last two. She caught herself before she fell, then held up a finger asking them to wait until she caught her breath. They exchanged worried glances as Addi breathed heavily for several moments, then sat heavily on the floor. "Guess what?" she finally asked.

Ursula rolled her eyes. "After that entrance? What?"

"They're building street signs."

"Who is building street signs?"

"The SS soldiers have ordered the men who normally work elsewhere in the camp to build street signs."

Ursula pulled a face. "Why?"

Addi shrugged. "Come outside and see."

The three women descended the stairs to find men carrying handmade sawhorses in the direction of the Town Hall. They followed them and found the open area buzzing with hushed excitement. The only other times Ursula had seen the quadrangle so busy was right after a train unloaded its cargo of confused, scared travelers. But unlike the wide eyes and palpable fear Ursula always noted in the new arrivals, here the men smiled and joked. The sounds of metal teeth sawing through wood carried to her ears, and the aroma of freshly cut pine invigorated her. She approached a young man. "What's happening?"

He turned to her and his entire face lit up. "Haven't you heard? We're beautifying the ghetto. We're making it into a true town. There are to be shops and currency. Food will be more plentiful, and we are to live more freely. It's wonderful!" He walked away, his enthusiasm apparent in his bouncing stride.

Ursula watched warily, then turned to Addi and Ilse. "What do you think?"

Both women's faces reflected her feelings of doubt and distrust. "Can you talk to Edvard Svoboda and get the truth out of him?" Ilse asked.

Addi shrugged. "I could ask."

Ursula stared at her. "It won't cost you anything?"

"Things have changed, Ursula. The information will come freely."

"How can you be so sure?"

"He seems to genuinely care for me."

"How do you feel about him?"

Addi twisted her mouth. "He's good to me, and I suppose that's enough . . . for now, at least."

Ursula was pleased that Addi had negotiated a sense of security for herself. In so many ways Addi was more mature than she was. "Good. Let us know what you discover."

A woman hurried past them carrying a bundle of fabric and a teapot. They watched her enter an administrative building, drop her load on the floor, and exit again. As she passed them, Ilse muttered, "I believe that teapot belonged to Frau Hekker, may she rest in peace."

"The fabric was Marika's," Ursula said with disgust. "It was stolen from her a week before she died."

"I wonder if they plan on opening stores with merchandise that we already own?" Ilse mused. The woman passed them again, this time carrying several pairs of high-heeled shoes. She dropped them on top of the fabric and vanished again.

Ilse rubbed her palms together and smiled. "Excuse me, ladies. I need to get some supplies for the children's costumes." She dashed to the building, grabbed the roll of royal blue fabric, and ran back to Dresden barracks, cack-ling as she made off with the material.

Ursula smiled. "Marika would be proud of us."

Addi scoffed. "For stealing?"

"It's not stealing if you're restoring something to its rightful place."

Ursula observed the woman return holding an armful of ladies clothing. As she deposited her load, the woman noted that the fabric was missing. She stood, turned around, and made eye contact with Ursula. "Did you take the cloth?"

"Me? No."

The woman eyed her suspiciously. "Did you see someone else take the cloth?"

"Yes."

"Will you tell me who it was so I can get it back?"

Ursula stared at the woman and decided that she had been wrong about the dual nature of life in the ghetto. It wasn't just good and evil. Not just light and dark, or black and white. It was a dull, practical gray that ruled daily decision making. Morality was no longer binary. It existed on a sliding scale.

Ursula raised her chin. "No. I will not."

45

Willy glanced out the window as they approached the Copenhagen airport. His only experience flying had been in his uncle's smaller, private plane, and he was awed by the power of the larger U. S. government plane that now circled the airport. He had spent the entire trip pouring over European maps that outlined where Allied intelligence had located internment camps. He was determined to visit all of them until he found Ursula . . . or her body.

He sat back in his seat and wondered if he was on a fool's errand. His uncle had said that Ursula was dead, and he had told Otto that he believed it to be true. *But what if she's not?* a voice whispered. *What if she's waiting for you to find her?*

Willy sighed heavily and shifted his attention to the events of the last few weeks. He felt as if he'd been drinking from a fire hose in learning his role as Wallenburg's assistant and how the War Refugee Board functioned in relation to the International Red Cross. When he reached the point of feeling somewhat informed, he turned his attention to understanding the U.S. role on the international political stage. Many felt that the United States should have intervened sooner and done more to aid the plight of European Jews. Others seemed eager to maintain closely monitored borders to ensure that America wasn't overrun with foreigners. Willy found the latter idea amusing, seeing as U.S. growth and success was built largely on the shoulders of foreigners' ideas and investments. Despite his personal opinions, as Wallenburg's assistant he was to be seen more than heard, so he found himself taking a crash course in diplomacy and etiquette as he negotiated the varying viewpoints.

Bridget used some of his speaking money to purchase him three new suits, with coordinating ties and shoes. She also secured an apartment in Fairfax, Virginia, not too far away from where Willy worked in Washington, D.C. She and Otto had grown even closer since coming to the States, and Willy suggested that while he was abroad, she sell her house in England and investigate purchasing a home with money he'd earned from the speaking tour.

"I wouldn't know where to begin," she protested.

Willy placed his hands on her shoulders. "I've done some research, Mum, and I think being close to New York would be amazing."

Bridget scrunched her nose. "Too busy."

"Not New York City, but more north. The rest of New York State is beautiful. Maybe while I'm gone you and Otto can take a trip to investigate."

Otto smiled. "It sounds wonderful to me, Willy. We'll find a home that can fit all four of us. Bridget, Ursula, you, and me. And perhaps some grandchildren as well." He winked at Willy as Bridget playfully slapped his arm.

Willy smiled at the memory as the Boeing 314 touched down in Denmark. He and Wallenburg disembarked, collected their belongings, and traveled to Christiansborg Palace, the seat of Denmark's government. They were shown to a reception room that was befitting the name of the building in which it was housed. After only a few minutes, Willy recognized Franz Hvass as he entered the room with his hand extended in greeting.

"Mr. Wallenburg, what a pleasure to finally make your acquaintance. Your fine reputation precedes you."

"You're too kind. It's my pleasure to meet you. May I present Willy Hitler, my assistant."

Hvass turned his appraising eye to Willy "It's a pleasure, Mr. Hitler."

Willy shook his hand. "Thank you for hosting us."

Hvass raised his eyebrows. "Well, as you know, the king has instructed Juel Henningsen and me, along with someone from the International Red Cross, to visit Terezín to ensure our citizens are being treated well."

"Yes, and I'm glad that we have the opportunity to tag along as representatives of the WRB," Wallenburg said.

"I trust your travel was satisfactory?"

"It was. Thank you."

Hvass turned to Willy. "You had no problem getting through the Nazi checkpoints?"

"No, sir. It would seem that my uncle is treating Denmark with the respect it deserves."

"For now, at least. Everything can be negotiated, apparently. When the Germans attacked us in April, we quickly realized that the Nazi forces were too great. We had to make a choice. Fight and most likely lose or allow German occupation and carry on fairly normally. The government, in agreement with the king, chose the latter and, so far, hasn't regretted the decision."

"I understand that your Jews are not required to wear a yellow star on their coats."

"That's correct. That was part of our negotiation. The Nazis know who is

Jewish and who isn't, but we Danes don't need to know, do we? Our citizens are Danish, regardless of their religion."

"If other leaders had taken the same stand, their countries might be in better bargaining positions," Wallenburg commented.

Hvass threw his hands wide. "Yet here we are. Now, tell me, Mr. Hitler, I understand you know someone who is incarcerated in a camp."

Willy told Hvass the story. The Danish diplomat was attentive, nodding now and then as he listened. When Willy had finished, Hvass slapped his knee. "By God, we must find your Ursula. If she's as beautiful and talented as you say, she should be sharing her gifts with the world."

"There's nothing I would like more."

Wallenburg asked, "Can you tell us more about Terezín?"

Hvass cleared his throat, stood, and clasped his hands behind his back. "Well, first you should know that in German it is called Theresienstadt. Terezín is the Czech translation. Thirty miles north of Prague, Emperor Joseph II of Austria created a fortress in the late 1700s and named it after his mother, Empress Maria Theresa. He called it Theresienstadt. It became a holiday getaway for local nobility. In late 1941 Hitler ordered his chief of the Gestapo, Reinhard Heydrich, to create a settlement to house Jews who were over sixty-five years of age, who had served honorably in the Great War, or who were of notable enough character that foreigners might inquire as to their whereabouts. Heydrich worked with Eichmann to convert Theresienstadt into what he called a spa town and claims that the inhabitants are being treated well. Hundreds of Danish Jews have been sent there and about fifty have died. We were told that they succumbed to diphtheria, but we questioned the care they received and the conditions in which they lived. At first, we were ignored. Our further inquiries were also ignored, so we contacted the International Red Cross, who began putting pressure on the Reich to address our outstanding questions. Finally, we received permission to visit Terezín."

"So, you are going with us to the camp?"

"Yes. I'm going, along with Dr. Juel Henningsen, the head physician at our Ministry of Health, and Maurice Rossel, a representative of the International Red Cross."

"Why visit just one camp?" Willy asked.

"I requested to visit Terezín because that's where the Danes died."

"But would it be possible to expand our visit to other camps as well? I understand that there are several in the same general vicinity."

Hvass shook his head. "Impossible, Mr. Hitler. I think you're underestimating the effort it took to secure this visit."

Willy held up his hand. "Of course. My apologies. I'm just anxious to find Ursula. If she's not in Terezín, I can't imagine returning to the States without her."

Hvass nodded. "I appreciate your predicament, but my mandate is to ensure my countrymen's security."

"Of course."

"May I ask you a question?"

Willy nodded. "Of course, sir."

"What will you do if you find her?"

Willy blinked several times and then looked at Wallenburg, whose curious expression indicated his interest in the answer. Willy had imagined seeing Ursula again, scooping her up, and smothering her with kisses. He had envisioned her arms around his neck, and her laughter ringing in his ears. He had imagined them back in the United States, in their tidy, brick home with a white fence around the front yard, tulips popping up through the fresh earth in the spring. But he hadn't created a vision for how he would rescue her from whatever hell she was in. He was embarrassed to admit that he hadn't even considered it. *How utterly ridiculous*, he thought.

"You do have a plan, don't you?" Hvass asked.

"Willy?" Wallenburg said. "Are you alright?"

The gilded door to the reception room opened, and a uniformed soldier appeared holding a silver tray with a folded piece of paper on it. "Please excuse the interruption, but I have a message for Mr. Hitler."

Hvass nodded. The soldier walked briskly toward Willy and extended the tray. Willy took the note and read it, then folded it and placed it in his pocket. The soldier waited patiently. "Will there be any response, sir?" he asked.

Willy's mind raced, and his heart beat wildly. "Yes. Please tell the Führer that I'll be in Berlin on the next available train."

46

Weeks had passed since the first *Brundibár* rehearsal, and the show was coming together. Addi had become the de facto leader of the children, herding them when their attention strayed and keeping their spirits up by leading them in games during downtime. Hans Krása attended each rehearsal and remained true to his word that Ursula could coach the cast. Originally fearful that she would miss being on stage herself, Ursula found that she enjoyed the effort it took to draw strong vocal performances from the children. The more time she spent with them, the more satisfaction she gained. She had cultivated a sense of trust and love that was returned to her through laughter and hugs at the end of each rehearsal.

Of course, it didn't hurt that their meals had improved dramatically in the last few months. The children came to rehearsals with full bellies, the boys often competing in belching contests that left them doubled over in laughter. Like its inhabitants, the ghetto had transformed as well. Addi had spoken with Edvard Svoboda, who verified that the beautification was real and would be long-lasting.

"Is that all he said?" Ursula asked.

"Did he say *why* the ghetto is being made into a real town?" Ilse had pushed.

"And why now?" Ursula added.

Addi shook her head. "He wouldn't tell me. I think he knows the reason, but he won't tell."

Street signs had been erected, followed by shops stocked with merchandise. As Ursula and Ilse had feared, some items had been obtained from the prisoners. But after the initial stock was arranged, weekly shipments started arriving that contained items such as perfume, books, and linens. The trains that had brought only despair and fear now became harbingers of hope and new beginnings.

Additionally, movement restrictions had been relaxed. People could now wander about the complex without a curfew. Children, when not in the newly furnished school, played tag among the gardens or rode swings on the new playground. Buildings had been painted and proper bunks had been erected in the barracks. Each prisoner had been allotted new clothes. Warm bathing water became the norm rather than the exception. The general mood in the camp became jovial as conditions improved. Although the SS guards still roamed with their rifles at the ready, even some of their smiles came more readily.

For her part, Ursula remained skeptical and reminded Addi that they were still prisoners as they prepared for rehearsal. "Don't delude yourself. We're not free to walk through the gates. Until that day comes, we're in shackles. They may be invisible, but they're there. And they're very, very real."

Addi rolled her eyes. "You should be more grateful, Ursula. We're now living in a true town, and we're staging a performance. For once you should focus on what's good."

Ursula set her mouth. "The other shoe will drop, Addi. Mark my words. It's only a matter of time. Hitler wouldn't allow this beautification to occur without an ulterior motive."

"Has it ever occurred to you that the Führer knows nothing of what occurs in Terezín?"

Ursula guffawed. "Now I know you're truly delusional! He orchestrates everything, down to the finest detail."

Addi crossed her arms. "Ursula, I understand that he has an extreme need to control. But honestly, think about it. According to you, Hitler's goal is to run the entire world, so why would he concern himself with our little corner of it?"

"Because *I* am in this particular corner."

Addi gave her a look of disdain. "Well, someone has a mighty opinion of herself."

Ursula shook her head. "My ego has nothing to do with it. Hitler is so insecure that if he can't control everything, down to the smallest element, he will implode. This has nothing to do with me, per se, but it has everything to do with Hitler. He sees the world from only his perspective. He's incapable of appreciating someone else's point of view. I understand him and how he thinks. I wish I didn't, but I do. Something's coming, Addi. Something bad."

"If what you say is true, then I plan on enjoying myself until something bad comes. My suggestion is that you do the same thing."

Ursula twisted the chain of her necklace, a habit that had started as a reminder of Willy but had become a nervous tic over which she had no control. Addi watched Ursula's quick fingers worry the chain. "What about Willy?"

Ursula paused. "What of him?"

Addi held her arms wide. "Where is he in all of this? You've been here for almost two years. Why hasn't he come for you?"

"He doesn't know where I am."

"Anna knows. Do you think she hasn't told him?"

The same thought had occurred to Ursula on many occasions, especially late at night when she couldn't sleep. Why *had* he not come for her? Anna had said that he wouldn't stop until he found her. She'd seen the conditions in which Ursula was living. Surely, she had found a way to break from her gilded cage to communicate with Willy. Yet still he didn't come, and Ursula had no answers.

Addi saw the distress in Ursula's eyes and softened her tone. "Ursula, you know me. I'm an optimistic pragmatist. I'm hopeful that Anna has communicated your whereabouts, but she may not have for fear of Hitler's wrath. On the other hand, if she did tell Willy where you are, and he hasn't yet appeared, the question is why?"

Ursula wiped away a tear and stared at her hands. When she spoke, it came out as a whisper. "Perhaps he has forgotten about me. Perhaps he should."

Addi sighed and drew Ursula in for a hug, holding her tightly until she felt Ursula's heartbeat match her own. "I think he's out there somewhere looking for you. Or, if he knows where you are, then he's devising a strategy to get you out of here. And when he does—" She drew Ursula away and smiled, "—please take me with you."

Ursula paused and then burst out laughing. She wiped her eyes and nodded. "Deal," she said.

Hans Krása bounded up the stairs but stopped when he saw the two women. "Everything alright here?"

Ursula wiped her nose with her sleeve. "We're fine. Are the children coming?"

"They're on their way as we speak. You should know that they're especially eager today and have extra energy."

"How come?"

"Because each has a coin in his pocket."

Ursula shook her head. "You mean the useless currency we're given for our work? The money that holds no value except in this ghetto?"

Krása shook his head. "No, Ursula. New currency has been created that can be used inside the camp and *externally as well*."

Ursula's heart sped up. It was the first time she'd allowed herself to feel a surge of hope that they might see beyond the fort's walls. "Why would they give us money?"

Addi turned quickly. "You see, Ursula? I knew it! This is all leading to our release! They're preparing us to rejoin the outside world once again."

Ursula squinted in thought. "What did they say when they gave each of the children a coin?"

"Commandant Rahm told them to spend their money at the toy store or the candy store. Of course, they chose the candy store and loaded up on sweets. Now they're coming to rehearsal. Hence, the extra energy." He smiled broadly.

As if on cue the door burst open and the horde of children stomped up to the attic, chatting and laughing. Their colorful new clothes matched the red in their cheeks, a result of playing outside in the warm sunshine. They dropped to the floor and settled down, eventually all turning their bright eyes toward Ursula. She had never seen the group so content and didn't want to spoil their mood. Yet the recent changes in the camp left her with a growing discomfort. She wanted to urge them to enjoy their current circumstances but maintain a sense of caution in case the kindnesses dried up.

"We're going to do something different today at rehearsal. I want you to tell me the story of *Brundibár*."

Confused glances flew around the room.

"I know that we've sung through the story many times, but who can *tell* me the story?" Ursula urged.

A boy of no more than nine years stood. "I can tell you, Fräulein."

Ursula smiled. "Please remind me of your name."

"Fritz." Ursula's smile froze as she recalled her friend who had died in the snow. "Go on, Fritz."

The boy twisted his hands and shifted his weight. "Well, the story is about a brother and sister who go to the market to buy milk for their ill mother. But they have no money. So, they raise money for the milk by singing in the street, much like Brundibár, the old, mean organ grinder. But he is loud, and their two small voices can't be heard, so they make no money and are chased away by the evil bully. The next morning, they make a plan to become louder by joining forces with some other children, a cat, a sparrow, and a dog. The new, larger chorus is louder than Brundibár, and the children make enough money to buy milk for their mother."

Ursula was impressed at Fritz's summary. "Well done. You'll become a fine teacher one day. Perhaps a music teacher." Ursula winked, and Fritz sat, his cheeks flushing crimson. She felt a surge of joy at witnessing such camaraderie and fleetingly wondered if she might become a music teacher after rejoining Willy. She realized with trepidation and sadness that it was the first time she'd thought seriously of life after the ghetto. Until this moment she'd been focused on living only one day at a time. *Hope can be dangerous*, she reminded herself. *Stay the course.*

"Fritz summarized the story of *Brundibár*. Now I want someone to tell me the lesson that lies within the story."

Blank stares greeted her, and Addi stifled a laugh. A hand crept into the air. "Are we going to sing today, Fräulein?"

Ursula smiled patiently. "Not today. Who can tell me the lesson, the very important life lesson that *Brundibár* teaches us?" Her eyes swept the room. She made eye contact with every member of the cast. When no one offered a response, she said, "The story of *Brundibár* is one of perseverance and teamwork. The group is always stronger than the individual. Always. When a situation seems hopeless, one need only seek out a group of like-minded people in order to defeat a bully like *Brundibár* or—"

"Ursula!" Addi interrupted. "I think the children understand your point. If we work together, we can fight injustice." Addi's eyes held an unspoken warning. One never knew when evil ears were listening.

"Can we though?" A young man stood. Ursula had noticed him, not only because of his beautiful tenor voice, but also because he was a natural leader. He reminded her of a young Willy. He addressed Addi. "This children's opera is all well and good, but our reality is different, isn't it? There are so many of us in this camp, like-minded people, as Fräulein Ursula said. Yet we don't fight the injustices we experience every day."

Small heads turned in unison from the young man to Ursula. The younger children didn't know exactly what was happening, but they appreciated that the tone of the meeting had shifted.

Ursula stepped forward. "You make my point for me. What's your name?"

"Petr Ginz."

"Petr, the fact that we are here, that we exist at all, flies directly in the face of—" She paused and glanced at Addi, who shot a warning with her eyes. "Those who would rather we not exist at all," Ursula finished. "It's quite remarkable that we have the chance to perform *Brundibár*, whose underlying lesson cannot be extinguished or ignored, but rather points to the precise situation in which we find ourselves. I want to ensure that we harness this opportunity."

Someone cleared his throat, and all eyes swiveled. In the heat of discussion no one had noticed that Commandant Rahm had quietly entered the building and climbed the stairs. The camp improvements had begun under his leadership, so many people viewed him as fair and kind. But through Addi's conversations with Edvard Svoboda, Ursula had learned that Rahm was anything but kind. To that end, she had steered clear of direct interactions with him.

"Don't mind me," he muttered. "I'm a fly on the wall." He walked toward Ursula and stopped directly in front of her. "And to think I was looking forward to hearing the children's melodious voices."

Ursula lifted her chin and held his steady gaze.

"We were just about to sing," Hans Krása interjected. Rahm held up his palm toward Krása, silencing him. The tension hung heavy as the children waited for direction. Rahm glared at Ursula as he towered over her, his breath rustling her hair as he exhaled. "You and I have not been acquainted yet, Fräulein, but the former commandants told me all about you. Let me just say that your *reputation* precedes you." His dark eyes bored into hers, and although she tried, she couldn't hold his gaze. Her cheeks burned with insinuation. She was grateful that the innuendo seemed beyond most of the children's awareness. But not Addi, whose eyes betrayed her understanding.

He turned from her and faced the cast. "Did you know, children, that Fräulein Becker was an opera star in Berlin?" Murmurs waved through the group. "Yes, she was quite something. But now look at her . . ."

He turned to face her. She pictured the scar under her eye that sat aside her misshapen nose, and her unruly, uneven hair. A look of distaste crossed his features. "How far your star has fallen. What Commandant Seidl saw in you I will never understand."

At the mention of Seidl's name Ursula forced herself to stare into Rahm's dead eyes. They reminded her of pictures she'd seen of sharks. Dark, cold wells devoid of feeling or soul.

He wheeled around and clapped his hands. "Good news, children. Your debut will be held exactly two weeks from today when the International Red Cross comes to visit. Many important people will be in attendance, maybe even the Führer. Over the next two weeks you'll be instructed on what to say and how to act. It's imperative that you follow directions. We want the international community to understand how well you're being treated. Tell me, children, are your stomachs full?"

"Yes," they called out.

"Did everyone enjoy some candy?"

"Yes!"

"And how about the rousing game of tag in the sunshine?"

"Yay!" The children laughed.

He clapped his hands. "Who wants to go outside right now and play some more?"

The children turned to Hans Krása and Ursula, silently begging permission.

Rahm waved his hands in the air, drawing their collective attention. "You're to take a day off and enjoy the sun. Go, now go!" He laughed.

Addi ushered the children down the stairs, leaving Ursula, Rahm, and Krása in the rehearsal space. Rahm's mouth twisted into a smug grin. "Like I said, we don't know each other well, Fräulein, but you really need to understand only one thing about me." He stepped forward and grabbed her face with his hand, squeezing her cheeks until her mouth was forced open. She stood on tiptoes to lessen the strain as he pulled her toward him. She could feel his words enter her mouth and slide down her throat as he whispered. "I know under whose orders you are here. I know that you are protected. But . . . do not test me. Unlike my boorish predecessors, I can find ways to make you hurt that won't ever be visible." He shoved her away. She stumbled but righted herself. Rahm examined her withered, haggard body, then met her eyes. "You cannot ever win this game. Ever."

47

The 355-kilometer trip from Copenhagen to Berlin gave Willy many hours to imagine the confrontation with his uncle. By the time the train screeched to a slow halt in the Berlin station, Willy had worked himself into such a state that he inadvertently forgot his fedora that sat above his ticketed seat. Realizing his mistake, he returned to the platform to retrieve the hat, but the train had pulled out of the station. Willy watched it disappear around a corner and then cursed in frustration. He turned to find a mother hugging her young son against her leg.

"Please excuse my outburst, madame. I left my hat on the train. I didn't mean to scare you or your son."

"It must be some hat for you to be so upset about losing it."

Willy smiled sadly. "It is, actually, an exceptional hat. An amazing hat. I'm afraid that it might be lost to me forever."

The woman looked at him for a long time, as if she were reading his thoughts. Her son pulled on her skirt, yet her gaze remained on Willy. "Are you certain that it's your hat you're missing?"

Her words found their mark. Willy realized with embarrassment that he was displacing his concern over Ursula to his fedora.

"Why don't you speak to the stationmaster inside the terminal. He might be able to retrieve your hat for you."

Willy touched his hand to his imaginary brim in thanks and went to the ticket desk. He spoke to the stationmaster, who assured him that he would look for it.

"Your name, sir?"

"William Hitler."

The stationmaster's head shot up quickly.

"Did you say William *Hitler*?"

"Yes."

The man's entire demeanor altered in a second. He straightened and threw out his right arm. "Heil, Hitler!" he screamed. Willy physically recoiled at the man's ferocity and the wild look in his eyes. He couldn't decide what offended him more—the fear, or the loyalty exhibited in the gesture. Willy nodded in thanks and walked outside to hail a cab.

Berlin had changed substantially in the two years he'd been gone. Huge pictures of an unsmiling Hitler loomed over each square. Swastika flags had been prevalent before, but now they were everywhere. Large and small banners hung from balconies, and SS soldiers marched the streets in strict formation, their legs shooting out in exacting goose-step unison. The cab parked in front of the Chancellery and Willy paused, considering for the first time that he may not make it out of Berlin alive. He whispered a silent prayer, told the cabbie to wait, and exited the car. He straightened his coat, smoothed his hair, and strode up the steps, looking far more confident than he felt.

He entered the building and was immediately stopped and searched by two very thorough SS officers. Satisfied, the taller one ordered, "This way," and turned on his heel. Willy followed him through several heavy steel doors, noting that the older, wooden doors had been replaced. At the end of a narrow hallway were two massive guards who stood shoulder to shoulder, blocking a door. Willy's guide nodded and they parted. The guide stepped forward, opened the door, and motioned Willy to enter. He did, expecting the guard to enter behind him, but when he turned around, he was alone in a vestibule no bigger than a tiny elevator. He turned and tried the door through which he'd entered, but it was locked. He twisted the handle on the door in front of him but it, too, was locked. He was just starting to panic when the door in front of him opened, and Anna appeared.

"Willy!" She rushed forward and embraced him. "Come in. Come in! Adolf will be so happy to see you!"

She acted as if they'd seen each other yesterday. Willy held his ground as she motioned for him to follow. "Anna, do you know where Ursula is?"

She ignored his question. "Willy, come, please. Adolf is waiting to see you." She let go of the door and started walking. It was closing on its own, threatening to lock him inside again. He had no choice but to follow.

"Anna, stop for a moment and look at me."

"We must go to Adolf."

"Anna!" Willy grabbed her wrist and forced her to stop. "Where is Ursula?"

Anna averted her eyes. "I can't tell you that."

"You knew I was searching for her. Why didn't you reach out to me?"

"Because I knew the end result would be this conversation, and I can't have this conversation with you, Willy . . . even if I want to." She started walking again, faster this time.

"She's your sister, Anna."

"Stop, Willy. I will not speak about her."

Anna had sold her conscience for a life of luxury and false hero worship. *How could two sisters be so incredibly different?* Willy thought. He wanted to grab her and throw her against the wall until she told him Ursula's whereabouts. But he knew that she would never betray Hitler, so he decided on a different tack. "It seems like there's a lot of protection around Uncle Alf these days."

Anna stopped to face him, and tears rushed to her eyes. She dabbed them away with a silk hankie that appeared from nowhere. "There have been several attempts on Adolf's life. It's astonishing considering all he has done for this country! We're almost there." She turned a corner and entered a tunnel that became so narrow they had to walk in single file. "Anna, where are we going? Was this tunnel always here?"

"No. It's new. Adolf had it constructed so he could access the Chancellery gardens without walking outside. People are crazy, Willy. It's remarkable what Adolf has had to do in order to keep us safe. Ah, here we are."

She opened a thick, wooden door, and sunshine spilled into the tunnel, momentarily blinding Willy. After his eyes adjusted, he saw a lush, beautiful garden filled with approximately twenty well-dressed people who turned in unison. Willy's mouth dropped as he recognized several famous film directors and composers. To his left, actresses Leni Riefenstahl and Erichtina Söderbaum stared at him, clearly deciding whether he was worth their time. Anna laughed as she followed his gaze. "Yes. Much has changed since you left, Willy. Adolf likes to spend time with people who understand him and his goals for the Reich. The group in this garden have not only funded his rise to power but continue to support his goals, as he supports theirs. It is a mutually beneficial relationship."

A loud crack broke through the chatter and silenced the crowd. Nervous twitters and light laughter followed as the Führer stepped from behind a tree. In his hand he held a whip that he flicked in coordination with his stride. Hitler's penchant for theatrics shone as he took his time approaching Willy. His deep blue eyes, always intense, held a mania Willy had never seen.

"William, how kind of you to join us." Hitler cracked the whip and those closest to him jumped.

Willy flinched but held his ground. "Uncle."

Hitler circled him as the partygoers looked on. Willy felt like a lab animal awaiting the first cut in a dissection. He glanced at Leni Riefenstahl and noted that her mouth was set in a small smile.

"I shall get right to the point, Willy. I did not care for your article. It was slanderous and mean."

Willy swallowed, unsure how to proceed. He wanted to say many things, but he hadn't considered that he might speak to Hitler in public. Nor had he ever imagined that his uncle would be brandishing a horsehair whip during their conversation.

"Now that you have vented your apparent anger at me, I expect you to move on."

Willy closed his hands into fists.

"And I trust that you will no longer tour that wretched country spewing venom in the guise of telling the United States what a madman I am."

Willy couldn't help himself. He smiled. Hitler had been following his American speaking tour.

"Stop smiling!" Hitler seethed. He twitched the whip, and a split second later a crack sounded. Willy flinched and became stone-faced.

"That's better," Hitler said as he resumed circling Willy. The guests shifted their weight and exchanged nervous glances. What had started as a party game was deteriorating into a debacle they weren't certain they wanted to see.

"Have you nothing to say, William?"

Willy slowly met Hitler's gaze. "Is this why you called me here, Uncle? To berate me in front of your sychophants?"

Hitler's lips curled into something resembling a smile. "You are an ungrateful sloth. I gave you every opportunity to excel in the Reich and you threw it away. Then you have the audacity . . . the *audacity* to speak ill of me overseas?" His anger spiraled, twisting his paranoia into a tale of treacherous woe in which he was wrongfully accused. "I am building glory here, William! I am building an empire in which the Aryan race prevails! It is imperative that we move forward according to the intentions of God! I have been chosen, and your mean-spirited words not only blaspheme me but fly in the face of everything I am trying to achieve for the Reich!"

Hitler looked away and caught his breath, then glowered at Willy. "You will stop, William. It is that simple. You. Will. Stop."

Willy could feel the guests' collective breath being held. He took a step forward. "Or what?"

Hitler didn't hesitate. "I will kill her myself."

Anna gasped but Willy ignored her. "So, she is alive. You told me through your spy that she wasn't alive. But clearly, she is." Willy smiled. "That's all I needed to know, Uncle." Willy turned on his heel and walked toward the door.

"WAIT!" Hitler shrieked as he cracked the whip at its full length. A woman screamed and the crowd pressed together in an effort to find reprieve from Hitler's fury. Willy turned around and noted that Hitler's moustache twitched. His fury was palpable and fueled Willy's anger.

"I swear that I will kill her, Willy. There will be no gunshot through her temple. It will be slow and painful. Men will enjoy her beforehand, as they have already. Count on it."

His words painted a grim picture, and Willy started shaking. The harder he tried to control the tremors, the more violent they became. Like any apex predator, Hitler took note and went in for the kill. "Yes. You should know, Willy, that Ursula has enjoyed the company of men since she entered the ghetto. Several times, in exchange for clothing and food. Your fiancée is a whore. Not surprising, really, given her lineage. But nevertheless, probably somewhat disappointing for you I suppose."

Willy's hands balled into fists. He felt his fingernails digging into his palms. "You're lying."

Hitler scoffed. "I assure you that I am not."

Willy's stomach seized and bile rose in his throat. He stepped forward quickly. A guard appeared and threw his hand on Willy's chest, stopping him from getting closer to the Führer. Willy felt his lips pull away from his teeth like a wild animal whose killing instinct must be tamed. "Hear me when I say that if you hurt Ursula, I will tell the world about your affair with Geli, and how she was pregnant with your child when she committed suicide."

Gasps erupted from the guests. Rumor had run rampant about Hitler's affair with Geli, before and after her demise. The coroner had quickly ruled her death a suicide, and the body had been rushed to Vienna for burial. The Bavarian Minister of Justice, Frank Gürtner, had halted any more investigation, and Hitler's propaganda machine had gone into overdrive to spin stories about what might have driven such a beautiful young woman to take her life.

Hitler's eyes became wild as he lifted the whip, then cracked it centimeters away from Willy's left side, taking the heads off a row of blood-red begonias. Willy didn't flinch. He was beyond feeling or surprise. All that mattered was finding Ursula. He glowered at Hitler and was astounded to find that his uncle's eyes had become dewy.

"I loved Geli and I was sick when she died. You need to understand that Ursula is my second chance. She's my Geli. Mine!" A tear ran down his cheek and he swiped it away.

"She's not Geli, Uncle!"

"I know that!" he screamed. Hitler tugged his bangs away from his eyes and wiped his mouth. His hands were shaking as he pointed the handle of the whip at Willy. "I will not hesitate to kill her, Willy. I'll kill her and then take my own life if you write one more word about me!" His anguished eyes scanned the garden as he raved.

Willy felt his adrenaline drain, and he felt suddenly exhausted. "I just want Ursula back, Uncle. I promise that I will remain silent if you allow Ursula and me to return to the United States."

Hitler, still wrapped in his own grief, paused and wiped his eyes, then stared at the anxious crowd as if seeing them for the first time. Their fear seemed to embolden him, and his sadness instantaneously evaporated. He stood straighter and smoothed his hair, then turned to Willy. "I will not return her to you, nor will you write another bad word about me. I have stated my terms, and you will abide by them or Ursula will pay the ultimate price. Now, get out and never claim any familial bond with me. I disown you as my nephew. As far as I am concerned, you are deceased." Like a petulant child who has spoken and won't await a response, he turned quickly and muttered something that made the captivated crowd laugh. Everyone relaxed and returned to sipping their wine as if nothing had happened.

Willy watched them for a moment, marveling at the ease with which this group had compartmentalized their lives, banishing reality to the less fortunate. He returned the way he had come and entered the cab that awaited him outside the Chancellery. He smiled broadly as he recalled Hitler's exact words. "You should know, Willy, that Ursula has enjoyed the company of men since she entered the ghetto."

The ghetto, Willy repeated in his mind. In the weeks leading up to his trip to Denmark, Willy had researched each of the work camps. There was only one that was referred to as a ghetto, and that was Terezín. The other prisons were referred to as concentration camps. By using the term "ghetto" Hitler had inadvertently revealed Ursula's location.

The driver gazed at him in the rearview mirror. "Forgive me for saying so, sir, but you seem rather happier than when you entered that building."

Willy met his eyes. "I am, my good man. I am."

48

Ursula spent the morning watching a run-through of *Brundibár*. As promised, Ilse had cobbled together splendid, colorful costumes that allowed the children a further imaginary escape from the camp. She had bartered, bribed, and stolen the necessary material and had worked tirelessly to ensure their completion. Addi had prevailed as well, creating false moustaches and finding stage makeup for some of the cast.

For their part, the children had exceeded Ursula's expectations, and she felt humbled by their trust in her. Their excitement was infectious, yet they undertook their roles with a mature focus, determined to meet their vocal director's exacting standards. Her heart soared when she thought of them, a rambunctious group that had become her new family. She felt like a mother to the younger ones and a big sister to the teens. She couldn't wait to showcase their talents!

"Ursula, why are you smiling?" Ilse asked.

"I'm so proud of our group, I could burst!"

Ilse grinned and sewed the final stitches of the cat costume. "Three days until our performance. The time has passed quickly."

"Why do you think Rahm has ordered a mandatory roll call today?" Ursula asked.

Ilse shrugged. "Who knows? We haven't had one for a week or so. Honestly, I think some people could have walked out of here, and the guards wouldn't have noticed. They've been so busy overseeing the ghetto's beautification."

"There's nowhere to go, even if we did leave."

"I know, but you understand my point. Things feel different. Although I was initially skeptical, Terezín feels almost like a real town now, not a camp."

Ursula's eyebrows came together. She, too, had felt the positive change. Not only in the living conditions, but in the attitudes of the guards and the Jewish Council. The air smelled fresher, and people seemed kinder. Money changed hands for goods and services. People felt proud once again as they contributed towards something bigger than themselves. But beneath the painted buildings and relaxed attitudes, Ursula still felt an undercurrent, a hidden riptide that threatened to drown the peace.

"You don't agree?" Ilse examined her. "What is it, Ursula?"

"I can't shake the feeling that all is not what it seems."

"Well, I hope you're mistaken."

"Me too."

"What do you make of the Red Cross coming to visit?" Ilse asked.

"After Rahm told us they were coming, I spoke to Jakob Edelstein of the council. He reinforced what we'd been told. The world wants to know that we're being treated well here. That's why the recent changes have taken place."

Ilse blinked. "But what happens after the visit? Did Jakob talk about that?"

"I asked the same question. Apparently, Rahm assured him that the positive changes would be maintained for the duration of our time here."

Ilse sighed. "That's good to hear."

"Yes." Ursula didn't share her concern over the phrase that Rahm had used, "the duration of our time here." As if the time were short-lived. *Are we going to be moved? Killed?* The uncertainty was the undercurrent of tension, the riptide. It seemed as if she were the only person who felt it, so she kept her apprehension to herself.

"What do you think?" Ilse held up the completed costume, and Ursula's concerns melted away.

"Oh, Ilse. You have truly outdone yourself. It's beautiful."

"I made a promise to the children, and by God, I was going to keep it." She beamed.

A claxon call interrupted their conversation and reverberated throughout the camp's loudspeakers, followed by Rahm's booming voice. "Everyone will report to the town square in five minutes." The directive repeated two more times, and the speaker fell silent. Tension crept into Ursula's jaw, and she noted that Ilse, too, moved more stiffly as she packed away her sewing supplies.

Five minutes later they joined thousands of other inmates on the lawn in front of the Town Hall. Without being told, the crowd arranged themselves so that the quad was covered in seemingly endless, perfectly straight queues. They remained silent as the guards counted them, tensing when the dogs walked by, and then relaxing when they moved on. Twenty minutes later everyone had been accounted for, and Rahm spoke into a microphone.

"Good afternoon. You did a fine job today organizing yourselves. As many of you already know, we will have visitors in three days' time. The International Red Cross will be spending an entire day in our little town, and I expect you to be good hosts and hostesses. They will follow a predetermined path. Those of you who will interact with them have been made aware of your roles. Those of you who will not interact with them will not speak, even if spoken to. Is that clear?" Thousands of heads nodded silently. "If you choose to speak, there will be consequences. If not to you, then to someone you love. Is that clear?" People nodded again, this time staring at the ground.

"There will be a football match and a performance by the children while our visitors are here. If you are on the two teams that will be playing, or if you are in the children's opera, please step out of line."

Well-trained, the individuals Rahm mentioned took one step to the right so that they stood out to the commandant, who gazed at them before continuing. Ursula noted that the football players were mostly Danish and in very good physical condition. They had been in the camp only a relatively short time. "The people involved in the performances may not speak to our visitors, even if spoken to. Is that understood?" He looked directly at Ursula. Her eyes bored into him, but she nodded. "Good. Now, another order of business. I know that conditions here in Terezín have become more crowded in recent months, but we are now prepared to send some of you to Theresienstadt family camp, located slightly east of here." Murmurs bubbled through the crowd. Rahm held up his hands. "Now, now. Don't worry. Much like Terezín, the new camp has been restructured to accommodate larger numbers of Jews. You will like it there, and you're guaranteed to remain with your family. Over the next two days many of you will pack your belongings and board the train for your new home. Any questions?" Blank faces stared. They knew that Rahm's question was rhetorical. "Good. Dismissed."

People disseminated as they discussed the upcoming Red Cross visit and the family camp. Ursula and Ilse linked arms and walked slowly as they watched a woman walk by with her three young children in tow, all of them holding hands. "I don't have a good feeling, Ilse."

"Me neither."

* * *

Ursula awoke to the clatter of train wheels on the tracks. A whistle blew, followed by Rahm's voice over the loudspeaker. "An officer will collect you from your barracks if you are to travel today. Be ready." Everyone jumped up and stood in front of their bunks. They listened as heavy boots climbed the stairs and paused on each floor, bellowed some numbers, and then continued upwards. When the boots appeared at her door, they were occupied by Edvard Svoboda. Ursula watched him scan the room. He caught Addi's eye and smiled. She smiled back, and Ursula realized that they genuinely cared for each other. What had started as an "arrangement" had blossomed into something from which each party gained. She supposed many successful marriages were based on the same premise.

Svoboda cleared his throat and reviewed the numbers on his list, then called them out quickly. "Gather your belongings and get on the train if your name was called."

Forty-five people from their room exited the building and stepped into the almost-full cattle car. As the train slowly pulled away, Ursula examined its occupants. Rahm had kept his word. Families remained together.

"Fräulein?"

Ursula turned to find Rahm staring down at her. A sliver of ice slid down her spine, and she shuddered. He took no notice. "I'm glad that you remain here." Ursula said nothing. He stepped closer. "I believe that working with the children has been good for you. You have color in your cheeks."

"The ample food and regular bathing have done their part as well."

"But of course. My point is . . ."

She strained to look past him, but his frame was too broad. She ended up staring at his chest. He cleared his throat. "You're being rude. I was saying that—"

"I understand what you're saying . . . or what you're not saying."

"Fräulein, I suggest that you alter your tone. You—"

"Are not for sale."

"What?"

She focused on the buttons of his coat, not trusting herself to look anywhere else. Perhaps it was the recent freedom that she'd been granted, or the fact that she found herself dreaming more often of life after the camp. But somewhere, deep down, she'd made a decision to stand up for herself. She couldn't avoid all of the daily, personal degradations, but she could draw the line at being violated. Or she could try. An unexpected calm descended upon her. Her emotions flatlined, and she exited her body so that she was looking down at the two of them from above.

Rahm chuckled. "You're not for sale? As I mentioned, I'm not interested in you. At all, actually. You repulse me."

Her shoulders relaxed.

"However, I don't care for your tone, so I suggest you alter it."

Relieved, she smiled, a real smile, and looked into his eyes. "That's better," he said. "Now, I have gotten word that the Führer, who has never visited a camp, will be attending the children's performance. He has requested that you wear the green dress he gifted you when you performed Verdi."

Ursula felt her insides flip, and she started shaking. It started in her belly and worked its way outwards until her entire body trembled. *He's going to kill me*, she thought. She couldn't explain how she knew it, but she had never been more certain of anything in her life. *He's never been to one of his torture centers, yet he's coming here to murder me.*

Before she could stop herself, she said, "No."

He leaned into her and spoke evenly, without emotion. "You will play the role I assign to you or suffer the consequences."

She forced herself to look into his black eyes. "I will not."

Time slowed as she watched Rahm lift his heavy arm. He drew it across his body and lifted it high above his head. It descended, and at the height of its momentum, landed against her head, which jerked to the left. The force of the blow lifted her from the ground and smashed her against the wall. She observed from above as the shell of her body crumpled to the ground, and onlookers shrank in fear.

She listened to Rahm's breath as he bent over her and felt for a pulse. Satisfied that she was still alive, he hissed, "What a bitch you are! Look what you made me do! Now you're going to be damaged when the Führer arrives. He will *not* be pleased."

Although she fought it, her mind reentered her body and processed the pain. She wished she could exit her body again, but the momentary break with reality that had allowed her to stand up for herself relinquished its protective hold, and her self-awareness returned. Exhausted, she lay there, hoping for the final blow that would end her misery. But in her soul, she knew that it wouldn't come. She was Hitler's prey, and his conquest would never be denied. Edvard Svoboda appeared and lifted her from the ground. He carried her to Dresden and placed her on a bunk, then turned to Addi, who had trailed behind. "She'll be okay, but she was hit very hard. Take care of her. She needs to look presentable for the upcoming visit."

Svoboda exited the room, and Addi rushed over to examine her face. "Oh, Ursula. Your cheek is split wide open. I hope the bone isn't broken."

Ursula winced. "Well, something is broken. It hurts to breathe."

Addi gingerly touched her left side and Ursula screamed. "I think several ribs are broken, Ursula. You hit the wall very hard. Your face is bleeding a lot. Ilse, can you please sew Ursula's cheek?"

Ilse appeared with a needle already threaded. "This is going to hurt, Ursula."

"No more than my pride."

Ilse inserted the needle into the skin on both sides of the open gash and pulled the skin flaps together.

Ursula gasped through clenched teeth. "I don't know which hurts more. Breathing or being sewn back together."

"Sorry. I'm doing my best," Ilse whispered.

Edvard Svoboda appeared at the doorway again and called out more names for the next train. When the chosen had left the room, he asked how Ursula was doing.

"She'll be alright," Addi answered.

"Another train already?" Ursula asked.

"It would seem so," Ilse said, her face a mask of concentration as she stitched. They listened as Svoboda called out another twenty-five names, leaving only eight people in their bunkroom. When he'd gone, Ursula whispered, "They're cleaning house."

Addi nodded. "Many people who are going to the new camp are older or sick."

Ilse shook her head. "That's not true. There are plenty of children going."

"But they're leaving with their parents because Rahm said that families would stay together," Addi countered.

"That's the only way people would get on the trains so readily," Ursula whispered. "As long as they're together, they think they're safe. But they're not."

"What do you think Rahm is doing, Ursula?"

Her heart sank as she fully realized the brilliance of his plan. The ghetto had been spruced up, and the prisoners had been fed, bathed, and instructed on what to say and how to appear. Two performances had been prepared for the upcoming visit—a football match and a children's opera. What better way to fool the world than by showcasing healthy, happy children? The final step, of course, was to lessen the ghetto's overpopulation and weed out those who appear physically compromised in some way, thereby completing the picture of a content, well-cared-for Jewish community. Rahm's words played through her memory. "You will play the role I assign to you or suffer the consequences."

"We've been preparing *Brundibár*, but that's not the actual performance that matters. When the International Red Cross comes, we will be acting on a global stage. The reward for a mediocre portrayal will be death." She turned her head to the side, wincing at the pain. "The role of a lifetime."

49

Trains had run day and night over the last two days and carried away more than eighty percent of Terezín's inhabitants, leaving approximately seven thousand within the fortress walls. The result was that the camp seemed almost empty. With only eight to a bunkroom, guards had ordered the remaining inmates to scrub the walls and floors until they shone, then installed real beds, bookshelves, and desks in each room. The more effort put into beautification, the more nervous Ursula became about the Red Cross visit. The unspoken tension was felt by most remaining inmates who moved about quietly, afraid to draw the attention of guards who found themselves with extra time.

The *Brundibár* cast ended up performing their dress rehearsal in front of the entire camp administration. When it was over, the soldiers and guards— led by Karl Rahm—leapt to their feet and whistled and cheered.

Hans Krása addressed the audience. "Thank you so much for coming. We hope you enjoyed the show!" The crowd erupted again, and Ursula was reminded of her curtain call after playing Adele in *Die Fledermaus*, only eleven years prior. *How far I've come*, she thought. *How far I've fallen.*

Rahm locked eyes with her. She glared in return and unconsciously touched her stitched cheek as he approached.

"You did a fine job with the children. The performance was well done."

"Thank you."

Rahm kept his eyes on her.

Ursula fidgeted. His stare was disconcerting. Unlike Seidl, whose motivations were clear, she didn't know what Rahm wanted when he looked at her. "The Red Cross will arrive soon, yes?"

Rahm looked at his watch. "Any minute. Do you remember the schedule?"

"Yes. They arrive at eleven a.m. and meet with you until twelve p.m., when they have lunch, then a tour of the camp, followed by the football game, a short break, then the opera, dinner, and then they leave. Did I miss anything?"

Rahm squinted at her. "You missed nothing. Remember, you must wear the green dress for the performance. I trust we will not have any more issues surrounding the Führer's request?"

She bit her lip and forced a response. "Yes."

"Remember, do not speak, even if spoken to. Is that clear?"

"Yes."

He looked at her again, and she met his eyes. In them she noted something she'd never seen before. A slight crinkle at the edges, a small lift of the eyebrow. She didn't recognize it at first, so when the realization came, it perplexed her.

Fear. He's actually scared. But of what?

50

Willy returned to the Copenhagen hotel and shared his news about Ursula's location. Although he desperately wanted nothing more than to jump into a car and drive to the camp, Wallenburg reminded him that arriving with the Red Cross would place him in a more powerful position than arriving on his own. "Besides," Wallenburg reasoned, "have you formulated a plan to get her out of there? Take the two days before we arrive to plan, Willy."

Willy agreed and spent the next two days writing letters. His first letter was to Bridget and Otto, updating them on the meeting with Hitler and his locating Ursula. He then wrote to anyone he thought might help his case: United Kingdom Prime Minister Winston Churchill, American President Franklin Roosevelt, King Christian X of Denmark, and Max Huber, President of the International Red Cross. He also penned a note to William Randolph Hearst on the off chance that he had some influence with any of the others. Willy knew that his letters wouldn't arrive until after the Red Cross visit had occurred, but he was laying the groundwork in case the situation developed into an international incident.

After sealing the letters and leaving them with the concierge, Willy turned his attention to the plan to free Ursula. Because Hitler had known that Willy was in Copenhagen, he also presumably knew that Willy was on his way to Terezín with the Red Cross.

Would Ursula be there? Willy wondered. *Would Uncle move her somewhere else? Hide her? Or would he parade her as a prisoner in front of me?*

He was fairly certain that Hitler wouldn't actually kill her, at least not before Willy arrived. Hitler would hold her as a bargaining chip for as long as he could. Besides, Hitler held a sick fascination for Ursula, a kind of twisted, possessive passion. Willy's greatest fear was that his uncle's passion would morph into a vicious hatred that could spiral out of control.

Bribing the guards was a distinct possibility, so prior to coming to Europe Willy had withdrawn a significant amount of cash. If that didn't work, then he would devise a way to sneak her out. Perhaps in the boot of the car? A disguise?

Willy shook his head. Without knowing the exact layout of the camp and the number of guards, there was no way he could proactively plan their getaway. He would have to get there and think on his feet. Improvise.

Then a terrible thought struck. *What if Ursula is crippled? What if she can't walk?* Willy dropped his head in his hands and started to cry. He was so close to her, yet in some ways was no closer than when he didn't know where she was.

No! He corrected his thoughts. *You know where she is, and you* will *bring her back with you, or die trying.*

* * *

The small caravan carrying Willy, Wallenburg, and the Danish and International Red Cross representatives approached Terezín. Willy's heart hammered in his chest as the cars passed through the gate labeled Arbeit Macht Frei.

"That's a sick joke," Willy commented. "These people are incarcerated."

Wallenburg translated the phrase. "Work sets you free. Probably not true in this place."

"No doubt that was Uncle Alf's idea."

"Remember, Willy, keep your wits about you and let me do the talking. Alright?"

Willy nodded. "I promise. Thank you, by the way, for all that you've done. I know that you gave me this job so I could find Ursula. But I hope that I've been an acceptable assistant."

Wallenburg put his hand on Willy's shoulder. "You've been exceptional, actually. I was hoping that when this visit is over you might think of staying on."

Willy was touched. "Thanks. I'll think about it."

The car drove past several freshly painted buildings, then around the quadrangle to park in front of the Town Hall. Karl Rahm stood at the base of the stairs with his officers and soldiers arranged behind him. Two well-dressed prisoners stepped forward and opened the car doors. Wallenburg exited, followed by Willy. The other car parked, and its occupants exited as well. When the visitors had gathered, Rahm lifted his chin. In pristine unison, one hundred uniformed guards slapped their heels together and stood at attention. Rahm stepped forward and shook each visitor's hand. "Welcome to Terezín, an artist and retirement community for Jews."

Willy's eyes wandered around the square, but the only inmates he saw were the ones who had opened the car doors. He tried to catch their eyes, but they looked straight ahead or at the ground. Rahm wasted no time.

"Please, gentlemen, come in and let us enjoy a nice lunch."

51

From a window on the fourth floor of Dresden barracks, Ursula scrutinized the two black limousines filled with strangers who would pass judgment on the treatment of Jews in Terezín. She pressed her face against the glass to better see the visitors as the cars drove by. One man turned toward her, but the glare of the sun bounced off the window, momentarily blinding her. When she regained her vision, the car had passed.

52

Willy's stomach was in knots, but he forced down the lunch of beef stew, potato dumplings, and a spätzle. He declined dessert, hoping that the group might start the tour a bit early. He was disappointed when Rahm announced that they would be strictly adhering to the preorganized schedule out of "respect for the townsfolk who had labored to ensure a fine visit." Willy smiled repeatedly at the women who served their lunch but, once again, they kept their eyes either on the plates or on each other. Not once did any of them make eye contact with their guests.

"Tell me, Herr Rahm, the people serving us today. Are they servants or paid employees of the town?"

Rahm offered his most winning smile. "They're compensated for their work."

Wallenburg shot Willy a warning glance. Willy ignored him. "I see. I find it interesting that they don't interact with us in any way."

Rahm stiffened. It was a tiny change, but Willy noticed it. "Well, Herr Hitler, here in Terezín we have trained our staff to be respectful of authority. That's not to say that they're scared of us. Quite the contrary, I assure you. They simply know their place and feel fortunate to have work."

A young female server approached with a steaming cup of coffee. As she placed it in front of Willy, some liquid sloshed over the side and into the saucer. The woman drew a sharp breath and glanced fearfully at Rahm. Willy saw the glimpse and knew that the niggling he felt deep down held merit.

"It's alright." Willy smiled and placed his hand on her arm. She looked at him, and his smile dropped. He saw terror, sorrow, and pathetic gratitude for his graciousness. Time paused as they shared a silent conversation, but it was over in a second. Willy's insides hardened, and he turned to find Rahm glaring at him.

Willy returned the glare. "I'd like to take that tour now. Please."

53

Ursula, Addi, and Ilse peeked around the corner of Dresden. Although forbidden to exit their barracks during the visitors' tour, they had snuck out. They were aware of the punishment if they were caught, but the impulse to see people from the outside world, where things were not upside down and everyone was free, was irresistible. They walked quickly down the street, turned left, and then right so they were staring at the lush green grass of the quad where the football players were warming up. They hid behind a large tree and saw guards standing in front of the Town Hall, stomping their boots in appreciation when one of the young men performed a particularly talented trick with the ball.

"Ursula, stop swishing," Addi scolded.

Ursula pulled at her dress, which hung on her gaunt frame. "I can't help it, Addi. This dress is far too big, and it drags when I walk."

Ilse looked at her. "You do look beautiful."

Ursula rolled her eyes. "I look ridiculous. He wants me to look ridiculous."

"He wants you to stand out," Addi said.

"But only to make fun of me," Ursula finished.

"Hush! They'll hear us. Oh, they're leaving the Town Hall."

The doors to the Town Hall opened, and eight men emerged. Led by Rahm, they walked down the steps and paused at the edge of the grass, watching the players practice. Rahm said something and they all laughed.

Except one.

One of the men stood stoically, his arms folded across his chest. Instead of watching the athletes, his head swiveled, examining far-reaching corners as if searching for something. Ursula noted that he was well-dressed, but he was too far away to discern individual features. He was tall and stood out from the rest of the group, not because he was dressed differently, but because of the way he carried himself.

He seemed proud and confident. And determined. And familiar.

She leaned forward and squinted. Without thinking, her right hand found her neck and started twisting the chain that hung there.

"He reminds me of Willy," she whispered.

"What? Who? Which one?" Ilse and Addi spoke at once.

"The one that's hanging back from the group. He has Willy's stature and . . . his walk. It's so much like Willy's."

Ilse rubbed her back. "You know that's not Willy, don't you? There's no way that the Führer would allow him to come here."

"Unless the Führer doesn't know," Ursula breathed.

"As you so aptly pointed out, Ursula, the Führer knows everything that has to do with you. Do you really believe that Willy could sneak in here without his uncle knowing about it?"

Ursula's heart sank as the man reluctantly followed the rest of the group across the grass to start their tour. She turned to her friends and covered her face with her hands. "Of course, you're correct. My imagination is playing tricks. I feel like I'm losing my mind. Besides, I would never want Willy to see me like this. Broken ribs and bumpy nose, a scar like a pirate across my cheek. I'm hideous."

Ilse smiled. "Ursula, don't you realize that you're more beautiful now than when you entered the ghetto?"

Ursula choked back a sob and wiped tears from her eyes. "You're wrong. Kind, but very, very wrong, Ilse."

Addi shook her head. "No, Ursula. Ilse is correct. You are more beautiful now."

"But I'm broken."

Ilse smiled. "That's precisely what makes you so stunning. Like a broken vase that has been glued back together, your light can now shine through the cracks that have been made, allowing those around you to see the real you, your goodness."

Ursula looked intently at her friends, frightened to utter her thoughts. After several moments, she gave them voice. "But if I ever see Willy again, will he be able to see through my cracks?"

Ilse started to cry and ran her finger along Ursula's cheek. "From what you've told us, Willy has always been able to see through your cracks, even before they were visible to you or the outside world."

Ursula smiled through her tears. "I'm very fortunate to have you two as my friends."

Addi nodded. "Yes. You are. Now, let's stop being worrisome women. You *will* see Willy again, and we *do* have an opera to stage, so let's get to it."

54

Willy thought he would lose his mind as he straggled behind the tour. He took every opportunity to peek around corners and into windows. Several times Rahm caught him lagging and called him to the front of the group. Willy always complied, but he found his impatience growing as the hours ticked by.

During the football match he was able to enjoy himself for minutes at a time as he got caught up in the rivalry and excitement. The match ended in a tie, with both teams urging for more time to properly determine a winner. But Rahm insisted on moving the visit along, so Willy waved to the players and followed the group toward the Town Hall for a brief respite before the opera.

Rahm had not left Willy's side during the second half of the tour. But when the commandant was called into the Town Hall for a moment, Wallenburg sidled up to Willy. "Any sign of her?"

Willy shook his head. "No, but it's a large area. Have you noticed that the only people who answer our questions are the Danish prisoners? I think they're allowed to speak because King Christian is the person who insisted on this visit. But no one else responds to questions. They always look at Rahm when we speak to them, and he answers for them."

"Yes. I have noticed that."

"I'm wondering if the entire town has been whitewashed for our visit. Something seems very . . . wrong."

Wallenburg's eyebrows came together. "I'm not sure I agree, Willy. It seems like the Jews are being treated well here."

Willy pulled back. "Please don't tell me that you're falling for their ruse."

Wallenburg looked around. "The people look happy, Willy. They're fed and clothed. There are cafés and bookshops. A school. Football games. Not one person has said anything negative about their living conditions."

Willy shook his head. "I think they can't speak or they'll be punished. Can you really not see past the paint and rosebushes?"

"What are we discussing, gentlemen?" Rahm approached and tilted his head in Willy's direction. "I trust everyone is happy?"

Willy looked away, not trusting himself to speak.

"Good news," the commandant continued. "I just received a phone call from Adolf Eichmann. He and the Führer will be here in time for the opera at four o'clock."

55

The children's excitement was barely contained as they sang vocal warm-ups. Afterwards, Krása gave them a rousing, pre-performance speech, and Ursula gathered them around her for a final word before they took the stage. The drone of chatter from the audience seated in the newly constructed auditorium carried to the cast and made them even more eager to showcase their hard work. Ursula smiled at Addi, who clapped her hands twice to silence the animated children.

"Ladies and gentlemen," Ursula said. "It's been my pleasure to be your vocal coach. I can't think of anyone else with whom I would rather work on this fine day. Each of you has surpassed my high expectations, and it's been my honor to get to know you. Your ages range from five to seventeen, yet all of you have carried yourselves with the utmost professionalism and dignity in these trying times."

Ursula noted some blank stares from the younger children.

Addi intervened. "Dignity is the manner in which someone carries herself with pride and respect."

Ursula smiled. "Yes, and you need to know that each one of you is very dignified."

The children grinned broadly as Ursula heard the audience become quiet.

"My point is, we are about to go on that stage, and you should be proud, so very proud of what we have accomplished already." Ursula stopped and started to cry. "I guess I want you to know that working with you has been the most wonderful time of my life." She paused to gather herself. "Now, go out there and continue to make me proud!"

Gideon Klein sat at the grand piano that had been brought into camp the previous day. Ursula poked her head out from behind the curtain and nodded to him, the predetermined sign for him to begin.

56

Willy was chatting quietly with Wallenburg when a hush fell over the crowd. He turned to see the Führer enter the auditorium, followed closely by Adolf Eichmann. The officers and soldiers in the room rose quickly and saluted. Hitler walked to a chair at the end of the first row and glanced dismissively at Willy, then sat and crossed his legs. At the same time, a dark-haired head peeked out from behind the curtain and nodded to the pianist. A surge of adrenaline rushed through Willy. His breath came shallow and fast. Although it had been only a glance, and the woman looked older and thinner than Ursula, Willy wondered if he had just seen his lost love.

57

The opera lasted forty-five minutes. During that time Ursula took several opportunities to steal glances at Hitler. If he recognized himself in the bully organ grinder character, Brundibár, he didn't show it. Seeing him again made her feel physically ill, so she forced herself to pay attention to the show. At the end of the performance, the entire cast of Jewish children turned to Hitler and raised their right arms, offering ironic homage. Ursula peeked at Hitler again and saw him smile at the children. But the smile seemed forced, and she could tell by his eyes that something was bothering him. *It's me*, she thought.

The audience jumped to its feet and applauded as the children took their bows. Once the cast had been recognized, Hans Krása emerged from behind the curtain and crossed to center stage.

"Good afternoon. Thank you so much for attending today. I am very proud to have written *Brundibár*, but I couldn't have staged it without help. The creative costumes were created by Ilse Weber, and the makeup was done by Addi Lutz." Ilse and Addi came out from behind the curtain and bowed, then joined the beaming cast.

"I would be mightily remiss if I didn't introduce our wonderful accompanist, Gideon Klein." Klein played the introduction to *Brundibár* before waving to the cheering crowd.

"Finally, allow me to present our vocal coach. These children have performed *Brundibár* many times in the past, but they have never sounded better than today, thanks to her hard work. No stranger to the stage, please welcome diva Ursula Becker."

Ursula stepped from behind the curtain and waved at the audience. The applause crescendoed as she kissed her palms and threw them to the crowd, relishing the acknowledgment. She hadn't realized how much she missed it. At this sublime moment, her preposterous dress didn't matter. Her battered face and bony frame faded to the background. Nothing mattered but the music, the crowd, and the joy she felt. Her eyes landed on Hitler, and she felt a surge of anxious adrenaline. Wanting to extend the happy moment, she turned away from him and faced the right side of the audience.

Her breath caught as she saw Willy. His hands were at his sides, and he was smiling through his tears. She closed her eyes, confident that her imagination was torturing her. When she opened them, Willy had taken a step toward her. A sob burst from her throat, and she brought her hand to her mouth. Everything around him fell away as she took in his clothes, his smile, his eyes. The eyes that she had dreamed of and craved for two endless years. An eternity of hell.

The applause continued, and he lifted his hand to his cheek, silently asking about her stitches. Her hand went to the gash, and she nodded, unsure what else to do. Slowly she returned her gaze to Hitler, who stood perfectly still. His head was tilted, and his hands were clasped in front of him. A Mona Lisa smile sat on his thin lips.

58

Willy did nothing to stem the flow of tears. He felt weightless, a balloon that might float away on a gust of wind. Ursula seemed like a dream to him, more so because of her appearance. She was at least ten kilos lighter than the last time he'd seen her. Her pallor bordered on sickly, and she wore an extravagant dress that highlighted her weight loss. Her limbs looked too long for her lean frame. Her elbows and wrists seemed like knots in a thin piece of pine. Her glorious hair was shorter and listless, hanging heavy and straight. Her nose had clearly been broken, and she had a gash on her cheek that had been roughly sewn together with black thread. The overall appearance was that of a lightweight boxer who hadn't simply lost a match but had been pummeled.

But her eyes. They radiated the same passion and brightness that he remembered, shining like beacons through her otherwise shocking appearance. Those eyes bored into him now, expressing everything she couldn't say. *Take me home, Willy. Please.*

59

Hitler took the stage to cheers and applause from the audience. As he crossed to center, Ursula drew the children close to her, instinctively wrapping her arms around as many of them as she could. He ignored her and lifted his hands to calm the raucous crowd. After several moments, he cleared his throat.

"What a wonderful performance we were privileged enough to see today. Thank you, Herr Krása, for such a fine example of how children can perform the highest art form. Your music was melodious, and the acting was first rate." He turned around and held out his hand toward a little girl named Greta. The five-year-old didn't hesitate to go to Hitler, who wrapped his arm around her and asked her name.

"Greta," she answered shyly.

"What a beautiful name. You did a fine job today, Greta. Now, tell me, do you think that the entire cast of *Brundibár* should receive a surprise to celebrate their hard work?"

Greta nodded eagerly.

Hitler beamed at her. "Would you like to go on a train ride?"

Greta paused and looked at Ursula, whose terrified eyes were locked on Hitler.

"Don't worry, Greta. Do you know how some families from Terezín recently went to a new camp? Well, you'll be going to the same camp. It will be a great treat. There's a glorious playground there. There are swings and ice cream."

Greta's eyes grew to saucers at the mention of ice cream. Ursula lurched forward and grabbed Greta's shirt, dragging her away from Hitler. "Don't do this!" she hissed.

Hitler laughed and glanced at the officers in the audience, who all started clapping.

He addressed Greta once more. "Should the entire cast go? Hans Krása, Ilse Weber, Addi Lutz, the children? Everyone except Fräulein Ursula, of course."

Hitler stared at Ursula, and his smile transformed from kind to cruel. She glared at him, imagining tearing his eyes out. His pupils were dilated, and he appeared manic. He was sweating and jumpy. She wondered if he had taken some medication before coming to the camp. *Coward!* she thought. *He can't face what he's done. Or perhaps what he's about to do,* she finished. She stepped forward while pushing Greta behind her. "No." The crowd's encouragement drowned out her words, so she took another step and yelled, "NO!"

The cheering ceased. Willy started to approach the stage, but Hitler turned abruptly. "Do not move, William," he ordered. "Eichmann, gather the cast and get them on the train. It's right outside, children. Hurry, or you'll miss the ice cream."

Ursula raised her arms. "No, children! *Stop!*" But they didn't hear her and scampered off the stage. Ilse, Addi, and Krása stood frozen in place, unsure what to do. Rahm shot them a glance and jerked his head to the door, indicating they should follow the rest of the cast.

Wallenburg stepped toward Hitler. "What's happening here, Herr Hitler?"

Hitler's face was a mask of innocence. Only his excited eyes hinted at his sadism. "I'm sure that I don't understand your implication. Have the conditions in this camp not exceeded your expectations of how the Jews are being treated?"

"Yes, but—"

"But what? Now, please excuse us. My nephew, Fräulein Becker, and I must speak in private." He nodded at Rahm, then turned and exited the building.

Willy and Ursula shared a long look. So many words to be spoken, yet neither knew where to start. He approached the stage and held out his hand. She took it, then stepped off the stage into his arms. She gasped, and he gently released her. "What is it?"

Ursula looked away, embarrassed. "My ribs. They're broken."

Willy's face became beet red. "Who did this?" he growled.

His depth of feeling touched her heart. How could she begin to explain the horrors she had witnessed and experienced, the deals she'd struck, the sacrifices she'd made. She lifted her hand and caressed his face. "I can't believe that you're here."

Ursula felt something jab into her back and turned to find Rahm holding his pistol. "Outside. Now."

"How dare you—" Willy started.

"Do not test me! She's been nothing but trouble," Rahm hissed. "You go too!"

Willy turned to find a confused Wallenburg gaping at him. "It's alright. I'll be right back."

Rahm, Ursula, and Willy exited the building and crossed to Hitler, who leaned against his car and picked lint from the sleeve of his coat. Ursula saw

Hitler's driver, Erich, sitting inside the limousine, smoking a cigarette. He glanced at her and did a double take, then averted his eyes and resumed smoking.

"Did you really think I wouldn't know your every move, you *stupid* boy?" Hitler spat each venomous word. "Did you think I would let you ride in on a white horse and steal her away from me?" He laughed, a high-pitched, deranged sound that resounded in Ursula's core.

"Please, Uncle, just let me take her with me—"

Ursula noted that Hitler's intense blue eyes were glassy, as if he were feverish, or had taken complete leave of his senses. "Oh, the time has passed for all of that. Perhaps if you had not shamed yourself with false accusations and claims against me. Maybe if you had not spread lies across the United States or if you had respected my wishes and left well enough alone. But you did none of that, and once again, Ursula will watch as others die in her stead." He turned to Eichmann. "Is everyone on board?" he called.

"Yes, Führer."

Hitler nodded, and Eichmann raised his hand above his head and moved it in a circle to indicate that the train should leave.

As it started to move, Ursula looked at Hans Krása, who stood quietly in the cattle car, alone amidst the sea of people. He stared straight ahead, clearly resigned to his fate. She heard her name and turned to find Ilse leaning out of an opening. Her eyes were desperate as she screamed, "The children, Ursula! Please!" Faces ran through Ursula's mind: Markus, Marika, Fritz, the choir members. She had caused every one of their deaths. They lay in her heart like stones weighing her down. She looked at the children, so trusting and innocent, and realized that her conscience couldn't abide one more death.

"Wait!" Ursula screamed. "Please wait! I'll go. Take me! Please!" She ran toward the slow-moving train, then turned back to Hitler, who held up his hand to stop the train. Out of breath, she started sobbing. "Take me. In lieu of all of the children. I can't play this game anymore." She turned to Willy. "I wanted to see you one more time before I died. That was my nightly prayer, Willy, and you came." She smiled through her tears and walked toward him. "You came. I love you so much." Then her smile dropped, and her tone changed. "But I am tired. Tired of fighting, of being afraid, of not knowing whether I'll live through another day. I just can't do it anymore, especially if my living means that the children are sent to their deaths."

She turned to Hitler and held his gaze. He was smug, defiant. He knew that he had won, but she didn't care. Nothing mattered except saving the children. She dropped to her knees and joined her hands together in supplication. "Please. I am on my knees in front of you, just as you always wanted. I'm begging you, *imploring* you to take me instead of the cast."

Hitler's lips twisted into a look of complete disgust. "God, but you're boring," he said. "This isn't how I envisioned this at all." His visage changed into one of fascination. "You are truly broken. I honestly thought it would take more than a group of young Jewish brats to bring you to your knees. How utterly disappointing."

He turned to Willy and pursed his lips. "I will grant your whore of a fiancée her wish, and you'll watch as the train carrying her pulls away."

"No!" Willy took a step toward Hitler, but Rahm stepped between them and backhanded Willy across the temple, sending him sprawling to the ground. Ursula rushed forward, but another guard intervened and held her from behind.

"Willy!" she screamed.

Hitler shook his head. "What was I thinking?" He examined her with a look of disgust. "Look at yourself. You're pathetic. At least Geli had the dignity to end her own life. She was a woman of action. She never would have allowed herself to wither away as you have." Hitler threw a pistol at her feet and laughed. "I will give you the same privilege, Fräulein. Shoot yourself and the children may live."

"You are insane!" Willy hissed.

Hitler ignored him as he stared at Ursula. "You say that you are willing to die so the children may live. Pick it up." She stared at the gun and imagined using it to kill him. As if reading her mind, SS guards surrounded the cattle car and aimed their weapons at the children.

She glared at him and slowly bent down to retrieve the gun.

"Ursula, don't! Uncle, please . . . please don't do this!" Willy begged.

A tear traced her cheek. "It's alright, Willy. It's my choice. I can't stand it anymore." She turned to Hitler, who had turned suddenly solemn. "Do you give me your word that the cast will live?"

"I do."

She faced Willy. The desperation in his eyes broke her heart. "I love you so much, Willy. Thank you for never giving up on me." She brought the gun to her temple.

"Ursula, do not pull that trigger!" Willy ordered.

"What's happening here?" An angry Wallenburg appeared with the two Danish dignitaries trailing him. His mortified eyes went from Ursula to Hitler.

Hitler whipped around. "This is none of your concern. It is an unresolved personal matter. I strongly suggest that you and your Danish colleagues take your leave. I trust you've had a pleasant day here in Terezín, and that you will report that the Jews are enjoying a lovely town." It was an order, not a question.

Wallenburg looked at Willy, who had risen slowly and was wiping blood from his face with a handkerchief. "I admit that your spa town seems pleasant, Herr Hitler. However, I'm concerned with what I'm witnessing at the moment."

Hitler waved a hand towards a guard, who snatched the pistol from Ursula. Willy rushed over and gathered her in his arms.

"You're misunderstanding the situation, Mr. Wallenburg. My nephew and I are having a disagreement. It happens in families."

Wallenburg pointed to the train. "And what of that? Where is the cast going?"

Hitler smiled. "Nowhere, actually. They'll be disembarking the train momentarily . . ." He faced Ursula. "And Fräulein Becker will be boarding."

Willy's head snapped up. "Absolutely not!"

Ursula felt lightheaded and realized that she no longer wanted the responsibility of anyone else's life on her shoulders. She just wanted everything to be over. She faced Willy. "I must go. So much has happened here . . . I can't explain. I've done things."

Willy took her chin in his hand and lifted her face to his. "Ursula, look at me. Nothing you've done here is your fault. Nothing. Do you hear me? You did what you had to do to survive."

Ursula pulled away. "No, Willy. You can't understand. I must go." She turned to Hitler. "Unload the cast and I'll board the train. But our agreement still stands."

"I give you my word."

She stared through him, defeated and exhausted. A melancholic peace replaced her fear and anxiety. She didn't want to die, but seeing Willy again had strengthened her, allowing her to make the decision to offer her life in exchange for the children. She had caused so much suffering to others. Now she could repay her debt. A warmth spread through her core as she realized that her life had purpose and meaning. Knowing that the children would live made her smile.

"I will not allow it!" Willy ordered. He turned to Hitler and lowered his voice. "Uncle, hear me. Please. I know you loved Geli, and I understand the guilt you still feel so many years later." Willy paused, and Ursula could see that he had reached beyond Hitler's glassy gaze. "Your fascination . . . your obsession with Ursula is unhealthy. It's founded on an unreasonable premise—that you can replace Geli with Ursula. But she is not Geli. She never will be, even if she agreed to love you."

Ursula watched Hitler absorb Willy's speech. His eyes darted back and forth as she imagined emotions competing for dominance in his troubled mind. He seemed to be softening, and, for a nonsensical moment, Ursula imagined that he allowed Willy to whisk her away. But suddenly his faraway look disappeared, replaced by hard, focused eyes. "But she didn't."

Willy tilted his head in Hitler's direction. "Who didn't what?"

"She chose not to love me!"

"Ursula or Geli?"

Hitler was no longer listening. "She had every opportunity to please me, and in each case, she chose to disappoint."

"Who are you talking about, Uncle?"

Hitler shook his head as a confused look crossed his features.

"Doing this will not bring Geli back!"

Several moments passed. The only sounds were birdcalls that sounded strangely happy in this most awful of moments. She saw a tear trace Hitler's cheek as he said, "Get on the train, Ursula."

"You're destroying all that's good in the world, Uncle. You know that? She's not going!" Willy gripped Ursula's wrist so tightly that she winced.

She placed her hand on his. "It's not your decision, Willy. It's mine. I need to do this. So many bad things have happened because of me. People have died. I love you. I'll always love you." She embraced him, inhaling his scent as the children clambered down from the train. Ursula watched Addi gather the cast in a circle while Ilse ran towards their barracks, obviously overwhelmed with emotion.

"Then I'm going with you," Willy announced.

Hitler's eyes cleared. "Don't be ridiculous, William."

Willy stepped toward Hitler. Rahm went to restrain him, but Hitler held up his hand to allow the approach. Willy leaned down to whisper in his ear. "If it were up to me, she would be walking into freedom through those iron gates. You can shoot me if you like, here in front of the International Red Cross and Danish authorities. But I'm getting on that train with Ursula."

60

Hitler pursed his lips and narrowed his eyes. "I have a better idea, nephew. You and Ursula will not get on the train. You shall be driven. Commandant Rahm has overseen Ursula's stay in Terezín. It's only fitting that he see her to her new home."

He glanced at Wallenburg, ensuring that the Swedish diplomat was witnessing his magnanimous gesture. Then he faced Ursula.

"Unfortunately, I won't be accompanying you, as I must return to your sister. Although she wanted to attend today, of course I couldn't allow it. You understand." He smiled, enjoying the drama he had created.

He turned to Rahm. "Commandant, you will take my personal car to ensure that you travel without being stopped. The more quickly you deliver your passengers, the better. Choose an officer to drive you."

"Ja, mein Führer!" Rahm turned to Edvard Svoboda. "Get the car!" he barked.

"I want to go too." All heads turned to Addi. She was staring at Ursula as she spoke. "I have no family. Ursula is my family. She promised me that when she left, I could go with her. Remember?"

Ursula's face crumpled. "Of course, I remember, but surely you don't want to—"

"I want to go with you."

Hitler regarded her for a moment, then laughed lightheartedly. He turned to Wallenburg and spoke loudly. "Who am I to ignore the desires of a young girl? As you wish, Fräulein." He motioned her dismissal, then turned his attention to Willy. "Now go, William. I'll call ahead so they know you're coming. Be assured that a special greeting will await you." His eyes danced as he spoke.

Ursula turned to face Hans Krása and the children. "It's been my honor working with each and every one of you."

Tears streamed down Krása's face. "There will be songs written and sung about you, Ursula. On my honor." His hand went to his heart. Ursula smiled, kissed her hand and threw it to the cast, then crossed to the car, where Rahm had opened the door for her.

Willy turned to Wallenburg, who wore a confused expression. "Willy, what's going on? What can I do? I could contact the—"

Willy shook his head. "Listen, the last two years have taught me that I don't want to live in a world without Ursula. I'm not sure exactly what we'll be facing when we arrive at our destination, but at least we'll be together. But you can do something for me."

"Name it."

"I wrote letters to several powerful people in case events unfolded in exactly this way. I'm not sure if you can reach President Roosevelt in time, but please try. And William Hearst and Churchill as well. They'll all take your call. I know they will. Even if Ursula and I perish, at least there will be a record of my uncle's actions. You're a witness to the farce we were shown today, and what just transpired here. I'm counting on you." Willy squeezed his shoulder.

Wallenburg gave him a disbelieving look. "Things like this don't just happen, Willy. I'm a diplomat, and you're under diplomatic status when traveling with me. I'm not going to let them take you away to God knows where."

"I appreciate it, but I can't let Ursula face her fate alone. That's not who I am. It'll be alright."

Wallenburg took in the scene. "It doesn't look alright to me. None of it."

Willy smiled sadly. "It's my choice to accompany Ursula. Please understand."

Wallenburg looked doubtful. Finally, he gripped Willy's extended hand and shook it. "I'm going to raise hell, Willy. The world will know. Count on it."

As Willy walked toward the car, he saw Wallenburg talking to the confused Danes.

Suddenly Ilse appeared, out of breath from running. "Can I please say good-bye to my friends?" Rahm stepped in front of her, but Hitler nodded to indicate she could approach. "I would like to give them a memento if that's alright."

Unable to give up an opportunity of false kindness, Hitler nodded as he glanced at Wallenburg and the Danes. "Of course."

Ilse reached through the window and handed Ursula the cap the character Brundibár had worn in the show.

Ursula cried as she accepted the gift. "Thank you for being my friend. I'll never forget you, Ilse."

Ilse gazed at her intently. "You're correct. You will never forget me. Take care of this special hat and what it represents. I'll miss you and Addi." They held hands until Svoboda started the engine and the car crept forward.

As it gathered speed, Ursula turned around and held up her hand to Ilse, who waved back and pointed to her head. Ursula paused, wondering what the gesture meant. As Ilse faded away, Ursula settled into the seat she shared with Willy.

61

Ursula and Willy sat huddled in the back seat of Hitler's bulletproof limousine. Addi sat next to them, staring out the window. Rahm positioned himself sideways in the front passenger seat so he could keep an eye on everyone in the car, including Edvard Svoboda, who wore a sour expression as he drove. Rahm assumed that he resented being chosen for the trip. The long drive to Auschwitz meant that he wouldn't be home for dinner.

Ursula looked at Willy's profile, trying to memorize it. His gentle forehead developed into a strong Roman nose that sat above a full mouth. She stared at his ruby-red lips. "Why did you come with me, Willy?"

"Because I can't imagine my life without you."

"Even if it's a short life?" she whispered.

He squeezed her shoulder in response.

Ursula closed her eyes and tried to imagine what awaited them. A sob sat at the base of her throat, but she knew she wouldn't stop crying if she started, so she held it at bay. "I'm so grateful that you're here."

"I've never stopped looking for you, Ursula. It's been a winding road, but I'm here now, and I'm not going anywhere without you ever again."

Ursula glanced at Svoboda in the rearview mirror. His unreadable gaze alternated between the road and Addi. The Czech guard genuinely cared for her, and now he was required to chauffeur her to her demise. But Ursula knew that, regardless of his personal feelings, he was an obedient soldier and would follow orders. Her attention turned to Rahm, whose hard eyes flitted between her and Willy. "You don't have to whisper. You may speak openly. We all know what your future holds."

Ursula ignored him and thought about how much she'd changed during her captivity. She wanted to share so much with Willy, but she was content to curl into his side and inhale his intoxicating scent. She closed her eyes and ran her hands over the cap Ilse had given her. The wool felt rough under her fingers. "It was thoughtful of Ilse to give me this hat."

Addi took it and smiled. "Yes, it was. She did a beautiful job on the costumes, didn't she?"

Ursula nodded. "She did."

Ursula looked out the window, taking notice of how lustrous the trees appeared. The fat, green leaves against the bright blue sky reminded her of a painting she'd seen at an art gallery as a child. Her mind wandered to Otto, and she wondered how he would react when he heard the news of her death. She hoped that Anna would keep her word and take care of him. Otherwise, she feared he would die of a broken heart. Unless he had already—

"How is Papa, Willy?"

Willy turned to her and smiled. "He's fine, Ursula. He misses you, but he's fine."

She swallowed hard, determined not to cry. Her thoughts returned to Terezín, her makeshift home for what felt like an eternity. A wave of longing swept over her, for her real home, for normalcy, for a future denied. The feeling overwhelmed her, and she wanted to pour out all of her memories to Willy, to paint him a picture of daily life in the ghetto. Suddenly it became imperative that he understand why she'd made certain choices, and how they'd changed her for the better. How she'd become less selfish and more caring. How she'd finally come to understand that the whole was so much more important than the individual. How the importance of life came into stark focus when faced with death. How art could transcend a thousand bullets.

She tamped down her instincts and forced herself to create a gestalt picture for him. "There are many wonderful people in Terezín, Willy, and so much culture. To think that many of them may not survive . . ." The emotion rushed forth and she was unable to stop it. Years of frustration, humiliation, and anger broke through the dam and tumbled down her red cheeks.

Willy pulled her closer. "But those children will survive, Ursula. Because of you."

"Do you think your uncle will keep his word?"

Ursula watched Willy as the fields of grass whizzed by. He breathed deeply. "Oddly, yes. He has a bizarre sense of loyalty, so he'll keep his word to a woman who was willing to sacrifice herself for others. Even if it was you." He kissed her head.

Ursula glanced at Rahm. He glared openly; his anger at her brief happiness was palpable. She wondered whether he'd always been vindictive or whether Nazi ideology had created him. Then she dismissed him, with her eyes and her mind. She took Willy's hand and turned her gaze outside.

It had recently rained, making the grass a deep green punctuated by flashes of colorful flowers. The trees were in full bloom, and the sky was painted a light blue dotted by fat, puffy clouds. She had never seen such a beautiful sky. Her mind wandered to what lie ahead and she fought a rising panic. She closed her eyes and focused on the *Brundibár* cast. Knowing she had saved their lives calmed her somewhat. *My sacrifice will not be in vain.*

She looked at Rahm again, who watched her intently, as if she might flutter away at any moment. *Where could I go?* she wondered. As she watched the world fly by, she contemplated opening the door and throwing herself out. *Even if I managed not to kill myself, I wouldn't know what to do next. Besides, Rahm would shoot me.* She glanced at Willy and realized that she was only fantasizing. She could never leave him. Nevertheless, her eyes flitted to the door handle.

Rahm smiled. "If you're thinking of jumping, I wouldn't recommend it. You would break something in the fall. Besides, if you were to leave us, Fräulein, I would shoot your friends." His smile dropped and he abruptly turned around to face front.

"How much do you want?"

Rahm faced Willy. "What?"

Willy's jaw tightened. "How much will it take to let us go?"

Rahm's face was expressionless. Ursula tensed, wondering if they would be shot on the spot. She felt Addi take her hand and squeeze.

"You are asking me if I would defy my Führer's direct order and release you?"

Willy shook his head. "I'm not asking *if* you would ignore his order. I'm asking how much money you require to free us."

Ursula met Svoboda's large eyes in the mirror and saw his apprehension. She sensed what was coming but could do nothing to stop it. In a millisecond Rahm unholstered his revolver and pointed it at Willy. She screamed. Addi covered her face with the hat and bent forward in her seat.

Rahm sneered. "You're playing with words, Herr Hitler."

Willy glared at him and spoke evenly. "You're playing with our lives, Herr Rahm. How much?"

Ursula listened to Addi breathe in short bursts as she twisted the cap in her hands.

Rahm stuck out his lips and placed his index finger on them. "Hmm. This is an interesting question, don't you think, Svoboda?"

Svoboda's knuckles whitened as he tightened his grip on the wheel, but he remained silent.

Ursula felt Addi stiffen, then felt pressure on her leg. She glanced down to find Addi pressing the hat into her lap. She absentmindedly grabbed it as she stared down the barrel of the pistol that was pointed at Willy's face. As they rounded a curve in the road, Svoboda slammed his foot on the brake. All of them lurched forward as the car came to an abrupt, violent halt.

62

"Damn it!" Rahm said. "Move that obstruction, Svoboda. The ground is too moist. We can't drive around it, lest we get stuck."

Svoboda exited the car and approached a huge branch that lay across the road. He pulled and dragged, but the branch moved only centimeters. "I need assistance," he called out.

Rahm turned to Willy. "We can continue our discussion once the branch has been removed. Go! Help him." He turned to Ursula and Addi. "Do not even think of exiting this vehicle, or you'll be shot on the spot."

Willy exited the car and approached Svoboda. Ursula and Addi watched as the two men negotiated the best way to gain some leverage against the branch.

"Hurry up!" Rahm yelled from the car. He glanced at his watch.

Willy and Svoboda took turns in various positions but were unsuccessful. Willy turned to the car. "If you want to keep going, Commandant, you need to help us."

Rahm sighed heavily and glanced at the back seat. "Don't move." He waved his gun in their direction, then exited the car.

Addi turned quickly. "What did Ilse say about this hat, Ursula?"

Ursula's eyes were riveted to Willy. "What?"

Addi grabbed her arm. "What did she say?"

Ursula faced her. "She said, 'Take care of this special hat and what it represents.'"

"What do you think she meant by that?"

Ursula resumed watching Willy while running the hat through her fingers. "I don't know, Addi. Maybe it represents our teamwork, our ability to persevere under—" Ursula stopped short when she felt three small bumps. She looked at Addi, who smiled and nodded. Ursula glanced at the men who were slowly making progress on moving the branch. She turned the hat over and carefully tore open the underside seam, then shook it. Three glistening stones spilled into her palm.

Addi gasped. "Oh, my God."

They looked at each other. "We can use these to bargain for our freedom," Ursula said breathlessly.

A loud burst punctuated the air. They looked up to see Rahm writhing on the ground. Svoboda stood above him, his pistol still aimed at the commandant. A shocked Willy stared at the two men, his hands in the air.

Ursula and Addi jumped out of the car and rushed over. Rahm had been shot in the gut. Blood oozed slowly across the rocky dirt road. He moaned, "You fucking idiot! You shot me!"

Ursula turned to Svoboda. He seemed as surprised as Rahm.

"Are you alright?" Ursula asked Willy.

"Yes, yes. I'm fine," Willy answered. He was shaking his head in disbelief. "I don't understand . . . why did you . . .?"

Addi finished Willy's question. "Edvard, why did you do this?" She approached Svoboda slowly, her hands in front of her, palms up.

He turned to her slowly, as if just realizing she was there. His eyes were wild and his head shook back and forth. "I could not abide him anymore. I can't abide this any longer." He swung the pistol wildly, causing the others to duck for fear of being shot. "This insanity. The killing. The torture. I can't . . . I can't . . ." He broke down sobbing. Addi crossed to him and gently removed the gun from his hand. She gave it to Ursula, then returned to Svoboda and embraced him.

Ursula stared at the Walther in her hand. Its dull black color matched Rahm's fathomless eyes. She bounced the gun up and down in her hand, testing its weight. It felt heavy. It felt like control. Power. Revenge.

"Do it," Rahm wheezed. His breaths were short, staccato. "I know you want to. Do it."

Ursula looked at Willy, whose kind eyes held empathy but not direction. She spoke very quietly. "I was violated. Many times. Not by him, but . . ." Ursula's voice faltered as she gazed into the past. "It may as well have been him. They're all the same." She returned her focus to Rahm. "You're all the same, you Nazis."

She heard Willy's voice from somewhere far away. "It wasn't your fault, Ursula."

She whirled to face him. "I made the choice, Willy. I let him do it!"

Willy shook his head. "No, Ursula. In a situation where one person holds more power than the other, your ability to choose is taken away. It's not your fault."

Rahm smirked. "Seidl said that you loved it."

Ursula pulled the trigger without hesitation. The gunshot resounded across the field yet was muffled to her ears. She watched Rahm's head bounce in slow motion against the ground. His body twitched twice, then lay still. She looked at the gun, amazed at how easy it was to end a life. A sound drew her attention, and she lifted her gaze to the sky. A bluebird flew past, and she tracked its flight until it vanished. *How does beauty flourish amidst chaos? Perhaps the chaos highlights the beauty.* She realized she was smiling, and she wondered what that said about her. Willy was speaking but she couldn't understand his words. She felt him remove the gun from her hand and guide her back to the car, where she picked at a small tear in the leather seat.

Several minutes later Willy returned wearing Rahm's uniform. Ursula's eyebrows furrowed as she focused on the large bloodstain near the hem. Willy took the driver's seat, then instructed Svoboda to sit in the front passenger seat. Willy started the car and drove back the way they'd come. No one spoke for some time. Finally, Svoboda said, "You were right, Ursula."

Ursula blinked several times. It took a full minute to return from the safe, dark space where she'd found refuge after killing Rahm.

"What?"

"A long time ago you told me that I wasn't a Nazi, just a simple Czech policeman caught up in the chaos." He turned to face her. "I'm not proud of many of my choices, but I am proud that I shot that pig. That disgusting, awful man." He glanced at Addi, who held out her hand. He grabbed it like a lifeline and held on.

Ursula nodded. She didn't know what else to do.

"Where are we going?" Addi asked as they drove past the turn-off for Terezín.

Willy caught Ursula's eyes in the rearview mirror. "We're going home."

Home. Where is that? Ursula wondered. It had been a lifetime since she'd been home.

"But we'll have to drive through many checkpoints to get to Switzerland," Svoboda said.

"I know. But in this car we won't be questioned. And if we are, I'll use Rahm's uniform to bluff my way through. If that doesn't work, I have five thousand American dollars to use for bribes."

"Your uncle will hunt us," Ursula said quietly. Her entire body was shaking, but she felt nothing. She was numb.

Willy swerved around a large hole in the road. "That's true. But if we drive through the night, I believe we can be in Switzerland before he realizes that we escaped."

The setting sun shone through Addi's window and bounced off the three diamonds that lay on the hat Ilse had given them. An impossibly bright rainbow of color burst onto the seats. Ursula retrieved the hat and stared at the stones.

You will never forget me, Ilse had said. Ursula smiled. She was correct. Addi and she would never forget her. Nor would Willy or Svoboda when they discovered their good fortune.

Although she knew they had a long way to go, for the first time in years Ursula felt free. She rolled down the window and inhaled the warm, fresh air, then reached across the seat and squeezed Addi's hand. She held up one of the diamonds so it caught the light. The flash drew Willy's eyes in the rearview mirror, and he slammed on the brakes.

"Is that . . . what is that?" he asked breathlessly.

Ursula's eyes twinkled. "There were three of them sewn into the seam of the hat Ilse gave us. They are our assurance of freedom and a future. All of us."

1957

EPILOGUE

"No, no, no! Please, Mom! More! You can't leave us hanging like this," eleven-year-old Margaret whined.

"Yeah, Mom. You do this all the time," Elizabeth chimed in. "Please, for once, finish the story! What happened to the woman who shot the commandant? Was she caught?"

"No. She was not," Ursula said.

Margaret huffed. "But where did she go? And what about the other guard and the girl?"

Billy lay in his bed, covers up to his chin. Ever thoughtful, he examined his mother carefully. "Leave Mommy alone," he said. "She'll tell us when she's ready. I don't think she's made up the rest of the story yet."

Ursula gazed at her youngest. The five-year-old had been born prematurely and barely survived birth, then beat the odds again by living well past the two-year mark that doctors had predicted. His eyes were a reflection of her own and held wisdom well beyond his years, as if God had given him a sixth sense to make up for the physical prowess he would always lack. She winked at him and stroked his hair. "Thank you, Billy."

"You need to write this stuff down, Mom. It would be a great book," Margaret offered.

Elizabeth blew out a mouthful of air. "You're an idiot, Maggie. No one would believe that four escaped convicts shot a Nazi officer and bribed their way to the Swiss border without being caught. It's ridiculous."

"They weren't convicts and don't call me an idiot! You're the idiot. They were running for their lives, and don't you know that a lot of concentration camp victims sewed jewelry and stones into their clothing? Just like Anastasia in Russia. Remember the little princess who died with her family?"

"That's stupid, Maggie!" Elizabeth retorted. "And not true."

"You're just mad because I know stuff you don't!"

As the girls bickered, Billy held his mother's eyes. She stroked the cowlick in the center of his forehead, and her mind wandered back to Markus, the teenager on the train. So many people, so many friends gone. She had recently sent her monthly correspondence to Ilse in Berlin, only to receive a letter from Ilse's niece stating that she had suffered a fatal stroke the previous week. The niece wrote that many of the *Brundibár* cast had appeared at her funeral, now grown and some with children of their own. She had enclosed a picture that Ursula devoured, trying to place grown faces with names. In all, twenty-eight of the forty cast members had survived Terezín.

Ursula had saved those children's lives just as Ilse had saved hers, Willy's, Edvard's, and Addi's. It had taken the car, the uniform, the money, *and* the three diamonds to make it to Switzerland. If they hadn't been in possession of the diamonds for the final checkpoint, all four of them would have perished less than six kilometers from freedom.

Ursula silently thanked Ilse and leaned down to kiss Billy good night. "I love you so much."

He smiled crookedly, his crossbite causing a lisp as he whispered, "I know it's all true, Mommy. I know that it's you and Daddy in the story. I'm glad you're my Mommy."

Ursula stifled a sob that threatened to unleash a torrent of long-packed-away memories. She stood abruptly, then kissed all three of them. "Remember, tomorrow we're going to Auntie Addi's art exhibit."

Margaret rolled her eyes.

Elizabeth asked, "Do we have to go? Art shows are so boring!"

"She is family and we're going," Ursula said.

"She's not really family," Elizabeth countered.

Ursula paused, trying to figure out the best way to express her feelings. There was no effective manner in which she could communicate her depth of commitment for those with whom she'd fought for her very existence. "Some family you are born into. Other family you choose based on shared experiences that bind you. Both bonds are unbreakable and priceless. So, we will go to Aunt Addi's art show and support her gallery opening because she is family, and we love her."

"Will Theodor be there?" Billy asked.

Ursula smiled. "Of course. He's your cousin."

Elizabeth rolled her eyes. "Not by blood."

"Are Aunt Addi and Uncle Edvard married?" Margaret asked. "Neither of them wears a ring but they live together and have a son. It's kinda weird."

Ursula made a face. "So many questions this evening, children! They are a strong couple who care for each other very much. Again, bonds make family. Now, girls, go to your room. It's time to sleep. I love you." She blew a kiss to each of them and exited the room to find Willy standing in the hallway, his arms spread wide in invitation.

The girls burst from Billy's room, running down the hallway in a race to their bunk beds.

"Good night," Willy said as he jumped out of their way. Their door slammed shut. "I love you too!" he called after them.

Ursula laughed and snuggled against Willy's chest. He enclosed her in a warm, long embrace, rocking her like Otto used to when she was a child.

"They're becoming more curious, aren't they?"

Ursula nodded against his chest. "They sure are."

They stood contentedly near the hallway window, listening to the mesmerizing drone of cicadas as they searched for a mate.

"I miss my father, Willy."

"I know you do. I do too."

"I wish he were here to see his grandchildren grow up."

"At least he got to meet them before he passed."

"True."

Willy kissed her forehead, then traced the scar on her cheek. "Besides, my mother will be around forever. She's enough grandparent for fifteen kids."

Ursula's mind wandered to Billy. The way he had looked at her . . . as if he saw through her. "Billy knows that all of my stories are true. That's what he told me."

Willy pulled away and looked at her with concern. "Really?"

"That's what he said."

"Maybe that's why the girls are starting to ask more questions."

"Do you think we should tell them the truth?"

Willy sighed heavily. "We changed our surname to Stuart-Houston so no one would know our past. I'd like to keep it that way. Besides, how do you tell a child that his true last name is Hitler?"

NOTE TO THE READER

Thank you so much for reading *Swan Song*. As I continue to grow my readership, reviews are like gold. I would be grateful if you could post a review on Goodreads, Amazon, and/or your preferred reading website. Additionally, I would love to hear from you through elizabethsplaineauthor.com. I will get back to you if you take the time to write me a note.

When I read historical fiction, I always want to know what is based on fact and what's created in the author's imagination. Let me clear that up for you, point by excruciating point.

Ursula Becker is loosely based on Lotte Schoene (1891–1977), a soprano of Jewish descent who sang with the Vienna State Opera, Salzburg Festival, and Berlin State Opera (where Ursula sang). As the Nazi regime gained power, Ms. Schoene wisely decided to relocate to Paris, where she sang with the Opera-Comique and the Paris Opera. She remained in France until her death in 1977. She was not affiliated with Willy Hitler and never interacted with Adolf Hitler to my knowledge. There were many artists and musicians who emigrated from Germany, Poland, Czechoslovakia, and other countries in an effort to avoid persecution and retribution. Ms. Schoene was one of them, as was Carl Ebert, who emigrated to England to protest Hitler's obsession with performing only German/Austrian works. It's of note that other directors were forced out due to Hitler's prejudices as well.

Otto Becker is fictional, although the practical decisions he makes most likely represent the terrifying situation for so many families in Nazi Germany. Anna Becker is also fictional, but as I wrote, she became Eva Braun in my mind. Many descriptions of Anna's behavior and decisions were based on similar actions taken by Eva Braun.

Fritz Rosen is fictional and represents the hardworking people in opera houses all over the world. People who work tirelessly behind the scenes to ensure that the people on stage are successful. Likewise, Hilde, the makeup and hair artist, is fictional. Finally, Marika and Addi (Ursula's Terezín friends) are fictional and represent the sisterhood that must have been developed to maintain hope in an otherwise bleak situation.

Anyone with the surname Hitler was based on real people: Willy, Adolf, Alois, Bridget. William Patrick Hitler (Willy) was the son of Adolf's half brother, Alois, making Willy the Führer's half nephew. I refer to him as Adolf's "nephew" for ease of reading. Willy's mother was Bridget Dowling Hitler, an Irishwoman who married Alois Hitler. Alois did go to Germany on a gambling tour and did abandon Bridget and Willy in England, where

Bridget raised Willy on her own. Alois remained in Germany, where he married bigamously and had another son. When Willy was grown, he went to Germany and worked in the banking and automotive industries. Uncle Adolf wanted him to join the Party, but he declined, leading to a disagreement between them that culminated in the cocktail party scene where Hitler brandishes a whip. All terrifyingly true—embellished but based on Willy's account of events in *Why I Hate My Uncle*, which was published in *Look* magazine. It's also true that William Randolph Hearst sponsored Willy's U.S. speaking tour. Stranded in the United States when World War II broke out, Willy received special dispensation from President Roosevelt to join the U.S. Navy and returned to Germany to fight with the Allies. After the war he married Phyllis Jean-Jacques and settled in New York, where he ran a home-based laboratory business and had four sons.

The story Willy tells about Hitler's niece Geli Raubal (the daughter of Hitler's half sister Angela Raubal) is based on real events. Adolf and Geli did have a tumultuous relationship, and Willy claimed that the extended family knew that Geli was pregnant when she died. She was twenty-three when she was found in Adolf's Munich apartment, dead of a gunshot wound from his pistol. It was quickly ruled a suicide. Her body was quickly removed, and the incident was covered up, so no one knows exactly what happened. Verbal and written accounts following Geli's death confirm that Hitler was distraught to the point of suicide. He retreated to a friend's home and spent weeks wallowing in guilt and melancholy. When he emerged, his demeanor changed abruptly and dramatically for the worse. One can only imagine (as I have) what might have happened if Hitler came across someone who so closely resembled Geli, a young woman whom he couldn't control, and with whom he was, by all accounts, obsessed.

The descriptions of changes made within the Berlin Opera were all real. Hitler removed seats in the auditorium so that he could have a better view. Hitler was an avid operagoer and actively followed famous actresses and opera singers of the day. Given his nature, he would have wanted, at the very least, to be surrounded by them, if not adored by them. To have one of them dismiss him as ridiculous (as Ursula did) would be untenable, especially given her physical similarity to Geli, who had given him the ultimate humiliation by killing herself.

The *Drottningholm* was a real ship that Great Britain purchased from the United States in order to repatriate English citizens. Its Swedish registration allowed it safe passage, even in the midst of war. The description of the stateroom was based on the SS *New York* that ran between Hamburg, Southampton, and New York prior to World War II.

At the height of his power, Hitler had at least three planes for his personal use. Cabin pressurization came into use in 1938. Hitler's planes were some of the first to take advantage of it, thereby no longer needing oxygen masks to fly above fifteen-thousand feet.

The story that Joseph Goebbels tells Ursula of the Chancellery rug being purchased by Hitler from the League of Nations is also true. Hitler liked to tell that tale because he came out as a hero, saving the League from embarrassment.

Hitler's personal limousine was spacious and bulletproof, but it had only a front seat and a back seat. Hitler liked to sit in the front seat with his driver, often referring to maps or chatting.

Elizabeth Layton was Winston Churchill's secretary from 1941–1945. To my knowledge, she never met Willy Hitler.

Blondi, Adolf's beloved German shepherd, was real. It's also true that Eva Braun (Adolf's mistress and then wife) was jealous of the time Adolf spent with Blondi and would sometimes kick the dog under the table. Adolf had several German shepherds, but Blondi was his favorite and was with him when he died in the bunker in 1945. In fact, Hitler gave Blondi a cyanide capsule prior to swallowing one himself (and then shooting himself to ensure his death). Eva Braun (Anna Becker in this story) married Hitler two days before joining him in suicide via cyanide.

All artists (composers, conductors, singers, actresses, and authors) with whom Ursula comes into contact are based on real people, except for Addi. I have used their real names when I was able, but I have taken some artistic liberties with their actions and mannerisms.

Rafael Schächter was a Czech composer and conductor who led the cultural effort within Terezín. While there he directed several full operas, as well as conducting Verdi's *Requiem* at least sixteen times. He was sent to Auschwitz after the final Verdi performance and died on October 6, 1944.

Hans Krása was a Czech composer who wrote *Brundibár*, which was first performed in an orphanage prior to his being sent to Terezín. He managed to smuggle the piano score into the ghetto and reconstructed the rest of the musical score once imprisoned. Krása was integral to cultural life in Terezín. He died on October 6, 1944, in Auschwitz.

Gideon Klein was a Czech pianist and composer who, along with Rafael Schächter, was an integral part of cultural life in Terezín. Some of his compositions were smuggled out of Terezín and survive today. He did accompany the *Brundibár* rehearsals.

Ilse Weber was a German poet, composer, and playwright who wrote primarily for children, including the book she reads to the children in this story. She died in Auschwitz on October 6, 1944.

Jakob Edelstein was president of the Jewish Council in Terezín and was responsible for the administration of the camp under the direction of the SS.

Raoul Wallenburg was a Swedish diplomat who launched rescue operations for Jews during the Holocaust. He saved thousands of lives by issuing Swedish passports and hiding Jews in rented buildings in Budapest. Because of his activism, he was named an honorary citizen of the United States, Canada, Israel, and Australia. Mr. Wallenburg was captured and jailed by the Soviets in January 1945, where he is assumed to have died approximately two years later, but accurate records are impossible to obtain. He has a tree dedicated to his memory and heroism on the Avenue of the Righteous in the area of the Yad Vashem memorial in Jerusalem. Mr. Wallenburg did not attend the International Red Cross visit on June 23, 1944, and, to my knowledge, never met Willy Hitler. Visit https://sweden.se/society/raoul-wallenberg-a-man-who-made-a-difference/ for more information.

The descriptions of Theresienstadt (in German) or Terezín (in Czech) are as true as I was able to discern having not been there. Please feel free to refer to the books listed in the references to learn more about the ghetto that imprisoned so many talented people. When the camp first opened, primarily Czechs were housed there. It was only later in the war that Germans, Poles, and Austrians were sent there as well. Most of the artists referenced in the book were of Czech descent, which is why it was imperative that Ursula speak the language. Using only one score, Verdi's *Requiem* was performed sixteen times under Rafael Schächter's leadership. More on this amazing feat can be found at https://www.defiantrequiem.org. The quote in Chapter 40, "whatever we do here is just a rehearsal for when we will play Verdi in a grand concert hall in Prague in freedom," is taken directly from Schächter's speech to his choir prior to one of the performances.

The International Red Cross did spend a day in Terezín on June 23, 1944. The Nazis created a façade of a perfect village, and thousands of inmates were shipped to Auschwitz and elsewhere in order to lower the population prior to the visit. Hans Krása's *Brundibár* was performed, and the children did offer an ironic Nazi salute at the end of the show. Although there were many SS officials in attendance, Adolf Hitler was not there. Several months after the Red Cross visit, the entire cast was sent to Auschwitz, where a few children managed to survive. The little girl who is singled out by Hitler after the show was based on a picture of one of the cast members named Greta. I can only hope that Greta was one of the children who survived Auschwitz, but in this re-imagined version of events, she definitely survived.

Finally, I have a personal link to *Brundibár*, the children's opera that was performed during the International Red Cross visit to Terezín on June 23,

1944. When I first became aware of the Central Pennsylvania Youth Opera (CPYO), its director was a bright, energetic woman named Addie Appelbaum. She told me stories of growing up in New York and meeting Leonard Bernstein. Addie's enthusiasm was infectious and drew me into the children's opera world. Her cast was performing *Brundibár* when I met her. One of the cast members was my voice student, and she took it upon herself to contact a woman who had seen a *Brundibár* performance as a child in Terezín. This incredible lady spoke before the CPYO performance and, of course, there was not a dry eye in the house. Literally. Although I didn't know it at the time, the seed of *Swan Song* was planted that day. Since that time Terezín has haunted me, causing me to read multiple books about the ghetto and its inmates. In the meantime, I ended up performing several shows with CPYO, and Addie and I became friends. She was invaluable in the creation of this book, as she very kindly read through and commented on two versions. *Swan Song* would not be the novel it is without her insight, wisdom, and guidance.

In addition to Addie, I am indebted to my beta readers, my editor, and my publisher, as well as Steve Eisner, who believed in *Swan Song* when I was still mulling over how to accurately capture the enormity of the story and its characters. And to my wonderful family, without whom my writing would not be possible, I love you and thank you for your unending support.

I am in awe of the Terezín inmates' tenacity in the face of unspeakable suffering, and their ability to create beauty where there should have been only terror and fear. Nothing can bring back the millions who perished in the Nazi reign of terror, but we can honor their memory by not allowing the world to forget.

Humbly,
Elizabeth B. Splaine

RESOURCES

Beer, Edith Hahn. *The Nazi Officer's Wife: How One Jewish Woman Survived the Holocaust.* William Morrow, 1999, 2015.

Berenbaum, Michael. (July 20, 1998). Britannica. *Theresienstadt Concentration Camp, Czech Republic.* Retrieved 2019, from https://www.britannica.com/place/Theresienstadt..

Encyclopedia.ushmm.org. *Aryan.* Retrieved 2021, from https://encyclopedia.ushmm.org/content/en/article/aryan-1..

Encyclopedia.ushmm.org. *Theresienstadt: SS and Police Structure.* Retrieved 2021, from https://encyclopedia.ushmm.org/content/en/article/theresienstadt-ss-and-police-structure..

Facing History and Ourselves. *Defying the Nazis: The Sharps' War. America and the Holocaust.* Retrieved 2019, from https://www.facinghistory.org/defying-nazis/america-and-holocaust..

Facing History and Ourselves. *Holocaust and Human Behavior/The National Socialist Revolution. Targeting Jews.* Retrieved 2019, from https://www.facinghistory.org/holocaust-and-human-behavior/chapter-5/targeting-jews..

GG Archives. *SS* New York *Passenger List—3 November 1938.* Retrieved 2019, from https://www.gjenvick.com/Passengers/HamburgAmericanLine/NewYork-PassengerList-1938-11-03.html..

The *Guardian.* (March 1, 2015). "Business and Finance News from Guardian US." The *Guardian.* Retrieved May 21, 2015, from http://www.theguardian.com/us/business..

History Learning Site. *Causes of World War One.* Retrieved 2019, from https://www.historylearningsite.co.uk/world-war-one/causes-of-world-war-one/causes-of-world-war-one/

RESOURCES

The History Place. (1996). *The Rise of Adolf Hitler: Hitler Runs for President*. Retrieved 2019, from http://www.historyplace.com/worldwar2/riseofhitler/runs.html

Holocaustmusic.ort.org. *Rafael Schächter*. Retrieved 2021, from http://holocaustmusic.ort.org/places/theresienstadt/schachter-rafael/

HolocaustResearchProject.org. *Mischlinge: Nazi Classification for Germans of Mixed Race*. Retrieved 2021, from http://www.holocaustresearchproject.org/holoprelude/mischlinge.html

Holocaust.cz. *Anti-Jewish Policy after the Establishment of the Protectorate of Bohemia and Moravia*. September 5, 2011, from https://www.holocaust.cz/en/history/final-solution/the-final-solution-of-the-jewish-question-in-the-bohemian-lands/anti-jewish-policy-after-the-establishment-of-the-protectorate-of-bohemia-and-moravia/

Jewishvirtuallibrary.org. *Anton Burger*. Retrieved 2021, from https://www.jewishvirtuallibrary.org/anton-burger

Lundmark, Thomas. *The Untold Story of Eva Braun: Her Life beyond Hitler*. Self-published, 2019

Njaco. (May 7, 2014). WW2Aircraft.net. *Hitler's Personal Aircraft*. Retrieved 2019, from https://ww2aircraft.net/forum/threads/hitlers-personal-aircraft.40725/

Payne, Robert. *The Life and Death of Adolf Hitler*. Praeger Publishers, 1973

Penn, Michelle. Study.com. *Danish Red Cross: Theresienstadt Visit & Nazi Deception*. Retrieved 2019, from https://study.com/academy/lesson/danish-red-cross-theresienstadt-visit-nazi-deception.html

Rosenbaum, Ron. (September 3, 2013). *Vanity Fair. Hitler's Doomed Angel*. Retrieved 2020, from https://www.vanityfair.com/news/1992/04/hitlers-doomed-angel

Salship.se. *A Tribute to the Swedish American Line*. Retrieved 2021, from https://www.salship.se/drott.php

Smith, Kristan. (updated March 20, 2020). Quora. *In Nazi Germany, What Was the Difference between the Gestapo and the SS? Was It Possible to Be a Member of Both?* Retrieved 2019, from https://www. quora.com/In-Nazi-Germany-what-was-the-difference-between-the-Gestapo-and-the-SS-Was-it-possible-to-be-a-member-of-both

Stratigakos, Despina. History Extra. (November 2015). *Where Did Adolf Hitler Live? The Homes of the Führer and How They Were Used as Nazi Propaganda.* Retrieved 2019, from https://www.historyextra. com/period/second-world-war/where-did-adolf-hitler-live-berlin-munich-home-germany-nazi-propaganda/

Sweden.se. (updated January 24, 2020). *Raoul Wallenburg—A Man Who Made a Difference.* Retrieved 2020, from https://sweden.se/ society/raoul-wallenberg-a-man-who-made-a-difference/

"Terezín: Children of the Holocaust." *The History of Terezín.* Retrieved 2019, from http://www.Terezín.org/the-history-of-Terezín

United States Holocaust Museum, Washington, DC. Holocaust Encyclopedia. *Theresienstadt: Red Cross Visit.* Retrieved 2019, from https://encyclopedia.ushmm.org/content/en/article/theresienstadt-red-cross-visit

United States Holocaust Museum, Washington, DC. Holocaust Encyclopedia. *Theresienstadt: Establishment.* Retrieved 2019, from *https://encyclopedia.ushmm.org/content/en/article/theresienstadt-establishment?series=18010*

Vagabond, J. YouTube. *Hitler's Former Reich Chancellery in Berlin. A Detailed Then and Now Video Tour.* Retrieved 2019, from https:// www.youtube.com/watch?v=zGAZvpmdjKs

Vulliamy, Ed. (April 5, 2013). The Observer. *Terezín: The Music Connected Us to the Lives We Had Lost.* Retrieved 2019, from https:// www.theguardian.com/music/2013/apr/05/Terezín-nazi-camp-music-eva-clarke?CMP=twt_gu

RESOURCES

Weinstein, Frida Scheps. *A Hidden Childhood: A Jewish Girl's Sanctuary in a French Convent 1942–1945*. Hill & Wang, 1985

Weiss, Helga. *Helga's Diary*. W.W. Norton & Company, 2013. The Wiener Holocaust Library. *The Holocaust Explained. Theresienstadt Ghetto*. Retrieved 2019, from https://www. theholocaustexplained.org/the-camps/theresienstadt-a-case-study/ conditions-within-theresienstadt/

Wines of Germany. *The Kurpfalz-Weinstuben (Wilmersdorf)*. Retrieved 2019, from https://www.germanwines.de/tourism/wine-places-in-berlin/the-kurpfalz-weinstuben/

ABOUT THE AUTHOR

 **Elizabeth B. Splaine** is a retired opera singer who enjoys reading and writing WWII stories that focus on tenacity, hope and the indomitable human spirit. Prior to writing, Elizabeth earned an AB in Psychology from Duke University and an MHA from University of North Carolina, Chapel Hill. She spent eleven years working in health care before switching careers to become a professional opera singer and voice teacher. When not writing, Elizabeth teaches classical voice in Rhode Island, where she lives with her husband, sons, and dogs.

SWAN

SONG

A NOVEL

ELIZABETH

B. SPLAINE